Reveille

A Story of Survival, War, Family

George S. Smith

PublishAmerica
Baltimore

© 2009 by George S. Smith.
All rights reserved. No part of this book may be reproduced, stored in a retrieval system or transmitted in any form or by any means without the prior written permission of the publishers, except by a reviewer who may quote brief passages in a review to be printed in a newspaper, magazine or journal.

First printing

This is a work of fiction. Names, characters, places, and incidents either are the product of the author's imagination or are used fictitiously. Any resemblance to actual persons, living or dead, events, or locales is entirely coincidental.

PublishAmerica has allowed this work to remain exactly as the author intended, verbatim, without editorial input.

ISBN: 978-1-61546-364-0
PUBLISHED BY PUBLISHAMERICA, LLLP
www.publishamerica.com
Baltimore

Printed in the United States of America

PROLOGUE

Historical fiction: Truth mixed with assumptions, fleeting mental images, and make-believe. *Reveille* is an historical fiction novel is about a young man I never knew but to whom I am indebted nonetheless. In dealing with history before the electronically recorded word became the reality-god, there is no such thing as absolute truth. There are recollections, perceptions, first-hand accounts (muddled by time and circumstances), and second- and third-hand stories. There are written records—official and plebian—but "facts" in one document are often changed, diluted or ignored when transferred to another. Seldom when digging into the artifacts of historical events do you find absolute truth. Under that premise, *Reveille* is as close to truth as I could make it.

In March of 2006, the Andres clan, descendents of a slight man who lived a majority of his life as Charles Montgomery Andres—just a sad-faced image in need of a shave that was imprinted in old, sepia-toned photos—began planning its first real reunion in more than a decade. Far-flung family members met spur-of-the-moment only on certain occasions…usually following the death of a revered aunt or uncle. Pleas were made to gather family stories to create a reunion keepsake. The project, named after the small community in Southwest Arkansas in which the modern Andres family story began, was titled "Memories of Sutton."

As the stories rolled in about the Andres clan, only stories by the three remaining Andres children—Betty Ann Andres White, Jack Wayne Andres, and Wanda Ruth Andres Collins—contained any mention of Charles Montgomery Andres and his wife, Nancy Ann Hines Waddle. Except for a handful of hand-me-down family pictures in which he appeared, an old, handmade, long-stemmed pipe, some county land records, and his scrapbooks of newspaper and pamphlet clippings (mainly dealing with religious issues), firm evidence of his existence was slim. Before 1870, there seemed to be no official record of Charles Montgomery Andres. All the family knew were from the stories of his early years that he had told.

His personal imprint is evident in his three remaining grandchildren and the hundred-odd great-grandchildren, great-great-grandchildren, and great-great-great-grandchildren, scattered around the United States.

Who was Charles Montgomery Andres? The family stories about the man known as Grandpa Andres were flimsy and without concrete detail:

    1. C. M. Andres was an orphan from New Orleans.

    2. His father and mother were from France; his father was a doctor.

    3. One story had his entire family being wiped out in a "plague"; another had two brothers being in the orphanage with him, both leaving the institution to join the Confederate Army at the onset of the Civil War. If he ever mentioned the names of his parents or siblings, that information had been lost.

    4. To get out of the orphanage, at age thirteen to sixteen (depending on the story), he tried to join the Confederate Army and was rejected because of his age. He hied himself off to join the Union Army. He was a drummer for *some* Union regiment, stationed *somewhere* for a couple of years.

    5. After the war, he came to Arkansas, stopped to work at the Archibald Waddle "plantation," married the family's second oldest daughter, and had six sons and a daughter.

    6. He was born June 25, 1847 and died January 18, 1929—it is so stated on his marble marker in Harmony Cemetery in Nevada County, Arkansas. He is buried in a family plot shared by his wife, several children, grandchildren, great-grandchildren and great-great-grandchildren.

    7. He was hard-working, protective of family and friends, loved to read, embraced simple, no-frills, by-the-Word religion, and was considered something of a "healer" by locals. In his later years, he made patchwork-type scrapbooks out of odds-and-ends articles in newspaper and church bulletin clippings.

That was all. The life of a man was summed up in a few hundred words.

More than eighteen months of research revealed that much of the family "fact" was fiction—contrived or believed, but fiction nonetheless.

The man later known as Charles Montgomery Andres was born July 3, 1846 in New Orleans. He was christened Charles Adrien Jean Baptiste Andree in St. Louis Cathedral.

His father—Georges Adrien Andree—was a merchant; his mother was Josephine Laumonne (or Laumont, as it was spelled on another document). He had two brothers: Charles Gustave Constant Andree and Georges Hyacinthe Andree. His parents and his brother Charles died of either yellow fever or cholera in late 1849 or early 1850. The entire family was listed in the city's 1850 Census (counted in October of 1849), but only Georges, his brother, was listed in the 1860 Census. Charles was placed in a New Orleans orphanage in early 1850 and his name was shortened, probably due to mouth-to-pen transfer, to Charles Andre.

He left the orphanage in early June 1863 and apparently tried to join the Confederate Army, although no record of such an attempt could be found. If he did, he was rejected. (It would make sense that he made that attempt. New Orleans was under Union control and life for the regular populous was hard; the life of institution-bound orphans was doubly hard.) If the Confederate Army rejected him, it was not because of age. In the early summer of 1863, the Johnny Rebs was accepting boys as young as twelve in infantry units, as young as ten to serve as musicians. Charles was less than a month shy of sixteen at the time.

Within a few days he made a life-changing decision. He walked about ten miles northeast and joined the Ninth Connecticut Regiment stationed outside New Orleans. He served till the end of the war as a drummer, first for Company H, then, when the entire regiment was reformed, for Company C.

With *Reveille,* Charles Montgomery Andres finally has a voice. A blank shroud of uncertainty is lifted from his life, even if only in an historical fiction sense. It is the aim of this account to replace that shroud with a literary tableau of colors and identifiable and understandable circumstances that helped define the boy that went to war and shaped the man who emerged at the end of it.

It is a sincere hope that Private Charles Andre, musician, Ninth Connecticut Regiment, would be proud of *Reveille.* His pride in the end result would not be because of any by-happenstance factual depiction of him, his actions, attitudes, motivations, or attempts to build his life-story. The pride would come from the effort expended to make his life more complete than simple words carved on a tombstone in an isolated country cemetery, or as a dour image in ragged-edged photographs hanging in a hallway or stuck in an envelope.

GEORGE S. SMITH

The hundreds of hours doing research for this book was not a lonely quest; Charles Montgomery Andres, my great-grandfather, walked by my side every step of the way. For any assumptions made about this quiet, unassuming man and his life that are incorrect, I sincerely apologize. He assuredly deserved better than I had to give.

CHAPTER 1

Running the Streets

A story can't be told until a story's done.
Galen Gilmore

At fifteen Charles Andre didn't know much for certain.

He knew he was an orphan. He knew he had a stand-by-his-side-no-matter-the-consequences friend named Ian, whom he considered a pure-dee idiot.

He knew he had a friend named Sarie Beth that he wanted to be more than a friend, but they were both too young to do anything about it. And, them being Catholic, even if they were older and if they were so inclined to do something about it, couldn't do it anyway without something bad happening to them both.

He knew he wanted to grow up quicker than he was doing and make decisions for himself rather than have others make them for him.

And he knew he was better than people thought he was, or thought he could ever be. Someday he would prove those people wrong.

Or die trying.

Summer. New Orleans. 1860.
The city held the stink of old, wet garbage close to it, like a grieving woman clutching her stillborn baby. Rotting fish heads with skin cracking across the bones. Spoiled cabbage. Rancid, maggot-encrusted table scraps. Decaying

ooze from dead animals. Metallic stench of dried blood. Thunder mug residue.

Charles Andre wrinkled his nose and shook his head as if to sling the stench away. Then he shook his head again, slowly, sadly, knowing what he was trying to do was impossible. Nearing the alley behind Fettermann's General Store, the smell intensified, taking on a more ominous interpretation. Charles chanced a look down the alley. Huge bones, including one intact rib cage from a butchered cow carcass were strewn about the alley; a dozen snapping, growling dogs fought over the tendrils of meat hanging from the bones, and slitherings of worm-like tendons and gristle.

It surprised him that he actually stopped to watch the spectacle. It was not a sight he should want to remember. Putting his sensibilities and common sense aside, he focused on four dogs fighting over a denuded hindquarter, the hoof barely attached by a single, sickly white tendon. Charles' eyes jumped back to the rib cage; curlicues of meat hung from it like wisps of Spanish moss from a flooded cypress. The dogs were oblivious to this unclaimed prize, seemingly content to fight and bite and growl over a single, greenish chunk of decaying meat.

What is 'bout those dogs that they gather up and focus on that lone hindquarter?

It was a rhetorical mental spasm. The answer was clear. It was the same instinct, same urge, same force, that made him think about fighting on occasion. In his darkest thoughts, he could see himself—lips curled back, neck and chest ligaments taut, hands forming claws—to defend the simplest of principles or possessions, like his open-sided ticking mattress stuffed with dung-strewn straw centered under the huge south bay window at St. Mary's Orphan Boy's Asylum.

But, in his simplistic reality, Charles was not a fighter.

What would I fight for? Is there anything? Life and territory! Simple concepts of survival.

If your life was threatened, or you "owned" something or thought you did, you protected it, fought for it, and, if necessary, died for it. Next to breath and food and being loved, owning something, anything, was a driving force of life. His life, for certain. He had breath, enough food to survive (*never enough, but...enough*), and he had his place under the window. In his position, at this time, three out of four was certainly acceptable.

Placing his mattress under the big south-facing window at the overcrowded orphanage was a simple, common sense thing to do. And Charles Andre, by all accounts including his own personal analysis, was a simple boy, blessed with an abundance of common sense…and an overwhelming, sharp-edged sense of survival.

The south side of the orphanage caught a night breeze that, sometimes just for a few precious moments, cleansed the air and eradicated the smell of the inner city and the large sleeping room filled with other orphans from his nostrils. Charles lived for that breeze, for those few breaths before the gut-roiling smell beat back the freshness of the ocean's perfume.

An orphan with lower social status than a shanty house whore, his world encompassed the worst of smells, sights, and sound. His eyes were constantly downcast, limiting his view to legs from the knees down, discarded cigar butts, wet, lumpy chunks of masticated plug tobacco, and feces—always feces, animal and human. He, like the city's other orphans, homeless vagabonds, and unattached coloreds, walked in the gutter. The street was for the buggies, wagons, and horses carrying passengers participating in acts of commerce or for pleasure; the sidewalk was for the gentry—highbred men and women and those who attended to them. They, he knew, thought they were born to rule; they carried themselves in a manner that left no doubt they were peacock-proud of their position, not ever walking in the gutter. It was not expected—by them or others.

Sometimes, Charles watched them in the reflections of storefront windows: The men with the slick, polished shoes (sometimes tipped with silver, filigreed toe-taps) shiny, striped pants, waistcoats, ruffled shirts, gold and silver watch fobs, and high-top hats with saucy ribbons at the bottom of the crown; the women with the tiny, pointy-toed shoes with bright ribbons for laces, billowing, brocaded dresses with tiny flowers on a field of white lace or heavy, iridescent stripes of contrasting colors…purple and yellow, red and blue, green and brown.

He thought it interesting that he confined his clandestine viewings to clothing, not facial features.

Why do I do that?

He did not covet anything the gentry had.

Not a single thing.

He had convinced himself of that personal truism time and again. But he could not understand why, then, he hated them so.

Is it hatred? Or envy? Can't be envy. I hate envy!

The moneyed gentry (or life-scammers who pretend to be just that) had fine clothes, lived and partied in beautiful homes, owned high-stepping, shiny horses with plaited manes, had enough money to buy a fine meal, and even leave a coin or two for the liveried help.

Rich people expected others to be subservient. Few (only those richer) denied them that fundamental pleasure. They threw money away and never missed it. Most of the boys at the orphanage regularly begged metal crumbs from finely fitted-out ladies and gentlemen. But not Charles. Never Charles.

"I'd rather die than beg," he once told his best friend, Ian O'Rourke.

"Dah-die, then, you old sah-sot!" Ian stuttered, as he ran off, zeroing in on two young, rich gentlemen, both weaving a bit unsteady as they exited a fashionable saloon and bawdyhouse.

The fact that one of the gents threw a three-cent piece in the gutter and both men laughed as Ian got down on his hands and knees in the natural sluice brimming with vegetable leavings riding on black water didn't seem to bother Ian a bit. It was all Charles could do to keep from crying.

He didn't consider himself especially strong-willed, overly righteous, or particularly principled. He also didn't think himself weak the previous afternoon for taking a hand-out from Ian: The slab-ham sandwich made with meat that was more fat than lean and two tough-as-nails slices of week-old bread offered as a handout from the back door of a fancy restaurant off of Chartres Street.

Je ne prie jamais. Comme Dieu est mon témoin, je fichu sûr ne mendiera jamais.

I didn't beg. As God is my witness, I damn sure will never beg.

When he thought profanity-laced thoughts, he unconsciously made a quick sideways movement as if the sisters at the orphanage read his thoughts from across town and materialize in a black-and-white swirl to box his ears for even thinking a curse word.

He gratefully took the sandwich from Ian and chipped away a tiny imprint of mold with his teeth before intentionally spitting it in almost the same place the three-cent piece had come to rest.

Yes, rich people could buy and sell us a hundred times, thousand, even.

But he surmised they would never know about the simple pleasures one could find without money. Like leaving the orphanage in an instant and visiting sun-baked islands and fishing in clear, cool streams. Or being treated as royalty in palaces of kings with the pyramids on the horizon. All scenes from a world history book in the orphanage's small library. All accomplished in thoughts and dreams.

As Charles watched the dogs, he wondered where Ian was, and if he had found anything worth taking back to the orphanage. Ian, the only orphan who had been at the orphan's home longer than Charles, was like a brother—closer even. As Charles watched the dogs, he thought back a few weeks. It was a typical spring day in New Orleans—tolerable temperature, but with compressing humidity higher than an arched cat's back. The pair found themselves walking along the Mississippi River levee and had just crossed the street in front of Miss Sadie's Place, a hot mattress house with more than twenty girls—white, blue-black, octoroon, high-yellow—that claimed to service more than a hundred men a day. More, when boatloads of immigrants hit the docks. The gregarious, eclectic mixture of Mattress-back Janes made Miss Sadie's a must-visit destination for customers from the most affluent New Orleans residents to a just-off-the-boat, piss-poor French, Italian, or Irish immigrants digging whatever money they had out of their shoe, each yearning for a quick wick-dip as a Welcome-to-America present to themselves.

The boys were on a foraging trip trying to find something for breakfast and had come up empty except for a large, wilted lettuce leaf stuck to an newspaper advertisement for ship hands for a voyage to the Orient. The leaf was stuck at the bottom of the obituary page of the *Picayune*, one of the town's two daily papers. Charles spit on the dirty, ink-stained leaf, wiped it off on his shirt, carefully tore it in half, taking into consideration the leaf's top was twice the width of the bottom. Ian took it grateful, slapped it in his mouth and chewed. At some point in his life Ian had broken his jaw; when he chewed Charles always had an image of a cow chewing its cud.

Charles watched Ian chew the leaf until he saw his Adam's apple bob up and down twice. Without realizing he had been counting, he knew the number of times his friend had chewed the portion of leaf until he swallowed: twenty-two.

Charles unconsciously chewed the top half of the leaf twenty-four times before swallowing.

Without mental warn-up or reason, he remembered what John Ryan, the old man who sometimes worked at the orphanage, said just yesterday: "Life's a contest. And you better fookin' play it to win."

Right now, in an alley just off Royal Street, he didn't care about playing to win. He just wanted to live another day. Period.

To Charles, being alive, right here, right now…that *was* winning.

It was Ian who spotted the well-dressed drunk sitting upright between two garbage barrels in front of Sean LeForche's Gala Girls Saloon just off the east end of Royal. He hadn't been there long: A gold watch chain ran across his ample stomach and the winder stem and the top third of an engraved gold watch was clearly visible in his left vest pocket. The man's eyes were open, but unfocused. He sat there, limp, as if the alcohol had robbed him of his motor skills.

Of course, the boys (independently, not as a cohesive unit) thought about robbing the man. The pickings were easy and the money that could be made from selling the watch would feed hungry mouths at the orphanage for a week or more.

"I-I think I know where we mah-might get some old potatoes. Eh-if we hurry."

"Let's go, then," Charles said as he starting running down the street, Ian hot on his heels.

Neither boy ever brought up the lost opportunity.

Charles pulled himself back to the present. The alley. The dogs.

Without thinking, without giving himself any mental warning, he pulled off his tattered shirt and started running down the alley, swinging it over his head like a rock-and-sling in the direction of the closest animals, screaming "Aiiiiiiiii-EEEEEEEEEE!" All of the dogs stopped what they were doing—crunching bones, licking at blood-soaked fresh scraps, snarling, fighting—and looked up, half tucked tail and took off down the alley. Five of the dogs started to follow, then stopped and looked at Charles over their shoulders. Then, as if directed by a single mind, they turned to face him, teeth bared, neck-hair bristling. A chorus of low growls (like summer thunder bouncing over the bay) stopped Charles in his tracks.

The shirt dropped to his side as he skidded to a stop about five feet from the first dog, a mangy, catahoula-looking critter with gold eyes and a bad case of mange.

REVEILLE

This was a bad idea.
The catahoula took a tentative half step in his direction, the snarl pulling its lips so tight the lips went from black to an off-blue with white ridging. Two other dogs quickly came up in support, covering the catahoula's flanks; the remaining two, as if guided by mental commands, went to the east wall of the alley and, shoulder to shoulder, started inching toward Charles.

Frantically looking for a more suitable weapon than his shirt, Charles' eyes latched on a short, solid leg bone ripped from one of the cow chunks. He threw the shirt at the lead dog, and quickly grabbed the bone, and started swinging it like a dervish, back and forth, moving forward a few inches on each slashing motion. The lead dog hunkered down and refused to move, but the other four dodged backward slightly with each swing.

"Aiiiiiii-EEEEEEEEE!" Charles screamed. The alley echoed his war cry.

He felt a push of air behind him and for an instant thought that a dog had crept up behind him. "Ah-ahiiiiiii-EEEEEEE!" Ian screamed in his ear as he busted past Charles on his left, swinging a long, stout tree limb. Ian slammed the limb down on the catahoula's head and the dog dropped hard to the cobblestones, front legs akimbo.

The other four dogs were already high-tailing it out of the alley, when Ian turned, leaned on his stick, threw Charles his lopsided grin. "So, old sah-sot. Cain't you gah-get through one lah-lousy day without me rescuing your ah-ass?"

"I figure I was doin' jist fine 'thout no help from you, yes."

"As u-u-usual, you done figured wrong," Ian said. "Let's dah-do a duel, right here and right now. Your sha-shirt and that sta-stubby bone against my sta-stick."

They laughed until they couldn't laugh any more. Tears of joy mixed with tears of relief fell and were quickly diluted in the alley's bloody slime.

It took only a few minutes for the boys to rig up a couple of slings by tying together several pieces of severed ropes found at the other end of the alley. They loaded up parts of two bony hindquarters and a forequarter on their backs, and set out for St. Mary's.

"I hate to leave that other lot back there, yes," Charles said, adjusting the foul-smelling cargo on his back.

"Wah-well, one thing's for certain. They wah-won't be there lah-later."

Too many hungry people, just too damn many.

Less than fifteen minutes later, their backs starting to blister in numerous places by the rubbing bones, Charles and Ian entered the orphanage grounds by the back alley. Located as it was on Mazant Street, between Royal and Chartres, it was an easy-in and easy-out journey from just about any place in the city. The merchants in the area didn't like the orphanage or the gaggles of raggedy urchins that seemed to cover the streets at times. Because the orphanage existed on the site due to an agreement between the city and the church, the merchants couldn't express their feelings in any way but muttered curses; offending the church—or the city on most topics—was not an option.

Charles and Ian went directly to the kitchen, a separate building just to the west of the huge three-story orphanage. Jeannine LeTreau was standing at a counter, her back to the door. "Miss Jeannine" was the red-faced, chubby cook who regularly prepared meals for a constantly shifting number of boys (sometimes upward of two hundred) from flour and vegetable scraps delivered to her by assigned and volunteer scavenging crews and the three Sisters of the Marianite Order of the Holy Cross.

The sisters and older orphans kept the asylum doors open through miniscule monetary donations from the Archdioceses of New Orleans, from handouts from a handful of benefactors, local and from as far away as Indiana, and through scavenging forays into the inner city. Everything picked up had a use; nothing was rejected. In a world where having *nothing* was expected, then having *something*, having *anything*, was considered more than a treat…it was a godsend.

"The saints preserve us," Jeannine said, as the two boys kicked open the partially open kitchen door with a bang. Ian banged his bundle of cow bones on the door jam as he entered, then eased backward to the large chopping block that dominated the center of the spacious room. Charles followed, carefully maneuvering through the door, making sure not to hit the doorway with his load.

"Mah-miss Jeannine, my lah-love," Ian said, giving a deep bow, "we have for you the mah-makin's of a fah-fine feast."

"A mess you got, a mess is right, yes," the cook said, putting her hand to her mouth to suppress a grin. And, Charles surmised, to hide yellow corn teeth rotted into little, spiky shards. "But I swear that these bones, chopped up to pot size and boiled up nicely with some carrots, onions, celery and such will make a fine meal. Fine, says I."

She cocked her head and gave them a fat-faced grin.

"And where would the vegetables be?"

Charles jumped in: "What did you do with the vegetables, Ian? Didn't you have them? I swear you had handfuls just a moment ago."

Ian began patting his pockets, one by one. "I nah-know they must be here somewhere. Wha-where could they be?"

The cook laughed the laugh of the roly-poly clan, holding her hips as they shook like side-by-side billowing willows in a wind-gust. "I betcha plenty the Sisters bring some back. Those nuns can talk cats outta trees, I'm telling you, me."

Charles and Ian started a clamor about which nun would bring home the biggest bounty from a day of begging—Sister Mary Calvary, Sister Mary of the Nativity or Sister Mary of the Five Wounds (or Sister Cavalry, Sister Baby and Sister Bloody, as they were known to the orphans). Both sought to bet on Sister Bloody, because she was the best "bah-beggar, because she was the pah-prettiest," as Ian put it.

Charles relented and took Sister Baby for the bet—a hard lick on the loser's shoulder by the winner. It was Sister Baby who just a fortnight before brought home eighty dollars cash money after talking a rich gent into giving his solid gold snuff box to the orphanage to sell for food. The gentleman suffered through two stories about the "starving orphans" before he anted up. At the time Ian said she got the snuff box "'cah-cause she tha-threatened to cah-kiss him." Both boys agreed—Ian loudly and often, Charles only in thoughts—the word "comely" and Sister Baby were not even nodding acquaintances.

While Charles usually restrained himself from making harsh statements about anyone, he did enjoy hearing Ian when he got wound up. "Sah-sister Baby is as uh-ugly as the inside of a wah-wharfman's boot. Sha-she's so uh-ugly a uh-ugly dog would bah-bite itself afore it bah-bited her."

Charles loved it when Ian amused himself to the point of letting loose an addled donkey laugh that rattled the rafters.

CHAPTER 2

Measured Blessings

> *But is there for the night a resting-place?*
> *A roof for when the slow, dark hours begin?*
> Christina Georgina Rossetti

Ian had a hole in his heart, Charles instinctively knew. Like most orphans there was a missing piece that Ian—and others like him—were constantly trying to fill by different measures: Introverted determination, acute shyness, heightened sense of bravado—all offensive mechanisms while searching for a connection, a bond, with another human being. Even strangers were not excluded. It was not uncommon for a charge of St. Mary's or the girls' orphanage near the levee, slipping in and out of shadows, to follow strangers, to make up stories about how they were related. To many, that was better than the alternative: No family and no one to care whether they lived or died.

A vast majority of orphans had a common need: To find or claim missing family members. Many found comfort, at least at some point, by finding a relative to two, even if the person or persons existed only in their minds.

Charles, too, had a heart hole that was large. At times it seemed so big he would swear he could hear the wind blowing through it. The sound it made…dreary, soulful, low…seldom left him, even in sleep. And the mournful sound always hinted at the same unspoken questions.

Family? Why don't I have a family?

Sister Bloody knew the hearts of most of her charges, and tried to compensate for what was missing in each. She was a tender mother figure to those that needed special attention. She played the role of ritualistic matriarch when called upon to do so. To others she was religious instructress, giving plausible options to what some youngsters believed to be unanswerable questions. To Charles she was more of a big sister or young aunt than a religious scion or mother figure.

His quietness troubled her, exactly why she could not fathom. She watched him as he approached everyday life at the orphanage with a methodical sameness—eyes on the goal, hands at the ready, back bent to the task at hand. Whatever she wanted done, he did. Not happily. Not grudgingly. He just did it. When she praised him (which was often), he would smile or nod, or both, his eyes fixed on her face, so she could see the glassy reflections of the scene before him.

Only when she scolded him, or when one of the sisters or brothers did so, did emotion show in his face. Hooded eyes. Furrowed brow. Thin lips crushed thinner still. Anger, perhaps? But she didn't really believe that. Disappointment for letting others down, she decided. Her, the other nuns, or the brothers? she wondered. Hard way to go through life, she thought more than once.

She often marveled at the bond between Charles and Ian. Due to circumstances that placed the boys in similar life-scenarios—needy youths, authority-figure helpers, and older sibling role models—they had been inseparable for several years. At first, Ian detested the slight, quiet introvert with the wiry hair and funny eyes. The initial feeling was mutual. Charles thought Ian a bombastic, blow-hard who worked aggressively at being annoying, rude, and profane.

Over time—working hip-to-hip scrounging for scraps of food and usable items in the dank, dark city alleyways—without even realizing it, they began looking out for one another. Ian was street smart, wise to the whims and waves of the cobblestone pathways and dirt alleys that crisscrossed New Orleans; Charles was just plain smart, a reader, more studious, but much more naïve about the human heartbeat and bloodstream of the city. He was always surprised about the human nature aspect of aberrant situations in which the two often found themselves. Ian reacted immediately to such situations; Charles liked to study on things for a bit before taking action.

It was more than a partnership, more even than a kinship. It was an existence born out of individual desires for survival…and to be needed. On some level. By someone.

Life at the orphanage was like a woodpecker's tapping: Repetitive, with no apparent change in rhythm or purpose. For most of the older charges at St. Mary's, each day was a mirror image of the one before: Get up by six o'clock, roll up a thin blanket-pallet, help the little ones any way that was needed, eat something—pieces of cold hoecakes, flour milk, stale bread, coffee boiled with old grounds for the older charges, water or watery milk for the younger ones—go to the school room to practice reading and penmanship, listen to monotonic recitations on every subject from French history to simple principles of mathematics by sleepy-eyed priests, and do chores assigned by the priests and nuns.

For the older orphans the time spent in the classroom was diminished, the number of chores escalated. "Teaching responsibility," one grizzled brother intoned, after ordering Charles and Ian to remove the filled privy buckets, dump them in a nearby ditch, and give each a thorough washing before placing them again under the three irregular holes.

After chores, the charges went off scrounging, in pairs or organized packs.

For the most part, the priests at St. Mary's—Brother Vincent, the director, and Brothers Basil, Theodule, De Sales, Aloysius, and Gonzaga—assumed the role of harsh taskmasters and stern, by-the-rote teachers. The boys quickly learned any coddling (or, simply, kind words) would come from the nuns. One, actually: Sister Bloody. Holding forth a stern demeanor and a foreboding attitude were not in her.

Ian had come to like Charles' company because the slight, dark boy didn't talk much. Talking was Ian's forte, the one thing at which he excelled, despite his stammer, despite his disinterest in book learning, or learning anything that didn't have to do with minor adventure and survival. Over time, Charles found a familial contentment in listening to his stammering friend talk about nothing and everything. But then, again, he seldom listened with a full ear as he was always watching his surroundings, listening for out-of-place noises, looking for opportunities to make survival more of a certainty.

As Charles walked, his eyes constantly flitted side to side, like a swamp panther harried by a passel of hounds. His peripheral vision was passable, but was limited by the wide-brimmed hat he had heard some refer to as a Messkin

Gigolo. The hat was a rather fancy affair with short rear brim and longer brim in front. Six months earlier he had slipped it off the head of a dead man of undetermined heritage slumped in an alleyway. Charles circled the body and thought the man was probably a robbery victim or, perhaps, the end result of botched kidnapping by a crew of hard billys looking for seamen—willing or unwilling—to crew-out a whaling ship set for a voyage around the tip of South America and then head west across the Pacific Ocean.

The man had been beaten severely about the head. Charles took the hat without a single negative thought; he certainly didn't consider himself a thief.

You can't steal from a dead man.

That thought and others of a similar vein bounced around his head as he rescued the hat from under the man's blood-encrusted head. Water from a spitting summer shower, a little saliva, and elbow grease removed much of the stains congealed in the crown and sweat band.

Even thought Ian constantly made fun of his odd-looking hat, Charles liked it. It kept the sun and rain out of his eyes; and few people had one like it. While the hat kept him from seeing the entire world around him, it also prevented the world from seeing details of his face, which was in a constant shadow.

It's not that there was anything wrong with his face. It was, for lack of a better description, an ordinary face bordering on pleasant...serene even. Like most faces, it was a face of parts: Fleshy nose, a bit large for his small features; small ears, standing at attention at a forty-five-degree angle to his head; soft, brown eyes partially hidden beneath heavy lids; a straight mouth with thin lips; medium-brown hair hacked off short with a kitchen knife to hold lice at bay.

What most people saw first when they looked at him were his eyes. Highlighted as they were by a prominent high forehead and cheekbones with abrupt angles, their color (light cocoa, like the underside of a well-washed brown flannel shirt) was emphasized by the subdued, outside teardrop eyelid folds; golden flecks of color radiating from the edges of the cornea. His natural dark complexion, wiry, unruly hair, high cheekbones that hinted of Basque or Indian influence, and, again, those distinctive eyes, caused people to stare. Those eyes. That dark coloring. The dominant cheekbones. More than one person immediately thought of him as a mixed-breed, a blending of races. French Cajun-Oriental-Negro? Negro-Caucasian-Indian? Mexican-Oriental-Caucasian? While the possibilities seemed endlessly suspect, the truth, which he did not know, was quite simple.

REVEILLE

What he was or where he really came from, he didn't know for sure. Charles, like many of the St. Mary's charges, didn't remember his parents or the two brothers a nun told him he was supposed to have had. He didn't have a middle name, as far as he knew. It stressed him that he could not remember the names of his family, that when he tried to visit them in his dreams, most of the time their faces were blank slates. He was four when the dreaded Yellow Jack descended on the city like a swarm of viral locust. More than two thousand residents died from the distinctive smothering, choking, and agonizing death of the mosquito-borne disease in less than four months.

Sister Bloody had picked up a short, and quite unsensational, tale from a well-meaning neighbor woman who had delivered the mewling toddler to the orphanage. When Charles was eight and had started asking questions, the nun said his father was a doctor who came to this country a few years before Charles was born. He and his wife and his brothers died in a wave of the creeping sicknesses that hit the Crescent City every couple of years.

Although she did not know for certain, Sister Bloody felt sure that his family (like the French-born nuns and brothers at the orphanage) only knew that the "Port of New Orleans" was as close to living on French soil as you could get anywhere in the world.

Charles believed he was born several years after his family came to New Orleans. He was told he was four when he was dropped off at the orphanage but he thought he must have been younger.

At four, wouldn't you remember the names of your parents and brothers?

He tried to remember his family, to recall a name, any detail of his life before St. Mary's. He thought he could remember his father laughing and wearing a funny little hat. He thought he remembered two brothers, one bigger than the other.

Memories of his mother were different. Occasional vivid visions of his mother holding him tight, nuzzling his neck, swarmed his thoughts. She had brown hair, like his own, with a face of angles and light. Small eyes, assuredly, also like his, and clean hair as thick and unruly, tied up in a swirling topknot. In dreams and stray thoughts, she was called Josephine; her smile was small, yet captivating; flickering candlelight danced in her eyes. In his mind, she was always looking kindly at him, smiling.

Always.

CHAPTER 3

Intrusion of War

War can only be abolished through war, and in order to get rid of the gun it is necessary to take up the gun.
Mao Zedong

February 4, 1861.
War came to New Orleans fast after Louisiana seceded from the Union. It was only two months and eight days after succession that General Pierre Gustave Toutant Beauregard and his Louisiana regiment attacked Fort Sumter in South Carolina. When word reached the city that Louisiana boys, most from New Orleans or hamlets to the north and west, had attacked Fort Sumter, the communal pride at the feat was palpable.

For a time, Beauregard's name was toasted in every tavern in town. Newspapers carried various descriptions of the one-sided battle, with the single similarity being the heroic act of the general and his Louisianans.

But in a certain section of the city, many residents—the social outcasts, the illiterate, the poor and those that worked with them, including the brothers and nuns at St. Mary's and the older charges like Charles and Ian, didn't understand what the hullabaloo was all about.

Despite what warmongers from both the North and South said, the conflict was over slavery. States rights were the cloak issue; the real reason was hidden in even gloomier shadows. Those that had slaves were, by God, going to keep them, and expand the practice to the New West. Those that vehemently opposed slavery, didn't want the practice continued under any circumstances.

As it was throughout the South, slavery was evident in New Orleans. But it was simply a blink in the kaleidoscope of New Orleans' daily activities. There were more free black men and women in the city at the start of the Civil War than in any other in the United States. Many "freedmen" were the blood-children of the city's founders and myriad passers-through that helped create the city's vibrant, colored under-culture. White. Black. French. Cuban. Chinese. Irish. German. Italian. No color or culture were missing from core societies of New Orleans.

Many coloreds were classified *gens de couleur libre* (men of free color) and noted as such in official documents, including the Census; background, education, and obtained wealth bought many negroes and those of mixed races a special place in the city's elite upper class.

In New Orleans society's color spectrum, there was not a profession in the city—from blacksmiths to butchers, from doctors to bookbinders, from musicians to engineers, from masons to carpenters, from cooks to clerks—that did not count free negroes among its members.

Despite the local truism concerning the number of free coloreds and slaves in the city, the announcement of a rebellion against the uppity North ignited a feeling of us-versus-them pride in the city. The excitement was short-lived. Two months after Fort Sumter, Admiral David Farragut, a Tennessean who had been raised in Louisiana, was named Union Flag Officer for the West Gulf Blockading Squadron. In that role he commanded a force of eighteen wooden ships, a fleet of mortar boats, and 700 men.

The news that Farragut was intent on capturing New Orleans was not unexpected. Farragut was a military legend, having been appointed a midshipman at age nine, and assumed command of his first United States naval vessel at twelve.

Now, fifty years later, he was preparing to sail a small armada up the Mississippi River and fight its way past two well-armed Confederate forts (Forts Jackson and St. Philip). It was his lone aim to enter New Orleans Harbor and demand the surrender of the city.

The Federal ships entered the mouth of the Mississippi, laid anchor, and its officers began debating the best way to pass by the two forts. In less than two days, word filtered upriver about the progress of the Union ships. The city's rumor mill started working overtime.

"Six Union ships sunk by Fort Jackson guns!"

"Union ships were driven back to the Gulf!"

"Did you hear? Farragut tied trees—full-grown trees—to the masts of his ships to make the batteries at the forts think they were trees on the far shore."

"I heard the ship's crews hand-painted the ships with mud to make them harder to see at night!"

"An armada of Union ships made it past both forts and will be arriving in a few hours!"

The blow-by-blow fight downriver between the shelling of ships and the two forts, delivered via fishing boats caught upstream of the fight, and riders on horseback, caused a near panic throughout the city. Families dispersed to reside with relatives and friends inland; husbands sent spouses and children to sanctuaries set up in churches far north of the city; prices of goods spiked; citizens hoarded goods (everything from dry goods to nails to food destined to spoil before being consumed), with the practice decried in the street and from church pulpits. An active, compliant society with a live-and-let-live attitude, quickly degenerated into an every-man-for-himself attitude.

Despite admonitions from Sister Bloody and the strict, brittle brothers, Charles and Ian went to the southernmost levee several times a day hoping to catch a glimpse of the invading armada. The Confederate naval force at New Orleans was a mishmash of vessels—a handful of trade schooners fitted with a three or four small cannons, several bobbing flatboats with mortars lashed to the bow, plus assorted fishing vessels manned by musketeers.

April 28, 1862.

Charles and Ian were sitting on the top of the levee just south of St. Louis Cathedral. The pair were watching seven, no, eight, smallish boats flying the Confederate flag form up a ramshackled, floating barricade in the middle of the Mississippi. The boys were talking about the war, about how life was going to change for everyone. At first, Ian thought "An orphan's lah-life don't change. Eh-it just keeps on bah-being life." After thinking on it a bit, he then decided, "Ah-I guess everything is gah-going to change, even the life of orphans."

Nudging his friend, Charles pointed to the far bend in the river. The sails of a three-masted schooner could be seen over the low roof of a foundry. Soon after, the tall masts of three other ships, knotted up tight, came into view.

Charles' heart bird-fluttered as the four ships, all flying the Stars and Stripes and West Gulf Squadron battle flags, came down the river, two abreast.

"Wah-we've got more bah-boats."

Yes, Charles acknowledged. "But they's be bigger."

The battle was short-lived. Less than an hour later, with the Union ships flinging cannon balls high and on target and the Rebels answering with smaller guns, most of the shells splashing harmlessly in the river, six of the small Rebel boats were keeled over or were lying in the mud in the bottom of the river. The remaining two Rebel ships, both damaged and limping under partial sail, fled to the north, staying near the south river edge to avoid the heavier current flow.

By the time the boys returned to the orphanage, the city leaders had surrendered, and Farragut announced New Orleans was, once again, Union soil. The city was on edge…and would remain so for more than four long years.

When Farragut accepted the surrender of the city without a shot being fired in the town, New Orleans was the largest cotton market in the world and was, by far, the wealthiest city in America. It had been an American city for barely more than fifty years before it found itself a city captured in wartime.

Charles would never forget the sight of the first Union soldiers he had ever seen. He, Ian and Sarie Beth McPhee from the Academy of Holy Angels on St. Claude Avenue (known by locals as the Female Orphans Asylum), were scavenging through holey Crocker sacks and barrels of discarded trash. It was a messy, but necessary task and all three of the youths tackled it with grit; outright enthusiasm was held in abeyance until something of real value—thrown-away vegetables still good enough to eat, scraps from local bakeries or restaurants—was rounded up to take to the orphanages.

The trio was a team that was not supposed to be. The same three French nuns at St. Mary's started the girl's orphanage a few years after their arrival in America, and quickly took responsibility of more than a hundred female orphans. They were openly adamant about their male charges not fraternizing with the female counterparts; they were just as adamant, albeit covertly, about certain boys accompanying the older girls on foraging trips. The city streets were rough, and wartime anxieties and bands of occupation soldiers did nothing to smooth them out.

The nuns, and certain realistic brothers, looked the other way when Ian and Charles waited for Sarie on the corner of Frenchmen and Esplanade Streets near the orphanage. It would be unseemly, Sister Bloody had told them, to go directly to the orphanage. "Mind your manners. Be discreet. Be respectful to Sarie Beth at all times." Those were her instructions, words they took seriously.

Sarie was thirteen and claimed she had been born at the orphanage. Charles did not correct her, even though he believed babies were never, ever born at any orphanage, only left at them when they were unwanted for a variety of reasons. Though Sister Bloody told the orphans over and over again that orphans were gifts to God from people who could not take care of an infant, Charles had his own ideas about why babies, toddlers, and even older children were sent to orphanages: They were deformed, ugly by some unknown standard, or an untimely death of a parent or parents led to the decision to deposit a child as a ward of the church.

That initial theory didn't hold water, he readily admitted, when he learned from Sister Bloody that some of the orphans were *paid* residents; some relative actually paid hard money—albeit a small sun—for the orphanage to raise a child. He was shocked to learn that more than fifty boys—a fourth of the total number—actually paid rent for the *privilege* of residing at St. Mary's. It's not like the monthly stipend paid to St. Mary's for each orphanage bought any special favors; whatever was available to eat the nuns made sure was shared equally.

What kind of person would pay to put a kid in this place?
Charles's second thought was more disturbing.
What's so terribly wrong with a kid that someone would pay to put them here?
For the first time, he took comfort in his being at the orphanage.
At least I am here because I don't have a family.
A solid, sobering thought hit him like a two-by-four between the eyes.
If I had family, would I still be at St. Mary's?
Dieu nous sauvent!
God save us!

Charles couldn't put into words how he felt about Sarie Beth; she was a friend who seemed shy and extroverted...sometimes at the same time. On occasion she gushed on and on about everything…and nothing. Above all, he knew Sarie Beth trusted him implicitly.

Charles was of the age when he liked looking at women and girls, dreamed about them, and wanted to be in close proximity to the opposite sex whenever possible.

He didn't know what to make of his thoughts about Sarie Beth. But he was sure that if she could read his mind, she would run as fast as possible back to the Academy of Angels (as the orphanage was sometimes called), and never come outside again. He had kissed her once, he thought; she might have kissed him. But the experience, as brief as a cat sneeze, was often resurrected in his pre-sleep thoughts and deep-sleep dreams.

Wish we were more than friends.
But if we were, could we still be friends?

Ian first heard the commotion and told Charles and Sarie Beth he thought it was on Iberville, a couple of streets over. The trio hustled over in the direction of a cacophony of noise, mixed cheers, and jeers. Cutting through an alleyway, they emerged from the other end. The sight greeting them was profound: Union soldiers took up the entire street, gutter to gutter. Each marching soldier, save the lads holding flags and drums, shouldered cap-and-ball rifles with fitted bayonets, looking all the world like a moving, gigantic blue pin cushion.

At the front of the column were two men on horseback, one in the lead and one in a slightly subservient position off the lead horse's right flank. The second rider had a Union flag strapped to a pole, the end of which was firmly grounded in a pouch-like contraption on his right stirrup.

What caught Charles' eye was the lead rider's hat, an off-white, big-brimmed affair, the left side pinned up. Sprouting from the pinned-up crease was a long, flowing, dark-red feather. The conscious attempt at color coordination—red, white and blue—did not escape Charles' notice.

The officer was holding a long, shiny sword with gold-and-silver guard decorated with an interlaced, indescribably intricate, web-work design. His uniform was tailored and pressed; buttons caught sunbeams and sprayed them in all directions. The horse's saddle and bridle were punctuated with silver, embossed circles of light.

Just as the rider and horse got even with them, Ian pointed directly at the officer and said in an overly loud voice, "Wha-what a pah-poppinjay."

The rider slowly turned his head, looked directly at Ian. A toothy wolf-grin slid onto his face. He nodded at Ian, then purposefully took his sword, held straight out in front of him, then slowly twisted in the saddle and swung the sword to the side until it pointed directly at his verbal tormentor.

His grin expanded as he made a slight stabbing motion with the sword, and then popped it smartly back to his shoulder.

"Fah-fooking popinjay," Ian said in a subdued undertone, before quickly making the sign of the cross. Sarie Beth hit him hard on the arm before she and Charles mimicked Ian crossing motion.

The solders that followed were in perfect step; their uniforms were pressed, perfectly matched with white bandoliers, and white belts with copper buckles, shined bright.

The troops marched to a cadence pounded out by four drummers, and it was at them that Charles stared. An older soldier, the obvious leader, marched in the front left column; the other drummers, obviously younger, cast nervous glances at him from time to time. They all looked anxious, overwhelmed. They glanced around in a nervous way, squinty-eyed, lips as tight as their drum heads.

Marching out in the open in enemy territory might do that to a person.

The drum line was split by two flag-bearers, one with the Union flag, one holding the regimental flag of the Thirteenth Maine. The drummers beat out a syncopated rhythm that was easy to follow: *Barrumm, barrumm, barrumm, rumm, rumm.* Line after line of the soldiers passed, eyes to the front, in step, chests popping, proud as peacocks.

"They do look grand, don't they?" Sarie Beth said in a whisper, obviously comparing the Union soldiers to the rag-tag outfits of Confederates who, until recently, had been bivouacked throughout the city and at watcher-camps up and down the Mississippi.

When the Federals moved into the city in force, the Confederates took off in various directions, mainly North and East. Pockets of Grays wandered around in the vicinity of New Orleans, mainly to probe and pry and see how serious the Union Army was about New Orleans' occupation. The occupation was serious business for the North. Dead serious. And the Confederates knew it.

Any talk about a Confederate attack on the city was just that: Talk.

CHAPTER 4

When the Worst Is Over...

Good and evil are repaid in kind, just as shadows follow bodies, and echoes follow sound.
Chinese proverb

May, 1862.
Charles loved New Orleans in the springtime. He was walking his normal looking-for-handouts grid off Jackson Square, with no luck as yet. He raised his head a notch, sniffing the air. A fresh southern breeze tempered the usual unpleasant stench, as well as early heating spells waiting to spring into action; humidity was at its lowest except for the dead winter months; yards and window boxes were profuse with an artist's palette of flowers.

A column of starchy Union boys marched by, their columns stuck dead center in the middle of the street. For the past month the townspeople had seen columns of Union soldiers marching from here to there, from there to here. In his fine mood, Charles thought the column looked sprightly, in an almost-elegant sort of way.

Those boys stand out right smart.

Over the next several months, Federal companies and brigades would be scattered around the city; tent cities would spring up overnight in the strangest places—parks, consecutive empty lots, cemeteries, near the docks—like the eruption of toadstools after a shower.

Charles had started out on the food hunt with Ian, Sarie Beth, and Sister Bloody. They had split up just east of Canal (with Sarie and Sister Bloody staying together) to quicken the search for suitable leftovers. Ian headed north while Charles worked his way east, crisscrossing the narrow alleys between Bourbon and Royal, searching, always searching. On this particular foraging trek, he found a recent four-page edition of the *L'Union*, the city's first paper owned and operated by a negro, Paul Trevigne. From his first issue, the editor stirred up quite a controversy with his outspoken commentary. Charles picked up the discarded paper, read over a couple of the single-column headlines before folding it and sticking it in his back pants pocket.

Reading material for contemplation time in the privy.

Exiting a narrow alley onto Royal, Charles turned left toward Lafayette Square and abruptly stopped. For the first time, he noticed Union pickets standing on the southwest corner by St. Louis Cathedral. They didn't seem overly serious about their duty; they were just standing, looking, watching the stream of carriages and strolling shoppers entering and exiting the square.

Planning to stay to the outside of the square to avoid scrutiny—just why, he was not sure—Charles caught the eye of one of the soldiers, who stiffened slightly. Charles nodded, put on his best I-belong-here look, and turned the corner. It was not the direction he had intended to go (his normal route would have taken him directly in front of the cathedral); it was the quickest line away from the sentries.

It had been a week since he had been to the square, so he was unprepared for the sight: Forty to fifty small tents and one, two, three…six large tents were pitched on the square in almost perfect alignment.

The tents were dingy with age and wear; irregular gray blotches of mildew marred every tent he could see. But, even with the seediness of the miniature tent city, it was evident the soldiers had worked at trying to make the city-within-a-city unobtrusive, which was impossible due to the park-like surroundings. The entire area was clean, which surprised Charles. Why, he didn't have a clue. With such a gaggle, maybe he expected clutter. But any extra gear was stacked in neat lines along the north side of each tent. There was no trash that he could see.

Leaning against a wooden post holding up one corner of a second story balcony above a tobacco and pipe shop, Charles took in the scene with a subtle hint of excitement he really didn't expect and couldn't explain. This was, he decided, a day he was to be bewildered.

A day to be bewildered.
The thought amused him.

A group of about twenty soldiers, some in regulation uniforms, others in civilian dress, were marching with syncopated steps in the middle of the cobblestone street in front of the massive cathedral. They were under the harsh eyes and strong voice of a sergeant with unruly red hair that stuck out from under his forage cap at all angles. The soldier bellowed orders and insults with equal vigor.

"Your left! Your left! Not that left, you damn dummy! Where'd you learn to march? With the consarned Reb Army or your Aunt Bessie's quiltin' group?

"Your left! Your left!"

The soldiers passed by Charles, their eyes fixed on some distance street corner. A short soldier at the rear missed a step and was rewarded for the error with a swipe from the sergeant's broad brogan.

"Don't you miss a step in my platoon! You hear me? Do you hear me?"

"Yes, Sergeant."

Charles thought the young soldier was going to cry. Sadness nipped at Charles' hairline, threatening to fall into his eyes. He shook off the feeling and turned back toward the square. A flapping blue, red and yellow flag at the top of a long, thin, skinned tree caught his eye: *Ninth Connecticut Regiment.* A smaller flag, green with yellow letters followed the larger flag's lead: *The Irish Brigade.*

Wonder if they have a French brigade?

Word hit the street like a thrown stone: Lincoln, the northerner who called himself leader of the invading army, had named General Benjamin F. Butler as the military governor of occupied New Orleans. After a hastily called, strained meeting with a dour-faced audience of city officials and regional gentry, there were few kind words uttered about the man. Those that had heard stories about him repeated them. Those that had never heard the name mentioned believed the stories. In wartime, it somehow seemed better to believe what was spoken as the truth rather than simply "not know."

When Butler arrived in New Orleans several weeks later he made a show around town, riding up one street and down another with a contingent of officers, all well-armed—swords, pistols (some carried two) and filled rifle scabbards fitted flush between horse and thigh. As a rule, Butler led his men down the middle of the street as he made his tour, forcing other horsemen, dray wagons, buggies, and pedestrians to the street's edge. Many wagon and buggy drivers, seeing the group coming in the distance, quickly sought the comfort of side streets. In thinking about and dealing with Butler, fearing the unknown and acting irrationally was a continuous pastime among the townsfolk.

The general made his intentions known quickly. One of his first acts was to shut down a secessionist newspaper, the *New Orleans Daily Crescent*. Since New Orleans had surrendered, martial law—Butler's law—reigned, and the military governor drew hard on the reins. He followed the newspaper outrage by mandating all residents to swear allegiance to the Union; those that refused to so declare, some silently, others with inspired venom, saw their property—house, household goods, animals, slaves—confiscated. The legal plunder was either used for housing and feeding officers and the troops, or sold to favored speculators with open pocketbooks, few scruples, and no conscience.

Butler's hard reputation crystallized, Brother Bartholomew told Charles and Ian one day, when the general ordered the hanging of a man suspected of desecrating the American flag. The public hanging infuriated the townspeople. But overriding the fury was fear…the exact reaction Butler had sought to inflict with the hanging.

"At least the worst is over," a city official proclaimed at an impromptu street gathering. "It can't get no worser than this."

Then it got worse.

The most outspoken segment of the populous were certain womenfolk. Groups of them would meet and walk down board sidewalks or at the edge of the street, purposely going out of their way to confront Union officers and soldiers. The term "ladylike" did in no way reflect on members of the outspoken female bands that roamed the streets, looking for soldiers to harass. Soldiers were insulted, openly laughed at, taunted, cursed, and their manhood brought into question in various forums, from dining rooms to church meetings to street corners. Columns of marching soldiers were targets for garbage thrown by small, gloved hands with unerring accuracy.

And all the while, the men folk looked on in abject, but mostly silent, pride.

Charles and Ian would take back tales of such behavior and the Sisters would cluck-cluck, clutching their crosses with more religious fervor than usual.

General Butler warned city officials to set about curtailing the activities, telling them on more than one occasion that if he had to step in to solve the problem, no one would be happy with his solution.

The personal attacks continued unabated, culminating when a Bourbon Street resident opened her second-floor window and dumped the contents of a chamber pot on the passing Admiral Farragut. Various stories flew through the city on gossip-wings—"Not one pot, two, and both of 'em to-the-brim full!" and "I heard he was hit square above the left ear with the whole pot!"

Butler quickly issued General Order Number 28, which was posted throughout the city the next day. It was startlingly simple, intentionally antagonistic, and to the point: Any woman who insulted a member of the United States Army would be treated as a prostitute, in "the midst of plying her trade."

The action, the order, gave new meaning to the term "outrage" for New Orleans residents. The town's prostitutes didn't take it as a compliment either and let their soldier customers know about it. "Pillow talk" took on a whole new meaning when the subject of General Order Number 28 was raised.

Butler's actions were reviled in every business, household, brothel, and church and he quickly became known to all residents as "Beast" Butler.

Despite protests from city leaders, Butler refused to rescind the order, which resulted in the harassment of union troops ceasing. No New Orleans woman was ever arrested.

Butler's disruptive actions did not cease with General Order No. 28.

Charles and Ian were skirting Place d'Armes, which was becoming better known as Jackson Square, on a sunny Saturday when they noticed a gaggle of soldiers surrounding the elegant equestrian statue of Andrew Jackson, the hero of the original Battle of New Orleans. It was Jackson who was credited with saving the city from the British less than fifty years previously.

The boys sauntered closer to the statue. A slight man, hawk-nosed, with small eyes, was bent down at the base of the statue. Using a small, wooden-handled chisel and wood mallet, he was carefully, methodically, carving words into the statue's base. Working near the end of three lines, he stopped now and again to wipe his brow. When he reached for another, sharper chisel, Charles read the inscription: "The Union must and shall be preser…

"'Preserved', I reckon," Charles muttered to Ian.

"Git along now, boys," a soldier with two gold bars on his epaulettes said. "I'm sure you got business elsewheres."

The two boys decided the soldier was right.

After telling the tale to one of the orphanage Brothers later than night, he opined, "I guess they think that when you win you can do anything."

That thought never entered Charles' mind. He was thinking about what it would take to become a stone carver and how one went about learning the craft.

Butler's heavy-handed ways didn't stop at the boundaries of the city. Figuring friction between masters and slaves at area plantations had to be firestorm high, he issued an order declaring the plantation owners to be disloyal to the Union…and confiscated their property—their slaves. Adding insult to injury, he immediately declared them free.

Within a week, as soon as many of the slaves figured out the order was for real and would be enforced, they left the plantations by the hundreds and flooded the city looking for paying work. Some fled north and east behind Union lines seeking safety and the promise of freedom. To ensure there were no retaliatory actions by former slave owners, Butler proclaimed that any person "disloyal to the Union"—and his orders—would be hanged.

The citizens held rallies demanding due process under the ruthless rule of Butler. They quickly found out that due process under Butler's definition of martial law was what he decided it would be with the definition changing on a day-to-day basis.

In a pompous speech to city leaders about his actions, Butler said, "I was always a friend of southern rights, but an enemy of southern wrongs."

The Union occupation of the city intensified life-struggles at every turn: With fewer ships tying up at city docks, fewer goods were coming into the city, fewer items were for sale, commerce faltered, money tightened up. It was a vicious cycle that affected every resident, from the richest citizen to the wandering homeless and orphans, who were trying to subsist on a dwindling number of charitable acts.

Charles, Ian, and Sarie Beth redoubled their efforts in scavenging forays; they ate what they found if the findings were too small to make a difference at the orphanages; they brought other donations—week-old, hard bread, blinked milk, weevily flour, vegetable leavings—back to the orphanage, without exception.

Places where in previous days the boys could count on a donation of some sort—McIntosh's Saloon, Kurtmeyer's Market, Wu Sing's combination laundry and Chinese restaurant—were barely eking out a living. All three proprietors were so nice about turning them away that Charles and Ian conscientiously avoided the establishments so the owners wouldn't feel badly about having to take care of their own first.

Conditions worsened over the fall and winter...and into early spring. The trio was tired of scrounging and finding little or nothing at all to bring back to the orphanage. They were tired of trying and failing. They were just...tired.

June 2, 1963

Charles and Ian made a joint decision: They were going to leave St. Mary's. The two pals made the decision while on one of their wandering walks along the southernmost levee near the docks.

"But, what is Sister Bloody going to do without us there?"

"Sha-she'll get sah-someone else to take our place. John Menders is getting real good at sca-scrounging."

"John is twelve."

"Bah-but he's an old twelve."

They talked for hours, walking back and forth on the levee. As the sun was gasping its last breath of the day, the issue talked to death, the decision made, they trotted over to the see Sarie Beth.

Of course, they couldn't just walk up to the door and knock, so they wandered outside for a while until they caught the eye of a younger girl named Mildred and motioned her to the window.

"Would you please get Sarie Beth," Charles said. The dark-eyed girls smiled and darted off. Sarie Beth appeared quickly and could see by the boys' expression that something was wrong.

Charles was trying to think of how to form the proper words when Ian said, "Wha-we're leaving. Joining the Reb army, we ah-are."

Forgetting decorum and ignoring the fact her petticoat would show, Sarie Beth climbed out the window; with the boys help, she landed feet first. She gave both of them a quick look, and took off running down the street.

"Sarie Beth! Wait!" Charles said, before flying after her with Ian close behind.

Two blocks down there was a government building with a small green area in front, and a rickety latticework iron bench with bowlegs. When the boys got to it, Sarie Beth was slumped over on it, crying with the passion of the heartsick.

Charles sat down beside her, his hand on her shoulder. With a nod, he motioned Ian to the edge of the bench near her feet. Charles began slowly stroking her hair, which was pulled back tight and dropped into two perfect pigtails.

"Don't cry, Sarie Beth," Charles said. "Please don't cry." The wails intensified.

Charles looked at Ian, who was sobbing, his face in his hands.

With the shadows of dark closing in, and the tears of all three flowing freely, they held onto each other with a desperation bordering on total depression.

After several minutes, Sarie Beth sat up, wiped her eyes on her jumper sleeve and pulled both boys into a heart-felt hug. "I knew you were going, you know. Boys are so…what's the word…?

"Stupid?" Charles queried.

"Yes, that's true enough. But you are, what is that word? Easy to see through? Transparent! You can see right though boys if you are a girl. I knew you were plotting something and I thought I knew what it was, but I didn't want to believe it. Not you two. Not now. Not ever."

Ian was not longer crying; he had traded tears for hiccups. "Wha-we better be—*hic-ough*—getting you bah-back," Ian said.

"That's right, Sarie Beth. We don't want to get you in trouble with the sisters."

"Posh and bother! I don't care if I get in trouble. What are they going to do, slap my hand with a stick! Slap it, then. I don't care! I'll go back when I'm ready."

Over the next thirty minutes, the boys told her their mighty plans and hopes and made promises to come back to visit. "And, one day," Charles said, "we'll all be living somewhere close so we can visit and be friends forever."

Sarie started crying again. This time the boys were silent, just touching her arms to let her know they were…close.

"No, we won't," she said, between dry heave-hiccups. "That isn't what happens in life and you know it. You can make all the pretty plans you want, say all the right things to make me feel better. Then you will just walk off and join the danged old army and you'll both be killed and I'll never see either of you again."

The depressive feelings boiled like thick fog.

Hours later they walked Sarie back to the girls' orphanage. They stopped within sight of the sprawling house. Two nuns, silhouetted by the lamplight coming through the window, were sitting on the front porch, looking nervously up and down the street.

"Stay here," Sarie Beth said, and went barreling down the street toward the orphanage, skirt tail and pigtails trailing in her wake.

The boys saw both nuns jump up when Sarie approached. Frantic voices, loud and raucous, and extravagant waving of hands greeted her—spastic sign language of the harried female kind. It looked to the two boys as if Sarie Beth was trying to insert an explanation into the double-barreled harangue session. Whatever she said calmed the nuns down enough for her to exuberantly wave to the boys to come closer.

They walked and stood politely under a lit streetlamp, voiced appropriate greetings to the two nuns—Sisters Cavalry and Baby—and waited for their verbal punishment.

Sister Baby stepped forward. She gave the boys a look reminiscent of Solomon at decision time. "It's not proper for a young lady to be out unaccompanied. You know that and should respect Sarah Elizabeth, even if you don't respect yourself." Her face softened. "She has said that you are going to join the army. Is that right?"

"Yes, Sister. Tomorrow."

"Have you told Sister Mary of the Five Wounds?"

Charles faltered and Ian pitched in: "Nah-no, Sister. We aim to lah-later."

"Be sure you do. Now, it's time you got back to St. Mary's. Go along now."

"Bye, Sarie Beth," Charles said. "We'll be seein' you, yes. Count on it. And we're not goin' to git killed either. Ian's too mean to die and I'm too pretty."

"Tha-the runt's got that bah-backwards, is all."

Despite her evident sorrow, Sarie laughed. "I love you both. Be safe and come see me. If I'm not here, I'll leave word with the sisters. Come back. Promise?"

"Promise!"

"Dah-double promise."

CHAPTER 5

Hard Life Decisions

Leaving home in a sense involves a kind of second birth in which we give birth to ourselves.
Robert Neely Bellah

Charles and Ian slipped down the creaky stairs in the dark, staying to the inside by the wall where the boards were tight. They maneuvered down the long front hall, through a small dining room to the kitchen, moving in the pitch darkness like blind men in familiar surroundings.

In the kitchen, Ian stood by the door listening, while Charles opened a cabinet door and pulled out two fist-sized chunks of hard bread he had placed there the night before.

He *psssted* to Ian and moved quickly to the back door, pushed aside the floor-level, wooded, door stop with his foot and slowly opened the door. He took a step down onto the small stoop and stopped dead in his tracks, feeling rather than seeing a presence on the miniature porch.

"Sit down, Charles," Sister Bloody said, her lilting, accented voice hitting his heart like a railroad spike. Charles sat, his legs off the edge of the porch. He heard a scuffing noise as Ian came through the door: "Sit down, Ian," Sister Bloody repeated.

"Gah-gah-gawd-a-mighty!" Ian said in a whisper. "Why dinit ya scare the bah-bejeezus out of somebody?"

Charles could feel the nun's dismay in the silence that enveloped them.

"Why—?" was all she got out before she started quietly crying. Charles couldn't see her but he could "feel" her, sitting on the top step, holding her head in her hands.

"It's not you, Sister. It's this place. Ian and me have been here our whole lives. This is all we know. There's got to be somethin' out there better, somewhere, yes. We left you a note—"

"I know," the sister said, "in the big Bible, in the chapter about the prodigal son. Appropriate in a way, wouldn't you say?"

"We're gah-going to jin up wah-with the Confederate Army, see us a big chunk of tha-the country," Ian said, his voice shaking as if he were cold.

Sister Bloody sniffed once, again, then exhaled loudly. "So, you think fighting in this stupid war that's split the country, split families, and has already left thousands and thousands of good lads dead and rotting on fallow fields is better than living here with people who love you?"

"Not better, Sister," Charles offered. "Different. New." He didn't say the thought ricocheting inside his head.

Loves us? Who besides you?

Charles felt her hand touch his knee, move to his arm and down to his hand. She held it, gave it a squeeze, pressed something cool and familiar into it and stood up. He took the rosary with the small crucifix and stuck it deep in his pocket.

"Come here, you two," she commanded between gulping sobs. "I'm just being selfish. You've been such a big help in gathering food for the little ones. I'll just miss you, that's all." Dry sobs racked her body.

The trio hugged on the tiny porch for what seemed like hours, but was still not long enough for Charles.

"You be safe, you hear me?" she said harshly, finally loosening her grip around their necks. "Be gone with you, if you're going. Remember your lessons, especially the ones from the Church. Be safe and God protect you. And come back to see me after the war when you're all grown up. And don't forget your rosary and Hail Mary's."

"We will. We assuredly will, me and Ian," Charles said, knowing for a fact that probably was a lie.

The boys slipped down the alley, willing themselves not to look back. Both stopped at the street corner and glanced over their shoulders. They could see nothing but shadows in various shades of black.

Charles put his hand in his pocket and directed his thumb and forefinger to gently stroke the small cross.

Daylight was breaking as Charles and Ian trudged along the well-worn path at the top of the levee. A soft summer breeze blew off the river cool and clean. Their destination was several miles east of the French Quarter; they were headed toward an old boarding house that had been converted into a Confederate Army recruitment center. The irony that the recruiting center was within three or four long rifle shots of the Union encampment located just up the river at DuCrois Station, not to mention the two battalions located in the city center, was lost on the two boys.

They had hiked to the Confederate camp the previous day to check it out and were amazed that the soldiers went nonchalantly about their business as though Yankee troops were not encamped less than five miles to the north and not more than six miles to the west. Tents sprouted in a vacant lot next to the old boarding house that had served as a wagon stop for east-west travelers before train tracks cut through the backcountry like dandelions after a spring shower. Uniformed soldiers stood about, rifles close by, but few at the ready. Two soldiers sat over a small fire, cooking something on a spit. Ian pointed to the pair: "Dah-don't that look like a cah-cat carcass to you," he said. Charles forced the image and the ensuing thought to retreat.

He pointed out to Ian a smattering of civilians going in and out of the boarding house.

"Wah-well, ol' sah-sot," Ian said, "Here we are. Let's go gah-get our sah-soldiering gear and go kill us some Yah-yanks."

Charles wanted to wait a bit and observe the surroundings, but found himself trudging along in Ian's footsteps. Confidence was one attribute Ian had in abundance, Charles thought as they entered the building.

Be nice if he had some common sense to go along with it.

Inside they were directed to the courtyard to the rear of the house and there they got in line behind a tall, lanky man, who looked to be in his early twenties.

"How old do you have to be to get into the army?" Charles whispered to Ian.

"I'm tellin' 'im I-I-I'm sah-seventeen," Ian said.

Charles looked up at Ian and encountered his goofy grin. "What does that make me look like, nine?" Charles said.

"Tha-they only want men, ya dog dah-dick! Not Frenchie runts!" he finished with a chuckle.

The man in front of Ian made his mark on a long sheet of paper, said, "Thankee Sergeant," and moved aside. Charles watched as he was directed to follow a soldier who also had an upside down V on his sleeves.

Ian stepped up and said in a loud voice: "Eh-Ian O'Rourke rah-reporting for duty, Sah-Sir!" He finished by standing at what he thought was attention and popping a salute, which ended up looking like he was trying to shield the sun from his eyes.

The sergeant looked at Ian like he wanted to spit in his eye. "So, ya wanna be a soldier in the best army in the world, do you, Snotnose!"

Ian relaxed and nodded his head up and down like a dog with an earful of ticks. "Yah-you betcha. Indeedydo I do."

"So you say you're at least sixteen. That be right?"

"Sah-sixteen, it is. How'd ja know?"

"Sign right cheer," the burly sergeant said, pointing to a long line at the bottom of the page. "Ya git eleven Confederate dollars a month, a uniform when some more come in, a blanket after a while, some other trinkets, and you get half a tent to share. You get to do a lot of walking and take in the beautiful countryside. An' you kin pitch yore half-sheet anywheres ya a mind to inside a set area. How's that for a deal?"

Without reading the document, Ian signed his name in a perfect cursive script.

"Why, that's a fine hand, indeed," the sergeant said, showing it to a younger, less-secure soldier standing to his right. "I don't think I've ever seen such a pretty handwriting. You'll do fine, son. Get on with yourself with the corporal there," he said as he pointed to a fat soldier leaning against the fence, "and he'll get your gear and get you sit-e-ated. Welcome to the By God Johnny Reb Army."

Ian jumped out of line and the sergeant leveled his eyes at Charles.

"What ya want, boy?" the sergeant growled as Charles took a step up to the table.

"My name is Charles Andre and I want to join up, me," Charles said, his voice cracking.

"We don't take nigras nor runts, in that order. We ain't in that bad a shape yit. Next!" the sergeant bawled.

Charles didn't budge. "I ain't no nigra an' I ain't no runt!"

"I said 'Next!' Now git!" the corporal said, loudly and with meaning.

Charles remained still, the tops of his thighs pressed firmly against the table.

"I want to join up and fight Yankees," he said in a measured tone, staring straight at the soldier.

Charles felt footsteps behind him and instinctively tucked his neck into his collarless shirt as a protective reflex.

"What's the problem here, Sergeant?" a rich baritone voice rang out.

Charles glanced over his right shoulder and saw a tall man looking down at him. The man was in a tailored, clean uniform with gold braid, epaulets, and a shiny sword in an ornate scabbard. His hair was long, to his shoulders; a mustache perfectly framed his mouth on three sides.

The sergeant stood quickly and snapped to attention.

"No problem, Major. This here quadroon or octoroon tis tryin' to jine up is all. I was just sendin' him on his way."

The major's kind eyes stayed on Charles.

"So, boy, are you a nigra like the sergeant says?"

"No, sir, Major-sir. I's French, me."

"How old er ya be, boy?"

"Seventeen, sir," Charles said, stretching his age more than a year.

"So, you small for yore age, er ya?" the major said, looking sternly.

"All us Andre's is small, then we shoot up quick-like. My spurt is about due."

"Sergeant," the major said, "what makes ya'll think this young'un's a nigra?"

"Wah-wah-well, just look at him. He's a half-breed if I ever saw one. Part Messkin and Chinneyman, I suspect, and looks like he probly got some black blood, too. Zits obvious, ain't it?"

The major turned back to Charles as he spoke to the corporal. "Did you happen to notice his eyes? Did you ever see light brown eyes in a nigra's head? I did once, but it was only one eye and it was just part of that one eye. No, Sergeant, this lad is no nigra. He may have a little mix in 'im, but nigra blood, if he got any atall, is a dribblin'. But he's a bit small to offer up as cannon fodder to the gawddamn Yankees."

He put his hand on Charles' shoulder and gently pushed him out of line.

"Go home, boy. Go home and thank God that you was not taken in this army this day. Come back when you are much oldah and much biggah."

The major turned to leave, but Charles' voice stopped him: "I'm an orphan. I got no place to go,."

Without turning around, the major, his chin seemingly resting on his chest, said, "Then go back to the orphanage. Now. Git away from this camp and when you git where you are going, git down on your knees and pray that you never have to fight in a war such as this. This is a bad-feelin' war, boy. Go away from this camp. En don't come back."

Charles watched him march off, back straight, left hand on his sword to minimize the swing.

The officer disappeared in the shadows of the house's entryway. Charles set his shoulders square and marched after him. He dodged a backhand blow thrown at him by a sentry stuck like a pike by the front door. Charles skidded into the house. The major was halfway up a stairway to the right, just passing a large portrait of a bloated man with billowy white hair. The man in the portrait looked kindly and evil at the same time.

"Whatcha doin' back, heah, boy?" the sergeant from the courtyard said from a part of the room that direct sunlight could not reach.

Charles stepped two steps forward and snapped to attention: "Charles Andre, sir, at your service, I am."

The sergeant walked out of the darkness and spat, the glob of dark brown tobacco juice speckling the cypress plank floor just to the right of Charles' foot. "Go home, boy, go home now. And don't come back around here no more."

Charles felt his arm gripped in a death-claw as he was hustled out the front door and shoved toward the street.

He looked around the camp and thought he saw Ian in a long line of disheveled and uncoordinated recruits, marching down the wagon road toward a tent village barely visible in the distance.

Ce qui maintenat?

What now? I can't go back. I have no place else to go.

CHAPTER 6

The Devil You Know vs. …

> *I did not direct my life. I didn't design it.*
> *I never made decisions. Things always came up*
> *and made them for me. That's what life is.*
> B.F. Skinner

June 17, 1863.
Charles was stopped three times as he worked his way toward a tent that had been pointed out as the Union Army regimental command tent. Each time, a young soldier bearing a big gun, held diagonal across this body, braced him. All the soldiers sounded alike, fast-barking their "Halt! What's your business?" in a high, nasal Irish brogue.

Charles was disappointed in the dress and manner of the soldiers of the unit. In June in the Deep South the high humidity in the swampy land surrounding New Orleans created sweat pools that drenched straight through even the thickest of uniforms.

The soldiers he could see—sentries, soldiers lying in tents with the flaps open, men hunkered over tiny cooking fires—were shabbily dressed, not like other Union soldiers seen marching through the streets of New Orleans, or frequenting Sadie's Place, or on sentry duty at the docks or at key city government buildings. Some seemingly had no coats, wearing threadbare shirts and ragged pants; many were without shoes, their feet wrapped in pieces of leather (not unlike what Charles wore) tied together with small, loopy strands of hemp twin or thin strips of leather. Holey shirts and pants were commonplace.

The entire scene seemed surreal to Charles. He was used to seeing Confederate soldiers in threadbare clothing. In the South, underclothed and underfed soldiers were commonplace. But to see Union Army soldiers without proper clothing and equipment seemed a sacrilege on a monumental scale. These men looked nothing like the spit-and-polish soldiers seen marching down the streets in New Orleans in a daily show of force.

Finding himself in front of the tent with a huge America flag flapping from a skinned tree trunk, Charles stared at a smaller blue flag with *Ninth Conn. Regiment* in perfect, cursive embroidery. Another flag, this one blue and yellow, shared the rope at a lower level. He put his mind in overdrive, remembering he had seen the same flags in Jackson Square some months back. He took a step forward, pushing against the urge to run back to the orphanage and Sister Bloody.

The devil I know or the devil I don't know.

Charles smiled wryly, thinking about the quote by Brother Bartholomew. Then he shook his head and felt like shivering.

What am I doing? What the holy hell am I doing here? Easy one: To get out of the orphanage and get two hundred dollars I heard you get for joinin' up. Two hundred dollars!

A shadow covered him, dragging him from his thoughts.

"Now, what do we have here?" a tall officer said. The man, standing straight, shoulders back, chin tucked in, hands clasped behind his back, had apparently walked up from the side of the tent.

Charles snapped to attention: "Charles Andre, me. Reporting for duty. Sir!"

"Well, well, well, what *do* we have here? Andre, you say. A volunteer with a mixed breed accent? French? New Orleans swamper? How absolutely odd." The officer wheeled to face the closest sentry: "Don't you think that's odd, Corporal? He could be a spy. Does he look like a spy to you?"

"I wouldn't know, Colonel. I'm just a corporal and have no opinions." Mimicking Charles, he added an emphatic, "Sir! Leastways that's what my sergeant told me."

The officer laughed loudly, hooted actually, putting both hands on his ribs as if to hold his sides together.

"Did you hear that, boy?" he asked. "The corporal has no opinion about whether or not you are a spy." He paused, leaned over toward Charles, winked and said, "Well, are you a spy?"

"I don't tha-think...no, sir," Charles said, perturbed that he stuttered. "I'm jist here to join up and fight for the Union."

The officer forced himself upright, put his hands behind his back and looked sternly at Charles: "Why do you want to fight for the Union?"

"Sir?"

"Why do you want to join the Union Army?"

At a loss for words, Charles stood stock-still, unconsciously trying to emulate the corporal: shoulders back, chin tucked into his chest, arms riveted to his sides.

"Why do you want to join the Union Army?" This time the question was softer, with pauses between each word.

"I-I-I..." Charles started, then stoped, hunched his shoulders and bowed his head as tears clouded his vision.

The officer stepped close, put a hand on Charles' shoulder. "Take your time, son. Just take it easy and take your time."

Sucking in three deep breaths, Charles looked at the officer. "What's yore name, sir?" he asked in a kitten whisper.

The officer seemed amused at the question. "Colonel Healy."

"Colonel Healy. Until day before yesterday I lived in an orphanage over near Ramparts Street. Despite the good people, most anyways, the nuns and brothers and the help, it was a pure-dee hell-hole. I was witherin' away in that place. Too much hunger. Too hard to stay alive. Sometimes you just get tired of something. And I'm past tired." He stopped and rubbed his nose on his sleeve.

"You want to join the army because the orphanage was a bad place?"

Charles started babbling. "Yes, sir. That and the fact that I tried to join up with the Rebs and they turned me down thinkin' I had nigra blood, which I ain't, and made fun of me 'cause I'm small-like but I'm gonna grow soon but they took my friend Ian and he stutters and is a idiot and I wouldn't trust him with a gun, me, and I don't have no place to go if you don't let me join up with you boys."

He took a big gulp of air. And squeezed back a couple of tears gathering strength at the corners of his eyes.

The questions came fast. "You didn't directly answer the question: Why do you want to join the Union Army, son? What can you do? Are you good with a rifle? Tend to wounded men? Can you scout trails? Got any experience as a scrounger? Can you write and do sums? Are you sure you want…"

Charles jumped at the opening: "I can write, read and do multipliers up to my twelves. Tens, anyhow. I ain't never shot a gun but reckon I can learn. I never been out of the *ville,* ah, city so don't know nothing about scoutin' trails, but reckon I can learn if someone teaches me. I don't know what a scrounger is, but bet I can be a good one with practice." He stopped to take a breath.

"Whoa! Whoa up, boy!" the colonel said. "Slow down a bit. I mentioned scrounging because I thought as an orphan you'd know how to do that. Can you go out wherever you are and find things that you or your mates might be needed…foodstuffs, pieces of metal for cooking utensils, other useful things, stuff like that?"

Charles face brightened. "Yessir, I can find just about anythin', I surely can. This one time Ian and me—Ian's my friend what done joined up with the Rebs, the one I said was an idiot, but didn't mean it—brought home some cow bones, enough to make a tasty soup for the littl'uns at St. Mary's. Did I mention I can read and write and do my sums up to my twelves?"

The edges of the colonel's mustache rose just a mite. "Yes, I believe you did mention that, didn't he, Corporal?"

"I think I heard something like that, yessir!"

"Now, here's the hard question: Could you take up arms against the South, even shoot your friend Ian if you ran across him in a battle."

Wondering what the right answer to the question might be, Charles stared at his feet for a moment, then raises his head. "Naw, sir. I could shoot some other folks, I reckon. I could shoot some folks, wouldn't like to but I'd do it if I had to. But I couldn't shoot Ian. We best friends and we worked hard and partnered up and kept each other alive over the last couple of years. He's me and I'm him. I just as soon shoot my ownself 'fore I'd shoot Ian."

"What if he's going to shoot you?"

"Don't matter. Wouldn't happen. Ian would no more shoot me than I'd shoot him."

"When's the last time you ate, boy?"

The change in the line of questioning shook Charles. He stopped to think. "I had a little piece of bread yesterday and another piece earlier today."

"Well, let's get you something to eat and then we'll talk some more. Corporal! Take this lad and find him something to eat and when he's through, bring him back here and find me."

With that the officer walked into the command tent.

Truth was, Charles was hungry, having had nothing to eat in more than a full day. An end piece of bread and the remains of a partially eaten chicken leg had refreshed him two days ago but in no way filled the emptiness in his stomach.

"Call me Corporal Roarke," the young soldier said as he ushered Charles toward a large tent splashed with mildew. Telling Charles to take a seat, the corporal went over to a large table and came back moments later with a tin plate heaped with field peas, a goodly chunk of sowbelly, and two slices of cornbread. Looking at the plate, Charles hesitated, glancing at the corporal.

"Eat up, boy, time's a-wasting."

In short order, Charles was mopping up the last of the pea juice with a cornbread corner. He wanted to lick the plate, but refrained.

A few minutes later he found himself in front of the colonel. Head down, quill pen scratching in a small journal, the colonel did not acknowledge his presence even though the corporal had announced him in proper military fashion.

Charles stood at what he thought was attention until the colonel finishing scribbling, preserved the writing by hitting it a lick or two with a rocking stamp pad.

He looked up and stared into Charles' eyes, his expression a solid enigma.

"Here's what I'm going to do," the colonel said, rubbing his face with his left hand. "I don't believe you are seventeen or sixteen or even fifteen. You're just too small. I think you believe that joining the army, any army, is better than being in an orphanage. Well, in an orphanage you don't get shot at and you don't look down all of a sudden and see you only got one leg and wonder what the hell happened and where the hell did your leg get off to.

"An orphanage may be bad, but it's sure not war and it's not being in battle. Now I want you to go back to the orphanage and think on this for a spell. And then if you are still all-fired struck on being in the army, get you somebody of age to come back here and guardian you in. I am not assuming blame for what happens to a youngster like you. Besides, it's hard to trust a Southern boy who just walks up and wants to join the Union Army. That doesn't make much sense. You hear me?"

"Colonel, sir," Charles said, trying to keep an unwanted quiver out of his voice, "I just want..."

"Wanting and getting is too different things, son. If you want to get in this man's army, then go do what I say."

Charles didn't remember leaving or even walking out of camp. He looked up puzzled when he realized he was on the road back to New Orleans and didn't have a clue how he got there.

"How old are you really, boy?"

Charles jumped straight up and seemed to levitate in mid-air to the right toward the ditch filled with scummy water. Turning quickly, he saw a smallish officer staring at him from about ten feet away. The man had some sort of bars on the shoulders of his uniform and he was standing squared-off, feet spread, hands behind his back. He didn't look much older than Charles and was not much taller...an inch, if that.

Recovering from his heart-flopping fright, Charles answered: "Sixteen. And that's Mary's truth."

"Catholic, huh? Me, too. Or was at one time. Probably still am if I stop to think about it."

Charles said, "Why do you want to know how old I am?"

"I'm 23 now. Was two years younger when I joined the army. Everybody who didn't know me thought I was younger. Way younger. Signed up with the Ninth when it was formed because I'm Irish by birth and it's like being what I think would be called...'home.'"

The two studied each other. The officer's face was off center slightly, the jaw and nose leaning to the left. A clear, hairless scar split his left eyebrow; his jaw hung, catty-whampus to the left; some teeth seemed to be missing on that side. Hair the color of moldy straw poked from underneath his forage cap; his small hands were ruddy and a mask of white fingerlings of scars were visible from his wrist to the finger joints.

Hot water? Open fire? Wonder how that could'a happened?

"You really want to join up?"

"That's what I came to do."

The officer lowered his head; a thatch of hair fell over one eye. Without looking up, he said, "I was raised in an orphanage, in Rochester, New York. I joined up to get out of that place, same as you're trying to do."

"What's yore name?"

"Joseph H. Lawler." He paused, twisted up one eyebrow and answered Charles' unasked question: "The 'H' stands for Henry. They told me it was the name of my father and grandfather."

Silence filled the void between the two boys. "If you want to join up, I might be able to help you. You want me to help? You sure you want me to?"

Always cautious, always thinking, Charles mused over the question a bit, chewing on the implications. "Yes," he said. "What can you do?"

"The plan ain't all worked out yet. But come on back to camp in the morning and I'll have it in my head by then."

Lawler turned smartly on his heel and walked quickly down the empty road toward camp. The night passed slowly. Charles snuck into a lean-to cow shed about a mile from the Union camp and slept fitfully. A dog—wild, probably—came sniffing around during the night and Charles kicked a milk bucket in its direction and the noise scared them both. An hour before dawn—when the first sign of false dawn silhouetted the treetops in the distance—he was up. Breakfast was a dozen or so squirts of fresh milk from a cow that complained mightily about his unfamiliar hands and stroke. The night before he had spied a nesting chicken near the shed; a raw egg robbed from a chicken's field nest took the edge off his hunger. A quick hand scrub of his face at a nearby pond cleared his head. Stopping to think a minute, he ducked his entire head in the blue-black water.

Wouldn't mind drowning a few lice, that's for sure.

Twenty minutes later, just as the first sunrays streaked across the low shrub brush surrounding the camp, Charles walked up to the two sentries watching the road. He politely asked to see "Officer Lawler" and asked politely again when a short, wide picket with a large gut told him it was "Second Lieutenant Lawler" he was looking for and to come back later. He asked again five minutes later and was refused. Charles walked ten yards back toward New Orleans and sat down at the side of the road, letting the sun warm his face. It was going to be hot later. Almost already was.

More than an hour passed before Lawler showed up. He was grinning. "Couldn't sleep, huh? I figured you'd be here early or not at all. Let's go get something to eat and we can talk during."

Over a breakfast of a lumpy flour-paste-ground-corn-and-sugar porridge, strong, boiled coffee, a stubby slice of ham, and a couple of fresh biscuits,

Charles heard Lawler's plan, to which, while he didn't understand most of it, he eagerly nodded agreement. Finishing breakfast, Lawler, with Charles in tow, went to the command tent and inquired about the whereabouts of Captain Sawyer. "Right here," a voice behind the men boomed. The captain was silhouetted in the A of the tent's opening. Charles could see no details of the man, just that he was short and wide. From the silhouette it was apparent the man had on one of the biggest hats Charles had ever seen—tall crown like a top hat with a pinned-up, flat brim on one side and a large feather of some kind trailing off to the back.

The lieutenant asked the captain's permission to talk to him in private and the two men went back outside. They returned quickly.

"So, Mr. Andre, is it? I'm Captain Sawyer. You want to join up with this man's army and you are going to get your guardian, Mr. Lawler, here, to vouch for you? Is that right?"

Panic slashed at his eyes. Charles gulped and shot a quick look at Lawler, who gave a short nod.

"Uh, uh, yessir. I want to do what you said. I surely do."

The captain motioned him to stand in front of an old, wobbling, folding desk, handed him a couple of sheets of paper withdrawn from a large wooden box, and said, "Fill out these papers. You can write?"

Taking the papers with a trembling hand, Charles muttered, "Yessir. Sure can. Can write. Good, too."

"First, you get two hundred dollars for joining up. You don't get than money till your hitch is up. But it's there for you. Trust me on that. And you get thirteen dollars a month. That money is paid within thirty days of the end of a month if we are where the paymaster can get to us. It adds up if you don't get it for a while."

Thirteen dollars a month! I get paid more than Ian!

Taking up a quill and reading over the paper, Charles bent to the task. The first paper was titled "Declaration of Recruit." The unfamiliar words blurred. Reading the printed script quickly, Charles, in his careful, cursive script (taught with a religious fervor by the nuns) filled in the blanks.

"I, *Charles Andre*, desiring to VOLUNTEER as a Soldier in the Army of the United States, for a term of THREE YEARS...

Three years?

...Do Declare, That I am *sixteen* years and ____ months of age (He drew a straight line through the space, not taking time to count the months): that I have never been discharged from the United States service on account of disability or by sentence of court-martial…

What is a court-martial?

…or by order before the expiration of a term of enlistment: and I know of no impediment…

Do I have one of those? Do I need one? Where can you get one?

…to my serving honestly and faithfully as a soldier for three years."

The captain motioned to a nearby soldier who signed under "WITNESS:" *Andr Cale Liritz. Ninth C.V*

Instructed to fill out the second part of the folded paper after it was handed back to him, Charles filled in more blanks: "*Charles Andre* volunteered at *Ducrois Stat. Bernard, La., 18th June 1863."*

His new friend reached over and slid the paper from in front of Charles and started filling in the blanks: "CONSENT IN CASE OF MINOR. I, *J.H. Lawler* DO certify That I am the *guardian of Charlis Andra*; that the said (Lawler stopped and looked at Charles; 'C-h-a-r-l-E-s. A-n-d-r-E.') *Charles Andre* is *Sixteen* years of age; that I do hereby freely give my CONSENT to his volunteering as a SOLDIER in the ARMY OF THE UNITED STATES for a period of THREE YEARS.

GIVEN at *Ducras Station Parish St. Bernard* THE *18th* day of *June 1863*

Lieutenant Lawler signed the paper and handed the dipped quill to Charles.

Joseph H. Lawler

Charles Andre

Witness

S.W. Sawyer Capt

Co. H. Ninth Rgt. Conn.

Charles straightened up and saluted. All three men, plus two other officers sitting at a table at the rear of the tent, laughed. Sawyer snapped off a bare salute and winked at the new recruit.

The captain handed Charles another piece of paper, this one titled "Volunteer Enlistment." Charles commenced to writing, when Lawler asked the captain's permission to assist. "Granted," the captain said. Charles swore the captain winked again as he said the word.

"STATE OF *Louisiana*, TOWN (Crossed out) *Parish of St. Bernard*. I *Charles Andre* born in…

Lawler whispered: "Rochester, New York."

"What?" Charles said, looking at him with furrowed brow.

"You were born in Rochester—R-o-c-h-e-s-t-e-r—New York and you were a baker."

"A what?"

"Baker. A cook."

I know what a baker is.

Charles' attention went back to the document.

"*...Rochester* in the State of *New York* aged *sixteen* years and by occupation a *Baker* Do HEREBY ACKNOWLEDGE TO have volunteered this *18th* day of *June* 1863 to serve as a Soldier in the Army of the United States of America, for the period of THREE YEARS unless sooner discharged by proper authority: Do also agree to accept such bounty, pay, rations, and clothing as are, or may be, established by law for volunteers. And I, *Charles Andre* do solemnly swear, that will bear true faith and allegiance to the United States of America, and that I will serve them honestly and faithfully against all their enemies or opposers whomsoever; and I will observe and obey the orders of the President of the United States, and the orders of the Officers appointed over me, according to the rules and Articles of War.

"Sworn and subscribed to, at *Ducras Station,* this *18th* day of *July* (Lawler coughed and Charles scratched out July) *June* 1863. *Charles Andre.*

After he signed his name with an emphatic flourish, he blew on the document to dry the ink and then handed it to the captain, who glanced at it, padded the inked parts with a cloth roller and rolled it up. He handed the paper to a corporal, turned to Charles and said: "Welcome to the Army of the Righteous Way!"

I'm in the Army. Where did he say my two hundred dollars was?

CHAPTER 7

From One Life to Another

> *You cannot have an army without music.*
> Robert E. Lee

> *Every path to a new understanding
> begins in confusion.*
> Mason Cooley

    Charles' introduction to the other drummers in Company H was quick and performed with military precision. The sergeant led to a small tent just to the right and in the first row behind the command tent. The sergeant rapped on the canvas of a double-hung contraption he called a "dog tent" with a worn riding crop, which normally was kept neatly tucked under his arm.
    "Dunton. Johnson. Get out here!"
    There was a brief rustling inside the tent and a man in his late teens stuck his head out of the tent. He had a lean face, topped by hair the color of mildewed corn silk, twitchy, gray eyes, a short, wide nose, generous mouth, and a sprouting of peach fuzz above his lip and on the peak of his chin.
    "Samuel's not here right now, sergeant," the young man said. "He's gone to get our rations. He'll be back directly."
    The sergeant nodded. "Dunton, this is Charles Andre (he pronounced it "Ohn-dray") and he's a new drummer. He'll bunk with you two till we pair him

up with somebody else. It'll be tight, but you'll manage, I reckon. Show him the ropes and keep him from under foot and out of trouble."

The sergeant turned sharply and stomped back to the command tent and ducked inside.

Dunton (Charles still did not know his first name and dared not ask) ducked his head back in the tent, leaving Charles to stand outside and wonder what to do next.

The teenage veteran, Charles guessed, was a couple of years older than he. Dunton knee-walked out of the tent opening, pulling his suspenders up over his arms as he moved. He stood and stretched, then started walking south. Not knowing what else to do, Charles followed. Dunton skirted one large, open-sided tent, then cut in behind it and headed out down a long line of small, off-white, mud-splattered tents. He turned to Charles and in a conspiratorial whisper said, "Avoid that big tent there. It's the surgeon's tent. Them sawbones like to have folks do for them worser than anybody else, even generals. Hang around there and they'll have you whittling off legs and carrying out buckets of lung blood."

Charles closed his mind to the picture and looked at the line after line of tents.

How odd they look. Like little, skinny, peaked pillow cases.

Dunton stopped, looked over his shoulder, and said, "Hurry it up, now, ya hear?" Without waiting for an answer, he strode off again; this time Charles ran to gather in close behind him.

"Ohn-dray," Dunton said. "That English or Welsh?"

"Andre, actually, *oui*," Charles said, "French."

Dunton tried to pronounce it the way Charles did; the word came out *On-a-dree*. Charles thought about correcting him, but let the thought strangle itself. He wanted to ask where they were going but did not give in to the urge.

The pair moved past the last row of tents and entered a stand of woods. The grayness of the day went a shade darker as Charles followed Dunton through the close stand of live oaks, which were splattered with an occasional spindly cedar.

Dunton gave a single hoot that died among the barren trees and ground cover. *What is he doing?* Charles thought, just as Dunton stopped near the edge of a trench that was three feet wide, two feet deep and about twenty feet long.

Without a word, he placed the heels of his overrun Jefferson brogans on the edge of the trench, shucked his pants, spread the buttonless back fly on his gray union suit, and squatted like a skinny toad preparing to hop. His face scrunched up like he was in pain, the tendons in his neck popped out, resembling end-to-end cordwood.

Charles, standing less than six feet from him, averted his eyes, centering his focus on a vivid red male cardinal sitting on a limb as if waiting to have its picture painted.

"Had to show you the latrine area, On-a-dree. Next to the command tent and the quartermaster's, it's the most important part of any army anywhere in the world." Charles studied the bird with more intensity. "If you need to piss or shat, better get'er done now. Don't know what the sergeant has in store for you."

Without looking in Dunton's direction, Charles skittered along the latrine's edge, about ten feet from his guide. Loosening the drawstring of his coarse, too-big trousers, he pulled out his johnny and directed a split stream toward the center of the trench. Dunton was wiping with a handful of leaves when Charles glanced in his direction.

This is no better than a thunder mug in the middle of the orphanage.

"Privacy ain't no big thing in the army, On-a-dree," Dunton said, as if reading his mind. "You gotta do what you gotta do when you got time to do it. Don't forget that. Makin' water in the middle of a charge up a hill ain't a likely option. Unless, that is, it's down your pants leg."

Over the next few minutes, Charles learned Dunton was from Norwich in Connecticut, having joined up in the fall of sixty-one. He originally enlisted in the Second Regiment Infantry Rifle Company but was reassigned as a drummer. "I guess they needed good drummers more than poor rifle shots," he told Charles as they walked back to camp. He also told Charles that "when the war started we had a real regimental band, 'bout twenty or so boys. Most of 'em left when boys started dying from disease and such. Now we just use drummers."

Arriving back at the camp, Dunton introduced Charles to the third drummer. Samuel Johnson was a tall drink of water, hitting six feet and then some. He was also from Norwich; he and Dunton had lived on the same street, grew up chasing each other in endless games of tag, red rover, and hide-n-seek. A quiet youth of twenty, Johnson nodded at the introduction, offered his hand and then went back to writing on a stack of small sheets of paper.

Walking away, Dunton said, "He writes home all the time. He talks all time about going home and I wake up most nights expecting him to be gone. But he's always there."

Dunton showed Charles the quartermaster's tent and waited outside until the new recruit emerged with a look of bewilderment on his face.

Carrying only his one wool blanket and a mouthful of promises for his uniform when "the next shipment" arrived, Charles followed Dunton across the road to a meadow carpeted with a miniature city of off-white tents.

There must be a thousand tents here.

As if he could read Charles mind, his guide said, "There are almost two thousand tents in this one field."

Two thousand! So many.

"A lot of the men don't even bother with putting one up, even if the order comes down to do just that. They stuff their tents in a friend's pitch or hide them in hollow logs or sneak off into the woods when it gets dark and tie them to trees as a cover."

"It does get close in those tents sometimes."

Looking at the darkness between the distant tree trunks. "Sleeping in the woods might be better than having to put up and take down a tent every few days," he said, tryin to sound self-assured.

Charles had been a soldier for less than twenty-four hours. There had been no time for developing what he thought might be *normal* soldierly feelings; he felt lost, and even though he was part of a company, a brigade, a division, an army with more than a million men, he viewed himself as being isolated. He conjured up a picture being encased in a glacier at the top of a distant mountain, something he had read about in a well-used geography book at St. Mary's.

He didn't know what to do, when to do it, or even how it should be done. It didn't know what "it" was, and feared he would fail the first time anyone told him to do "it."

But, as he had with every other life lesson, he listened, paid attention, repeated important items in his head, and, when learned, the items were never forgotten.

He quickly learned there was much to learn, starting with the camp regimen and how musicians played a hearty part in it. Soldiers' Reveille was sounded at five o'clock each morning (sometimes later on Sundays as an officer's favor to the men), followed by a morning roll call, then breakfast call. Sick call followed breakfast, and either a call to march or to assembly for change in guard duty.

Drilling in a muddy field, the drummers kept the men in step; same on a march, but the drummers were expected to keep the men in step for just a brief time. Drummers and buglers (depending on what outfit and in what brigade musicians were assigned, and the personal preference of commanding officers) gave signals for certain battlefield maneuvers, and related orders when soldiers in ranks should prepare to fire a coordinated volley.

Solitary musicians often combined with regimental or brigade bands to provide music for parades, inspections, and review by dignitaries. For the first year after being formed, the Ninth had a regimental band. But first-year fervor was quickly extinguished and the majority of band members either were transferred to ranks or went home.

Charles tried to learn all the calls quickly, to show his worth in this man's army. The task was hard to do without a drum. With extra sticks provided by Dunton, he mimicked out the beats the best he could on flat rocks, tree trunks, fallen logs, or even on his thigh during inspections or the short marches inflicted on the men daily to "keep them alert," as Sergeant John Burke said.

I feel as useless as hen's teeth.

There was a wave of excitement flowing in the camp, tent by tent, soldier by soldier. Members of the Ninth Connecticut—five companies, C, E, G, I, and K—had been in a what one soldier described as a "minor mix-it-up" upriver at La Fourche Crossing. Charles had heard of the place in New Orleans and as far as he knew, the crossing was just a rope-and-pulley ferry across the Mississippi. He had also heard the railroad from Vicksburg to New Orleans ran through the small town but did not know if it were fact or a story of the times.

Wonder what anybody would even want it for?
Maybe to ferry supplies across? Or move men against New Orleans?
Or, most probably, just trying to gain more ground.

The word was that Ninth companies, about 400 men with Captain John Healy commanding, had loaded on rail cars but were forced to leave the railroad due to destruction to rails and underpinning, the work of enemy soldiers or local saboteurs. The companies continued north by forced march. Healy endeared himself to his men and became a local legend by commandeering heavy plantation wagons and horses and ferried the Ninth men overland in order to arrive at La Fourche more quickly with rested troops.

A short engagement followed, with two Ninth soldiers (Sergeant Peter Donnelly and Private Charles Reynolds of Company C) being captured. Three men were wounded.

Upon returning to camp, the three wounded men were treated as rich relatives, with visitors asking them time and again for stories about the battle. Charles was enthralled with the concept of battles and fighting. But, even in his naiveté, he could not help but notice how the stories of the battle and individual acts of heroism grew with every telling.

The next day, both of the captured men showed up, saying they'd been "paroled."

I don't know nothin' about war, but this is just crazy, the way things is done.

CHAPTER 8

Embracing the Newness

*Harsh necessity, and the newness of my kingdom,
force me...to guard my frontiers everywhere.*
Virgil (Publius Vergilius Maro)

"Get up and get 'im ready for the day, boys," Sergeant Daniel Murphy said in a straightforward manner as he marched by the two, conjoined tents housing the company's three drummers. As he always did, Charles watched the sergeant march away and marveled, as he always did, at how sergeants and officers marched to a silent, personal rhythm.

The sun was still below the early July horizon, the air humid and hot. Dunton had gone to the latrine, Johnson was squatted on his knees in front the left-side tent, and Charles was sitting near, thinking about how to keep from sweating.

"Where we goin', Sergeant Dan?" Johnson asked in his natural sing-song voice.

Sergeant Murphy stopped in mid-stride, his left boot heel firmly planted in the soft earth. As he slowly lowered his left foot to complete the step, he said in voice barely above a whisper: "How long you been in this here army, 'Skin Thumper' Johnson?"

It was obvious to Charles that Johnson knew the signs and looked quickly around for help. He really didn't expect Charles to help and if he did he would have been sorely disappointed. Charles had eased backward into the tent like a turtle pulling its head into its shell. "I jined up in sixty-one, Sergeant Dan," Johnson said, trying to forge a solid bridge of familiarity. "You know that. We jined up on the same day. Me and you and James and Peter Doyle and Daaggghhh—"

The speech met a straggling death. The sergeant had spun around and with snake-strike quickness grabbed the young soldier by the throat and hauled him upright. The drummer made a noise that reminded Charles of the sound of water running down the middle of the street in front of St. Mary's after a summer garbage-floating drenching. Gurgling. Bubbling. Mucousy water mixed with rushing air.

Sergeant Murphy put his bulbous nose right up against Johnson's and mashed in close. The youth could feel the big man's breath cascading down his cheeks; the twin wind ripples sent a snake of fear through his bowels.

"When I ask you a damn question, Private Samuel Johnson, my sister Jean's dearest and darlin' oldest boy, I expect a respectful answer followed by the imperial word 'Sergeant'. What I do not need is some damn warblin' converdamnsation about who jined up and when. Is that clear?" Samuel's left hand flew up to grab his uncle's hand but was quickly swatted away.

"Is that clear?"

The youth blinked twice rapidly, forcing tears to emerge and make tiny mud-tracks through the dirt on his swollen, red cheeks.

Charles, peering out of the blackness of the small, upside-down V of heavy canvas, couldn't believe the tableau being played out not four feet from his hidey hole.

Is this what the Army is going to be like?

He thought back to the occasional strapping he had received from the brothers at St. Mary's.

A strapping is bad enough, but being slowly strangled to death by an uncle is worse.

Right off, he couldn't think of anything much worse. He heard his next thought loud and clear.

I just wish I had an uncle, even if he did strangle me.

He launched a following thought.

That's a lie!

REVEILLE

It was more than three weeks before Charles was called to the quartermaster's tent and handed a uniform. "We got two sizes, one's small, the other ain't. This'un here is small," Charles was told. Getting the uniform was a simple operation: Walk in. Get handed a bundle of clothes and some square-toed shoes. Walk out.

After examining the clothes—obviously hand-me-downs two or three times removed—down by the shrub brush near the murky backwater, Charles, tried on the loose, cotton drawers with pull-tight strings at the waist and at the bottom of both legs.

This the smallest they got?
Trop grand. Beaucoup trop grand.
Too big. Way too big.
But that's what the strings are for, I reckon.

The faded blue flannel shirt was also *beaucop trop grand.* The light blue trousers didn't come close to fitting in the waist, and the legs were several inches too long. The coat, a regulation nine-button affair with several tattered holes in the chest and shoulder area, was, all things considered, not a bad fit. A tattered, non-military, free-collar vest was stuck into a coat sleeve.

Looks like it will fit fine.

Except for the holes, the coat was in pretty good shape; most of the men had them, although many were barely hanging together. The shoes were square-toed Jefferson brogans and, obviously, had last been worn by a Union Goliath.

Charles dressed in everything but the shoes, tying the pants to his waist with a piece of rope he finagled from the quartermaster. He pretended to check himself over in a mirror, turning this way and that, imaging what he looked like all dressed up.

A fine fiddle of a man, yes. A fine fiddle, indeed.

He walked back to camp, carrying his old, hand-me-down, holey, tired clothes in one hand and the shoes in the other. Within a couple of minutes, he had traded the shoes with George Dashwood, a New Orleans recruit, who signed up within days of Charles and had also just received his army clothes. His shoes, he said, "would fit a midget...and I ain't no midget."

It was another week before Charles received his forage cap, and haversack and canteen. The haversack was an ugly chunk of dead cloth with black tar spread unevenly on it as a water repellent. The canteen was a simple, tin affair, with rippled sides supposedly to add strength. Charles felt lucky to have the canteen, which looked new; some of the Ninth men had wood canteens, which tended to leak in cooler weather.

It would be weeks more before he was given a double knapsack (a bruised piece of limp canvas), a shelter half, and a gum blanket—a simple, tacky affair that was said to be water-proofed on one side.

The quartermaster's aide told him that "other stuff you need, get it from the sutler."

Surely will do. What am I supposed to buy it with?

The word around the campfires was that various regiments of the Confederate Army were stationed in the shrub brush outside the city, preparing to attack. Some said to the east, some south, most thought to the west, due to the proximity to Texas and Mexico, if a long-distance escape route was needed.

Residents of the city spent much time and effort debating on what form Confederate action to drive the Yankee army from New Orleans and the surrounding area would take. Many could not understand why the entire Confederate army, including those troops dedicated to "hang around Washington and harass Ol' Abe Lincoln," as one city councilman declared, didn't march right down to south Louisiana and take the city by brute force. After all, the city was the most continental of all cities in North America. It was also the largest foreign trade port in the country; in military terms, it was the key to controlling traffic on the Mississippi.

The street talk took on a common theme: Where are our boys? When they comin'?

Most of the talk was due to frustration. The lack of constant river traffic, of foreign ships landing and unloading as fast as the docks could be readied and cargo stacked, of the hordes of travelers passing through the city heading…somewhere…was a major economic distraction and personal frustration for the city's merchants. In small pods, by ones and twos, then with entire wagon trains, residents headed north where the insanity of the war was less virulent; more headed west to Texas and beyond. New territory, new sights, new start, new lives.

It's not that the Confederates were doing nothing. Harassment tactics occurred throughout the region from small, seemingly disjointed bands of rebel soldiers, along with the occasional, concentrated push from entire regiments.

One earlier battle in particular intrigued city residents: the Battle of Baton Rouge. Charles had heard about the 1862 battle, had read some slanted accounts in a local paper, and heard the telling of tales from people who were not there, but were merchants of a fashion, dealing in selective gossip.

Many of his new comrades were at the battle and had vivid stories of individual and regimental actions. In late July 1862, a Confederate force under the command of Major General John Breckenridge, former vice president of the United States, made its intentions known far and wide that more than eight thousand men would attack the Union army encamped at Baton Rouge. Charles had first heard the story between two top-hatted dandies passing the time on a Chartres Street corner. The account was muddled, he thought at the time, but he heard the first-hand story at a campfire session within a month of his enlistment.

The Ninth regiment had arrived to support the Baton Rouge contingent aboard one of four sternwheelers; the regiment, along with part of the Sixth Massachusetts Battery, arrived on the *Louisiana Belle*. The Union commander, General Thomas Williams, was not a favorite of the soldiers; nary an officer would come to his aid in fireside groaning sessions.

One of the veterans of the Baton Rouge dust-up, Corporal Michael Cronin, told Charles, "The boys truly blued the air ever' time General Williams' name came up. I be lyin' if'n I told you I could stand that stern, persimmon-mouthed son of a bitch." A rigid disciplinarian, Williams had the men drilled daily (sometimes twice a day) despite adverse weather conditions. Close-order and parade drills (including uniform inspections) were conducted despite temperatures of a hundred or more and humidity so high it took concentrated effort to even draw a breath. It was not unusual for twenty percent of the soldiers involved in such exercises to "fall out"—literally—and remain prostrate on the parade grounds.

"Maybe," another soldier involved in the battle told Charles eleven months after the battle, "he knew what was coming and was toughening us up." That statement met with a barrage of profanity from several of the soldiers who had suffered under Williams' hard-line rule. Timothy Buckley, a Boston man who had no fond memories of the Baton Rouge campaign, said, "There's a gawdamned difference in being strict 'bout rules and just plain mean. Ol' Williams was arse-sucking mean."

In his old life, now a single month in his past, cursing, even by Ian, which was frequent, didn't sit well with Charles. And, even though few curse words ever passed his lips (and only occasionally in his thoughts), in his short time in the army Charles had learned the difference in cussing, cursing, and blasphemy. His church upbringing (and memories of head-knocks and squeezed ears when he transgressed) kept his profanity at a minimum. Some of the men had no such restraint, many none at all. Cussing, cursing, and blasphemy...some did it all, often in a single tirade against bad food, bad conditions, or bad decisions by those ranked above them.

His new comrades fell into three distinct groups in regard to this subject: Those that did, often and loud; those that didn't and who shot reproving looks at those that did; those that did on occasion and usually ended the verbal blast with "Forgive me" or a quick "Hail Mary."

The air often turned blue when the men of the Ninth talked about past scrimmages with Confederates. In those cases, the curse words were of a friendly, positive nature because unlike most Union regiments or battalions up to mid-1863, the Ninth's soldiers considered themselves to have always been on the winning side. And few campfire sessions ended without some mention of the Battle of Baton Rouge.

The expected attack came on August 4, 1862 and was a nip-and-tuck affair—feint, attack, counterattack, feint, attack, retreat, hold ground. General Williams didn't get to witness the end of battle, being killed by a bullet not long after the initial attack by the Confederates. "No loss to my way of thinkin'," Buckley said, confident he spoke for many of the soldiers. "And the killin' shot may have been from a Reb sharpshooter. May have been, I said."

Colonel Thomas W. Cahill, commanding officer of the Ninth, assumed command of the Union force; this part of the story was told with noticeable pride in the voice of the narrator.

"There we was, sitting down in Baton Rouge, waitin' on the Johnny Rebs to hit us. They was comin' in from the north, they was," Buckley remembered. "We was fighting a lop-sided battle. We had more than five thousand troops on the muster rolls, but a'most half were down due to being sick with the Southern runs. Some were choleric. We had some nigra spies out and from what they brought us we put the Johnnys at about eight thousand men. Shucks, we had less'n half that many."

Charles learned the brief, but fierce battle gave the out-manned Union army two victories: One was a physical reality—they whipped the Rebel army; the other was more of a mental victory—they won despite being grossly outnumbered, thus temporarily taking the spotlight away from the Confederacy's claim to rolling up victory after victory back east with fewer soldiers, warships, and artillery batteries.

Once Charles heard the facts of the battle—Union casualties, fourteen, Rebel casualties, almost five hundred—his respect for his new unit inched up perceptibly.

Can those numbers be right? True? Or not? How can you tell one from the other?

Campfire talk was a time for reflection for many of the men. From his first day as a soldier, Charles had a hankering to know more about the men with whom he spent his days, the battles in which they had fought, and the inner workings of the regiment. It was not his nature to intrude, or to ask inane questions, so he did what he did best: Listen and learn.

Over time he found out when the regiment was formed, how it landed in Biloxi, Mississippi in April 1862, and spent a few days going back and forth between Pass Christian and Biloxi—"As if some durn fool couldn't figure out where we was supposed to be," as one soldier said. There was a two-week period in late April where the regiment was involved in the did-not-do-much-of-anything capture of Forts St. Phillip and Jackson in Mississippi before the unit moved on to New Orleans.

Two weeks of rest in the city included a public display of precision marching by the Ninth; General Butler ordered the regiment to march along major streets as a show of strength. While in New Orleans, Charles learned, various companies were spread out—stationed around the Mint, in St. James Parish, and on the shores of Lake Pontchatrain.

That adventure precluded a two-week stay around Baton Rouge, which was nothing more than a reconnaissance tour of nearby Warrenton, where a corps of rebel soldiers was supposed to be hanging out.

To that point, Corporal John Donahugh said one night just before time to turn in, that, "It seemed for all the world like we was a green checker in a black-and-red checker game. Go here. Go there. Now that yore back here, go 'way over yonder."

A month later the regiment was assigned to hit up the Mississippi to Vicksburg. That month-long stay was "no fun at all," one soldier remembered.

The Ninth was given "fatigue duty," which included trying to dig a canal—dubbed "Grant's Canal"—to divert the mighty river away from the wharves of Vicksburg, further isolating the town.

The ill-conceived plan was a disaster, as hundreds of men died from artillery fired from within the city's fortification, disease (swamp fever), and collapse of a coffer dam. More than twenty men from the Ninth died or later left the service as a result of the horrible conditions. Those veterans of Vicksburg's ill-conceived dig-and-die expedition considered duty back in the New Orleans area "southern Heaven."

Charles didn't know when it was supposed to be payday. He knew that the majority of the men got paid each month, but he didn't know when it was *his* payday. He watched men of the Second Brigade—Ninth Connecticut, four companies of the Twenty-eighth Maine, and the boys from Massachusetts (the Twenty-sixth, Forty-second and Forty-seventh)—go the quartermaster tent single file to get paid.

No one had bothered to explain the rules or intricacies of how a new recruit received his monthly stipend. And, as was his nature, Charles didn't ask. He had clothes, food—overall much better than he had at St. Mary's—and was able to keep relatively dry when it rained.

Relatively speaking, life was good.

Now, if I only had a drum so's I could quit pecking on rocks and such.

At Dunton's constant urging,
Nagging is more like it.
Charles made the short trip each day to the quartermaster to see if his snare drum had arrived on the most recent supply wagon or dropped off at a railroad spur used by the Union Army to ferry supplies as close to the spaced-out camps as possible.

More than two months passed, more than sixty days of following the leads of the other drummers and practicing countless hours on his own thigh and any handy object before the regiment's new quartermaster, Thomas Fitz Gibbon, said, "Well, young Andre, it's finally here!"

Fitz Gibbon handed him an odd-shaped package wrapped in muslin and overlaid with heavy brown paper.

Holding the package tenderly, Charles turned to go back to camp but was stopped by the quartermaster's voice.

REVEILLE

"Open it here, boy. I got use for the wrappings."

He carefully laid the package on the table made from two tree stumps and two shaved boards and took his time untying twine and easing back the cloth-and-paper covering.

Charles unfolded the last flap of muslin. The small, rope-tension snare drum fairly snapped with newness. The taut deer skin heads, rubbed smooth and thin, stretched over the open ends of a round wooden shell. Charles knew, from talking to the other drummers and examining their drums intensely, that the edge of the skin was soaked in water with lye mixed in, then tucked around circular flesh hopes. The hoops were held in place by wooden counter hoops, which controlled the tension on the drum skins. Leather braces—"They be called 'ears'," Dunton had informed him, "why I surely don't fathom."—adjusted the tension to set the right tone for the drum.

Charles couldn't tell what type of wood was used as the decorative shell, but most likely, he had heard, it was either ash, holly, maple, or rosewood. He believed his was from rosewood. Because he had been told it was the best wood, and he wanted it to be.

Dunton and Johnson, reveling in their chore of "teachers" had drilled him on the parts of the drum. He could easily recite the facts that the top head of the drum was the "batter head," and the bottom was the "snare head." The snare head on his new drum was fitted with five strands of rawhide clustered to the center to create the reverberation—the "snare" sound. Charles knew that some "snares" were made of catgut, but he knew rawhide when he saw it and was relieved that his drum did not have catgut, which was known to soften up in inclement weather and produce a "soggy" sound, one detested by those that considered themselves "good" drummers. He was also glad it was rawhide because, simply, he couldn't think of a good reason to be happy about having the gut of anything attached to something he was going to carry around.

He had seen a drum carried by Thomas Cavanaugh with F Company that was fancy—red centerpiece with gold stars scattered here and there. Charles' new possession—the first "new" thing he remembered ever owning—was rather plain, with a burnished tan paint that reflected light in a subtle way. He carefully unwrapped the four drum sticks (made of ash, assuredly), stuck two inside two rope tighteners as he had seen the other drummers do, slung the drum sash over his left shoulder and carefully pecked up a tentative beat. He hit a quick lick of reveille, then switched easier than he would have believed into sick call.

"Sounds good and solid," Fitz Gibbon said. "Get rid of that leather sash quick-like. They get wet and fall apart. Let the boys show you how to fashion a strap from old tent pieces; they last a long time and you can sew two stick holders on it out of canvas leftovers."

Charles nodded as he increased the tempo on the new drum. "Sounds good and solid. It does just that," Charles said.

C'est l'amende reelle.

"It's real fine."

And meant it.

The next few days, every spare minute between assigned duties as a quartermaster or surgeon helper, Charles wandered away from camp and practiced different calls he had learned from listening to Dunton and Johnson and from pecking out various beats with short, rigid tree twigs or borrowed sticks.

Despite the offers of both drummers to assist him in learning the calls on a real drum, Charles deferred. "I 'preciate it. I truly do. But I just want to get comfortable with the drum I'm gonna be playin' first."

The statement made little sense to the boys. It made perfect sense to Charles, who always carefully calculated moves before making decisions. It was his cautious way of coping with life. It would always be his way. Nothing—not living the life of an outcast, not war, not ridicule—would ever change it.

On the third day after receiving his new drum, Charles asked Dunton and Johnson if he could join in sounding reveille.

Less than a minute later, three drums began a synchronized rumble of the familiar call, all loud, all in rhythm. To the men of H Company, the morning ritual not only sounded different, it *was* different. Three drums sounded as one. On this morning, men seemed to get up more quickly with less grumbling about the early hour or claiming to need more sleep. The drummers had a smile in their performance, which carried over to the ranks.

"Sounding fine as frog hair this morning, gentlemen," Sergeant Burke said loudly, looking proud as he stood, hands clasped behind his back, swaying back and forth, heel to toe. "Yes, three does sound better than two. And that's a pure-dee fact. Dunton, you and Johnson did a right fine job teaching young Andre here."

Both experienced drummers beamed. Charles stared straight head, lost in his own thoughts.

Don't mess it up now. Whatever you're doin' right, keep doin' it.

It was late in the day, supper call done, taps still a couple of hours away. Charles was playing solitaire mumbly-peg with a single-bladed Boy's Easy Opener knife he had bought for a nickel from a peddler. Against his better judgment, he borrowed two bits from Dunton, promising a first-thing pay-back from his first pay. The peddler, sitting atop a rag-tag outfit drawn by a sway-backed piebald, had no more than set up shop when a sentry ran him off. The regimental sutler, attached to the unit by order of Brevet Major General William H. Emory, had the Ninth concession—no ifs, ands, or buts.

The peddler, believing it was bad luck not to make a sale after a stop, sold the knife to Charles at slightly above cost as he was moving at a steady clip down the road. Charles reckoned it was a good knife, with a curved, metal handle that more or less fit his hand. The metal handle was a see-through affair...no wood, just curved pieces of metal forming a nesting place for the blade. It was reasonably sharp when he got it but ten minutes of being slapped against a flat creek rock in a combination flat-and-curve-out motion and the blade edge shown like beveled glass hit by a dart of sunshine.

Charles was hitting right along on a solitary game of mumbly-peg ...one flip, two flip, fingertip flip, straight stick, one flip, two flip, fingertip flip, straight stick...when he heard a loud rumble of voices beat a path up from the creek. In no time at all, he extracted the knife blade from the pebbly dirt, snapped it closed, stuck it in his right pants pocket, grabbed his drum, and quit the cool shade.

Two men were scuffling on the ground,

Joseph Somebody and Something McTierney.

kicking and rolling and throwing ineffective punches. From Charles' vantage point looking through the circle of men, more damage was done to the ground that either of the men. Just when it seemed the two men were tiring out, McTierney grabbed Joseph by the hair, pulled his head back and walloped him right in his walnut-sized Adam's apple. Joseph made a sound like a neck-roped hound as he hit the ground and flopped around in a chicken dance.

"Teach you to cheat me!" McTierney said, stomping on his opponent's shoulder before he was pulled away by two look-see-ers.

"He didn't cheat no one," a lean man with a hawk nose said. "How can you cheat rolling lamb bones, for gawd's sake!"

Lamb bones. Dice. Charles knew that some of the soldiers had fitted sets of dice from small rectangular bones pried loose from a lamb's foot. Some men had the bones from back home; a couple of others had pried them loose from captured and slaughtered livestock along the trail. Even though the bones were a tad longer than wide (one and a half to two inches in length and about the diameter of a woman's finger), they rolled fairly well and were considered better suited for rolling than the knee joint bone that some of the older soldiers preferred.

Charles didn't cotton to playing dice. Handling bones, regardless of origin, did not interest him.

Too many picked up in alleyways, most likely.

McTierney held up the two die, squinting at them in the fading daylight. "There's somethin' wrong with 'em, all right," he said, dropping them on the hard ground and stomping them into shards with one powerful heel. "That bastard rolled four sixes in a row and God hisownself couldn't roll three sixes in succession, much less four."

Another good reason not to roll bones.

The grouping around the campfire was in a middling mood. Not happy, not sad, just middling.

One of the soldiers, a New Yorker who let his fiddle do his talking, started sawing on a start-up, and was quickly joined by two spooners, a private with a jaw-harp, and two thigh-slappers keeping time. The tune didn't sound familiar to Charles. It was catchy, haunting, even. Toes started tapping and heads started nodding. A couple of hangers-on jumped in, clapping to the beat.

From out of the darkness came the happy twang of a banjo as Joseph Douglas, a sharpshooter with the Twelfth Maine, slide out of the darkness, picking up the tune and demanding a faster pace.

The men slipped through a couple of runs before Corporal John Thrall, a former Hartford merchant, who, rumor had it, taught voice at some college thereabouts before the war, began singing:

REVEILLE

'Twas the night before battle: and gathered in groups,
The soldiers lay close in their quarters;
They were thinking no doubt, of the dear ones at home.
Of mothers, wives, sisters, and daughters.
With his pipe in his mouth, sat a dashing young blade,
And a song he was lilting so gaily:
It was honest Pat Murphy, of the Ninth Brigade,
And he sang of the Sprig of Shillaly

Jeff Davis, you thief! if I had you but here,
Your beautiful plans I'd be ruinin':
For I'd give ye a taste of me bayonet, be damned!
For tryin' to burst up the Union:
There's a crowd in the North, too, an' they're just as bad:
Abolitionist spouters so scaly,
For troubling the nigras I think they deserve,
A whack from a Sprig of Shillaly!

By this time every man-jack within hearing distance began softly clapping in some sort of rhythm so as not to drown out Thrall's delicate Irish tenor.

The morning soon came, and poor Paddy awoke,
On the Rebels to have satisfaction:
The drummers were beating the devil's tattoo,
Calling the boys into action.

Thrall paused and hollered over the music: "All together, laddies. Let's sing it like we mean it and then slow it down a bit. Sing lustily now or hie yourself off to spade out the pit!"

Then, the Irish Brigade in the battle was seen,
Their blood, in our cause, shedding freely;
With their bayonet-charges they rushed on the foe,
With a shout for the Land of Shillaly!

As if on a conductor's cue, the men shushed themselves, the music slowed, and discordant voices hit forlorn notes.

The battle was over, the dead lay in heaps:
Pat Murphy lay bleeding and gory:
A hole through his head, from rifleman's shot,
Had finished his passion for glory;
No more in the camp, shall his laughter be heard,
Or his voice singing ditties so gaily;
Like a hero he died, for the Land of the Free.
Far away from the land of Shillaly!

Charles liked music in general and fine singing in particular. He went to bed that night not liking war music in general and *The Land of Shillaly* in particular.

CHAPTER 9

The Mettle of a Man

*Far off, men swell, bully, and threaten;
bring them hand to hand, and they are feeble folk.*
Ralph Waldo Emerson

Private Wilmer Scoggins was not someone Charles would ever seek out as a confidante or to pass the time in a friendly game of Wisk. Scoggins was not a man to sit around a campfire and enjoy a give-and-take round of casual conversation. Every time Charles saw the burly former bullwhacker he had the same reaction.

If he were on fire, I'd go to the creek to get some water to put him out. But I'd walk damn slow going and coming.

The hulking private had the face of a bully: Flat face, squashed nose slumping to one side like a wind-whipped, thick-trunked willow, and tiny, black river-pebble eyes lost in a face puffed from countless bottles of bad whiskey and the hammer of bare knuckles. Scar tissue dotted both cheek bones; busted ear cartilage, bulbous and fiery red, pulled his expansive ears away from his head.

If'n he could flap those things, he might soar like a buzzard.

Scoggins was a loud, profane dullard, who thought being drunk was as close as he would ever get to Heaven. He hated the army, hated the officers of the Ninth, and only got along with two or three men in the company, all of his ilk—

tough men, with the brains of moles, eyes always on the look-out for prey, fists always clinched in response to some indescribable internal rage.

The men of C Company acknowledged Scoggins' strength was a blanket of unwavering courage he wore into battle. Or, his audacity in battle could be because, as one solider said in a whisper, "He's just plain asylum-bound."

Scoggins took an instant dislike to Charles for the smallest of reasons: The youngster's slight stature.

"You're too small and buggery looking to be much good for nothing," Scoggins said more than once, eyeing Charles like a corn snake sizing up a crib mouse.

For the most part Charles consciously stayed out of the bully's way. Like all slow-to-focus, dull-eyed, mouth-breathers, Scoggins' attention was easily scattered and could be swayed from an intended target with relative ease.

It was fall and there was a faint chill in the air. The regiment was still encamped just south of the small village of Ducroix Crossing. Charles Jacob Skimmer, a newcomer to the drum corps from the Twenty-first Michigan (who was reassigned to the Ninth "on an accident," as he put it), was sitting under a chestnut tree near a small creek. Charles lightly tapped out sick call on a flat rock for practice while Jacob twittered on about life in Michigan. "Shore, it can get cold back home. But heck, it gets cold everwhere. The coldest I ever got in my life was in Mississip last winter. Damn near froze off my twig and berries! But it don't get hot up home like it gets down here. Lord, but it's hot. I hate wet heat worsen I hate the wet cold of the South."

Scoggins stumbled onto the pair and quickly decided that tormenting the young drummers would be perfect pre-supper fun.

"Well, well, well," Scoggins said, running blunt, dirty fingers through his bird's nest of a beard. "If it ain't the Rebel squirt and that other skin-beater. Whatcha doin', boys, beatin' on your skins!" He hee-hawed at this own joke.

Charles jumped up like he had sat on a hornet's nest. Putting his right hand to ear, he said, "Hark! Hark, I say!"

Jacob squinted at Charles like he was about to have a fit. Scoggins's beady eyes shrunk to the size of lentils.

"Hark!" All three held their breath. "I swear that's cannon fire. Sounds like the Rebs are coming up the north road. Come on, Jacob! The colonel will be wanting us quick-like."

As they ran back toward camp, Jacob looked hard at Charles. "I didn't hear nothing. What did you hear?"

"Nothin'!" Charles said, laughing. "But it was the best nothin' I never did hear."

They ran on toward the camp, laughing the frenzied cackle of men jerked back from the edge of the grave.

"Hark?" Jacob said, wheezing between gulps of breath and forced laughter.

"I read it once in a book," Charles said. "It sounded like the right thing to say at the time." He paused. "Hark! Yep, that's a right fine word."

Thirty minutes later, as Charles and Jacob gathered up their supper rations, they saw Sergeant Rooney, a round-headed Irish tough squared up with Scoggins. The sergeant was screaming. "The fooking Rebel Army is a-comin', now ya be saying? Well, where they be, that's a question I'll be askin' you?"

"Sergeant, that damn squirt—"

"You be shuttin' your face, Private Scoggins. But since you think that the entire Rebel By Gawd Army be comin,' I'm going to let you dig us a nice, deep hole so we can all hide in it. I want that nice, deep hole right next to the nice, deep pit at the end of that nut orchard. And, while you're at it, cover up the old pit.

"In fact, get in the hole that you be coverin' up. I'm sure you'll feel right at home in that nice, deep, shitty hole with all your relatives."

The sergeant stomped off toward the mess area and the two boys ducked quickly behind a tent as Scoggins scanned the area, his face a thunderhead of hatred.

"Best you stay out of his way for a spell," Jacob said, rolling his eyes.

"Oh, yeah," Charles answered. He tried to sound fear-free and knew he failed.

Over the next several days, Charles spent a goodly amount of time on the lookout for Scoggins. When he went about camp on errands for the surgeon, the quartermaster, or one of the company or regimental officers, he blended in with groups of men going somewhere, or walked fast along the road running alongside the bivouac area, keeping to its center and away from covering brush.

He admitted to himself that he should be afraid of Scoggins; any sane man would be. He convinced himself that keeping away from the man was good, solid, New Orleans, Catholic, orphan common sense. Being hurt at the hands of a bully served little purpose.

Am I afraid of Scoggins?
He asked himself the question more often than he realized.
Not afraid, exactly, more like...cautious.
No, maybe afraid is what I am.
Not having had much experience in rough-and-tumble and none at all in what Brother Bartholomew had called the "art of pugilism," Charles simply didn't see any reason to fight the menacing soldier. That left plenty of reasons *not* to fight the man.

A couple of months after his run-in with Scoggins, Charles was headed toward the quartermaster staging area to pick up some plug tobacco for Colonel Healy. A moisture-laded, steady breeze from the south nipped at his face and fingers as he burrowed further into his wool coat. His bedroll blanket served as a cape and scarf, but failed to keep the wind's icy fingerlings from digging at his neck.

A roar to his right straightened him just as a blurred force knocked him from his feet. The impact launched him several feet; a two-man tent, which collapsed under his weight, retarded his momentum. He later remembered hitting something solid inside the tent. An elbow maybe; a knee, most likely. Yelps and grunts of pain came simultaneously from Charles and the tent's occupant as Charles' momentum carried him over the tent and into a small circle of men squatted around a campfire.

Stopping just short of the fire, Charles jumped up quickly and turned just in time to receive a strong blow to his neck and shoulder. Backwards he stumbled before losing his balance and hitting the ground with his face facing the fire. Someone grabbed his leg and tried to flip him over onto the fire, but Charles kicked with his free foot, landing a squishy blow that elicited a startled grunt.

Rolling clear of the fire, Charles rose in a crouched position, ready to run if possible...or fight, if necessary.

Scoggins!

Anger scorched his brain, a heated flatiron left on a cotton shirt. Fiery sparks hit the back of his eyes and blossomed into white-hot embers, as his brain tried to comprehend a logical solution to the problem.

He could feel his brain sluggishly starting to evaluate all angles of the situation just as a fist swept by his cheek, connecting like an iron bar into his shoulder. The blow knocked him to the ground a third time. Gathering his feet under him, he launched himself at his tormentor. With a banshee scream and fingers extended forward—eight daggers searching for a tender target—Charles left the ground and felt a high degree of satisfaction as the straightened fingers of his right hand struck Scoggins' neck at the apex of his prominent Adam's apple. An instant later, his left hand, fingers extended, sliced into the big man's right ear. Scoggins was trying to take a step backward to set himself firm, but caught his right heel on a root, causing him to bend to the right. He hit the ground hard. At impact he went ass over teakettle, turned a complete somersault, and ended up on his belly with his legs scattering the blazing campfire logs.

Scoggins grasped his neck with both hands; bawling noises accompanied by a gagging noise strangled their way out of his open mouth and nose. He only had time to make one feeble kick to disperse the flaming sticks when Charles started kicking him in the head with both feet.

(One soldier, recalling the scene in a letter home, wrote, "The young'un was poundin' on him with both feet and it made a thumpin' sound, like mess call on a little drum." Every time he told that story to a new audience, the laughter was loud, raucous, and sustained.)

One kick connected with Scoggins' chin and another was headed at the same target when Charles felt his feet leave the ground; his breath whooshed out by a chest-crushing weight. A feathering of red hair sprouted over his right shoulder; he grabbed the hair with both hands and yanked forward. A sharp yelp slapped his right ear like a blow from a flat stick.

Charles went airborne, hit the ground on his right side and rolled twice before his hip slammed into the trunk of a small pine. He lay still. Very still. He wanted to move, felt he should move out of a survival instinct, but his muscles refused to obey brain commands. He shook his head, trying to clear it, and took stock of the extent of the damage to his hip. The intense pain and dizziness quickly eased. Despite the confusion gripping him, he jumped to his feet and ran at Scoggins, still sitting on the ground, still holding his throat, screeching like a swamp cat beset by a pack of hunting dogs.

A heavy hand grabbed a headful of hair and jerked Charles off his feet. Pain sliced through the back of his head; a bubbling of tears hit the corner of both eyes. Grimacing and grinding his teeth so hard they ached, he forced his eyes open. Through a thick veil of tears, he stared into the wild eyes of Sergeant Phillip Reilly of I Company.

The soft voice belied the crazed look in those eyes. "I'm trying to help you, boy. Now calm yoreself down."

Trying not to move, Charles nodded with his eyes, blinked twice. The pressure on his hair eased. His feet found ground. "Now, git!" the gruff sergeant whispered loudly in his ear.

Charles turned to force his way out of the circle of soldiers. He stopped and slowly twisted his neck to stare at Scoggins, who was still on the ground. Charles noticed with satisfaction that there was blood on Scoggins' shirt and a red ripple of blood ran from his ear, down his neck and dripped onto the fine dirt of the camp. He inwardly grinned when he heard the man blubbering. Consciously trying to lower the tone of his voice, he said in a sawmill whisper: "Private Scoggins, if you ever touch me again—ever touch me again!—I will kill you. That's no threat, that. *C'est une promesse.* That's a promise."

He turned and walked away. A circle of men he didn't remember being there parted to let him through. More than one hand slapped him on the shoulder as he passed.

After Charles had been in camp a little more than five months, he worked up the nerve to ask permission to visit St. Mary's, to check on the sisters, to see if they had any word about Ian. And, he wanted to see Sarie Beth. Colonel Cahill overheard his plea to Sergeant John Burke and stepped out of the command tent. "If you're going to town, boy, stop by the tobaccary and get me some pipe stuffin's. Bailey's Finest, if they have it, Bennett's Prime, if they don't." He fetched a silver dollar out of his pocket. "They'll be a bit left over. Get yourself a hard candy."

"Bailey's or Bennett's. Yes sir, and thank you."

Three hours later, a tin of Bailey's Finest secure in his front left pants pocket, Charles stepped quietly up on the porch to the orphanage kitchen. Peering through the single windowpane to the left of the door, he spied Jeanine rolling out a wad of dough.

Bread! She's making bread! Oh, Mary, mother of Jesus, I have missed Jeanine's bread.

Slipping in the door without Jeanine noticing was easy. Trying to figure out how to scare Jeanine in a Christian sense was a whole different matter.

Charles eased into the room, leaned nonchalantly against the door and said, "So, what's for supper, Sweet Jeanine?"

The roly-poly cook jerked straight up and spun around, flour dough squeezed tight in both hands. "Saint's preserve us, if it aren't Master Andre in his new fine army clothes, even if they be a queer color for a member of the Army of the South. You scared me something terrible."

Charles spun around, arms straight out at shoulder height. "I went to join the Confederate Army like I said, but I decided that gray was not a good color on me. Blue is my color. But you have to admit, Great Cook of Catholic Orphans, I do look rather splendid, that I do."

As he knew she would, Jeanine started to laugh. Her hands seemed to be trying to anchor her hips, which wiggled side to side like two small rafts in a windstorm. The flesh pillows under her bodice began shaking; her face turned blood red as she fought for breath between guffaws.

He walked over to her, grabbed her in a gentle hug, and joined in the laughter.

"Git, now," she said, pushing Charles away with flour-coated hands. Two nicely outlined handprints decorated the front of his blue shirt.

"Now look at what you've gone and done," Charles said in mock horror. "The Union Army will not tolerate this type of behavior. We'll…we'll have to…"

"Well," Jeanine said, "what will you have to be doin,' yes?"

Forcing himself not to give her another big hug, Charles said, "The Union Army, upon my command, you see, will just have to recapture the city all over again and make everybody surrender a second time. And, that's not all. My real good friend, General Beast Butler will issue an order that any and all orphanage cooks named Jeanine must do anythin' and everythin' any member of the Union Army tells them to do. No exceptions."

"Even the ugly, short ones with the given name of Charles?"

"Even them. Especially them."

They hugged once again, each silently willing the moment to last forever.

After Charles told Jeanine about his misadventure in trying to join the Confederacy, and what he had to do to join up with the Federals, he talked about his short time in the army. He apologized for not bringing some supplies because he hadn't yet been paid. Then he asked about Sister Bloody.

"She's fine, still working hard, still as happy as a person can be. She really misses you and Ian, I can tell you that. You two took a big load off her. Oh, land's sake, I forgot about your 'brother.' How's Ian doin' and where's he at this fine day?"

"The last time I saw him he was being marched off with a bunch of other new signers toward the Confederate camp not seven miles east of here. I imagine he doesn't even know I never got in."

"No, Charles," Jeanine said, "that's not right. He knows. You and Ian was real close. Even a war and fighting for opposite sides can't change that."

"That's what I told the sergeant when I joined up with the North," Charles said.

But will it hold if we ever run into each other down the road?

After spending a few more minutes with Jeanine and exchanging greetings with some of the younger boys who stuck their heads in the kitchen, Charles set out to see if he could find Sister Bloody, who was, as he expected, scrounging around the river district.

Two hours later, after picking up her trail on Canal and losing it in the alleyways off Iberville and Bourbon, he gave up on his search. Looking at the sinking sun and knowing he was going to be late getting back to camp, he headed to the girls' orphanage to see Sarie Jane. She was waiting outside in a nervous state, having heard from one of the St. Mary's boys that he was in the city.

She saw him turn the corner and ran to him, grabbing his hand and jerking him back around the corner. Once out of sight of the orphanage, she launched herself into his arms, hugged his neck, and kissed him. Hard.

His eyes wide open, his arms plastered to his sides, Charles didn't know what to do. Finally, Sarie let loose of her grip on his neck and slid down to the ground.

"I missed you so much! You can't believe how much. Where's Ian? Why are you dressed in a Union uniform? Why did it take so long to come back? How long are you going to stay? When will you be back?"

Charles smiled and rubbed his lips with the back of his hand. Kissing. Sarie Jane. The one other kiss they shared may even have been an accident. Or a dream. Not this time. His lips still tingled.

Over the next hour, they walked from the orphanage to the levee and continued east through the French Quarter. They tarried by the edge of the river for a time, then headed to Canal Street and back to the orphanage.

Charles knew he should be getting back to camp, but prolonged the inevitable as long as he could.

When they were back at the corner of the orphanage, Charles worked up enough courage to ask Sarie for another kiss. "I want to, Charles. I really do, and you know it. But I want you to think about that first kiss and I want you to have to come back to get another. I hope it'll make you hurry back."

She ran around the corner, pigtails flying. She did not look back.

I'll be back, Sarie Beth. Count on it.

CHAPTER 10

Sometimes Living Is...Existing

> *Living, just by itself—what a dirge that is!*
> *Life is a classroom and Boredom's the usher,*
> *there all the time to spy on you....*
> Louis-Ferdinand Céline

Activities in camp during late summer and early fall were mind-dulling. Wake up. Fetch breakfast. Assemble in a pre-determined area. Stand for inspection. Perform marching drills to the rolling tappity-tap-tap of the drummers' sticks. Divide into work camps—latrine duty, gather wood, unload wagons, fetch supplies, clean rifles and cannons, help take care of the livestock. And, always wait for orders to move. Somewhere. Anywhere but wherever they happened to be at the time.

Late fall turned to early winter in a rush. "Mother Nature is in a hurry this year, boys," Sergeant Reilly said one night sitting by a blazing campfire. By the time the temperature dropped to below fifty degrees, the men of the Ninth had constructed more than sixty shanty houses from logs, mud, split hardwood, tents, and more mud. Most of the houses, especially those constructed by the Connecticut men, had interior fireplaces made from stones and mud and grass bricks. A majority of the Louisiana contingent—those that joined the Ninth in 1862 and 1863—who knew the usually predictable weather patterns, built sturdy enough houses, but opted to build fireplaces outside, under a lean-to, or just out in the open near the front door, with a helter-half or two as covering.

"It don't get that cold," said Private John Falvey, who had lived right down the road in the village of Carrollton. "Leastways, it never has." Putting regional weather history aside, Charles, Falvey, John Lovett of Decroix Station, and Peter Devlin and Bernard Boylan, both New Orleans boys, teamed up to build their winter cabin.

The existence was simple: When it was cold, the men did their assigned chores, then stayed inside, talked, played games, ate, and slept. When it rained, if chores were ordered, they did them, then returned to the cabin. On clear days, they went on forays into the nearby scrub brush hunting for rabbits and other small varmints, or went fishing. Since Charles didn't have an assigned rifle, he spent down time fishing in the nearby bay and runoff streams. He knew being a rifleman was not in his future. He had fired only one shot at a stationary target and found the experience sorely lacking in building his confidence. He apparently did something terribly wrong and injured his shoulder, which turned black and blue within hours.

After a month, the cache of wild critters fetched for camp meals tapered off in dramatic fashion; more and more men took up stances along the bayshore in hopes of catching fish. Some men were choosy about what they caught…at first. Later, when the weather turned nasty, any old fish or amphibian would do—gar, blue catfish, buffalo, carp, even alligator…it made do difference. If it got hooked and landed, it went in a pot.

On cold, misty, or rainy nights the cabins were buttoned up tight; clear nights, even in the dead of winter, a hundred campfires lit up the surrounding countryside, like giant fireflies at a homecoming.

It was the clear nights, when the fires were blazing, the front of a person's body was toasty and the back was cold, that, at first, Charles didn't mind at all. It was these nights, when the boredom of winter camp set into a man's bones and worried his mind, that cut loose the spirits of the musicians, singers, and storytellers. He enjoyed the music from a banjo or flattop git-fiddle, as a couple of Southerners called the guitar. The ascension of creativity on such a small, isolated scale roused the spirit of men like Charles—life's natural audience members, its chosen listeners, its mental applauders.

After supper, after final visits to the latrine, after the officers found sanctuary from the troops, after bottles of store-bought whiskey or fresh and evil-tasting apple jack were consumed, stories and songs flowed…literary and musical wine from a broached cask.

Corporal Peter Walsh of Hartford (I Company) was a favorite of the men when it came to telling stories. True or not, his stories were imaginative mental etchings, vocal masterpieces of facts, foolishness, and inventive fancy. He had a gift; his approach to story telling created a need in his audience to truly *listen.*

"We was marching down the yonder road by Bayou Teche. Jake, you was there, 'member? It was a good day for a march if there ever was such a thing, and they was sugar cane everwhere and Colonel Birge told us all to take a break and get some cane to sweeten our disposition. One of the men—I think it was Edward Hawley…nope, that can't be right, he up and died later that same year. It was…I'll 'member later.

"We passed by the Porter Plantation, name of Eden Manor or somesuch. It was, for sure, a paradise. The mansion was the biggest and best around. There was more flowers that I ever seen in my whole life. There was orange trees! It was too early for oranges, but if there'd been some I'd had more than some, let me tell you."

He paused and relit his long-stemmed pipe.

"'Bout this time, Missus Porter herownself came out of the house and marched right up to Colonel Birge, waving a white hankie at him like she wanted to surrender something, if you know what I mean?"

Most of the men guffawed and slapped thighs and yahooed.

What are they laughing at?

The story continued as the gales of laughter trickled into wheezy chuckles.

"It seemed her young son, fourteen or thereabouts, was taken prisoner. Colonel Birge said he's see what he'd do and told the lieutenant to get the boy back home safe by the morrow. I thought she was gonna kiss him right there and I think Ol' Birge was hopin' she would."

He paused again to relight his pipe with a flaming twig.

"'Bout an hour later we was a-passin' the residence of another wealthy family, and this 'un himself was a quite right successful slave-owner. Now, the colonel knew this man…Did I mention he was a negro? No? Well, he was. Real dark. Blue gums and the whole cloth. Anyway, this slave-holding negro had equipped a whole company of white soldiers for the Rebs.

"I heard his wife was white, but we never seen her a little. Shore is funny how things get all a-twisted, don't it? The colonel never took a cotton to the man. First off, he was spendin' good money to outfit soldiers to fight us. He was a nigra and his kind was part of the reason we been doin' all this fightin'. Don't seem right, somehow."

A painful silence had time to settle and take root before a soldier piped up: "Tell 'im about the Reb planter. That's a good 'un."

Walsh took a deep draw off his pipe and let out a billowy cloud above his head. The heated air above the campfire scooped it up and flung it into the overhanging branches of a sweetgum.

"That same day, hours later it was, we was getting close to camp and this Reb farmer wanted Colonel Birge to assign some men to protect his place. Birge said he would do that (here he changed his voice to do an uncanny impression of the colonel), 'Ahummmm. Certainly, we can do that, can't we, Captain. Ahummmmmm. We can, that is, if you are a loyal citizen of the United States.'

"As Birge knew he would, the farmer said, 'I'm a loyal citizen of the Confederate States of America.' Birge looked at him queerly, then said, 'Ahummmmm. That just won't do, now will it? I can't furnish a guard for the property of our enemy.'

"We started marching on and about a half-mile down the road, somebody looked back and hollered. There was a big, black cloud of dense smoke coming from the direction of the man's home.

"'That's a shame, that is,' one of the officer's said.

"'Couldn't have happened to a nicer fellow,' Birge said, a small grin on his face."

It took a while for the group to calm down, jawing at each other as men around a campfire are apt to do.

Some soldier asked Corporal Joseph Bieker of K Company to do the "darkie song." With only a modicum of coaxing, the thin-shouldered, towheaded lad stood, turned his toes akimbo, lowered his neck like a turtle trying to pick up a grub and started to sing in a perfect tenor voice.

Say, darkies, hab you seen de massa,
wid de muffstash on his face,
Go long de road some time dis mornin',
like he gwine to leab de place?
He seen a smoke way up de ribber,
whar de Linkum gunboats lay;
He took his hat, and lef' berry sudden,
and I spec' he's run away!

REVEILLE

De massa run, ha, ha! De darkey stay, ho, ho!
It mus' be now de kindom coming, an' de year ob Jubilo!

He six foot one way, two foot tudder,
and he weigh tree hundred pound,
His coat so big, he couldn't pay the tailor,
an' it won't go halfway round.
He drill so much dey call him Cap'n,
an' he got so drefful tanned,
I spec' he try an' fool dem Yankees
for to tink he's contraband.

Bieker stopped and said, "Sing the chorus with me, boys, and all the rest that follow!" The men sang lustily.

De massa run, ha, ha! De darkey stay, ho, ho!
It mus' be now de kindom coming, an' de year ob Jubilo!

Dar's wine an' cider in de kitchen,
an' de darkeys dey'll have some;
I s'pose dey'll all be cornfiscated
when de Linkum sojers come.

De obserseer he make us trouble,
an' he dribe us round a spell;
We lock him up in de smokehouse cellar,
wid de key trown in de well.
De whip is lost, de han'cuff broken,
but de massa'll hab his pay;
He's ole enough and big enough,
ought to known better dan to went an' run away.

De massa run, ha, ha! De darkey stay, ho, ho!
It mus' be now de kindom coming, an' de year ob Jubilo!

The last note fuzzed out. The men hoo-ha-ed a bit, then sat in the silence staring into the fire until, one by one, they peeled off and headed for their tents.

CHAPTER 11

A Wrong Righted

> ...when all wrongs are righted and the
> united futures of hero and heroine
> are straightway assured.
> —Cambridge History of English and American literature

Late November, 1863.
It was early morning. A V of scudding ducks circled over the fog-shrouded clearing where the Ninth bivouacked, the men hunkered down in their sparse cabins, muscles rigid against the invading cold. Charles watched the flock.
How do they remain so evenly spaced. And why?
Which duck was chosen for the lead? And how?
Was it a coveted position or a dangerous honor, like being the point on a march through enemy territory?
Charles was outside getting some fresh air. Leaning back against a small willow oak, he pulled his thin wool blanket tightly around him and wiggled, trying to scratch an evasive itch out of his back. He licked at a lump of sugar in the bottom of his black and white splatterware cup. It was a hand-me-down cup from the sutler who tagged along with the regiment. "This is a gift because you ain't got paid yet. The next time you need something, it's cash up front!" The cup had no handle and when filled with coffee was too hot to hold. That minor life-problem solved with a piece of bark, peeled off a sycamore trunk and wrapped around the cup.

Charles smiled at his ingenuity, momentarily forgetting he picked up the trick from watching John McGrady, another handleless-cup owner who professed he could not get through a single day without his coffee. Charles flicked his tongue at the sugar lump lodged on the cup's bottom, He didn't like sweetened coffee but never failed to pour a clump of sugar in the cup after he had drained it. That way the sugar wouldn't completely dissolve.

Licking a sugar lump after a meal was like having a confectionary treat, something Charles had often thought about at St. Mary's but seldom ever had. The orphanage had sugar but it was reserved for the coffee and tea of the brothers and sisters. The orphans seldom had sugar, not even for the daily portions of whey gruel or flour porridge. It was the lucky ones who got the croup and had sugar added to quell the wretched taste of the sulfur mixture used to dose the malady.

Charles was in a contemplative mood. A week ago he had got up enough nerve to ask Lieutenant David Warner about his pay. "I'm not complainin', me," Charles said. "But I would sure like to buy a few things from the sutler."

"What do you mean, you haven't been paid? Is that what you're telling me? When did you join up?"

"June last."

"And you haven't gotten paid? Not once?"

Charles nodded and hoped he hadn't done something wrong in asking.

The lieutenant said he would check on it and for Charles to check back later. "Wait! Tomorrow might be better."

The next day, the lieutenant motioned to Charles after morning mess. "Come with me. We're going to settle this mustering-in mess right now."

Mustering-in mess. What have I gone and done now?

Charles followed the young officer to the command tent, where Colonel Healy was looking at some maps laid out on a rickety table. He took a slug of steaming coffee before looking up.

"Beggin' your pardon, Colonel, but here's young Andre. I told you about the mustering-in mix up."

Healy eyed him over the edge of his cup, took a long slurp and set it down away from the maps.

"I just learned that you have been a soldier for almost six months and have not been paid. The lieutenant here checked the records and apparently you were mustered in improperly by Captain Sawyer."

Healy saw the scared-rabbit look in Charles' eyes. "Nothing to worry about, boy, nothing at all. We'll straighten it out quickly. But we do have to re-muster you in to make everything legal. You will get all your back pay. By my figuring, the United States government owes you the sum of sixty-five dollars, seventy-eight counting this month. But that may take some time. In the meantime, Lieutenant Warner is hereby authorized to open you an account at the sutler's so you can get some supplies."

The colonel turned kind eyes on Charles. "You should have said something sooner, Andre. Why didn't you?"

Charles' started to speak. His voice failed. Clearing his throat, he finally forced out: "I thought maybe I had done something wrong, but I didn't want to be sent packin' if I asked anybody and made 'im mad."

"You've been a good soldier, Andre. And now you'll be a good, paid soldier."

Lieutenant Warner right away set Charles up with a five dollar credit with the sutler, who wanted to argue about giving credit, but a stern look and the mention of Colonel Healy's name nipped any objections to the quick.

Charles didn't pick up supplies then. He thanked the lieutenant and told the sutler he would be back later with a list.

Making a list to buy things. If that's not the best feeling in the entire world.

CHAPTER 12

Action of a Sort

> *A deception that elevates us*
> *is dearer than a host of low truths.*
> Marina Tsvetaeva

Early December, 1863.
Charles was put on temporary transfer duty with C Company in December. The unit was on alert for a forced march for "unspecified action" and needed an extra drummer, since the company was down to just one.

Charles was assigned to assist head drummer Charlie Brean. Like H Company, C Company also had three drummer slots, but there were only two in residence, Brean and James Lawler (Charles asked, but he was no relation to Charles' "guardian"), a seasoned drummer who had taken to his bed with the "southern runs." The company's other drummer, Bartholomew McCarten, had left the unit several months earlier due to a sustained illness; his slot had not been filled. H Company's Sergeant John McKenna, not expecting action and not wanting any more bodies to watch out for than necessary, was more than happy to support the drummer's move to C Company.

Charles didn't mind the transfer. Left to his own devices, he thought he would never feel comfortable being in charge of, well, much of anything. He was a natural follower and was very comfortable following the lead of an experienced drummer. So, why did it matter where he did it? He also didn't mind sharing a small tent with Brean, who did a lot of talking and a lot of laughing…mostly at his own talking.

Brean was what Charles came to think of as a "medium man": Medium height, medium weight, medium features—medium-size nose, medium-brown eyes, medium lips—not too fat, not too thin. Medium.

"Lookee yonder, Andre," Brean said, poking Charles in the ribs with his medium-sized pointer finger. He gestured toward the large command tent. Brean called his new trainee "Andre" because "I don't want to call you Charles 'cause I might think I'm calling myself."

Captain John Healy

There's a passel of Healy's in this here regiment, and it's hard not to get them confused.

and Lieutenant John Carroll were standing at the tent's mouth, conversing with a messenger who had ridden into camp a few minutes earlier. The messenger stood at ease, cupping hot coffee with one hand and picking pieces off chunks of a fresh-baked loaf of bread sitting on a table with the other. The two officers were animated. Carroll was holding an unfolded piece of heavy paper, nodding his head as he read aloud to Healy. The captain asked the messenger several questions that were lost in the wind.

Healy stomped a foot and swore loud enough for the two boys to hear. Two men slicing potatoes at the cook tent stopped and looked up, their knives motionless. Healy shook his head, barked something at the messenger, who snapped to and saluted. Without waiting for acknowledgement, he ran to his horse and departed the camp at a full gallop. Dust hung in the air like a pale tan cotton boll.

"Assemble the company, Lieutenant Carroll!" Healy barked, stomping his left foot for emphasis.

Usually the young officers dispensed with military protocol when more senior officers—colonels, generals and the like—were not about. Not this time. Carroll snapped to attention, his fingers peaking his kepi and he literally shouted, "Yes, sir." Healy returned the salute promptly. With a wink and a familiar nod, he went back into his tent.

Carroll looked around, spotted the two drummers and motioned. Brean jumped up. Charles followed his lead.

"Sound assembly," Carroll said sternly. "Now!"

Brean took off for his tent at a dead run, Charles matching his steps.

REVEILLE

"Wonder what's up?" Brean said without breaking stride. "Think we're goin' to go find us some Rebs?"

Charles didn't answer. "Golly. I hope we're not going to find us some Rebs. You know they put drummers and flag bearers up front, don'tcha know?" Charles didn't know and hadn't given it much thought. Till now. Now that he thought about it, he didn't want to know.

Brean rattled on: "If we gonna find some Rebs, I hope they stay hid up real good."

At the tent Brean hauled out his fourteen-inch snare drum, checked to make sure four sticks were in the two holders affixed to the shoulder strap and ran back toward the command tent. A full-color shadow, Charles traced his every step. He didn't know what else to do and figured if he didn't follow Brean, he'd get in trouble. That thought clashed with another thought: *If I do follow him without being told to do so, I might get in trouble.*

Words from Sister Bloody came back to him in a rush: *Doing something, anything, is better than doing nothing, even if doing something is wrong.* The first time Charles heard those words, he thought they were just plain wrong, or worse, dead-dog dumb. He had the same feeling as he followed the Brean.

Lessons learned young are hard to forget.

Another thought remembered from another Sister Bloody speech.

What the hell does that mean?

Brean took up a straight-backed stance in front of the officers' mess and started pounding out "Assembly" with a vengeance. Charles, not knowing what else to do, stood beside him in his tent-hut stance, and picked up Brean's rhythm. By the third note, heads were turning as if on swivels. By the second bar, soldiers were pulling on boots, grabbing shoulder packs, powder and ball pouches, and canteens, trying to distinguish individual rifles from the stacked teepees and generally running around like lop-necked chickens.

Gossip sliced though the company, hitting ears with the force of an open-handed slap.

"Better gear up! The Rebs are gonna try and take back New Orleans."

"Reinforcements are on the way from Baton Rouge and we're headin' up North."

"New Orleans residents have started torchin' the city."

"There are no reinforcements on the way and we're stayin' put."

"Replacement troops are comin'! We're heading' home!"

"We're gonna push back a Reb advance and it's gonna be a bad one."

"Beauregard's coming!"

"The Ninth has been ordered to relieve the Twenty-third New York at the siege at Vicksburg."

"The Ninth is joining the Twenty-third New York upriver and move on Mobile."

In less than two minutes, most of the members of C Company were in a ragged formation, rifle butts square on the ground, backs straight, chests out, eyes flitting around, searching for...answers. Any answers. A few stragglers, those who had wandered down to St. Cyr Creek to fill up their canteen or were making use of the pit, joined the line, all late-arrivals trying to appear invisible.

The company stood at attention in the icy air. Minutes were silently counted and seemed like hours in the chilled morning air. Murmuring ran up the straight lines like a lit cannon fuse. "Quiet in the ranks," a sergeant called out. Several corporals echoed the order.

Charles, standing right-center next to Brean and facing the company, angled his eyes up the line. The men looked nervous. "They's all nervous," Brean said, still beating out assembly with Charles keeping time, allowing time for stragglers to find a hole in the lines and slip in.

Lieutenant Carroll stood off to one side, hands on hips, an air of annoyance clouding his face. He spied a young private coming up from the pit, pulling on his galouses as ran up the hill. Watching the last man elbow into line, the officer about-faced smartly and stomp-walked to the command tent. Pulling aside the tent flap, he said something unheard. Captain Healy popped out and without acknowledging Carroll's presence, found a spot directly in the center of the company, stopped and then nodded for the drummers to cease the assembly call.

Charles did a four-note ending, then listened while his new friend hit a solid, loud seven-note flourish ending the call.

Healey let a long moment pass before speaking: "Men, we are going on a short march today on an important mission. I'm sure the rumors are already flying, but I can tell you it's not as a last-ditch effort to save the Union. That job will come later, perhaps."

A nervous trail of laughter trickled through the ranks. "What I can tell you now is we're heading south of New Orleans to Company Canal to help out a neighboring battalion. They're having a bit of a problem that only the glorious Company C of the revered Ninth Connecticut Regiment can solve? Think we're up to the task, lads?"

A roar went up that startled Charles. Gooseskin popped up on his arms like needles through cloth at a quilting bee.

A voice from the back of the company sounded out: "It's not digging them boys a pit, now is it, Captain?"

Lieutenant Carroll's face clouded like a summer thunderhead. "Quiet in…" Healey's hand and smile stopped the order in mid-syllable.

"Well, boys, I got to tell you. I asked that very question and before they could answer, I told them we'd not only be proud to dig an entire regiment privy but we would do such a good job of it that no one would ever want to leave that spot again, knowing they'd never have a place to pass water and shat that was that good in their entire lives."

Raucous cheers mixed a symphony of mouth and throat noises—yips, whistles, yeehaws and yahoos split the air. Healy raised his hand. Silence descended like a stage curtain with a broken rope. Healy surveyed the men, straightened his back and squared his shoulders. "We're moving out in ten minutes. Make sure you have your blankets, full canteen, and anything else you need for the next couple of days." Without looking left or right, he said, "Dismiss the troops, Lieutenant Carroll. We'll reassemble back at this spot in ten minutes. Ten. Not eleven."

"Yes, sir!" Carroll shouted. "Corporal Connerty! Make sure the company's rations for three days are laid out proper. Help line it up so each man can pick it up on the run. Brennan, pick up Connerty's kit and then go help him."

He popped to attention: "Dismissed. And be back in formation in ten minutes!"

The company broke ranks, a covey of quail spooked. Charles stood stock still, still thinking about what he had just heard. He looked to his right and Brean was gone.

"Come on, Andre!" Brean screeched from down the hill. Charles took off fast, tripped over a root, tucked and rolled to protect his drum and came up running. Ten strides more and he was running even with Brean.

"Whoa!" Brean said in a whistling breath, "you are fast! That'll come in handy when you're running from a passel of Rebs." Brean started laughing at his joke and Charles couldn't help but join in.

Five minutes later, Brean and Charles were back at the command tent, blankets strung across their backs, haversack straps criss-crossing the short rope holding the blankets, full canteens slung from a leather strap on their left shoulders.

"What about our rations," Charles said in a stage whisper.

"We'll pick it up as we march out," Brean said, nodding his head toward the supply tent where Corporal Patrick Connerty and a soldier Charles didn't know dropped wrapped items on the ground in little piles. "It's easier to divvy up the supplies when on a march. Some men will carry just coffee, some sugar, some fat meat, dried beans, and so on. Then we all put it together at night.

"And, of course, there's always hardtack. Mmmmmm. My favorite." He chuckled quietly.

From his first day in the army, Charles heard gripes about the flour and water biscuits called hardtack, which, actually, were seldom called that. More colorful names were often used: Hard crackers. Flat bullets. Toothbreakers, Flour hammers. Quaker shingles. Rock crackers. And those were the nice names. Devil's cannon balls. Skillet shitereens. Slabs o' hard turd.

The best descriptive terms came from men Charles considered to have imagination.

Charles remembered his first hardtack biscuit, offered up by a wizened veteran on his first night in camp. Biting at the edge of the biscuit, about half the size of his palm and a finger's width thick, was like trying to chip away at a chunk of shale. Egged on by good-natured ribbing, Charles tongue-larruped an edge of the biscuit until it loosened up.

Better than straight cornmeal mush. By a long shot.

He finally sogged it up sufficiently to saw off a big bite, and was appalled to find parts of two weevils, still wiggling in the part not in his mouth. He spewed hardtack into the fire. All the men hoorahed him; one said, "And that's a good biscuit...only two weevils!"

While they waited for the order to sound assembly, Brean related the details of a normal march. "We'll usually camp before dark to get the camp set up and then be moving afore dawn, especially in summer, to get ahead of the heat. Each company carries enough food for several days march and that included one pound of hard bread or hardtack, less than a pound of fatback or shoulder meat, beans, plus sugar, coffee, and salt. That's for every manjack of us, every day."

Charles knew that in camp, the food was better, more diverse, with beans, potatoes, dried fruit, pickles and even the occasional chunk of beef or boiled chicken and fresh vegetables on nightly menus. He didn't offer any comments, knowing that what he had eaten at the orphanage, on most days, it now seemed, was a lot less—a whole lot less—than one day's marching rations.

Within the hour, the company had all supplies—food, water, ammunition, extra weapons—loaded on two wagons and were in marching formation. The unit faced south, downriver, toward New Orleans. The newest rumor was outrageous, but the most out-spoken of the gossip-mongers were convinced it was true: A unit had mutinied and C Company was ordered to squelch the uprising.

With the two officers leading on two middle-sized, black geldings, C Company, numbering about ninety up-and-walking men, marched out of camp to the solid rhythm of drumbeats. Less than an hour later, the company was transferred by a trio of oar boats to a battered stern-wheeler—*Channel Queen*—anchored in the Mississippi backwash. The two wagons, with four riflemen assigned as escorts, headed southeast to join up with the unit at Company Canal by the overland route.

Few of the soldiers knew exactly where Company Canal was located. Some opined it was north of New Orleans; others, after observing which direction the stern-wheeler was heading, argued it was south. The mystery was cleared up just after the boat starting moving slowly downstream.

Less than a hour into the trip, a couple of corporals rounded up the men on the foredeck. Colonel Healy mounted an upturned barrel and all eyes riveted on him.

"We are assigned a difficult task, one that I do not relish and wish I could have refused." The comments could have been expected to start whispered comments or queries. The silence was complete. "We are going to Company Canal where a battalion of Union soldiers have rebelled against their officers and, by various accounts, civilian and military, are terrorizing the citizenry."

He paused, clasped his hands behind his back, and took a deep breath, puffing out his cheeks and exhaling loudly.

"We are charged, and will so commit all resources to so do, quell said uprising by any means possible. There are approximately two hundred and fifty mutineers. And, it seems, their officers are powerless to stop them." Healy paused, put his hands on his hips and threw his shoulders back. "They may be powerless, but C Company of the Ninth Connecticut Regiment is most assuredly not. We will do our duty and stop any tomfoolery and we'll do it up proud and damn quick, too!"

The men started cheering and Healy acknowledged their enthusiasm by sweeping his brimmed hat off his hat and waving it in circles over his head.

Twilight was sliding under a cloud bank on the horizon when the *Channel Queen*'s captain backed its engines to slow the boat to a lazy crawl. His target was a makeshift, ramshackled pier on the west shore. The tattered anchor-log-and-board structure looked like it had been beaten together by a bunch of one-armed, drunk carpenters. The short pier led to an area cleared of underbrush, adjacent to what Charles knew was a "prison road"—a trail cut through the backwoods by convicts wielding machetes, picks, axes, and crosscut saws.

On the trip down the river, the men had been told the Union camp was only a short march down the road, less than a mile. On horseback, Healy, with a two-man escort, and Carroll conferred in the road as the men assembled in ranks at the end of the dock. The soldiers could see the officers were in heated debate. After several minutes, Carroll snapped to attention in the saddle and saluted; Healy returned the salute and the three soldiers galloped off to the southwest.

Carroll watched them for a time, then pivoted his horse to face the men. He hollered: "Muster up! Sergeants and corporals on me." The men ran in disjointed unity to the lieutenant, and came more or less to a synchronized halt. In ranks. At attention.

"Men in ranks! At ease," Carroll shouted. "Colonel Healy has gone ahead against my recommendation, but then, he's a colonel and I am a lowly lieutenant. He has a plan and I by gawd hope it works. Check your gear and make sure your guns are loaded and bayonets fixed."

He looked at Charles and Brean. "No drums tonight. But keep 'em handy and focus on me."

He told the men briefly about Healy's plan and within a minute the company was double-timing down the road.

It was full dark by the time the company could pick out the sparkling flicker of about ten campfires and the ghostly waver of white tents set up alongside the river. Carroll dismounted and tied his horse to a low shrub. Without a word, the men eased canteens, bedrolls, and any other item they were carrying to the ground. Under hand directions from Carroll, soldiers even emptied their pockets of coins and knives and such to eliminate any potential noisemakers. Carroll indicated with a slicing motion with his hand for the men to follow him through the scrubby landscape cutting back toward the west. Following his lead, the men angled away from the river and moved silently parallel to the camp.

Within a couple of minutes, the company turned due south again, circling toward the rear of the camp. As they got closer, the campfires became larger and brighter; the lieutenant motioned them to go slow…and quiet.

The men moved like moonlit shadows through the spotty underbrush until they were right behind the first line of tents. From the firelight, they could see lines and lines of soldiers, all in seemingly neat uniforms, all at attention, all thirty yards out and away from the tents.

As Carroll had said, rifles were stacked in front of the tents and the soldiers, dark silhouettes against the flickering fire light, did not seem to be carrying any weapons, including the sabers cavalrymen prized. Carroll had told the men it was Healy's intention to enter camp as a commanding officer and request an immediate uniform inspection, which necessitated all weapons being stacked or otherwise stored.

Keying on Carroll, the company divided, half going left, the rest right. They eased through the lines of tents and regrouped in a long line between the first line of tents and the unarmed soldiers.

There is no way Colonel Healy and the other officers did not see us sneaking in. But they are givin' no sign.

Healy was talking about honor and duty. "There comes a time when what an individual soldier or group of soldiers might want doesn't really matter. What matters is the whole: The whole company, the whole battalion, the whole division, the whole army. And, yes, the whole United Sta…" He lopped off his speech in mid-sentence when he saw C Company was in place.

"I came here today under false pretences. I came here not as an inspecting officer, but to put down the rebellious nature of the so-called Louisiana Native Guard. And I will do just that."

The soldiers in ranks started squirming and muttering.

"Attention! Attention in the ranks!" Healy shouted. The brouhaha only increased.

In a booming voice, Healy shouted, "Company C! Make your presence known!"

Following Lieutenant Carroll's earlier instructions, Brean and Charles started banging out the long roll and Company C soldiers stepped forward in unison and thrust their bayonets and bodies in a synchronized lunge position.

At the first drumbeat, half of the assembled soldiers jumped and spun around. Even in the shadows, their features were clear. "They's nigras!" one Ninth soldier shouted in alarm. Charles, like all of the men in the company, was shocked. They all had heard about colored soldiers, but few had ever seen a single colored soldier, much less an entire battalion. Roaming the streets of New Orleans every day since the capture of the city, Charles had not seen a single colored Union soldiers in town. It never entered his mind that he would ever do so.

Free coloreds and escorted slaves were one thing, but colored soldiers as part of an invading army in the Deep South was quite another.

"Quiet in the ranks," the lieutenant shouted. "Horseshoe maneuver on my command. Move!"

With the centerline of the company remaining between the colored soldiers and their weapons, the left flank led by Sergeant Daniel Sullivan, and the right flank, led by Sergeant Dennis Glynn, split off. The men moved quickly to cover the sides of the subdued, but obviously nervous battalion. Colonel Healy and the officers around him covered the front with drawn revolvers.

The colored troops broke ranks and moved to huddle in several giant balls of men with every soldier facing outward. Although outnumbered three-to-one, Company C had the upper hand. and the weapons—all the weapons.

Healy screeched for quiet. "Men of the Native Guard. You are hereby under arrest for mutinous attitudes and failure to obey the orders of your commanding officer. You will sit where you stand."

No one moved to follow the order. Heads of the encircled men swiveled in assessment of the situation.

"Sit down! Or you will lay where you fall." Healy shouted. "It's your last warning." No one moved.

Healy took a step toward the cluster of men. "Men of the Ninth Connecticut. On my command, you will fire into the assembled ranks! Ready..."

Are we really going to shoot our own troops, even though they be colored?

A few soldiers on the outside of the large circle plopped down.

"...Aim..."

In groups of ten or more, like disjointed marionettes with busted strings, the men of the Native Guard sat down quickly. In less than fifteen seconds, the entire battalion was seated. It was cemetery quiet, the only human sounds an occasional cough or foot shuffle. Charles became instantly aware of a sudden avalanche of noise...a singing convention of *ribbit*-ing frogs at the nearby slough.

"Sergeant Glynn, take half your men and gather up all weapons—rifles and swords—and..." Healy stopped and struck a thoughtful pose. Motioning for Sergeant Glynn to approach, he whispered for a long minute in his ear, Glynn nodding all the while.

Glynn backed up, saluted, waited for the slap-salute in return, and returned to his men. "By alternates, the first ten men follow me."

Every other man through the first twenty peeled off to follow the sergeant. One man was dispatched to fetch the supply wagon, while Glynn instructed the others to gather armloads of rifles stacked outside the first row of tents, and swords stacked inside three consecutive tents.

Five trips by half the men, four by the other half, were required to move the guns and swords to the supply wagon, which was then driven south out of sight.

The seated soldiers started muttering among themselves despite repeated orders for "quiet in the ranks" by Healy and the other officers. When the guns were out of sight, Healy ordered "Assemble in ranks!" The Native Guard soldiers grudgingly obliged, albeit at a lazy pace.

When the men were in a semblance of order, Healy stared up and down the line. "ATTENTION!" he barked. The order was met with a mere hint of following the command. The colonel looked mean. Then his face softened.

"I sincerely regret having to be here in this capacity. But do not take my feelings of regret as a weakness, because my orders clearly state that I can use whatever force necessary to make sure you men understand you are soldiers of the Union Army and are expected to act as such in all circumstances."

Healy paused to let the message sink in.

"What happens from here on out depends on you. You can agree to start acting like soldiers or you can elect to be bound, gagged, and treated like irresponsible chattel. I understand you may think you have grievances but finding out what they may be or how to resolve them is not my charge. You will agree to act like soldiers, like men dedicated to preserving the Union and making freedom for your kind a priority, and agreeing that the only outcome of this war will be total victory—or death—and that you will follow orders to the letter. If you do not choose to do that, then you are prisoners and will bound and marched to a prison camp in Indiana or Ohio."

The eyes of the surrounded soldiers were locked on Healy. There was little movement in the ranks, no muttering, no unexpected overt signs of defiance. Just mean eyes and clinched fists.

"Some of you are probably thinking—I know I would if I were in your place—that you outnumber us, that all you have to do is rush my men and then just…take off. That may work—for some of you. But if you choose that path, some of us will die, more of you than of us. Those that do escape will be hunted down like dogs. No, even worse. You will be treated like runaway slaves while in captivity. Then you will be summarily shot or hanged for mutiny."

Healy, eyes still sweeping the ranks, moved closer to the subdued soldiers. "Shot." He let the word hang in the frosty night air. "Or hanged. Not choices I would consider reasonable options under most circumstances. Your other choice is to agree to start acting like soldiers, instead of like reprobates, mutineers, and malingerers. Start acting like free men willing to fight and die to secure a better future for you and those that follow you than you have had in the past and you will be honored for your decision."

He paused, drew in a deep breath and blew it out, causing the ends of his longish mustache to flutter.

A palatable silence spread across the camp.

"What's it going to be, boys?" Healy snapped, nodding at a colored sergeant in the outer edge of the circle.

"Beggin' yore pardon, Colonel," the sergeant said. "If it's all the same to you, we'd like to go back to the way it was before you and your mens showed up."

"You talking about going back to being shiftless, no-account, and lazy, refusing to follow orders, and raising pure hell in the countryside?"

The large sergeant hung his head, then looked up and down the Native Guard line. "Naw, sir. I'm talkin' 'bout goin' back to bein' soldiers. We were good ones and can be again, too."

The battalion's commanding officer leaned in to Healy and whispered in his ear. Healy nodded.

"Me and my men will be here for the next week or so. If in that time you show your commitment to becoming not just good soldiers but exceptional soldiers, we will leave you with our goodwill and blessing. And, we will be proud to consider you comrades, good men, all, fighting for the same cause.

"Is that understood and accepted?"

After looking up and down the ranks and seeing barely noticeable nods of acceptance from the men, the colored sergeant said, "I think I speak for the free men of the Louisiana Native Guard in saying, we accept yore generous and kind offer. And we will do whatever it takes to be the best soldiers in the Union Army."

Without another word or gesture, the sergeant took two steps forward, saluted Healy and, when it was returned, turned back to his troops. "Attention!" They snapped into precision position.

The sergeant pivoted once again to face Healy.

"With the colonel's permission, may I dismiss the troop to their tents?"

Healey glanced at the battalion's commanding officer, who nodded.

"Permission granted! But no one leaves camp without express permission from your commanding officer."

A collective sign of relief, from those with weapons and those without, rustled through the clearing.

"Men of the Native Guard, you are dismissed!"

Carroll quickly divided his men into guard details to ring the camp; two men were assigned to guard the wagon holding the weapons.

There was an uneasy undercurrent coursing through the tents throughout the night. But the next morning, the troops quickly gathered at reveille...pounded out by four drummers—two colored and two white—standing side by side in front of the command tent.

The sight of the four young drummers, going about their assigned duty, induced a sense of pride in the officers of the Ninth, and smiles on the faces of many soldiers in the Native Guard.

The white officers of the Native Guard ordered the men out for drill. For two hours, the men marched in the chilly morning, even hustling in double-time for more than two miles up and back the south road.

At Healy's insistence, the officers complimented the men for their hard work and dedication in trying to "wipe the slate clean."

Six days later, peace restored and communications opened between colored soldiers and white officers, the Ninth marched north, back to the makeshift dock, where they waited overnight for the steamer to take them back to their own camp.

CHAPTER 13

Life Lessons Learned

There are endless sufferings to endure and endless lessons to learn.
Chinese proverb

Late December, 1963

Downtime in the winter camp was filled with mostly mind-numbing activities. Any time away from chores or drills was an invitation for creative thinking for many of the men of the Ninth. Around roaring campfires—shortly after breakfast call to taps, between must-drills, other chores, foraging, finding, gathering, and splitting wood—the men talked or played card games (some with rules, others made up on the spot). They rolled bones for money (real and imagined), talked of their past and future lives, and made up tall tales for the sheer entertainment value.

Charles didn't often join in the games. Too many of the games demanded talking—bidding, over-bidding, being asked seemingly innocuous questions. The talk was mostly benign early in the day, but seemed to turn malignant and dark as livers floating in foul-smelling liquor when darkness descended. Offered a drink of "plum punch" on a lazy evening in the late fall, Charles took a tentative sip, then a healthy swig, smacked his lips loudly, and within minutes…was praying for a quick death.

The "punch" was concocted of plums gone bad and allowed to ferment in a community water barrel. The smelly mixture was then cut with grain alcohol snagged from the hospital tent when the surgeons and assistants were at mess, and sassafras root. It was like "drinking the Devil's piss," one soldier cried as his stomach tied itself in knots.

But, if the intent of the elixir was to graduate its partakers from sober to drunk in eye-blink time, it was a fine brew indeed.

Charles held his stomach as if he expected his guts to cascade on the cold ground. Trying to focus eyes that seemed to be struggling to meet each other at his nose, Charles floundered out of the campfire light. He made his way into a nearby pin cushion of oak saplings, and promptly puked. When his stomach was drained, he dry-heaved for what seemed longer than Job endured his trials. His guts in a twist, Charles groaned, cursed silently, cursed loudly, and screamed at man and God for relief.

A friendly soldier who had passed on the potent potion—"I done had it onest awhile back and that were 'nuff."—half-carried, half-dragged Charles to the hospital tent, roused a sleeping hospital steward, and asked for his assistance. The man—August Ruhl, a former rifleman from Norwich who was a recent transfer to surgeon aide detail—took a long look at Charles, shook his head and said, "This 'un he'll have to pay for. The cure may be worser than the ailment."

Ruhl walked to the backside of the tent and after rummaging around a spell in a large, plain, pine chest, produced a great dark bottle with a wooden stopper. Using his teeth, he extracted the stopper, which he spat on a nearby table. Charles, in severe pain and feeling he was going to pass out any minute, never took his eyes off the bottle swaying at the end of the man's long arm.

"What...is...it?" he asked between gulping breaths.

"Ipecac. It'll clear you right up, most prob'ly."

Ruhl pushed the bottle's mushroom lips toward Charles' mouth. "Hold his nose," the steward said to the soldier, "then grab his arms and hold tight. He's gonna fight some, most probably."

"Fight?" Charles said, "Why wo—"

Ruhl quickly pinched his Adam's apple as the soldier grabbed his nose. A large glug of the dark, sticky liquid slid down Charles' throat.

In spite of his best efforts, he coughed, sputtered, tried to spit, and then swallowed. His taste buds initially refused to register the taste but when they did...Charles felt his stomach roil once, twice, then a upside down waterfall of ipecac and bile came up twice as fast as it went down.

Once, twice…five times, Charles' body tried to turn itself inside out as the two men held him down and did funny, side-step dances to avoid the spewings.

When the series of incredible tidal waves of cramps had passed, Charles was awash in a swooning sweat. He fell down on the long table and was passing into blessed unconsciousness when he said, "Why did you give me…that? I had already throwed up?"

"You have to get the poison out, boy, or you will feel real bad for a long time. That's what ipecac does. Cleans you out."

There's gotta be a better way to go about it than poisonin' a fellow.
His last thought was partially lost in the slamming darkness:
How do them other fellas…?

The next day, well after reveille, Charles sat up. Or tried to. Then wished he hadn't. His head was a cannonball pressuring up to explode. He had apparently slept in a tight ball due to on-and-off stomach cramps; the muscles in his back, legs, neck, and arms were tight.

As tight as Dick's hatband. And sore to boot.
Oh, God!
Ruhl hovered nearby. "How're you feelin'?"

"Better than last night. But then, I was about to die, so anythin' has to be better, *oui*?"

"*Oui*, yes, and surely."

Charles was quiet for a spell, thinking. "So, bein' a surgeon and all, you know a lot of medicines and such, right?"

"I'm no surgeon, not even a 'sistant. I volunteered into the army but wasn't a very good soldier and knew it. I might want to be a doctor someday after the war. If it ever does end. So I volunteered myself to come over here and help out wherever I can. I could never be a sawbones. Cuttin's not for me. I know it and the army knows it. But the army needs to have a warm body fillin' a set slot in the ranks. I do the best I can and that's all I can do."

"Do you know medicine? Can you teach me some?" The question was direct, not hesitant; it was bold for Charles, but contained no hint of begging or pleading in his tone or mannerisms.

"You want to be a doctor?"

"Truly? I don't know. I seem to be goin' through life findin' out things I don't want to be and I want to find somethin' I do want to be even if I don't know what the somethin' is just yet."

Ruhl paused, staring at Charles, studying him.

"Hmmmm. That sounds right smart, when you get right down to it."

For the next several weeks, whenever Charles had a break from chores, from fetching water or firewood, or tapping out orders for drills, he shadowed Ruhl's every step. His presence, especially in winter camp when physical ailments did not include, for the most part, wounds with missing body parts, was tolerated. Even Rollin McNeil, chief surgeon, allowed Charles' presence; he seemed to take a liking to the small, quiet southerner, describing him to Colonel Healy as "unusually attentive for a lad his age. He studies right close on anything anybody does."

From general discussions with Ruhl, McNeil, and other doctors and aides, Charles quickly learned interesting tidbits, like why minie balls caused so much destruction on the human body ("wide bullet plus slow velocity tears up jack in a man"), the proper way to tie off arteries with silk thread if you had it, and horsehair, if you didn't, and why army doctors were called "sawbones" (a bastardization of the name of the instrument used to cut through bone during amputations—the bonesaw).

He learned the difference in the various ambulance wagons stuck around the camp and that two- and four-wheel ambulances were required to carry up to forty men per thousand soldiers. With prompting (and what else was there to do at night gathered around a fire?) he could recite the differences of the ambulance in a monotonous rote learned from pouring over a pamphlet printed by the "Department of the Army for the United States."

"The 'Moses' ambulance wagon can accommodate up to three supine wounded on the march. With only one in a recumbent position, twelve men can be seated, or with three lying down, six can be seated."

And, "The 'Finley' and 'Coolidge' are two-wheeled ambulances tested in the west in the Indian wars, but we have only a couple and they are seldom used because of the rough ride that does harm to passengers, wounded and non-wounded alike."

He knew, and told anyone who would listen, that the smaller "Rucker and Howard wagons could be used for up to four recumbent soldiers," while the "huge Tripler, Wheeling or Rosencrans wagons must be drawn by four horses due to the weight and the fact they each could carry up to four men lying down and six to eight or more seated."

Ruhl, and even McNeil, were impressed with Charles' ability to learn copious amounts of information and took pride in filling his curiosity bucket to overflowing with new information.

Fascinated by the seemingly endless stream of facts and homespun fancies about ailments and cures that worked "at least some of the time," as McNeil put it, Charles keep copious notes on butcher paper scavenged from the quartermaster's tent and folded into small "books." Each book contained two sheets of paper, each about eight inches by nine inches, cut carefully with a knife and folded twice. He sat with Ruhl, McNeil and other hospital staff during sick call, writing down ailments and accompanying recommendations for relief.

Some of the medicinal advice he already knew from St. Mary's sisters—you can treat warts by rubbing the offending bump with a sliced potato wedge; sprigs of lavender inserted in the crown of hats comforted the brain, preventing headaches; worms would skedaddle if you took a small spoon of castor oil and a single drop of turpentine; and, for colds, hot lemonade with a spoon of baking soda seemed to work at least on occasion.

Charles' little collection of "books," labeled carefully at the top of each page as "Medicines and Remedys," were as eclectic as they were fastidiously recorded.

- *Skin Cancer: Make poltise of violet leafs and bake soda.*
- *Open sores: buttercup sauve. Cook flower pedals in pork greas, ad sugar & soda.*
- *Lice: Lard & sulfur aplied til gone. Also good for 7 year itch & Ringworm.*
- *Mustard plastard: when whezin, mustard seededs, flour & water. Make paste &cover w/cloth. Sucks bad out.*
- *Spring tonick: 2 sml. Spoons dry dandylon leafs & cup of boil water. Cleans blood, heps indigestation.*
- *Spring cleaner: Boil potatos in water til soft. Pour off water for soup. Add whiskey or beer and boil til potatos gummy. Eat big heppin. Sistem cleaned out in a day & a night.*
- *Sore trote gargal: dryd rassbery leafs, boil water, honey mixed. Thro out after 3 day as it gets bad.*
- *Colds and such: red clover tea, boild bristly. No sugar or honey. Also rosehips boiled in tea. Do not mix the two.*

- *Bad gas, worms or shakes: red bud in middle of Quen Ann's lace. Pulp up and stick on Tongue, hold for spell, swallow.*
- *Inner pain or running heart: Young motherwort plant tops, mix up with sugar or honey.*
- *Boils: Bake half onyon. Move center and fix over boil. Comes to head quick like.*

Charles was mesmerized by the myriad recipes and remedies the hospital staff constantly threw out in casual conversations. In his rumbling no-nonsense voice, McNeil or Ruhl would interrupt normal conversations to impart another remedy, forcing Charles to keep stubby pencil and one of his books always at hand.

"Hand me the medicine kit, Andre," McNeil said one cold-snapping day when he was preparing to lance a boil on a private's privates. "I need…oh, I almost forgot: A good cough syrup can be had with a cup of honey, a little bit of water, two big spoons of dried hyssop tops—flowers, not buds—and a small spoon of aniseed. You have to boil the honey and water to a very movable slop and add the crushed tops and aniseeds and keep over low fire for a while. It'll keep a bit if you top it tight."

The recipe was dutifully added to the latest book

Coughs: cup honey, bit water, two b. spoons hyssop tops, flouers, sm. Spoon, aniseed. Boilwater&honey til cream-like. ad tops and seeds. boil slow for awhile. Can keep if juged tite.

CHAPTER 14

Building Friendships

Friendships in childhood are usually a matter of chance, whereas in adolescence they are most often a matter of choice.
                                                    David Elkind

Spring, 1864
Winter passed into spring, and an early summer was coming on. The Ninth Regiment stayed stuck in the backwoods Louisiana camp. Higher-than-normal temperatures, added to the high humidity, made camp life miserable. There was little to do but work and drill and sit and grumble. And wonder about some of the miserable soldiers in camp.

Charles Montgomery was a no-account; everybody in the regiment knew it. Those that embraced that notion kept their opinions to themselves. A hulking private from New York, Montgomery stood about six-foot-three and would have field-dressed out at about 180 pounds. Before the war he said he had been a carpenter, and supposedly made side money betting on himself in alleyway rough-and-tumbles.

His frame seemed a bit loose around the middle and a couple of the boys in the regiment—and in other unit as well—had thought that was his weakness. It might have been, but his strength was in his ham-sized hands and bulky forearms. As a carpenter, he had spent countless hours using a hammer to drive I-nails and square-heads. That exercise had sculpted his arms into veined cordwood.

A couple of the boys—an artillery man from the Second Ohio (Third Division, First Brigade) with the unlikely moniker of Big Gal, and a beefy, regiment quartermaster with the Seventeenth Pennsylvania named Spencer—at different times braced Montgomery, challenging him to a bout of catch-as-catch-can after supper call. Each fight lasted less than a minute. What Montgomery lacked in finesse, he made up for brute force: he used his ham-hands like clubs, whipping them around like windmill blades. His powerful legs and broganed feet were likewise lethal weapons. Each leg was like a knotted fence rail and Montgomery flailed with first one, then the other—pile driving, crashing, debilitating blows into the thighs of opponents. As far as anybody knew, no one walked away from a fight with Montgomery. More than likely they were carried; the lucky ones simply limped away.

It was a hot, sticky Saturday. Humidity steamed the air, making breathing a chore.

The regiment was bivouacked at the edge of an overgrown thicket. Few ventured into the closeness of the underbrush, even in search of shade. Any air movement, even if it moved through a heated cauldron, was better than no air movement. Summer was still a few days away, but the heat was already oppressive.

Charles leaned against a small pine sapling, wearing only his pants and long johns, the sleeves pushed high on his arms. He had tired of watching, well, nothing, and was daydreaming about Sarie and Ian and Sister Bloody and…images of imagined family members at a gathering.

He could see relatives, all finely dressed, all smiling, all enjoying the time together. The men were splendid looking in swallow-tailed coats, fine linen shirts, and beaver hats with black satin ribbons encasing the crowns. They bore a resemblance to the plantation owners Charles had seen on the cotton docks or entering restaurants on Iberville or Bourbon. The women, replete with towering hair (interwoven and decorated with bright ribbon), wore floral silk gowns, and carried small hand bags and parasols. The men and women sashayed around an open lawn, like so many ornaments on a verdant tabletop.

In his dream-sleep, Charles smiled. Parasol. It was such an odd, funny word. Two suns, he thought it meant. *How absolutely quaint!* His smile widened. *Quaint. Another odd word.*

"What'cha smiling at, Andre?"

Charles jumped and straightened up, hitting his head on a sapling tumor.

"Owww!" Laughter caused him to open one eye and he found himself stared at a black shadow of a man, outlined by the setting sun.

Shielding his eyes, he made out the uneven features of a man Charles knew from the Fifth New York Artillery. Montgomery. Charles. He remembered because of the shared first name.

Then he thought of something else. A spider web of uneasiness wrapped up inside him.

"Nuh-nothing. Just a dream."

The voice teased: "What's her name?"

"Her? Who?"

"The girl you were dreaming about, young mister. Every boy your age thinks about girls, right?"

"I think about Sarie some, a girl I knew in New Orleans."

"New Orleans? I thought you was from New York."

Trying to shrink his widened eyes to hide the mistake, Charles blustered: "I was, I mean, I am, but I joined up outside of New Orleans. Went down there on business."

Montgomery studied him more than a little. "Baker business, that it?"

The question lay between them, solitary and unanswered.

Clearing his throat, Charles eased off the ground, saying, "Well, best be getting back to the command tent. Never know when the lieutenant is thinkin' somethin' up for me to do."

Montgomery's gaze never broke. "I don't like asking favors of no one, but I got one to ask of you." He paused, looking down at his feet. Charles let the quiet take root.

Montgomery raised his gaze, staring hard into Charles' eyes. "I opened my mouth back yonder in camp, over by the creek. I told three men from the Twenty-first New York I could whip them in a bare-knuckle fight. I was more than a little het up so I told them I'd fight—all together or each to his own—one right after the other."

He paused, looking once again at the parched ground. "Well, I thought they would back down, but they looked at each other and took me up on offer to fight all three. All at once. I think I talked myself into a mess."

Charles' mind raced along a singular track.

He wants me to fight with him!

"What I need is a second." Pause for a deep breath. "And I'd be beholden if you'd help me out here."

A second? He definitely wants me to fight with him.
"I'm not a fighter, Mister Montgomery."

"Fight? I don't want you to fight. I want you to be my second." A splash of recognition hit Montgomery's face. "Oh, uh, I want you to help me when I need it, give me water, hand me a towel, and such things. The only smart thing I did was get them to agree that when any man went down, me or one of them, that we'd have a little break. Without that, they could wear me down pretty quick-like."

"When?"

"In a while. Afore supper. Will you do it?"

Charles studied Montgomery's face but could not read it. All he saw was a placid mask.

"Why me?"

The big man studied the teenager and then looked off in the distance. "I heard you were quiet—'dead quiet' one somebody said—but was straight with your words, straighter even with your actions. I heard you don't judge people. That when you say you'll do somethin', then you do it. I hope I heared right."

Charles worried the words. Then, his voice cracking, said, "You tell me what to do and I'll be glad to oblige."

The big man nodded and turned to go before stopping and looking over his shoulder. "Be down at the creek, by that big rock, in about a hour. If you don't mind, bring a pail to gather water. I've got some preparin' to do." Without another word or glance, he swung around and headed back toward the linear lineup of tents.

Well, if nothing else, this should be interesting.

An hour later, Charles snaked and elbowed his way through a large ring of men, several hundred it seemed. He used the empty wooden pail to get the attention of closely stacked men who parted when he said, "Let me through, please. I'm Mister Montgomery's second. I need to get through."

It was only after he had stepped into the center of the men that he realized he had not filled up the pail.

Montgomery was squatting, toad-like to his right, bouncing slightly on his haunches. His closed eyes opened and stared at Charles.

He stood up gracefully, eyes on Charles, and smiled. His gaze shifted to the bucket. "So, Master Andre, you going to magic up some water as my second or are you going to fill it from your own personal well?"

A howl of laughter pounded against Charles' chest and back. "I'll gah-go get some now," he said, starting toward the crowd of men nearest the creek."

Montgomery's calloused left hand fell on his shoulders. "Boys, pass that bucket back through the crowd and get it back up here quick. Me and my second got work to do."

The bucket was jerked from Charles' hand and he caught a glimpse of it being passed hands-over-heads as he followed Montgomery to the north side of the ring.

"I want you to wrap my hands," Montgomery said. On the ground, on top of his issue jacket were a bundle of torn cloth strips. The burly man grabbed a longish one and, telling Charles to watch, he tied a slip knot to the inside of his thumb and pulled it tight. Then he pulled the three-inch-wide cloth over and under alternating fingers, smoothing it as he went. After he wrapped it around the pinkie, he weaved it back in the opposite direction. The strip ended up in his palm, and he directed Charles to tie it off with a knot that settled between his thumb and first finger.

Watching every movement and listening to Montgomery's running commentary, Charles took a second strip and overlaid the first. A third, shorter strip was then centered on Montgomery's wrist, looped underneath, X-ed across the top and tied tightly, again with the knot to the underside. With Montgomery whispering every detail, Charles carefully placed the fourth strip twice across the knuckles, secured the wrapping by tying it off on the wrist wrap on top and underneath by passing it through the space between the second and third finger.

The knuckles were wrapped in four, then five even layers of clean cloth. The last two strips were different: Three knots, each layered by tying knots on top of knots, fit exactly in the hollow of Montgomery's knuckles. As he secured the first strip by tying it tight and securing it with a granny knot at the palm, Charles threw Montgomery a look.

"Protects the hand, and creates a little damage…if done right," he said softly. The small speech ended with a slight nod and wink.

A soldier walked over with the half-full bucket of water and sat it down by Charles. Montgomery looked in the pail and grunted his thanks.

Charles repeated the wrapping process on the right hand, with only minimal instructions—"A little tighter. Cross over that last loop. Tie it down tight."

Like tree frogs after a clap of thunder, the boisterous crowd quieted. The wide circle parted and three, bare-chested men stepped into view. Individually, there were impressive specimens, each tall, broad-shouldered, heavy-handed, with mirror chins resembling rock outcropping. Together, standing shoulder to shoulder, the trio looked way more than formidable. All sported beards (two blue-black, one middle-brown), which seemed to add to the broadness of their features. Confidence flowed from the trio like water from an artesian spring—fierce, steady, timeless.

One man, the oldest and tallest, looked the leader's part, stood the leader's stance. He was raw-boned and appeared gangly, but moved with no lack of grace. He had a prominent nose, ears too small for his head, and a bow-mouth that would have looked at home on a shanty-house whore. It was his hands that held Charles attention: Big—hamhock big—with gnarled knuckles and tiny white whippings of scar tissue. A thought crossed behind Charles' eyes: *He's fought before and liked it. Win or lose.*

"Well," the big man said, "at least you did show up. We thought you'd rethink this little adventure, we did, and decide to save your hide in the onliest way you could...by hidin'." He laughed at his little joke and personal jab. Fifty or so jittery men joined his pealing laughter.

Montgomery stood up, flexed his shoulders, and pounded his fists together. The thudding sound snapped the laughter shut. "I do believe, gents that I beat you to this revered spot. Therefore, it was I who was a-feared you'd turn tail and run back to the regiment of New York road walkers that have been keeping you safe and sound clutched to their marchin' bosom."

Some men with the Twenty-First New York booed with vigor.

Three on one. Not good odds. Never good odds. Just ask the Rebs.

Charles checked over all the knots and patted Montgomery on the shoulder. "Are they all right?"

Without taking his eyes off his opponents, he said, "Perfect. I've never had them done better."

He pointed at the trio and nodded in Charles' direction: "This is Charles Andre, and he's my second. He's a drummer for the Ninth Connecticut. Now, Mister Tall and Loud, tell the men here all the rules and let's get it done."

The man nodded. "First, I'm Damascus Plott. And this'un here is my kid brother, Amos, and the other'un there is our cousin, Spinny Burlingame. We be from up north from New York and we don't have no truck with no cannon shooters." He cast a mean eye on Charles. "Er Connetican drummer runts. As to the rules: There ain't no rules except we get to fight him, three on one, no hold's barred, catch-as-catch-can!"

Seeing Montgomery give him a hard look, he said, "There's onliest one rule: If a man goes down, him or one of us, we take a short breather. The fight continues until either him or all three of us cry 'Uncle!' or can't cry out at all." He looked at Montgomery. "That'll do?"

Montgomery nodded: "That'll do. Time to quit talkin' and take your thumpin'."

The three men hooted and laughed, and immediately started circling the inside of the man-made ring.

Montgomery dipped his hands quickly into the water pail and stood up, moving into the center of the circle. As the three infantrymen worked into a triangle attack position, Montgomery bent down and ground both fists fiercely into the sandy soil.

As he was rising, the youngest soldier—Amos—took two quick steps and launched an overhead right, which Montgomery dodged by moving toward the incoming man, inside the swing. The punch landed harmlessly on his back. Montgomery's quick right uppercut to the throat and chin popped the soldier's head back; his head hit the ground first, followed by his backside. Rolling over on his left side, he laid there, mouth open, groaning, blood from a hundred tiny puncture wounds on his chin and neck. The blood gathered in the hollow beneath his Adam's apple, and streamed around his left ear.

Montgomery straightened up and started back toward Charles when the shortest of the three—Spinny—jumped on his back, crisscrossing his neck with both arms. As Montgomery spun around, Charles grabbed the attacker's leg and tried to pull him off, shouting, "Man goes down, fightin' stops!"

The crowd rose up as one, picking up Charles' cry. "Man goes down, fightin' stops!"

Spinny, a mixture of anger and fear driving his actions, held on tight.

After trying to grab his tormentor by the hair and failing, Montgomery stumbled backwards and slammed Spinny against a good-sized water oak. Air and fighting spirit left his body at the same instant. His grip loosened. Montgomery stepped away to watch the soldier puddle at the base of the tree.

Montgomery turned quickly to confront Damascus Plott, who was standing near the edge of the crowd with his hands held in front of him. "Spinny's a bit high-strung," he said. "I heard and respect the rules. Care if I hep'em up a bit?"

Montgomery nodded once and walked to the water pail, which he picked up, tipped and drank in noisy gulps. He sat down the pail, dunked both fists in the water again, and quickly smashed them into the earth, twisting them back and forth fiercely.

"Now I know why you done that," Charles said quietly.

"Now," Montgomery said, "so do they."

Without another word, he stepped to the center of the men-circle and waited. Amos was sitting up, but his eyes were unfocused. Spinny was standing, but wobbly; fresh blood gathered on the back of his head. Damascus eyed Montgomery and made a display of stretching his back.

Montgomery, his hands at his sides, said quietly: "I'm up and ready. Let's get it done."

The tall family leader grinned at him in the same way cats grin at cornered mice. "Gettin' it done sounds 'bout right."

He turned his back on Montgomery, pulled the two other fighters together and whispered something. Spinny nodded; Amos blinked a couple of times.

The big man took two steps and squared up with Montgomery. "Whatcha' say to 'em?" Montgomery said, hands still at his sides.

"Just told 'em to sit tight. This ain't gonna last long."

The big man took half a step and feinted with his right, which Montgomery slid to his right to block. But the right never landed, as the soldier spun further to his right and hit Montgomery with a haymaker left. The blow missed his head where it was aimed and landed on his right shoulder. The blow lifted Montgomery off the ground; he landed on his left shoulder and head a good four feet from where he was hit.

"Man's down!" Charles yelled and ran to Montgomery's side.

"Damnation, but that boy can hit," he said, sitting up and trying to stretch his right arm over his head.

Charles helped him to his feet and walked him back to the pail. Montgomery eyed the big man and nodded in acknowledgement. A nod and slight smile was returned.

"Time to change tactics," he said quietly to Charles, sticking his wrapped fists back in the water bucket and smashing his fists once again into the dirt. "If he hits me like that again, it'll probably break something."

His opponent was standing in the middle of the ring, waiting. "Time to go," Montgomery said to Charles, ruffling his hair as he marched back into combat.

Both fighters, having seen the power and the fury of single punches, were wary this time. The big man had his right fist up; his left stuck to his side. Montgomery's fists were up, elbows down, protecting his face and midsection.

Montgomery flicked a left...again...a third. All three hit the big man square on the nose and lips. The first one shuddered him, the second popped his head back, the third drew a gusher of blood from his nose and serrated the inside of his top lip with his buckteeth. With every blow, an echo gasp from the crowd quickly followed. Damascus backed up, squinting his eyes and shaking his head. Montgomery popped another jab, a fifth. Both connected solid. Tiny cuts, leavings from the rough dirt bandages on Montgomery's fists, appeared at a hundred places—chin, left and right cheekbones, above both eyes. A steady stream of blood coursed out of his left nostril before hiding in his thick beard. His mouth sucked some in; he cleared his throat loudly and spat a bloody, chunky globule toward the edge of the man-circle.

Damascus shook his head and started backing up, only stopping when he hit the ring of men, who pushed him back to the middle. Pop. Pop. Two more straight left jabs. The soldier was now bleeding badly from both nostrils. Montgomery advanced cautiously.

The pair circled counterclockwise inside the ring. Montgomery was concentrating on uncorking another jab when his arm was stopped in midswing. A fist crashed into the right side of his head and then his chest was crushed in a bear-hug. The fight was now back to three-to-one and Montgomery was in serious trouble.

Spinny, the back jumper, had Montgomery around the middle, squeezing hard, restricting his air-intake. Amos was throwing alternating haymakers at his head, connecting about every third shot. Damascus was wiping his nose on his shirttail. Watching. Smiling.

With a straight left jab, Montgomery backed up Amos, then levered both hands backwards, where they latched onto Spinny's jug ears. With one fluid movement, Montgomery snapped his head back, flattening Spinny's nose, eliciting a shriek of pain.

Dropping to one knee, Montgomery arched his back and pulled mightily. Spinny went ass over teakettle over Montgomery's right shoulder and landed five feet away, flat of his back. And stayed there.

"Man's down!" Charles screamed louder than he meant to and ran to

Montgomery's side. His eyes widened as he viewed his new friend's face. The blows, those that landed, did some serious damage. A two-inch knuckle cut was open over the left eyebrow and blood was dripping steadily into his eye; his upper lip was swollen, with a blood pool forming at the left side of his mouth. A dark, elevated bruise was forming on his right cheekbone.

Aware of the stage on which the drama was playing out, Montgomery stood upright, shrugged off Charles' offer of help, walked over to the tree and leaned against it. A proffered sip of water was gratefully accepted; he rinsed out his mouth, spat, then drank noisily.

"You done good," Charles said.

"Yeah. I do that good again and you might have to help bury me. Time to change tactics again, boy. They are not coming at me one at a time again, that's for damn sure."

Once again dipping his blood-soaked hand-wrappings in the water, and then in the gritty dirt, Montgomery walked to the center of the ring and motioned the three men forward.

Only two—Damascus and Amos—walked out, one to his left, one to the right. Spinny was sitting up, leaning on the legs of two men. There was no fight left in him.

"Now!" Damascus screamed, and both men charged him from two directions. Montgomery stood his ground until the last instant, then, stepped left to face Damascus, and launched an overhead right that hit the big man right above his left ear. He went down like a pole-axed steer.

"Man..." was all Charles had time to say before Amos hit Montgomery with a charge. Both men immediately hit the ground and began wrestling and gouging. "Man's down! Man's down!" Neither fighter paid attention. The crowd's screams and yelps drowned out further attempts to stop the fight.

After rolling around in a clinch for several turns, Charles saw Montgomery's right hand slide through the arm wrap hold that Amos had on him. In an instant, Amos' face opened, eyes wide, mouth open, eyebrows bounced skyward; his hands relaxed and Montgomery rolled free. It was obvious that the two men were connected by Montgomery's hand, which was still clasped firmly in Amos' crotch. The knuckles of Montgomery's hand and Amos' face were the same, pasty-white color.

Montgomery stood, fingers still clamped tight, dragging Amos upright. "Do you know what 'Man down" means, you dumb pikey?" Amos nodded but so slight it might have been surmised to be a cold shake shudder. Montgomery checked on Damascus, who was face down in the sand. "Somebody might turn him over 'fore his lungs fill with sand fleas."

He swung his attention back to Amos, who was standing on tip-toes, his mouth wide open, his eyes wide. Tears trickled down both cheeks.

"Er ye deaf?" Montgomery asked in a playful scream. A scythe-wide smile slashed his face. "Do you know what "Man down!" means?"

A strangled, high squeak: "Yeth."

"Good. Glad we got that settled." He showered down on his grip and a gullet-rupturing cry erupted from Amos' throat. Montgomery loosened his grip, his left hand grabbing Amos as he started to fall to his knees. He straightened him up, raised his chin a bit, and stuck a right fist halfway through his head. Amos hit the ground and didn't move.

Montgomery looked at the crowd, casting his eyes from side of the group to the other. "Man wasn't down, now was he?"

An hour later, after Montgomery cleaned up and rested without saying much, he got up from a sitting rock and turned to go back to his unit.

He took two steps and stopped. He glanced at Charles over his left shoulder and winked.

"You can write this down, young Andre. You are the best second any fighter ever had. Bar none. If ever I get in another scrap, I want you by my side."

He waited a while for a response, before Charles said, "I 'preciate that, Mister Montgomery. But if it's all the same to you, I hope you don't get in any more fights like that 'un. You got some good licks on you, that's for sure. But, that fight durn near kilt me and I don't want no more part of it."

Montgomery tried to smile, but grimaced instead.

"Smart boy. Take care. And my offer still stands."

It was a few minutes before the thought jelled in Charles' head.

Fightin' for something is one thing. Fightin' just to be fightin' is somethin' different. If you are fightin' just to be fightin' it don't matter if you win or lose.

Either way, it's just dead-dog dumb.

CHAPTER 15

Right. Wrong.

> *Nor is the people's judgment always true:*
> *The most may err as grossly as the few.*
> John Dryden

Mid-April, 1864.

Jonathan Alter was a bounty man, and most of the men in the Ninth Regiment would have nothing to do with him. The regiment was founded during an epidemic of One Nation Fever and was comprised mainly of prideful, hopeful, good-intentioned volunteers. Word was Alter had been paid eight hundred and fifty dollars in U.S. By God Currency by a rich banker to replace his son for a three-year hitch. That was in addition to the three hundred dollars paid to the government for the substitution.

Charles didn't understand the intricacies or legalities of such an action, but he heard that a Union draft order passed in early 1863 allowed able-bodied men twenty to thirty-five years of age to evade the draft by hiring a substitute or paying a commutation fee.

It made no never-mind Alter kept repeating the story about having to leave a sickly wife and three small children—a toddler and twin babies. Most of the volunteers had families and could have put such money to good use.

"Pride's everything," James Bartholomew, a former store clerk from Hartford, said between spits of juicy Southern Twist plug tobacco. "You get a bounty for doing what's right, and it's no better than cheating or thieving."

Charles didn't pass judgment on Alter, or agree or disagree with Bartholomew's comments. He felt strongly about many things, but was cautious when it came to stating an emphatic opinion or passing judgment on others. In a sense, he considered himself a bounty man, too. The only difference he could see was that he wasn't sure there even was a bounty until after he had signed up. And it was two hundred dollars and not eight hundred and fifty. Slight differences, maybe, but differences still.

He thought about the situation a spell and said, quietly, "I am coming to the notion that a man does what he has to do at any particular point in time to get to the next point in time. That's why I joined up with you fellows and I guess that is a reason a lot of men here did the same."

Some of the men looked at him queer-like, for he seldom offered up a sentence at campfire sessions, much less two.

From the corner of his eye, he caught Bartholomew nodding slightly.

"Well, I joined up for a mighty stupid reason," an older man named William Meehan, said. "I had a fight with my wife's father over some hillside land I wanted to buy and asked him to loan me the money. He not only told me to go to hell, but said he would send me there with a smile on his lips. I decided I needed to get away for a while. That was close to three years ago.

"I sure did like that land," he said, double-timing on the plug to loosen it up.

Charles, taking up the thoughts of the other regulars, thought that being a bought bounty man, regardless of the reason, was not a good way to serve out the war. But he couldn't help but think that if taking a payment to fight was a bad thing...what did that make the many who paid a bounty *not* to fight?

He wanted to ask Mister Bartholomew about it, but his questioning might be taken as a way of taking up for bounty men. It was a question, like many others in his life up till now and many more in the future, that lay fallow on his tongue like a seed dropped on a small piece of shale in a fertile field.

CHAPTER 16

A Short Respite

All the average human being asks is something he can call a home.
Mother Jones

Early April, 1864.
Word spread through the Carrollton camp with the speed of a diving hawk: The entire regiment was going home!

The word about a lengthy furlough came down from Grant's command at the last minute, as was the custom; telling them early they were going home, then pulling back the carrot because some dispassionate Rebel unit decided to attack some strategic something somewhere, was not an option. Disappointed or disgruntled troops are not at their best in either offensive or defensive maneuvers.

Everybody was excited except Charles and some of the other southern boys. Most knew they didn't have any reason to go or places to stay in the small state with the long name even if they did. And several, Charles included, had been feeling poorly for days. Charles had taken to his bedroll with the dysentery and was barely subsisting on water and milky flour-and-some-sort-of-meat-for-taste broth.

Not askin' what meat they use for seasonin'. Somebody might tell me.

"You gotta go with us, Andre," Brean said. "The whole town of New Haven will come out and welcome us. It'll be the most fun you ever had."

Charles smiled weakly. "You will want to spend time with family; I just need to lie here and rest up. With all you fellas gone, I don't have to do nothing but lie around and get fat."

"You can stay with me. You'll love my folks and all my relatives. With you comin' though, I'll make Mother send my little sister Lucille off to visit relatives. I don't want a southern runt like you makin' a play for my sister!" His smile belied the words.

Two days later, those of the Ninth that were able boarded flat cars backed into a siding. The men were ordered aboard, with everything the Army let them own stacked on flat cars.

Charles was still in his tent, feeling as bad as he ever had in his life. The day before the regimental doctor told him he had the Southern runs and "you'll get better or you won't." A hefty dose of sulphur, sweetened with molasses, gave him severe stomach cramps. The doctor watched him wince and double over. "Like I said, you'll get better or you won't."

Barely able to raise his head, Charles heard the train's whistle blast. It cut through him like a knife.

I wish I was going home.
I wish I knew where home was.

Night and day. It was that different. The next morning Charles woke up feeling better: No cramps nor chills, and the runs had eased. By that afternoon, he felt well enough to take a walk around the almost-deserted bivouac, wash up in a nearby creek—the boys had named it the Odd Creek With No Name; even the locals called it "Creek"—and even took other sick men fresh water and gathered up soiled clothes and blankets.

The fifty or so men—the ill and those whose term of service was about up and who had no intention of re-enlisting—were left in camp under the protective wing of Captain Wright and a few non-commissioned officers. When Wright saw Charles up and active, he said, "If you're feeling better tomorrow or the next day and have a mind to, you ought to go catch up to the boys and enjoy time away from all this up in Connecticut."

"Don't need to go, Captain. Don't have nobody way up there and I can help around here."

"Help to do what? And, don't you go be telling me not one of our boys said you could stay with them and their folks. I know better and I know those boys better. You'd be welcomed like family, that's for sure." He started to walk away, stopped and turned back to Charles. A thundercloud was in his eyes. "Tomorrow. Or the next day. You're catching that northbound train and you're going to Connecticut. I may not make it home this trip, but, by gawd, you're not going to miss the pleasure of visiting the prettiest damn state in the union. And, that's an order."

Two days later, with his knapsack, blanket, canteen, shelter-half, and drum slung over his back, Charles boarded a train bound for Baltimore, where he would pick up another train heading to New York City. A third train would take him to New Haven.
Sure takes a lot of trouble to get...home. Even if it's somebody else's.

The train pulled into New Haven at 7:43 on a beautiful late April Saturday morning and Charles, after helping an elderly woman get her bag out to the platform, stood on the raised decking at the south end of the brick depot stared at the town. Two church steeples, one off to the west, one dead ahead at the end of what looked like a main street, rose above the one- and two-story structures—many businesses and a few houses scattered about.

With his uniform and floppy cap, both brushed up as much as possible with a handful of water, a grimy rag he found in a crack among the boxes on a flatcar, and a middling of elbow grease, he gained instant attention. Men, women, girls, boys, and even small children, walked up to him—some even crossed the street—to greet and welcome him.

The cacophony of "Welcome," and "We're proud of you," and "God bless you," made any comment beyond "Thank you," Thank you, kindly," and "I appreciate it, thank you," an impossibility.

He winced as his shoulder was pummeled by a stout man who said he was a local banker.

Seems awfully proud of it, too.

Charles asked, "Do you happen to know where Charlie Brean lives?"

Not only did the man know, he was going right by the Brean place and it would "be a pleasure" to drop him off. "A.J. Morrissey, New Haven Bank. I own it and operate it." The banker pointed Charles toward a nice surrey hitched to a stunning roan mare with a diamond-shaped white flare between her eyes.

"Fine-looking horse," Charles said, pulling himself up on the carriage seat.

"Best around here, that's for sure. Got her as a trade for a few acres back east of town. Man's thinking the town is going to grow back to the east. It won't, though. The main land for the town growing is back to the west; that's the way the town is going to grow. I own more that a few parcels out that way."

Not knowing what else to say, Charles optioned for, "Fine horse, fine indeed."

Morrissey, after settling his coat flat against his expansive chest and checking his watch (expansively displaying the large gold watch with its finely worked chain) said, "Named her Flossie Mae, after my wife who departed this world three years ago come July. Died in childbirth, our sixth. Took the baby with her. Didn't ever have time to name the baby."

Charles ruminated on the nameless baby before settling on a thought about the horse.

Naming a horse—even a pretty horse—after your dead wife. Is that a good thing?

The banker made two quick turns and gave Flossie Mae a loose rein to set out down a tree-lined lane at a pleasant clop. Short minutes later the banker whoa-ed the horse in front of a house flanked by two huge oak trees. It was a neat-as-a-pin two-story with an L-porch; a short, white fence ran around the front and both sides; the back was open all the way to a line of trees. The man followed Charles' gaze and nodded: "Morris Creek's back there. Real nice at the creek. The Breans have a nice place. I hope to be able to buy it some day. With the land bordering the creek, this area is prime development land. Or will be."

If I owned it, I wouldn't sell it.
If I owned anything, I wouldn't sell it.

Charles was stepping down and thanking his host when Brean burst through the door and hollered: "Charles! You dog! You came after all! Are you feelin' better? You must be! You're here!"

Brean swept Charles through the front door into a parlor full of smiling faces—mother, father, two younger brothers, sister Lucille. The women were smallish and fluttery; the men were cookie cutter semblances of the largish Yankee drummer. Despite the fact the family had long finished breakfast, Mrs.

Brean welcomed him like a long-lost relative. Nervously flapping her bright white apron (decorated with embroidered blue birds splashing around in an half-gone cherry pie) like a pillow case on a drying line in a high wind, she scurried off with Lucille in tow toward what Charles took to be the kitchen.

The Brean men folk flocked around him like chickens on a June bug. They flogged him with questions about army life, family or lack thereof, and his post-war plans. Sidestepping the family questions with well-worn generalities, he tried to answer the rest with veiled openness. Most questions centered on New Orleans, a city not unfamiliar to newspaper-reading citizens of the north country, but as far removed from their version of reality as Paris, London, or Bombay.

"I hear tell New Orleans is run by freed slaves," Brean's father said. "That true?"

"There's lots of colored freemen in New Orleans—merchants and labor men, mostly. There's one what runs a bank that caters to their kind," Charles said. "There's lawyers, doctors and even a colored newspaper."

"Coloreds can read down south? My, that's queer. Just a few northern nigras can read."

"Lots of coloreds down home can read. Cipher, too. Slaves don't read much, leastways when anybody can see. Got their own churches. Big ones!"

"What religion are you?" an old man introduced as Brean's great-uncle William said. "I'm a peace churcher myself. Don't have no truck with fighting for the sake of fighting."

"I was raised Catholic. Seems I'm kinda between religions right now," Charles said before he thought the statement through.

No one asked him to explain. The questions ceased. The silence slapped the porch like a released guillotine blade hitting the block.

The comfortable breakfast served Charles—eggs, slab-sliced pork, homemade bread, and canned blueberry preserves—and his obvious enjoyment of it, punctuated with many compliments, breathed life back into the gathering.

After breakfast, Mrs. Brean, Lucille, and another woman that Charles believed was kin to Mrs. Brean, stayed to clean up. The men marched out to the porch. Pipes were brought forth from the pants pockets of the older men. Bowls were stuffed with a wine-soaked tobacco from a pouch passed around by Mr. Brean; the soft cotton sack was covered with strange characters, not letters from the alphabet.

Catching Charles eying the pouch, Mr. Brean offered, "This is Turkish tobacco. There's an Englishman who has a tobacco shop down on Center Street. He gets it special from Europe on packet ships. With the war and all, getting good tobacco from the South has been worrisome. But I found this and it suits me just fine."

Another man, another great-uncle, added, "Suits me too. I like it 'cause it's free."

A blanket of good humor and gentle ribbing spread across the porch.

An hour later Brean told the group "Me and Charles is going fishing. Com' on, Charles."

Thirty minutes later the two friends were sitting on a bump of ground pimpling out into Morris Creek. Two slender, limber persimmon limbs, a hank of white cord and store-bought hooks threaded with bacon rind made for good fishing equipment. They dropped their lines in the water just downstream from a slow-water dam made with big rocks and felled trees.

"I helped Poppa and Uncle Milton build that dam," Brean said. "Four years ago, now. It makes for a right nice fishing hole, if I do say so myself."

Having not slept much the night before due to the anticipation of joining up with a bunch of the Ninth boys in New Haven, Charles leaned against a spreading chestnut tree and was dozing when Brean shook him

"Com' on. Nothin's bitin' here. Let's go over to the Beaver Ponds."

A short walk later, they were getting their hooks wet in what Charles saw was an odd-shaped series of ponds. "Beavers done backed up water from Morris Creek into this area and it's all flooded and useless. But big ol' pickerel come in here to rest up, I reckon."

Charles' experience with fishing was limited; other boys at the orphanages fished the channel at the levee in New Orleans. He had heard and believed that fishing was always good; it was the catching that was a bit tricky.

Both boys were delighted that the Beaver Ponds decided to give up its bounty and within an hour, they were en route to the house, each with a ten-pound stringer of fish (Brean, four fish, Charles, three) made from forked limbs.

"We're eatin' fish tonight, Charles. You done earned your keep today."

Charles remembered Sister Bloody saying that "pride comes before the storm."

If that is so, there's a big-arse storm coming, and that's a fact.

It was the third day of his visit in New Haven before Charles had a chance to say a single word of meaning to Lucille. He had been content to say things that polite society necessitated him saying—"Good morning, Miss Lucille," and "Don't you look lovely this fine morning," and "I hope you sleep well with nothing but pleasant dreams."

He wanted to say more to Brean's sister, but had no firm idea of what the message should be. He was, as he assumed every male was, struck by her uncommon beauty. She had a pleasant, round face, pert nose, straight line chin, snapping dark eyes, a perfectly set mouth, tiny ears that stuck flat against her head, and tri-color hair with light, medium and dark strands fighting for attention.

She was a *petit* girl, but far from fragile. Or, that's how she seemed. She told him she was used to rough-housing with her brothers. Brean had told him back in camp she once gave him a black eye when he was teasing her about how she was filling out.

"So,' I told her, 'What, you think you're gonna be a woman someday, Squirt?'" he said over a campfire back in the Louisiana backwater country. "I don't think I had the word 'Squirt' out before she hit me with her two-bit-sized fist. Damn near put my eye out."

He said it as a matter of fact, but Charles detected a sense of pride in the telling.

Charles was sitting on the porch, watching the late afternoon flow of people coming and going, some toward home, others toward town, thinking about the upcoming months and possible places the Ninth would eventually end up. Tennessee some said, to help drive the Southerners ensconced in those parts "way the hell home," as one soldier put it. Brean opted for the Carolinas—"we gots to control the seaports down there, 'cause if Early pulls some divisions out of the Shenandoah and hit the coast, they can bust up jack." The opinions of where the regiment would end up after the furlough were almost as numerous as soldiers in the unit.

"It's a mighty fine afternoon, isn't it, Charles?"

Jerked from his reasoning, Charles glanced up and felt his heart melt into Lucille's liquid eyes. He stood up quickly, barking his spine on the layered house planks. He tried to stifle the natural reaction to pain, but from Lucille's hand-over-mouth giggle, he was not successful.

"Yes, ma'm...Miss Lucille. It's about the best day there ever was." He paused and looked at her what seemed like a long time. "It's even better now."

"Why, kind sir, I will take that as a compliment. How long are you going to stay? I know Charlie is staying another couple of weeks. But how long are you going to stay? Are you going to try and go home to New Orleans?"

"There's really nothing to go back to there, Miss Lucille. (He thought of Sarie Beth, but quickly shrouded the thought.) I don't have any family to speak of. And I feel I'm imposing on the generous hospitality of Mr. and Mrs. Brean and the entire family. It's good to just have some slow downtime that is interesting. Camp life is either boring or too exciting, so I don't really want to go back to camp before the furlough's over, if that's possible."

Realizing he had switched from answering a question to prattling, he quickly said, "What do you think I should do, *en peu de mon*?"

She was coyishly showing her profile when he asked the question. Without turning her head, her left eye shifted in his direction. Looking straight ahead again, she asked, "You speak French, *mon nouval ami*? And, am I your *little one*?

"*Oui*. And *oui, un peu*. I learned a little in New Orleans. It seems everybody speaks a little bit of everything down there. So, am I truly your *mon nouval ami*?"

"*Oui. Special nouvel ami.*"

Special new friend. Yippee!

It didn't take long for Mrs. Brean to realize that Lucille was not in the house and she burst through the front door in a flustered flurry.

"Oh, there you are, Lucy. Goodness, I couldn't find you and I was worried."

"Goodness gracious, Mama. It's New Haven. I'm on my own front porch with a nice gentlemen who is a good friend of my brother's. What is the world could possibly be worrisome?"

The tone of voice and question slapped a quizzical expression on Mrs. Brean's face.

"It's just that I missed...couldn't find...didn't know where you had gotten off to is all. I was...yes! Needing help in the kitchen. Come along now, child. There's work to be done," she said with finality, and left the door open. A forceful invitation.

"I must go, Charles, Lucille said. *"Nous allons reunir a nouveau pochainement, oui?"*

Charles laughed. "Too much, too fast. I got 'meet' and 'yes.'"

"We'll meet again soon, yes?"

"It would be my pleasure, Miss Lucille."

"Lucy," she said, turning so quickly her hair sliced the air.

As she entered the house, Charles leaned against a support pillar. Another voice, this time from the side of the porch, startled him. It was Brean, who was peeking around the corner of the house. "Don't forget, Andre, that's my sister you're trying to court."

Throwing a fake punch in the tormentor's direction, Charles retorted, "She's not my type, really. Besides, she's got some kinfolks I don't much cotton to."

Brean laughed loudly and disappeared along the side of the house.

Lucy! Yippee!

Days turned into weeks and time became convoluted, a frozed, fast-moving blur. The entire town held event after event—town band concerts and homecoming-type dinners on the square, barn dances and house-to-house canvasses by residents intent on making sure they met every one of the soldiers of the Ninth on furlough.

Of course, the soldiers were the center of every activity, and lavish praise and attention was paid to them at ever turn. Just as Charles was starting to loosen up and feel a part of what was swirling on around him, word came that the regiment would regroup the next Saturday. Orders were coming down and new duty awaited.

Due to the natural closeness of the Brean family, time spent alone talking to Lucy was regulated by the comings and goings of family members. Stolen glances, a slight touch of fingertips on a wrist, bare moments of whispered French words and partial phrases…that's all time and proximity allowed.

Two days before the unit was to leave, Charles was sitting on the Brean front porch, his legs dangling over a squatty rose bush, when Lucy came bubbling out of the house. Without a by-your-leave, she plopped down next to him and as he turned his head toward her, she leaned up and kissed him right on the mouth!

"Miss Lucy! You can't do that. What will people think?"

"People! I don't care what they think. You and Charlie are leaving in two days and I'm going to be here missing you both and I just wanted to make sure I made at least one memory with you, Charles Andre."

He started to say something, but she put two cool fingers against his lips. "Hush, Charles. You don't talk much, but sometimes you talk at the wrong time and place. I like you, Charles. I know we're young, but I like you and I don't care who knows it. I'm fifteen. You're what? Sixteen? Seventeen? It's simple, really. I like you. I sense a sweetness and goodness in you that I don't see too much of around here."

She enfolded his left hand with both of hers. "I know you're leaving and I know we'll probably never see each other again. I know…"

"But, Miss Lucy, I—"

"Hush, Charles. It's not polite to interrupt a lady." Her eyes and mouth matched expressions—overt happiness, a comfortable feeling with a dash of less-than-covert sadness. "I'm not asking anything of you. I just want you to know that I like you and I hope you get through this stupid war and will come back to visit. That's all I wanted to say." She got up and started to turn, but stopped and bent down and kissed him again!

A distinct "Oh, my" butted its way into the pair's cloistered world. Their attention snapped to the street where a portly woman pulling a small wooden wagon filled with cloth sacks was…just standing and staring.

"Why, hello, Mrs. Ferguson," Lucy said, in a happy-as-you-please voice. "Have you met our guest, Mister Charles Andre from New Orleans? He's a fine soldier in the Ninth Connecticut Regiment with my brother Charlie. He's leaving Saturday. I just kissed him. Twice! Right out in public! Because I wanted to and it felt good.

"Have a good day, Mrs. Ferguson."

With that, she was gone, flowing into the house, petticoats bustling. Charles watched her leave then turned back to Mrs. Ferguson.

"She's a mighty pretty girl, don't you think, Mrs. Ferguson. Kisses nice, too."

"Why I never…!" Mrs. Ferguson said, storming away with her little wagon kicking up dust.

Probably not…and why is fairly obvious.

Over the next two days, in stolen moments in the Brean's hallway, on the porch, by the side of the house between two big bay windows, Charles promised a thousand times to return to New Haven after the war, and Lucy promised an equal number of times she would wait for him.

REVEILLE

They only shared two more kisses in that time, four total. But it was four kisses neither of them would forget for the rest of their lives.

CHAPTER 17

Soyez Sur, Mon Doux

Leaving me guilted on a moving stair,
Upwards, down which I regularly fell
Tail backwards....
Allen Tate

July 18, 1864.
The entire city of New Haven, it seemed, turned out for the Ninth's leaving. It was a Monday, normally the start of the business week. The only stores open were general merchandise stores, where quartermaster assistants were stocking up on last minute purchases. Every other man, woman, and child seemed to be lining the streets wanting to catch a last glimpse of local sons, fathers, uncles, cousins, brothers, and friends.

Boys scattered throughout the state joined up at the town square to fill out the ranks. The regiment formed up by alphabetized company near the courthouse. To a rousing, citizen's band rendition of "Battle Hymn of the Republic," they marched right through the center of town. People lined the streets from the courthouse to the Long Wharf, where the *Elm City* was docked. It took more than an hour to load the regiment and their kit and caboodle onto the packet ship.

Officers expected the loading to be done more quickly, but the arms of an armada of mamas kept some soldiers tied up until sergeants and corporals were ordered to intervene. More than a few soldiers boarded that bare ship with uniforms moist with tears.

The entire Brean clan followed the marching soldiers to the dock, shouting words of encouragement and love. Charles, popping licks on his drum in an attempt to line up the men and get them loaded on the ship, spotted Lucy at the edge of the crowd. He smiled at her as she broke from the crowd, ran to him, placed something small and flat between two buttons of his tunic, stood tall, and pecked him on the check before placing her lips on his ear lobe and whispering, "*Soyez sur, mon doux.*"

Be safe, my sweet.

She darted back to the crowd, where she was greeted by stern looks from both parents.

Charles heard someone yelling his name. He leaned out in front of the first line of four soldiers to see a grinning Brean. "Better watch it, Andre. That's my sister!" The older drummer then struck up a louder beat and started laughing like a lunatic. Charles echoed his friend's laughter and drum beat. They laughed as only close friends can laugh and played the drummer's game like competing brothers.

An hour later, leaning against the bow railing, Charles plucked out the flat item Lucy had tucked into his tunic. A tintype showed a stunningly serene and beautiful Lucy. She was seated in a chair in a photographer's studio, flanked by a pastoral scene painted on canvas. In the oily-looking finish of the tintype—flashing in light and dark shades of purple, black and gray—Charles imagined he could see the color of her eyes, hair, carefully rouged cheeks, and lips highlighted with face paint.

Soyez sur, mon doux.

The trip to New York passed uneventfully, except for the constant rumors that plagued any regiment headed anywhere.

"We're going to New York and be stationed there a good, long time. Riot control duty."

"Washington bound, we are. There's talk Early's getting' ready to make 'nuther move."

"Back to New Orleans is where we're headed. That's where we left and that's where we'll end up."

REVEILLE

The *Elm City* sailed into New York harbor and anchored at a central dock in the Battery area of the waterfront. Pvt. Michael Ring of Bridgeport, who had lived in New York City for a time, told a massed bunch of I and H company regulars the boat was docking "where they have the New York Regatta." Momentarily the center of attention, Ring painted a vivid picture of the 1860 race with "hundreds of boats" heading out from the Battery. "It was July Fourth, it was, just four years ago and they all headed thataway," he said, pointing to what he said was the New Jersey shore. To Charles, the place pointed out was just a river-wraparound from New York. That notion was dispelled when Ring said, "The Hudson River comes into the ocean around the bend."

Departing the ship, the Ninth was marched to a large, open field several miles from the docks and told to "make yourselves at home."

It was quiet in camp. Too quiet. The normal hoorahing and funning and loud accusations and louder damnations that were commonplace were dampened. Something was up, and men of the Ninth were surmising just what it could be.

"We're bein' pushed and pulled ever whichaway," a rawboned rail splitter from Vermont opined. "I bet we're headin' down to the Carolinas. It's a coast, like where I hail from."

"It's not the Carolinas," Private Heenan Greenhart, a former teacher from Hartford, joined in. "There's not much going on that way is the way I hear it. We might be going down to support Washington."

Another Hartford soldier, Daniel Gaffey, said, "No need for anybody to go to Washington to protect nobody. More than half the Union Army is up there now, protecting Ol' Abe."

As usual, Charles kept his opinions to himself, even though he knew where the regiment was headed: To Tennessee. He had overheard Lieutenant Garry Scott tell an officer of like rank in the Fourteenth New Hampshire that "Tennessee is having fits with marauders and I heard the colonel say we're going up to help out."

Words from an officer's mouth to a drummer's ears: As good as a gold piece in a New Orleans levee saloon.

"I heard it was Virginia where we is headed."

The tremulous voice caused casual conversation to cease. Few looked at the man; most knew the voice by heart. It was "High-Pockets," a former rifleman from the Twelfth Massachusetts, who had been transferred to the Twenty-Sixth Massachusetts. Rumor was that he was transferred after he had accidentally stabbed one of his fellow soldiers on a march over near the Mississippi line.

How do you accidentally stab one of your own while marching?

For some unknown reason, High-Pockets had affixed his bayonet, then stumbled and stuck another private in the left butt cheek. It was a painful wound, of course, but clearly not a deadly one. Leastwise until the wound turned bilious. Despite the efforts of the camp doctors the soldier died a week later screaming, damning High-Pockets to Hades.

High-Pockets was unofficially declared a "Jonah," a purveyor of bad tidings, a walking cloud of doom, a man to be not only ignored, but avoided. Not unlike Jeb Stuart's cavalry.

Charles, not being the superstitious sort, had heard campfire talk about High-Pockets, but hadn't ever seen him up close. While most of the men around the fire kept their eyes riveted on the companionable tussle between wood, fire, and air, Charles studied the gangly man—long face haloed by hair that fell below his shoulders, and seemingly mostly elbows and knees—leaning up against a slight water oak.

The man's face was etched with sorrow lines, long, deep, natural scars cut into both cheeks—razor lines of worry. The skin beneath his eyes displayed sizable bags, dark and mottled; a tight, set mouth lay atop a slight chin that served to hold a beard-bounty of prickly light-and-dark stubble.

It was easy to see where he got his name: His pants, affixed with both a twine belt and heavy suspenders, settled somewhere just south of his armpits. Pockets, two front and one in the rear, were well above his waist.

"I think we're going up north is what I think," the gaunt shadow said, the words hanging drearily in the moist night air.

A voice at the edge of the fire: "Nobody here much cares what you think, High-Pockets."

"Best be on your way. You ain't got no friends here," another voice said, a shaking urgency slapping the end of each word.

The man's image seemed to fold into itself—head bowed, arms flapped across his chest in a solitary embrace. Without turning, he melded back into the darkness.

The dialogue came fast and furious.

"That man just gives me the shivers. I cain't hardly look at him."

"Doom is what I see. Just plain doom. And dumbness. He's so dumb he's eat supper afore saying grace."

"I heard he stabbed that one buddy on an accident and then shot another one a while later and that's why he got transferred."

"Did you hear'd about what L'il Phil Sheridan did over near Washington? I got the news today when I was getting' some cough sap at the sawbones'. I hear'd…"

Life around the campfire was back to normal. The Jonah was gone.

The "home stand" lasted but three days, the first two with only blankets as ground cover, the last with cover tops, before being told to pack up and reboard the *Elm City*.

"New Orleans-bound. Told ya!"

"Naw, goin' down the coast, probably to Virginia or the Carolinas, then march into the Shenandoah."

Onboard the ship once again, and heading east to the sea coast highway, the officers were told by Colonel Cahill, who passed the orders downstream, that it had orders to go back to New Orleans as a marshal force. The next day, the orders were clearly seen as in error, when the *Elm City* turned up the James River north of Washington and landed at Bermuda Hundred, Virginia.

While the men of the Ninth were in hurry-up-and-wait mode to disembark, a former Bristol schoolteacher told those around him that Bermuda Hundred was the first incorporated town in America.

"That can't be right," one hearty soul responded. "I'd heard that or learnt it in school if that was so."

"Sixteen hundred and fourteen, it was," the teacher said. "Look it up if you don't believe me."

"What, ya got a history book in your pocket?"

"Then, just ask around town."

Later, several of the soldiers, trying to prove a school teacher wrong, did just that, and found out the teacher knew his history. Charles, who liked learning new things and knowing things others didn't, wondered if could someday be a teacher.

Gonna buy me a history book one of these days. And read it from cover to cover.

After reporting in with W.S. Hancock, commander of the Second Corps, Colonel Cahill sent the order to bivouac the men north of town. The tents were set up along a stand of skimpy hardwoods. A sparse camp city popped up within hours. And was torn down three days later, when the regiment was ordered to proceeded on a forced march to Deep Bottom, Virginia. There the regiment rested two days with nothing livening up the boredom of camp other than rumors and card or knuckle-dice games, and the occasional musical treatment.

On a lazy, hot July afternoon Charles was on stand-by at the officers' tent and watched Colonel Cahill and a couple of officers play a strange game involving ten "duck pins" and a top. Cahill was bragging that Sheridan himself invented the game and taught "it to some of the boys a fortnight or so ago." The object of the game was to wind up the top with a long string and send it spinning past the pins and knock down as many as possible when the top reversed course.

That makes no sense. Why not just hit them head-on? No wonder it's called Dutch Ten Pins. Damn dumb Dutch game.

Without realizing it, the young drummer worried his rosary as he watched several men shoot the top. He wandered off, scratching his head at the follies that existed in the minds of men at rest.

Plain soldiers don't have the solid claim to doing stupid things.

CHAPTER 18

Just Plain Miserable

> *The secret of being miserable*
> *is to have leisure to bother about*
> *whether you are happy or not.*
> *The cure for it is occupation.*
> George Bernard Shaw

August, 1864.

It was pre-dawn dark when the sergeant slapped Charles' feet with a persimmon switch. "Up you be, Andre. The morning's comin' and it's time the men were up and preparin' to greet this fine day."

Without a word, without a stray thought, Charles bolted upright, pulled on his broad-based, flimsy half-boots and started down the long row of tents, whacking on the sides with the flat of his hand, saying the same thing over and over: "Time to get up. Long march today." His words were met with exasperated yelps, long, imaginative tirades against his heritage, and absent-minded, general curses.

Charles smiled, thinking what Surgeon McNeil had said last week while working on a soldier's badly infected leg: "If a soldier is alive, he's miserable. If he's not balled up in a wad over something, chances are he's dead or just awaiting his Master to come pick him up. Then he's happy 'cause he don't have to walk no more."

Charles didn't mind the long marches. He treated most days as an adventure. For years he marched miles every day along the main levee, inner streets, and alleys of New Orleans, looking for scraps and items that could be used at St. Mary's. In New Orleans, few things ever changed: The streets were often filled with garbage; the alleys always smelled like overflowing chamber pots and sour feet; the pickings were always the same—slim to none. On a march, the scenery was different, the smells were expansive, often pleasant, the people they encountered were…interesting.

Most of the men in C Company swore they never got used to the way Southerners looked at them, with white-hot hatred shooting from normally placid faces. The looks didn't bother Charles: as an orphan, as a professional scrounger, he was used to being the receptor of looks of distrust, of malevolent dislike, even unwarranted hatred. Some of the womenfolk in the northern neck-end of the Shenandoah Valley, seen standing in the porch shadows of canted log houses, or working in small gardens near the house, looked at Charles with what he took to be pity. He was used to that look, too; being an orphan, a homeless, youthful scavenger pulled at feminine heartstrings.

And everybody knew that you could see a woman's feelings through their eyes, just like in a fortune teller's crystal ball.

Everybody? Everybody but me.

Like lines of slow-moving weevils, the men slid into the tendrils of early-morning fog; some stumbled toward the communal water bucket, others headed to the creek to wash sleep from their eyes.

Charles kept a little pan of water by his tent; a sip or two during the night, the remainder used for a quick face rub in the morning.

The Ninth men were tired after the long march and a short sleep. Most were heel-dragging tired, heads down, shoulders slumped. This was more new country for Charles and he kept his eyes open and roaming. A mockingbird skidded through the hot August afternoon, chasing a flying bug or moth. Whatever it was chasing, it caught in a side-down swoop, and settled on a rail fence for the well-earned snack.

The long column of men, four abreast in the sand hill road, not in step but in a shoulder-to-shoulder stumble, wrapped around an S-bend, before disappearing behind a lone stand of hardwoods off to the right. A small house, dwarfed by one of the biggest barns Charles had ever seen, stood in a rowed field green-gold with corn, peas, and other garden-variety plants that Charles didn't know.

A young boy, hollow-eyed, with a high forehead and pinched nose, walked out from between two cornrows and watched the army pass him by. Armed with a strange implement that was part hoe, part pickaxe, he held it in front of him, almost as if he patterning the order for "present arms." The youngster eyed Charles and they both nodded at the same time. A tiny curl at the corner of the boy's lip was the only acknowledgement of the silent greeting.

Charles sidled up on Sergeant Reilly's right side: "Sergeant Reilly, do you mind if I drop out of line for a minute?"

Without looking at him, the gruff sergeant said, "Can't you wait till we hit them woods yonder?"

"No, that's not it. I just want to hey that boy back yonder. Just to talk for just a minute. Is that all right?"

A cloud passed over Reilly's face. "Just a minute? Methinks it will be more than that, Laddie. But go ahead. We're going to camp up around the bend, I hear tell. Catch up quick so you don't miss your camp chores."

Charles ran a few steps ahead of Reilly and threw him a big grin and a flamboyant salute.

No smile, but almost. "Git on with ye, and don't be late for chores! You're heppin' the surgeon get all set up and then helpin' unpack the quartermaster's wagon."

Holding his drum close so it didn't rub his leg, Charles crossed the ditch and followed the fence back to the corn patch.

The boy just watched him coming.

"Hey," Charles said.

Without a sniggling of emotion or movement above his chin, the boy heyed back with just a simple chin-dip.

"You live here?" Charles said, head-nodding toward the smallish house with an ample dogtrot through the middle. He grimaced at the abysmal question. He could hear Ian's braying voice.

Wha-where else wah-would he live, ah-old sot?

"Me and mama and my baby sister, Li'l Bit." The youngster cast his eyes behind him and whistled softly. A large, mangy yellow dog with blood-red eyes eased out from under the porch and trotted toward the boys. He had matted, thick fur and a train of slobber hanging from his lips. "This here is Ben," the boy said. "He looks mean but he would just as soon lick you to death as bite ennybody."

"Hey, Ben," Charles said, instinctively squatting on his heels to get closer to the dog's level. After looking up at the boy, the dog took a tentative step forward, testing the air with its large, wet nose. Charles held out the back of his hand, allowing the dog to give a half dozen healthy sniffs. The dog's tail started beating a silent tune in the humid air.

"He likes you," the boy offered. "He don't cotton to many folks, 'specially Billy Yanks. One of you boys shot him a while back, thinkin' he was gonna bite, I reckon. Pshaw! The only way Ben would bite anything is if he'd thought it was a bone."

"Sorry someone shot at Ben. There's some good people in this army, the South's too, I reckon. But, likely as not, there's bad 'uns in both, just like about everywhere."

The boy looked down. "I don't know about there bein' bad southern soldiers. All that ever came by here was nice and nary a one of them shot at Ben."

Charles let the statement sit heavily between them as he petted Ben, who had squatted down in the shade; the dog's heavy panting and dripping tongue soon soaked Charles' knee. He laughed as he got up and went over to the porch step to sit down next to the boy.

"What's your name?"

"Ben Alouis Parmenter."

"Ben? Like the dog's name?"

"Yep. May be queer to some folks, but Maw says he saves her a bunch of time not havin' to holler at the two of us all the time. Just 'Ben! Get to the house,' and both of us show up."

Charles leaned back against a porch post, his smile a slash of joy.

He heard the house's front door open and he jumped up, grabbed his hat and turned around. In the door, hands on ample hips, arms akimbo, stood a large, red-haired woman whose features fairly spit venom.

"You, boy, you got some reason to be lollygagging on my porch? Shouldn't you be off down the road with your ragtag bluebellys, rapin' and killin' folks and stealin' evathing anybody done had? Burned ennybody out today? Killed any cows and such? Shot any dogs?"

Stunned, Charles took a step backward and was turning to leave when Ben Alouis said, "Maw, we was just talkin'. He wasn't doin' no harm."

"YET!" the woman screamed, throwing her hands over her head and pumping them up and down like she was trying to swim skyward through the humid air. "He ain't done nothin' YET! That don't mean he won't or that he don't. Those damn soldiers who took the cows a month back, you done forgot that? They didn't do nothin' till they did that, now did they?"

"Ma'm," Charles said while nervously rolling his kepi into a tight ball, "I—"

"You shut up! Not a damn nuther word! This is my home. My home, you hear me? You will not talk to me that way in my own yard, at my own house. You will git off this place and git off quick or I'll make you wish you did it quicker than that."

"Sorry to have upset you, Ma'm."

"GIT! GIT and stay git! And don't you come back, ya hear me? And, Ben, git in this house now. And I mean right now!"

The boy glanced at Charles, then hung his head and trooped past his mother into the house.

Charles nodded at the woman. Her face fired up into a red blow-cloud and she pointed her finger to the north down the road. "Your kind done kilt this valley and half the men folk in it. This here is our valley and I hope the devil takes every damn one of you and drags him kickin' and screamin' and hollerin' straight down to Hell!"

The slam of the door rattled the single-pane windows and spooked two yard chickens. Ben's face, frozen with an ugly brand of sad, appeared in the lower left corner of the window. He shook his head from side to side, closed his eyes, and slipped beneath the window sill.

Charles set out at a mild trot, chasing C Company's dust.

Lord, what did I do to deserve that? This damn war is gettin' totally out of hand if folks just cain't stop and talk to folks.

The entire camp was abuzz. Small groups of men stood chin-to-chin, whispering quietly, heads bobbing like a bevy of water-top corks stuck in a swarm of minnows. Charles heard the rumor from Private James Leary, who got it from Corporal Edward Garvey in C Company, who passed it along from an overheard conversation between Quartermaster Thomas Fitz Gibbon and Adjutant Henry Kattensroth. As military rumors went, it was as solid as a pound of feathers.

One conversation thread had Corporal John Reardon from New Haven captured by a marauding Reb cavalry unit. Another, according to a friend of an acquaintance, "He just skedaddled, absquatulated, deserted, dead gone." A third, waylaid by southern sympathizers, dragged into the surrounding thickets, killed, his body hidden under a tree fall and left to rot.

Some rumors done got way too many details to be true.

"I saw him yestiddy," Private Jacob Scamahorn said, pointing back down toward the heart of the valley, like that would enhance the validity of his statement. "He shore didn't say nothing about lightin' out. I bet he was kilt."

A low voice rumbled out of the darkness: "I don't reckon he's a-gonna tell you if'n he was gonna skedaddle, now would he?"

"We was friends," Scamahorn said, anger putting a cutting edge on the statement. "I wouldda knowed if he was planning on leavin'."

Sergeant John Burke walked up, stood in the glare of the small fire and squinted at the group of men. "Time to quit talking about Reardon, boys. What's done is done. If he's dead, talking about it don't do no good. In fact, it's doing the man an injustice. If he's lost in the mountains, talking about it don't do no good either. If he's running for home, well, men make decisions for many reasons. There's reasons I may could use to take off for home…but, none of them are good enough in my book. Not now. Not in this war. We got too much at stake, I reckon. This country's got too much at stake."

The silence was like a wool blanket in the dead of summer, thick, suffocating, drowning out even the krick-krick-krick of the campfire. The subject of Reardon didn't come up any more that night.

CHAPTER 19

'Fightin's A-waitin'!'

> *A battle won is a battle which
> we will not acknowledge to be lost.*
> Ferdinand Foch

September, 1864.
It was a glorious day. Despite the time of year, a cool front had created snappish air alive with smells: Wild flowers, moist, loamy dirt, piles of colorful leaves blown in random piles by niggardly winds, the pungent odor of animal and human leavings.

The line of men, most heel-dragging after a long, forced march, stretched from horizon to horizon; thousands of feet heeled up dust puffs.

As the sun stretched higher in the sky, Charles momentarily took his eyes off his feet and looked at the countryside through the dusty gold haze. The green slopes of the Bull Run Mountains were off to the right; through a gap in a sparse stand of hardwoods, Charles caught a glimpse of a slight section of railroad track, slicing into the mountain like a double spider web strand. From campfire talk, he knew the Shenandoah Valley had seen more fighting than any other section of the entire country: Manassas, Chancellorsville and Spottsylvania to the south, Kernstown, Harper's Ferry and Sharpsburg to the west and south. Charlottesville out to the west. It seemed every bit of ground in the valley had seen see-saw battles from one end to the other.

The second- and third-hand stories by the Ninth veterans about earlier battles around the mountains, rolling farmland, and deep valleys created an apprehension that bordered on hidden hysteria in Charles...and, he thought, in countless other soldiers in the regiment. Thought? More like he hoped he was not the only soldier to feel the chicken-skin lickings of fear.

Surely I'm not the only one scared.

Thus far, the Irish Regiment had been battle-lucky—or unlucky, to hear a couple of ambitious officers tell it—in either avoiding an all-out charge. The regiment was seemingly always selected for reserve duty in conflicts, or placed to the far outside of battle lines to protect a flank of the main attack force.

Word was that the Rebs were sitting, waiting, and ready. "Ready, hell!" Sergeant Thomas Johnson of H Company bellowed at such a notion. "Them bastids is always ready. In every fight they been in, they more than ready."

Not counting the Confederate units already in place, those in sections already scouted and mapped out, word was there was a bunch more. The word in the ranks was that there were tens of thousands of veteran Rebel soldiers, dead set on pushing the Union regiments out of the valley and driving them all the way to the Potomac, if the fighting went that way, or out the south-end funnel of the valley, over the roads on which they had been marching.

"Words are easily spoken, boys," Sergeant Johnson had said one night after supper as the men sat around the campfire, smoking, chewing, jawing. "I heard a visiting officer say just the other day: 'We'll whip Johnny Reb this time and they'll never be back in the Shenandoah.' Words is cheap chattel. Backing them up by bringing them to our lick-log will take some doing. But we'll by gawd do it.'"

One of the older soldiers in the regiment, a grizzled white-beard named Dolan, opined: "This valley has been lucky for the Rebs, that's for sure."

The sergeant eyed him. He shook his head as one eye closed as smoke from his pipe roiled around his head. "Lucky? Pshaw! How 'bout good. So far, the Rebs have wanted this valley more than our boys have. And that's a fact. But then our boys didn't have General Philip 'Little Phil' Sheridan to lead 'em. Now, by gawd, we do, and by gawd, we're going to make a full accounting of our being here. That you can count on."

The words "full accounting" hung in the air like an ax, as each man in sound of the sergeant's voice assigned to it an individualized meaning.

Charles heard a disturbing rumor a few nights later and went looking for Sergeant Johnson. He found him sitting against an oak stump, smoking his pipe. The stump was not axe-whipped or saw-worn. It clearly showed the effects of a direct cannon ball hit; four feet from the ground, the trunk ended in an uprising of massive, spiny splinters. Charles started at the tree.

A giant, past-its-prime broom.

As was his style, he walked up to within a few feet of the sergeant and stood there, waiting acknowledgement.

"What can I do for you, boy?"

"I heard something and it's worrying me more than some."

"Campfire rumor, was it?" Sergeant Johnson said, blowing an ethereal cloud of smoke that rose slightly and settled easily in a gauzy layer a foot over his head.

"It came from one of the men who talked to a courier, Sergeant," Charles said, trying to keep the nervousness out of his voice.

"Like I said, campfire rumor."

Quiet settled over the pair for a couple of heartbeats. "Well, what it is?" Johnson said.

"The Rebs are bringing up fresh troops from all over and are planning to keep this valley at all costs."

"That's what I'd do if'n I was them. That all?"

"No sir, not by half. I heard the First Louisiana Volunteers are headed this way, maybe already up ahead."

"Gawddammit, boy, get to the point!"

"Well, Sergeant, my best friend, Ian—we was in St. Mary's Orphanage together down in New Orleans—joined the First Louisiana just before I hitched onto the Ninth."

The sergeant was statue-still; he didn't even blink, just sat there with the pipe clinched tightly in his teeth, staring.

Charles stammered as he fought his way into the next question: "Wha-what do I do if we run into Ian in the fightin'?"

Sergeant Johnson took a long draw on the hand-made pipe before spitting in the bowl. He knocking the ashes out on top of a nearby rock. He studied Charles a bit, then got up and came over and put a hand on his shoulder.

"Boy, if we worried about what might happen but probably won't then we wouldn't have no time to worry about what's gonna happen for damn sure." He half-turned and stared at the distant mountains. "Do you know what 'fate' is?" Charles bobbed his chin. "Fate. It's like something happens on an accident, but it ain't no accident. Well, if'n you and Ian are supposed to meet up here in this valley, after the war in some saloon, or sitting next to each other in a church pew, then it was meant to be."

Seeing that Charles was still troubled, the sergeant said: "The fighting's coming, and there's no two ways about it. But the chances of you running into your pal in a battle is about as likely to happen as it is for a nekkid gypsy queen to come waltzing in here right now and give us both a show!"

Grins were traded at the image.

"Thank you, Sergeant," Charles said, as he turned to leave.

"No problem, Andre. Just remember, when the time comes to fight—and it will come—just do what you have been taught to do and do what you think is right. If you do that, everything will turn out just fine."

Charles walked away and was quickly swallowed up by the dark.

But, if I do run into Ian, what do I do?

The road cutting to the southwest through the Shenandoah curved now and again, seemingly following a clear but meandering line between stone and split rail fence lines. For the most part, the fences were only a memory; too many soldiers needing too much wood for too many fires had taken its toll.

Charles wondered which came first, the road or the fences.

Had to be the road.

He pondered the question, putting one foot in front of the other by rote.

The road probably followed game trails or those used by Indians.

Least ways that's what one man, a mouthy private, surmised at last night's supper of roasted corn and hardtack dipped in hot lard.

Charles thought it was amazing that not a hundred years ago, this was mostly Indian land.

Settlers drove them out just like we're trying to do the Rebs and the Rebs are trying to do to us. Somebody always seems to be tryin' to drive somebody out of somewhere over some reason or other.

The thoughts spun, thickened, and jelled into different forms as Charles scanned the hillsides and open pastureland. He watched dark, billowing clouds of smoke spiraling out of the horizon, building clouds upon clouds as the southwest wind pushed the plumes into a horizontal bank that roiled overhead. The clouds pushed toward the sea, toward the Capitol of half a wounded and bleeding nation.

"Can you tell me once again," Charles said to Sergeant Johnson, "why are we burnin' this place?"

The sergeant gave him a look reserved for schoolroom farters. "This here valley is what Honest Abe calls the South's bread basket. It is from the Shenandoah that most foodstuffs come to keep Johnny Reb fed. What we are doin' is what the general calls 'total war,' meanin' leave nothing behind. Torch it all."

Charles pondered on that a spell. "That don't make no sense. Don't we have to forage, too. Burnin' it means we can't get at it if we need to."

"This army has enough supply wagons to tide us over, and we are taking stuff afore we burn it. It's the best of both worlds, boy-o. We get it and leave nothing for the Grays."

But what about the people who live here? They can't help where they live.

Shenandoah Valley.

The name rolled off Charles' mental tongue smoothly, like a spoonful of fresh butter sliding off a straight-from-the-stove biscuit.

It's a pretty place. Never seen nothin' this green and pretty. Torch it all? Don't make sense. These people may hug up to the Rebs, but they got to eat, same as we do.

The farmsteads were few, mainly built near the road, but occasionally the columns of soldiers would come upon a house set back in a large clearing. All of the homesteads, without exception, were sitting on clear-cut ground; except for an occasionally shade tree or two; remaining woodland was well back from the main residences and barns.

Safety, maybe. To keep sneakers at bay.

After living in New Orleans, the houses passed by the ant-lines of soldiers seemed ramshackled and tiny. Most were lifeless, windows shuttered, doors shut. Closed tight. It was a right pleasant day. And it was like most everybody was hiding in the dark inside. Or picked up and left. Just waltzed off. Somewhere. Anywhere other than the Shenandoah Valley.

Occasionally, there were people, sitting, standing, watching. One old, lop-faced man with a tiny nose, one leg, and a hat that peeled his ears downward, sat on a porch in a slat-backed chair, whittling on a fat stick propped between his knees. He sat there, whittling away at nothing, just staring at the tramping invaders. He got up creakedy-like out of the chair, and using a crutch made from a tree branch cut off at a convenient V-split, roll-hopped to the spavined porch railing: "If you come to burn me out, then you jist might as well kill me. We'd be dead afore winter anyways." Not waiting for an answer, he turned and without a look back, went into the dark interior of his cabin. The door slamming had the double ring of defiance and defeat.

Two farms down, an old woman wearing a face-shielding bonnet despite sitting in the shade, seemed to be shelling peas. She stared directly at the marching army parading past her home. Her face was a series of ravines, running underneath billowing snowcaps of hair that poked here and there from under the bonnet. A few soldiers threw her a wave. The gestures were ignored.

Just off the other end of the porch, a younger woman, child on her hip, gathered peas one-handed from a side yard garden. She stopped when she realized the soldiers were staring...a thousand eyes focused on her and the baby. The small child—it looked to be a girl—dug its face hard into the woman's shoulder, away from the prying eyes.

The woman, more than comely with a full figure her loose shift and multiple petticoats couldn't hide, didn't smile, but did nod her head slightly. A soldier in the row behind Charles bowed his head to hide tears. A puzzled look hit the woman's face like a skimming shadow. Without a word, she pulled the little girl off her hip and held her aloft, face to the soldiers.

A great, discordant shout of appreciation from the massed men busted loose in a dam's flood of emotion. The child jerked at the waterfall of noise and then smiled at the hoorahs and shouts. Clapping her chubby hands, she threw her head back and gazed at the cloudless sky and laughed out loud. The woman joined in and within a heartbeat the whole section of valley reverberated in joyous laughter that was fresh, alive. The old woman took no heed, other than to bow her head deeper to her task, the bonnet lid hiding her face.

The pounding hoofs of horses dampened the laughter only slightly. Captain William Lee, accompanied by his aide, rode up and demanded an explanation on why the company was holding up the line. Sergeant Reilly spoke quietly to the captain, whose eyes drifted to the woman and baby.

Motioning for the aide to remain in place, the colonel maneuvered his roan through the loose ranks and pulled up at the fence.

"A good mornin' to you, Ma'm."

"And I wish I could say 'the rest of the day to yourself and your men', but under the circumstances, that may not be right. Major? Is that your rank?"

The captain and the men that could hear the exchange smiled.

"That'll do nicely, ma'm. Just wanted to thank you for...well, whatever it was you did to cheer up the men. We've had a long march and we got a longer one up ahead of us. Thank you kindly."

"I didn't do anything, really. Just let'em get a good look at Sarah," she said, her chin pointing to the hip-hugging child.

Sarah! Visions and memories of Sarie Beth flogged Charles' memory banks. He fingered his worn rosary, stitched inside his right pants pocket.

Captain Lee's face softened by a measure. "A fine baby, that one is, Ma'm. How old, if you don't mind me asking?"

"I don't mind. She's nine months...tomorrow, I believe."

"Mine are three years, a boy, and seven months, a girl." His voice faltered, his eyes clouded. "I haven't seen the girl yet, but I hear she's a dandy."

A pulse-pounding silence followed.

"Where're ya'll headed, Major?" the woman asked. The question was simple, but Lee treated it in a wary manner.

"Down this road a piece. We'll camp nearby but I promise not one man will set foot on your land nor take any provisions. Not these men, anyway Not this day."

"My husband is with the Twenty-ninth Virginia, fighting down in Georgia, last time I heard," the woman said. "That's been a while. I hope he's all right."

"For what it's worth, ma'm, so do I. I surely do. If you don't mind me asking, ma'm, what's your name?"

She didn't falter at the obviously personal question. "Elizabeth Blankenship Slocum."

"Mrs. Elizabeth Blankenship Slocum. I'll remember this day for quite a spell. I'll remember you and Sarah, you can count on that. Not much pretty and not much good comes out of fighting like this even if it's got to be done. And when pretty and good come along, one should enjoy them."

The woman was silent and held her baby close.

"May I ask you a favor, Ma'm?" A nod. "Would it be too much to ask if

I could hold Miss Sarah for just a minute?" With only a slight hesitation, the woman stepped to the fence and held her daughter at arm's length. The old woman's head snapped up, the motion of a frightened bird before taking flight. The baby looked at the dirty soldier with the wide hat and bird-nest beard and held out her arms.

Captain Lee took the infant, holding her gingerly, away from his dusty uniform. Reaching out, the baby snagged a fistful of wiry beard and yanked. Surprised, the captain jerked back and yelped. The sound of a hundred belly laughs vibrated across the rolling farmland.

"You little scamp," he said, using one hand to pry the baby's fingers from his beard. He looked over his shoulder at the men, then turned in a theatrical swirl and held the baby over his head, bobbing the small bundle back and forth like a cork on a wind-swept lake.

The men cheered and laughed and hoorahed and stomped their feet. Small pillows of dust gathered at their ankles.

Turning back to the woman, he gently handed the laughing baby to her. "I can't tell you how much this has meant to me and the men," he said. He leaned in close to the woman: "We've got to do some damage in this valley, Ma'm. To the Confederate soldiers somewhere out yonder and to the valley itself. We've orders to do things I don't want to do, but with orders, there's not much choice. And for that, I'm sorry. But I'm going to leave word that no unit is to touch your place. I promise you that."

Captain Lee went to his horse, opened up the right saddlebag, and came out with a sheaf of papers and an ink well wrapped in a heavy cloth. He pawed through the saddlebag and came out with a quill. With the woman holding the inkwell and with using a sergeant's back for a desk, the officer wrote a brief note.

Blowing the ink dry, he handed the single sheet over, saying: "Any soldiers comes here to burn your place, show them this. I hope it will help and I believe it will. And, for what it's worth, I hope your man comes back in one piece and finds you and the baby (he glanced at the old woman on the porch) and your family well."

At that, he swept off his wide hat and performed a theatrical bow with his hat stuck way out to the side and his head nearly in the dirt.

He jumped on his horse without use of the stirrup and galloped down the line of men, hat flashing back and forth in the air, like he was waving off a hornet herd. Some of the men tried to imitate the colonel's bow, Charles included, and their antics left the woman leaning against the fence, hand over her mouth hiding her grin.

All the men, every last one of them, waved and waved and kept on waving. And the woman waved with her free arm until Charles lost sight of her among the uniforms as the column followed a bend in the road.

After the last soldier in the long line had passed over the closest hill, the woman walked to the porch, holding the baby close. She gently laid the captain's paper on top of the pea-filled apron in her mother-in-law's lap. Without looking at it, the older woman wadded it up slowly, methodically, in one hand and dropped it to porch floor.

Without a word, Elizabeth Blankenship Slocum placed the cooing baby on the hand-hewn porch, picked up the rumpled paper and smoothed it out as best she could. She folded it twice and stuck in an apron pocket, patting it with a gentle but firm finality that spoke volumes between the two women.

That night in camp, the men discussed the day's march, dissecting the enjoyable interlude at the Slocum farm in intricate detail.

The discussion turned quickly to two topics that occupied many conversations these days: Expected fighting and the weather.

Weather was the perfect verbal foil for soldiers on the move. It was too hot or too cold, too wet or too dry. This time of year—late summer—discussions centered on the heat. Consensus was it was hot. Skillet hot. No breeze and none promised.

The only clouds were flitty high-flyers, promising no rain, only more of the same for the next three or four days. At least that was the prediction of Corporal Dennis Glenn, who read signs.

"No rain. No rain a-tall. None for a spell. Too hot even to push up a thunder-bumper or two. But when she breaks loose, it's gonna be 'nuff to strangle a herd of tree frogs."

"How'd you know, Den Glenn?" another soldier said as a way of making conversation.

"Leaves. That there mock orange bush has leaves that fold up a bit on the edges if there's rain a-comin' within forty-eight hours. I checked. They straight as a gigolo's pecker at first howdy at a bawdy house. No rain."

It didn't rain that night. Or the next.

Leaves? Who would have thought...?

CHAPTER 20

'Go Git Early!'

> *Our enemies have beat us to the pit.*
> *It is more worth to leap in ourselves*
> *than tarry till they push us.*
> William Shakespeare

September 18, 1864.
There was a fever of anxiety around the camp.
"There's gonna be a fight!"
Charles was washing his face in the communal bucket when the meaning of the pronouncement hit him in the gut.
"Wha…when?"
Charlie Brean had wandered over from C Company and his entire face was open…eyes, mouth, expression. "Soon. Maybe tomorrow. The word is that Grant met with Sheridan and told him to 'Go git Early.'"
"Just like that? Grant said, 'Go get Early.' What kind of orders is that? 'Go get Early?'"
"It's enough of an order to get Li'l Phil's blood boilin'," Brean said. "That's what I heard the sergeant say. It's been a month or more of just movin' here and goin' there and evabody is spoilin' for a fight."
Charles dried his face on his shirttail, put his hand in his pocket and started worrying his rosary.
Maybe evabody. But not me. Not yet. I may never be ready.

Colonel Healy was all *het-up*, as he marched past H Company at a rushed clip. His face was scowly, his jaw set. His wide-set eyes flickering from man to man. One by one, they straightened up a mite as he drew closer, relaxed as he passed them by. Lieutenant Lawler, Charles' "guardian," followed behind like a baby duck, then peeled off at a ninety-degree angle to stop right in the middle between the Ninth and the Seventy-fifth New York. Clearing his throat loudly, he shouted, "The time has come for us to show what the Irish Brigade and the New England boys can do. We're going to whip the lung-dust out of Early and all the damn Rebs he brought with him to this valley."

Pausing for the expected, and delivered, shouting and yahooing, he bounced up and back, heel to toe, a couple of times, then raised his hand for silence. The men were watching for the inevitable sign and voices froze in mid-yip. Lawler looked directly at Charles, gave a solemn nod and a half-blink wink. Charles bobbed his chin imperceptibly.

"We're startin' out doing some pokin' to see if we can get a rise out of the Rebs, then we'll serve a reserve role, close up to the Sixth Corps, and ready to back them up if they need it." Mumbles started but the lieutenant plodded on. "We've got orders and a job to do and we will follow them damn orders and do that damn job. There will be no shirkers, slackers or scofflaws this day. We will, by gawd, remember that we are the Ninth Connecticut Regiment and the mighty Seventy-fifth and we will make our comrades in arms, our states, our families, our president, and our God proud."

Lawler stopped, peered up and down the line, and shouted in a thunderous tone: "Are we ready to kick Old Jube Early's arse?"

The yells slammed down the valley, echoing off the close-by hills.

Colonel Healy was walking down the line behind Lawler and the outburst stopped him cold, a smile playing hide-and-seek in his mustache.

Warned by the wide-eyed looks on the faces of the men, Lawler spun around, popped his shoulders back and fairly shouted: "Companies of the Ninth Connecticut, the honored Irish Regiment, and the Seventy-fifth New York wish to report, Colonel Healy, sir, that we are ready for battle and don't plan on ending tomorrow with anything but a glorious victory!"

"If enthusiasm counts for anything," Healy said, softly so that only a few of the men heard it, "you are by gawd ready!"

"Attention!" the lieutenant said, and snapped to; the men mirrored his actions. "Salute!"

REVEILLE

Several hundred men popped a simultaneous salute, which was returned promptly by Healy. "Carry on, Lieutenant," he said, turning toward the command tent. Over his shoulder: "Get some rest, boys, tomorrow's gonna come early." He stopped as if considering the unintentional pun. "And, if we do it right, Early won't be around...later.

Sleep was not a common commodity that night. Too many days of idleness, too many nights with little to think about other than what the next day would bring. Too many thoughts of glory or of dying alone in a baked pasture or on the side of a mountain hillock or in a ditch beside a rutted road.

Charles and Dunton, who had re-enlisted and been transferred to ranks as an infantryman the past winter, talked for several hours, working up their visions of the expected battle.

It seemed to Charles he had just settled in when a whack on the tent covering startled him.

"Get 'em up, Andre," Sergeant Johnson said. "Quiet line. No banging this morning, just tent rapping and tell 'em to get up, get dressed, get fed. We're rising up in the middle of the damn night and the damn dark's gonna get lighter all the time."

Checking the position of the spilled teacup moon, Charles guessed it was an hour after midnight, no more. There was no other drummer to assist, so Charles quickly roused William Jaques, a private from Norwich sleeping in the next tent, and told him of the orders. Splitting the rows—Jaques left, Charles right—the two drummers went about their directed chore with a purpose, whispering loudly, making sure soldiers acknowledged their presence and were moving about before moving on down the line.

Two hours later the units were in marching position along the Berryville Road; thousands of soldiers lined up in some semblance of military ranks and headed north toward Winchester. Major General James Wilson's cavalry passed the assembled men at a rapid clip by circling around the wagons and stacked units to the east; some of the mounted soldiers dodging in and out of a stand of virgin timber. Wilson had two full cavalry brigades under his command with two respected leaders, Generals George Chapman and John McIntosh, being in charge of the first wave of Union soldiers.

The cavalry always made more noise than marching men; this march was no difference. When Wilson's horse artillery gained support from six batteries from the Second, Third, Fifth and Sixth United States artillery, the rumbling of wagons and normal horse noises made a raucous clatter.

Wilson commanded six regiments, and while he was proud of all under this charge, it was McIntosh's brigade that had the stagelights in the upcoming battle. McIntosh's men hailed from all over—Ohio, Connecticut, New Jersey, New York and Pennsylvania. McIntosh was not a just-comer to the valley, having arrived in early August. During a stop in Washington, his entire brigade was outfitted with the new Spencer carbine, a seven-shot, breech-loading marvel that had already wrecked havoc against a skittish bunch of Rebs in a skirmish along the smallish Opequon Creek several days earlier. McIntosh's brigade, on a reconnaissance look-see, had used its superior firepower to capture sixteen officers and two bits more than a hundred enlisted men from six Reb regiments. Wilson's troops suffered only two killed and three wounded.

That's the stuff legends are made of.

"Wilson's boys will wake up them Rebs, that's for sure," Charles heard somebody behind him say.

"You think we can sneak up on 'em?" Charles whispered to the nearest soldier, Oscar Durant, a wiry, angular, talkative soldier who had signed up just a month before Charles in New Orleans.

"They say we got more'n 35,000 men ready to fight today. I don't see how that many men can sneak up on anything."

Makes sense. But, then again, with 35,000 men, why do we have to sneak anywhere?

The mass moving of a mammoth military strike force is like that of an arthritic snake—one part moves, another part tries to move, but nothing much happens, a third, disconnected part moves, but then stops to allow another segment to slowly catch up. To the men doing the moving, it's a frustrating process; to those that are responsible for the movement, it's frustration compounded by focused anger. It's a battle just trying to get to the battle. With an army on the move, logistical plans and troop movements scrawled on maps with the ink still wet, cartography efforts that looked stunningly simple on paper just a few hours earlier, are about as useful as hen's teeth. Maps—good maps—are essential for seeing what you haven't seen; except in the cases of natural topographical funnels (ridges, ravines, creek beds) they are slightly better than useless in helping predict what opposing forces will do.

On maps obvious areas ripe for troop movements are easy to see; in reality, good commanders rarely obliged opposing forces by doing the obvious.

Following the advance cavalry units and the Sixth Corps, by nine o'clock Brevet General William Emory's Nineteenth Corps, which included the Ninth Connecticut, was still stutter-stepping not more than a mile from where they started. By that time, Wilson's riders had already busted through the Rebs' first defensive breastworks, dismounted, and taken cover and used the enemy's defensive wall to repulse several counterattacks. The cavalrymen, backed by two batteries, hunkered down, peppering the surrounding woods with rifle shot and canister rounds, waiting for full infantry relief.

The battle—popping and snapping sounds mostly, punctuated by the occasional cannon fire—could be heard by approaching troops. The massed army seemed to move even slower, if that was possible.

As with most major attacks, Winchester III (as Emory had labeled it several days earlier, or Battle of Opequon Creek, as a captured Reb soldier called it that first afternoon), had several key points of attack. While Wilson's cavalry and auxiliary artillery headed right up the gut of the Rebel lines, other cavalry units led by Generals Charles Lowell and George Custer forded the Opequon at different places, driving the Rebels guarding the crossings before them. Crossing the Opequon at just any point was not an option; the creek's high, clay banks gave little opportunity for men, horses, caissons or supply wagons to cross except at established fords. Overall, the cavalry advance went exceedingly well; at sunrise Lowell and Custer hooked up flanks, with other brigades following soon after.

Badly outnumbered and faced by a determined enemy on several fronts, various Rebel commanders simultaneously began methodical retreating…but with a purpose—delay the Union's rapid advance, while angling toward other Confederate units. Strength in numbers was the goal, solid defensive positioning to hold off direct assaults, followed by concentrated counterattacks. The day was starting to heat up as the Ninth Connecticut on the left flank of the Nineteenth Corp found itself some marching room between the Sixth and Eighth Corps. The sounds of battle were still confined to distant pops and whomps from rifle and artillery. Several men guessed two or three miles to the fighting. With the surrounding hills, the sound seemed to come from just about every direction.

"Whatcha doin'? Durant asked.

"What? Doin' what?"

"You were movin' yore lips."

"Oh, I was just tryin' to figure out how many steps till we're in battle."

Durant looked at him peculiar-like. "Countin' steps to the battlefield? Boy, you got too much time to think."

A few seconds later: "So, how many steps is it now?"

Charles smiled. "Don't know. Lost count when you asked me what I was doin'. But I'm gonna pick up the count at 3,970. 3,969, 3968…"

Charles cast a sideways glance at Durant who was nodding his head. He turned his face to look at the countryside in the direction of Red Bud Run to hide the smile that sidled over his lips.

Durant was obviously counting steps.

The Ninth was ordered forward as a skirmishing unit to find the forward lines of the enemy and keep them occupied. H Company was sent to the right flank, just west of Berryville Canyon. Seven regiments were stacked shoulder-to-shoulder for almost a mile. The companies to the far right were marching in lush fields, the companies on the left through heavy forests with little underbrush. Berryville Road was kept clear for artillery and ammunition supply wagons.

But that plan, as it was with many military maneuvers, simply didn't work, as the soldiers on both sides of the road could plainly see. Ammunition wagons, caissons, gun carriages, ambulances…all were swarming down the road, or more accurately, had swarmed into a pile on the road, without much forward movement.

It looks like more stayin' than goin'.

The Union's Sixth Corps, coming up from both sides of the Berryville Pike, began the attack with a strong surge on the right. The Ninth, Colonel Cahill commanding, was directed by General Cuvier Grover, division commander, and anchored the far right of the front line. The men saw they were to be supported by another Ninth regiment and shouted encouragement zinged between the two units.

The men of the Nineteenth Corps knew the attack was coming with only a minimum of artillery support. Despite the rumored railing of Sheridan at company commanders for the untimely traffic jam, up and down the line, the word was: "We goin' in without the big guns!"

REVEILLE

With officers shouting up and down the line and drummer boys pounding out the long roll, the almost mile-long line of blue-clad soldiers started the slow, methodical march handed down through the annuals of civilized warfare that was guaranteed to inflict maximum human carnage. But this day, the Confederates were playing the defensive game…hide, watch, shoot, and generally raise hell in the opposing ranks.

The Confederate goal was simple: Those Yanks on their feet, put them on their knees; those on their knees, put them on their bellies or backs. Get as many of the enemy as possible out of action as soon as possible.

Hidden in heavy woods at both flanks and hunkered down in cornfields and undulating farmland to the center, Rebel riflemen raked the advancing army with sustained and accurate fire.

Once the men were on the move in the open land battle, the drummers were ordered to the rear to join surgeon helpers bearing stretchers. Without orders, without outward gestures, and with minimum introductions, they paired up, two to a stretcher, following the last advancing regiment by about a hundred yards; their job was to pick up wounded men, not wind up among the wounded.

After walking more than two hundred yards, Charles and Edward Murphy, a lantern-jawed Danbury soldier in C Company assigned to medical duty, came upon a gut-shot soldier who was writhing and crying. He was lying on his side in a fetal position, his feet flailing the ground, moving his body in a tight circle like a cheap carnival pen-wheel.

In less than a minute, as other stretcher-bearers stopped to pick up and pack other wounded nearby, the wounded soldier was on the stretcher and the bearers started fast-walking him to the rear. The surgeon's wagon was being unloaded in a brace of trees a quarter-mile to the rear as the first wounded man was brought in.

Next to the longish tent were piles of filthy-looking blankets, folded in a fashion, like laundry flopped around by a husband trying to make a statement about doing women's work.

A small mountain of sheets—dingy, stained, and frayed—was carelessly thrown on the ground next to the main tent. The sheets were the color and texture of shirt cuffs of a traveling preacher, too much wear, not enough careful washing.

"On the table, now," Surgeon George W. Avery screamed. He shouted orders at the colored aides, assistant surgeons, and a few malingers forced into service. "Sheets! Water! Get another fire built, now! Where's the cabinet of instruments!"

The soldier...

From the Fourteenth New Hampshire, I believe. Benjamin...something.

was picked off the raised stretcher onto the thick oak table with folding legs. Charles and Murphy picked him up again when an orderly showed up with a blood-stained sheet.

Charles was amazed at the lack of blood on the wounded man and mentioned it to the orderly, who said in a thick German accent, "Goot shot. It all stay oonside. He not last mooch loonger."

"Don't say that," Charles said in alarm. "He can hear you."

Avery came up behind Charles, and after a cursory examination of the area of the wound, said, "Don't you think he knows he's dying, Andre? Don't you think we all know?" Turning to the orderly, the surgeon said, "Get him off the table and under that big tree. There's nothing anybody can do but God and He's gonna have his hands a little full today."

The wounded man started screaming, begging for relief, begging for water.

"And, whatever you do, don't give him water. That'll kill him quicker than a bullet to the head."

The soldier quit screaming like someone had cut his vocal cords. A series of loud, piercing, heart-squeezing moans splintered the air around the operating table. As they moved him back to the stretcher, the moaning ceased. By the time they had reached the tree, he was gone.

Charles sat down next to the body, pulled up his knees and held them tightly. He started rocking, staring at the smoky battlefield to the north.

Without saying a word, Murphy rolled the still body off the stretcher, which he immediately folded. "Let's go, Andre. There's more waiting for us to gather up."

He was a good fifty yards away when Charles found his feet and struck out to catch up.

Water wouldn't have hurt him none. How could he have died any quicker?

By the time they had reached the rear lines again, it was obvious that the Sixth Corps, along with Grover's division, had broken the Confederate line, driving the retreating Rebs several hundred yards to the rear. When the Reb line broke, the Union forces charged, screaming and firing at will. They outpaced their officers, who were sucked along as if in a vacuum. It was an odd assault, one of the few, some veterans said, not punctuated by batteries of artillery.

The initial force of the attack died quickly, allowing the Johnny Rebs to reorganize and counter-attack, forcing the scrambling Union units back. The initial probing attack turned into a full-frontal assault, with rifle and artillery fire pounding up and down the accordion line. The Union line, despite the pleas and threats from officers and non-commissioned officers bent, sagged, then broke in dramatic fashion.

Men, who just moments before were screaming in pursuit of a battered and retreating enemy, were now streaming to the rear in a mass exodus from the field of battle.

Without apparent rhyme nor reason to those who witnessed it, the retreating soldiers heard shouting, then rousing cheers. The mass of retreating men stopped. Then, in pairs, threes, then small groups, they turned (almost as if connected to a common swivel) to face the enemy.

The story told around camp that night was about two captains, one artillery, and one infantry, hooked up as the retreat turned into a rout and started an unlikely attack with less than twenty soldiers and two cannons. They formed an island of stubbornness, an oasis of arrogance and hope, and additional infantry gathered to them. With only a handful of officers giving instructions, the conjoined regiments began lining up for another attack. Seeing the resistance form, and expecting a forward movement, Sheridan ordered a reserve brigade into the battle, adding fresh troops to the Sixth and Nineteenth Corps.

The North's rally stunned the Confederates, officers and soldiers alike. The southern troops had turned the tide of battle; they were certain of a decisive victory. Then, in a short time, they were once again relegated to fighting a defensive battle against two invigorated, active, hell-bent-for-blood corps. But the Rebs held once again, slowing down, then stopping the Union advance with withering fire and a constant cannonade.

In what some thought was a belated move, Sheridan ordered up two more reserve divisions. Fresh soldiers were brought up from the main Opequon Creek Crossing via the Berryville Road. They double-timed more than three miles before teaming up with units already in the field. As the Federals pushed forward anew, Early's army was pushed back toward Winchester. The Reb army approached the town from the northeast, and most residents fled to the south and west. Those that wanted to head north for family or other personal reasons, found their attempts stymied by the retreating southern army.

Continuous pressure by the Union troops, brought about by an anvil-and-hammer maneuver slamming into the left flank of the out-maneuvered rebels, and the lack of communication from key battlefield commanders for the out-numbered Confederate Army, shut out any hope of victory...or even a battlefield draw.

After nine hours of fighting, the Rebs were in full flight toward Fisher's Hill. Delaying feints by southern cavalry did not deter Union pursuit because there was no pursuit.

The Battle of Winchester was over and done. Both armies had had their bellyful of fighting this day.

All day long, with no stopping except for an occasional drink of water and a few bites of hardtack (and a single fall apple—wormy and soft—found at the base of a small bush at the edge of a small orchard) Charles and Murphy carried the wounded from the field of battle to the surgeon's tent.

At first appalled by the blood, the crying, shrieking, cursing—and the dying—the natural anesthetic of repetition dulled Charles' senses until he operated in a quasi-conscious state.

Breathing. Moving. Working. He studied on not thinking in any semblance of stream of consciousness. Like staring at a single close object over time can create unfocused images, Charles sought to unfocus the events around him. For the most part, he succeeded. But failure—on some level—was a certainty every time he delivered a wounded man to the surgeon's tent.

The surgeons—three standing in a straight line working simultaneously on two tables and a third fashioned from a sawhorses and a simple, pilfered door—quickly evaluated injuries and tried to save those they could. Low- and mid-body wounds—from cannon shrapnel, bullets, or, more rare, bayonet wounds—were usually set to the side; they would either live or die and God, not surgeon's skills, would decide their fate. It was the same with head wounds that went in more than an inch from each side or on top. Facial wounds, while always disfiguring, were not usually fatal if major arteries and the brainpan were left intact; shoulder and thigh wounds, if not dead-center hits, could be debilitating, but seldom fatal at the camp. Those deaths were counted later, after infection had set in, after days of excruciating pain, with fever so high the skin turned a purple-red, and only after the wounded was reduced to screaming earnest, pathetic pleas for death.

The toughest wounds for most surgeons—to treat and to decide the course of action—were wounds to the extremities, arms and legs.

By Charles's third trip back from the battlefield, two legs and two arms (three lefts and a right, he noticed for some strange reason) lay like discarded cordwood under the operating table. The arm and one leg lay flat on the ground; the second arm was propped over the remaining leg, the arm's bloody stump resting on the bloody grass.

It looks like it's trying to wave.
What a strange thought.

Charles put a damper on his thought-images and jogged off toward the sounds of the constantly shifting battlefield.

Somewhere about the tenth trip across the open field to pick up the wounded, Charles was struck by the smell of battle.

Battle has a smell?

But there it was, as distinct and overpowering as honeysuckle in early summer. The smell was brassy: sulphur mixed with gunpowder and the underlying hint of hot metal. All mixed together in a swirl, capped off with a pungent, mean odor, the powerful musk of fear-sweat.

It was a smell like no other. And one he would never forget.

Hours later, Charles sat in the coffin of darkness, amid piles of rocks on the banks of a creek. He never remembered feeling so tired in his life.

Tired doesn't touch it. Numb. Dead with my eyes open is more like it.

The events of the day ran in slow motion in his mind: Rifle shots, cannon shells bursting, Rebel yells ricocheting off the hills, dead men, body parts, carrying the wounded, dropping twice from exhaustion, then levering himself upright for more runs for more wounded.

How many dead and wounded? Five thousand! Can't be that many, can it? Plus what the Rebs lost. Plus what will die from the wounds. It don't seem possible. It don't seem right.

I can't do this again. Nobody should have to.

Charles stared into the darkness on the other side of the creek. The darkness was complete, no light, no shadows; it was so dark he wasn't sure his eyes were even open. He blinked a couple of times. Or felt sure he did.

He blinked once more, but it was a half-blink, really. It was only then he realized it was still light, not quite full dusk. He wished for the dark to return.

"Andre!"

The voice sounded like it was far off, around a bend in a hollow, or shouted from the top of a hill.

Let me be. Just let me be.

"Got to get up, lad." This time the voice was clear, close.

Charles strained to open his gritty eyes, blinked as minimal light filtered in. He thought he could make out a hovering shadow.

"What...what is it?"

"We're movin' out, boy," Corporal William Parker said. "The sergeant is lookin' all over camp for you. Thought you mighta hung the big one yestiddy. We're off on a nice march on this fine autumn night. And we can't go without you leading us, don't you know."

Corporal Parker, I just want to...Wait! Parker wasn't a corporal no more. Reduced to ranks in...June, wasn't it? Why's he here? Why was he reduced in rank? Don't care. Don't matter. Just want to sleep. Please...

Without further urging, Charles pushed himself to his feet and took two lurching steps to the creek. He dropped to his knees and slapped double-handfuls of water into his face. Two more handfuls slicked back his wild hair and using both hands he pushed his kepi on front to back to keep it in place.

Bending down on all fours, he brushed the light green scum from the water's surface in the short eddy as the pleasant lull of water-and-rocks gurgle filtered into his consciousness. He took two quick gulps of water before Parker said, "I think I'd drink somewhere else if I was you, lad."

Casting him a queer look, Charles' eyes followed the man's finger upstream. Not thirty yards away to the west what looked like a humped rock in the middle of the flowing water. Charles blinked twice. His eyes widened. The body of a Rebel soldier lay facedown in the creek, a hole the size of a grown man's thumb was barely visible above his left ear,

Charles looked at the body, then down at the water. With little warning, his stomach turned itself inside out and he vomited violently into the creek. Once. Twice more. Six times total.

REVEILLE

Panting for breath, Charles tried to stand up. His legs refused the muscle command.

"Take your time, boy. I'll go tell the sergeant you'll be there d'rectly."

Charles nodded and said, "Might be a good idea to pass the word to the boys not to drink from this stream—downstream for sure—leastways for a while."

"I was just goin' to do just that."

Left alone, Charles scooted on his backside back to the rocks. He chose a single rock amid the moss-covered boulders—strewn here and there like a giant's game of jacks—and pressed his forehead against it. The coolness instantly eased his queasy stomach.

I coulda gone all day 'thout that, that's for sure and certain.

By the time Charles got to camp, the orders had changed. Bed down. Get rest. The regiment would find a more suitable bivouac tomorrow.

Well after sunup, the Ninth gathered up and marched just a couple of miles to a full field that backed up on the creek. Pickets were dispensed in all directions; orders were shouted to make camp, get something to eat, and get some rest.

Tired men sat around a tired fire, waiting for water to boil, coffee to be made. The musicians and newest recruits gathered up the day's rations—bigger portions because of the long day of fighting and victory.

Charles picked up a sack full of vittles, side meat, forty or so small potatoes, plus four loaves of bread that looked in pretty good shape. He was heading back to C Company when he saw a familiar figure walking down the Berryville Road. Another Healy (this one John E., officially designated as the regimental drum major), hatless and bedraggled, his eyes as old as the Jewish race, was leading a horse. It was a brass-colored gelding with four white stockings, a startlingly white Z blaze, and a straight white spot on its left flank. Charles thought the mark looked like a map of Louisiana viewed through the eyes of a professional drunk.

He ran up to the major. "Major Healy, where'd you get him? What's his name? Can we keep him?"

Healy eyed Charles with a quizzical stare. "I came across him a mile or so back, just standing near the woods near the hill yonder. He's been shot, as you can see," he said, pointing to the horse's thick and muscular chest.

Charles looked closely and could see a small entry wound high up on the horse's left side and a larger, jaggedy exit wound in the area of the right breast.

179

"Sharpshooter, probably. Shot a couple of times, hit the horse, then probably the rider. Or, just somebody shooting at something, anything. There was a body near the horse, and he didn't want to vacate the area, I can tell you that. I'm going to fix him up and keep him. Maybe let him pack our instruments and such when we're on the march."

"Maybe you could name him 'Lucky.'" Charles said. "You know, he was lucky he didn't get killed and lucky you found him."

"Lucky?" Healy said. "Well, I guess that'll do. Lucky he is and 'Lucky' he'll be."

The new horse owner ruffled Charles' hair and the three walked back to camp.

Findin' somethin' precious alive in all this...killin' is somethin' special, for sure.

CHAPTER 21

Uphill Roads Are Long

> *Does the road wind uphill all the way?*
> *Yes, to the very end.*
> *Will the day's journey take the whole long day?*
> *From morn to night, my friend.*
> Christina Georgina Rossetti

September 19, 1864.
Another battlefield was waiting around a close-up hill. Less than three weeks after Winchester, the smell of almost-battle was in the air. The feel of it was externalized in the frequent, animated conversations of officers and the jittery movements of men on the march.

The right side of the Ninth's line almost curled back into itself as the soldiers tried to march in a line over the undulating terrain leading toward Fisher's Hill. Charles was drumming away, unconsciously flipping his drumsticks in a perfect rhythm. He could heard a couple of the sergeants—Reilly
Y*ou could always hear Reilly*
and Burke—shouting orders (some contradictory) to the men, trying to keep them in some semblance of order.

The sounds of the battle could be heard deep in the woods to the north. The battlefield seemed closer when the occasional whirring of a spent minie ball split the air overhead. Charles, like a vast majority of the men, detested that sound, but all were glad to, at least, *hear* it. "It's the ones you don't hear that kills you dead," Sergeant Burke had said recently in camp, while discussing the upcoming fight.

Without thinking, without looking around, Charles walked into the fog of crystal-white gunsmoke to the sounds of expanded gunfire, which added extra half- or missed beats to his constant drum roll. A barrage of rifle and small-arms fire came from off his left shoulder, back toward the center of H Company's line. The bullets winging through leaves and popping into hardwood tree bark unnerved him; his body went into a series of unconscious twitches and jerks as he tried to dodge bullets already past him or spent into tree trunks or the ground. He felt a slight tug at his left shoulder, looked down and he could see where a bullet nipped the shoulder pucker of his coat.

A cat's-hackle of fear pawed Charles' heart and squeezed. Hard.

Could I be a drummer with one arm? Is there such a thing? Normally, I'd been ordered back to the rear by now. No orders. Where's them orders?

As another thought was starting to form, Charles was hit in the back as hard as he had ever been hit in this life and went sprawling behind a huge sweet gum tree. He ended up looking skyward. The top of the tree was simply…gone, like God had pinched it off about eight feet off the ground.

"Damn you, Andre!" Sergeant Burke said, slapping Charles upside the head with his beefy fingertips. "What the hell you think you're trying to do, get kilt? Well, laddie, you're not allowed to get kilt in my army. Now get up and ease up the hill toward your right, and stay behind cover!"

That's the kind of order I like, right there.

CHAPTER 22

'Dyin' Time's Not Yet'

*What we call luck is the inner man externalized.
We make things happen to us.*
Robertson Davies

The smoke was hot, thick, gummy. Akin to walking through burning snot. Charles' hands and face were hot. His neck felt slightly scorched.
Beelzebub's breath.
Every lungful of air took effort, with more acrid smoke than air slamming into his lungs. His back and knees were bent, his body trying to meld with the torn and ragged earth. A distant rhythm
Cannon, most likely; cannon, assuredly.
throbbed against him, a steady, sure noise that he followed as he dashed from tree to tree, all the while trying to keep up a steady drum-beat.
The wasp-whirl of a spent bullet went by his right ear and he swatted at it—much too late—with his right hand. His drumstick knocked his kepi a-winding. Half-questions ricocheted inside his head:
Stop get the cap?
Get trouble show up at muster without?
If stop, target for Reb sharpshooter?
Plastering his spine against a smallish red oak, Charles squinted into the wavering, roiling sheets of whiteness from cannon fire and half-regiment

volleys. He finally spotting his cap. It was twelve feet away, lying upside down, crumpled.

A soldier fallen, looking to heaven.

He checked the downhill slope. No comrades in sight. Between the rifle fire, *weengs* of tumbling minie balls and the occasional *boom-thuu* of a distant cannonade, Charles heard what he thought was thrashing of brush off to this left.

The boys are coming right along. Gotta keep them coming!

Intensifying his drumbeat to push the troops, Charles darted from tree to tree, serpentining his way through the choking smoke. Uphill he moved, sometimes at an angle, but always uphill.

Without a hint of a breeze, the smoke curtain parted. His eyes widen, his mouth dropped open. Less than fifteen yards away was a massive breastwork, a mish-mash crossing of a partial rock fence, an unnatural latticework of trees, and uneven piles of dirt. What seemed like a thousand faces—specks of white eyes, features blurred by burned powder smudges, mouths open—honed in on the lonely figure.

What the hell...?

Charles strained to hear...nothing except for the stray rifle shot and an avalanche of silence. A deep baritone voice: "Where's the rest of yore men, son?"

The voice startled Charles and he jumped. Laughter flitted up and down the line like popping worm waves on a levee.

Again: "Where's the rest of yore men, son?"

Charles slipped his right hand in his pants pocket and worried the rosary, then checked over his right shoulder. White. Waves and waves of white smoke shifted through spindly saplings and around huge oak trunks.

Realizing he was still keeping a quiet rhythm with his sticks, Charles quieted his drum.

"They'll be along directly, I reckon, tha-them," he stammered. Without another word, he slowly, oh, so slowly, took one step backward as he started pecking "retreat."

The relief laughter from the Rebs hit him in the chest like a whale log. A man wearing a fancy hat with snap-brim that seemed out of place with his ragged, gray uniform, held up a hand. The laughter sputtered, then died.

"You don't got no Yankee accent, son," the serious man threw out. "Where you be from?"

"Nawleans, sir." Charles said, keeping up the slow drumbeat.

Another voice shouted out, "Nawleans? Then, why the hell er ye...?

"The boy has a reason, I reckon," the officer said, stepping on the soldier's words with meaning. "Keep a sharp lookout, men. The smoke's startin' to clear." He paused, looked down at his feet and shook his head. When he looked up, his eyes had softened. "Best be gettin' on back to your friends afore some of these good southern boys decide to nail another hide to the barn."

Keeping steady eye contact with the sad-faced officer, Charles nodded, turned his back and walked in what he hoped was a calm manner back into the smoke pillow. Five steps. Ten. He looked back. The temptation to run overwhelmed him, but he kept an even pace. The left half of the Rebel line was obscured. One small-faced soldier at the edge of the smoke curtain, not much older than Charles, if that, flopped a hand up and threw him a single wave.

Charles' eyes caught the image of the solemn officer as he moved left to right down the line. The man seemed to be smiling and he flipped a two-fingered salute at Charles. Snapping his head to the front for effect, head up, chin tucked into his chest, and back ramrod stiff, Charles dissolved into the wounded, smoky forest canopy.

Checking over his shoulder one last time and seeing nothing but various snaking levels of smoke, he started running, shouting: "It's Andre! It's Andre coming!"

"Hold up, boys, it's the banty drummer a-comin," the voice of Sergeant Reilly blasted slightly downhill off to his right.

Veering sharply at a right diagonal, Charles picked up his pace, shouting over and over, "Andre's coming in! Andre's coming in!"

Dodging a large elm, Charles' flap-armed downhill flight was stopped like the second hand of a stomped pocket watch. His feet were still lunging downhill when he was hit across the chest. He ended up flat of his back, the wind knocked out of him, his eyes full of smoke and grit. Tears jumped up, trying to wash the irritants out.

The meaty, florid face of Sergeant Reilly filled his world. If mad were a color, the sergeant's face would have been mine-hole black.

"What in the hell do you think you be doin'?" the sergeant screamed, his nose so close to Charles' face, it was blurred. Spittle pecked Charles' cheeks. "You don't listen worth a damn, that's for shore. Burke told me that you durn near got killed just standin' up and makin' a target of your own self and now you go and check out the Rebs first-hand. Yore job, me laddie, is to bang out a tune we all can dance to, not waltz up to the gawdamn Rebs and have afternoon tea. Now get behind a tree and stay there until I tell you to come the hell out, gawddammit!"

He punctuated his screaming with a hard shove that put Charles flat on his back. Reilly started to crawl away, then stopped and stared at Charles mean. "You just better be damn glad, boy, that your dyin' time's not yet."

Lying there for just a half-breath, Charles bounded up and stumbled toward a blue blur scrunched down behind a big oak to his left. He was surprised to find himself next to Lieutenant Joseph H. Lawler, his "guardian."

"Don't hold it against the sergeant," Lawler said, clapping him softly on the shoulder. "You scared him when you disappeared into the smoke is all."

Charles willed the tears of relief not to come.

Then that's two of us what was scared.

Within minutes, Reilly reappeared and screamed an order: "Up, up, lads! Let's be on our way to run the Rebel off'n that ridge. Peck out the advance, boys," he said, staring down at Charles, his eyes searching for another drummer. "Peck it out good and loud and let's be about our business." He stopped and stared hard at Charles: "And, you…you stay behind trees, stay down! You don't have to lead by your lonesome, Let that racket you make on that little drum do the leadin'. Take us up together a little ways, then head back down the hill. No, wait, stick close to me till I tell you to skedaddle. We got to do somethin' to keep these boys gathered up."

For the next two hours, the battle forged up and down the single hillock, with the Ninth and Twenty-fifth Massachusetts finally swarming over the summit breastworks from different directions at about the same time. The Rebel line broke the attack, with hundreds of graycoats slamming through the heavy woods in a mass retreat. The Ninth flooded the wall and one of the first soldiers over picked up the Rebel regimental flag. He pried it from the clinched fist of the company flag-bearer who lay on his back, glazed eyes staring unseeing toward the forest canopy obscured by the heavy smoke. A tumbling minie ball had sliced through his throat.

A cheer went up as the soldier waved the captured flag, proof of the isolated victory rolled down the advancing line. Almost simultaneously, hundreds of Union soldiers jumped, crawled and climbed over the well-built wall and began an across-ridge charge after the fleeing Rebel regiment.

"We've got the ridge," Reilly screamed to Charles. "Stop 'em before they run them damn Rebs all the way to Washington. We've got the heights, and by gawd, we're going to hold it." Charles started to pound out the assembly call. James McGuire, with C Company, located down the line about thirty yards, heard the call and followed suit.

It took a while for the charged-up Ninth soldiers to realize the fight was over for now. It took even longer for them to climb back to the breastworks. The jubilation was evident: Soldiers hugged and danced solitary jigs, threw their hats skyward, and taunted the retreating Rebels, who were well out of earshot.

"Run home to mama!"

"Tell Mas' Robert the Ninth done said hel-the-hell-o!"

"Come back and fight!"

"Run away, li'l gray sheep! Baaaaaa!"

Charles listened to the banter, smiling as only those who are afraid of dying in battle and who survived can. Tentative. Nervous. Relieved.

McGuire walked over to Charles and they sat down on a fallen tree, watching a couple of officers standing on the downhill side of the breastworks. Colonel Cahill was pointing and Captain William Lee was nodding. Typical officer conversation. The captain called for Reilly, who came running. After a brief conversation, the sergeant hollered, "Andre! Uhhh, and you," he said, pointing at McGuire. "Front and center."

He told them to help carry the wounded down the hill and stay and help the surgeons at whatever tasks were assigned. It was an expected order, but never comfortable or pleasant duty.

The duo barreled down the hill, angling off to the south and west toward the edge of a cornfield where they had last seen the supply and medical wagons. They silently marked the location of several men that were down, systematically categorizing them:

That one will make it down on his own.

Get that one first, might be saved.

Check, but probably will be gone before we get back.

It took twenty minutes for them to locate the wagons and tents, now situated further to the northeast of the main battlefield. Putting their drums in a medical wagon, and grabbing a rolled stretcher, they took off back up the mountain. The first man they came to had already assumed the Death Curl, knees drawn up to his neck, his face buried between his knees, arms wrapped around his legs.

Charles touched the man's head, removed his hand quickly, and nodded uphill. Crossing the path of two older soldiers carrying a soldier with a bloody head wound, one of the stretcher bearers told them there was a "bunch in them trees yonder." The boys sprinted uphill toward a small stand of hickory trees. As they got closer, they saw one soldier leaning against a small tree. He was holding his left leg, or what was left of it. A cannon ball had snapped the leg off about four inches below the knee, and Charles was surprised at the lack of blood on the ground.

"Go get James," the man said, holding his leg off the ground. "I done packed the wound with mud from the dirt and blood, so the bleedin's slowed down a mite for now. Get James. He's gut shot." He hesitated and then said, quietly. "He's my brother."

The boys stopped. "Let us get you down the hill. The surgeons are waiting."

The man's eyes blazed. "Damn it, I said get James. He's my younger brother and I done promised Maw he'd come back home and by gawd he will. All the damn cutters are going to do on me is cut. You know it and I know it. Whether they do it now or an hour from now, don't make no never mind to me. Now, you done heard me. Go get James. He went down by that lightning-struck tree yonder."

The boys hustled off to the tree, about a hundred yards across the hill. "James!" Charles hollered. Silence. "James!"

A whisper floated out of the tall grass: "Here. Over here."

They found the wounded soldier in a natural depression left from a felled beech uprooted by too much rain and wind. The young soldier (he was no older than Charles, maybe younger) was lying on his left side, knees pulled up and midsection covered by his splayed hands. His dark blue coat was darker blue from the chest to the end seam. Charles focused on his face.

"How you doin'?" he whispered.

The youth looked at him and grimaced as a wave of pain wracked his body. A cloud slid in front of the sun. The shadow passed over the trio. The spasm eased and the youth said, "Been better. How's Matthew?" Following the thoughtful exchange of eye glances between his two rescuers, he said, "Matthew. My brother. I saw him go down from a cannon ball over yonder." A barely perceptible nod of his head indicated a location across the face of the slight hill.

"He's gonna be okay. He sent us to check on you," Charles said. "We're gonna get you down the hill and to the surgeon's tent. James, get his legs."

REVEILLE

The boy's head flopped back and forth violently. "Don't move me. I'm holding my innards and you move me and I'll die right here and right now. I got some prayin' to do before I go. I want to say goodbye to James and Mama."

Charles sat down heavily. Any energy he had for arguing seeped out of him into the ground.

The young soldier closed his eyes, took a deep breath and hollered as loud as he could, which was not much more than a cat's rumble, "James. I love you. Tell Mama I love her even though you don't have to 'cause she knows it."

McGuire stood up and looked in the direction of where they had left his brother. "I don't think he heard you."

Dismayed and angry at McGuire for being a damn fool, Charles stood up and yelled: "James, Matthew said he loves you. He wants you to tell his Mama he loves her."

Another spasm struck the youth, this time, turning him into a human pretzel, arms and legs compressing into an impossible tight ball. He took two gulping breaths, and his body relaxed. A long sigh. Then, stillness.

McGuire picked up a nearby forage cap and placed it over the youth's face, grabbed Charles by the arm and stood up. "Let's go find someone we can save." Carrying the stretcher, he started up the hill.

Charles touched the youth's hand, then followed McGuire at a lope.
Save them? Save them how and for what kind of future?

Charles and McGuire made four trips up and down the hill. On their last trip, they were loading up a soldier whose name Charles knew but couldn't recall. The private had two wounds, one off-center in his upper chest, the other sliced into his right hip, erupting a gout of flesh and bone. Charles heard rustling in a nearby thicket and told McGuire he was going to check it out. The senior drummer hailed a soldier he knew from the 138th New York regiment passing by and asked him to bear the downhill side of the litter.

Cautious by nature and necessity, Charles eased into the tangle of briars and underbrush skirting the thick forest. He heard noise uphill…and down the slope.

"Where are you? Are you hurt?"

The noise stopped instantly. Charles' neck hairs stood at attention. He looked up the hill and spotted two men on the ground, both sheltered by a stump. A patch of gray…
A sleeve!

caught Charles' eye and he turned to run out of the forest. A Confederate soldier stepped from behind a tree on the downhill slope and put his dirt-encrusted finger to his lips.

Fearing he would be shot if he charged into the open field, now painted a golden hue by the sunset, Charles hurled himself down behind a fallen tree. He took little time to figure out his next move, quickly spidering his way behind a long log. He began crawling over and under tree limbs not snapped off when the tree hit the ground.

Rustling from uphill seemed to track his movements. The tree's umbrella of limbs obscured his movements and he found himself alongside a shallow drainage ditch cutting across the face of the hill. Without thinking, he slithered into the ditch, ignoring the trickle of water still running in the meandering channel, and, staying low, crawled as fast as he could.

Every few minutes, he would stop and listen. It seemed as if the silence was always broken by the sound of rustling leaves and snapped twigs that came from…

Where?

Moving as quietly as he could, Charles stayed in the ditch, head flopping back and forth in search of pursuers, of movement of any kind.

Without thinking about it, without a conscious thought about the possibility, Charles suddenly realized two things: He had been moving away from the Union lines for quite some time, and it was dark. Not dusk. It had come and gone. It was inside-boot dark. Charles stopped, listened. Then plunged deeper into the woods.

Somewhere on that hill, in those woods, he stopped to rest. A sliver of moonlight filtered through the leaves, marking the limits of his known territory. He crawled over to a particularly large tree and settled on the downhill side, between two protruding roots. He sat quietly and listened to night forest sounds.

CHAPTER 23

Chancy Encounter

Coincidence may be described as the chance encounter of two unrelated causal chains which—miraculously, it seems—merge into a significant event...(the) two strings of events are knitted together by invisible hands.
Arthur Koestler

Charles awoke with a start and a yelp as if stuck by a pin above his left collarbone. All he got from his quick movement was another prick in his shoulder.

As his eyes adjusted to the darkness, he looked at the figure bathed in moonlight, first seeing a stained bayonet

Is that rust...or blood?

and followed it up the adjoined rifle. Two dirt-smeared hands with fractured nails the color of midnight held the rifle steady. Slowly, Charles' eyes took in the heavy, tattered, gray, wool uniform, then moved up to a face etched in lead. Dark, sad eyes poked out of a bird's nest of a beard that looked red in color with errant white hairs corkscrewing every which way.

The voice coming out of the beard rumbled, like an avalanche on a distant mountain. "Speak up, now, boy! And be quick about it. What are you doing out here all alone?"

"I-I-I—" Charles stopped trying to talk and swallowed. "We was in a fight yesterday," he told the man, whose eyes seemed to be closed. "I got separated from my regiment, the Ninth Connecticut. You happen to know where they might be? I think they be behind you over yonder."

The Rebel sergeant's eyes opened slowly and he blinked half a dozen times. Quick-like. "Lost, you say. And you want me to tell you where your regiment's at? If that don't beat all. That's real uppity. Or er you just plain dumb?"

The man's eyes closed again, then quickly reopened. The pressure of the bayonet on Charles' left shoulder did not lessen.

"How old you be?" the Union man asked.

"Seventeen, I think, sir."

"You don't talk like a Yankee. You talk like a southern gypsy to me. Where you from?"

"Nawleans."

"Nawleans? Bullshit! Ya gotta come up wid a better lie than that there. There's not a gawddamn Yankee soldier in this gawddamn army that's from the Deep South. You lie to me, boy, and I'll gut you like a carp." He pushed harder on the bayonet and Charles winced in pain.

"It's the God's truth," Charles said, trying to shift his weight to the right to lessen the bayonet's pressure. The move accomplished nothing; if anything the bayonet hurt even worse than before. "I tried to join you Rebs a year ago last June, but the major-fellow said I was too young. Too young and too little."

"How'd you get to be a Yankee, then?" the soldier said in a voice as tired as Job's. "And why?"

"You ever live in an orphanage?" Charles asked. There was no answer. "Well, I by God have, and I'd have done anythin' to get out of that place. And I'm never goin' back."

Behind closed eyes again, the man studied on that a spell and then said, eyes still screwed shut, "So ya jined up to be a Yankee druther an' live in a orphanage? You'd fight against yore own kind to get out of a orphanage? Hell, nuthin' could'a been that bad!"

"It was bad, badder than a shit flood in Hell at high tide, that's for sure. I wanted to do the right thing and join up with you fellows, but some uppity officer said that couldn't be, no. So I eyed around for an alternate plan and here I am. An' I don't fight nobody. I'm a drummer."

The weary soldier studied on that a bit. "So ya jist drum a good tune to make sure good boys march to their death. What kinda job is that?"

The question lay sour between them.

"So this here al-ter-nate plan you done come up with," the Reb said, stretching out the three-syllable word like a first-grader at a reading bee, did it 'clude bein' bayonet-stuck by a former sto-keeper from Cahaba, Alabama, who's out here on a purpose?"

He paused and shook his head and muttered something that to Charles sounded like: "Onlys I done forgot what the real purpose is, I reckon."

The Reb closed his eyes again. They stayed shut for an eternity. Charles didn't move an inch, his breathing shallow and fast, like a wide wet weather stream. He hoped the soldier didn't go to sleep and fall forward.

That would hurt. A lot.

As if he heard the thought, the Reb stood upright, removed the bayonet from Charles' shoulder, stretched and said, "Got any food?"

"Naw, sir. Had my last bite yestiddy, I did. But if I did have some, I'd sure split it with you, yes."

The soldier's lips cracked open, showing splintered teeth and the tip of his pink tongue. "That's a good 'un, boy. That's a good 'un."

He lowered the bayonet till it was pointed at Charles left foot and reached into the knapsack that was tied around his waist with a piece of rope. Charles saw one of the shoulder straps was broken, and trailed toward the ground like a tiny, thin, dirty white flag. The Reb handed Charles a piece of crinkled, red-black jerky that appeared as hard as frozen tree sap.

"Here," was all he said.

Reaching out a reluctant hand, Charles took the jerky. It felt like dried tree bark but the smell of the peppered dried beef turned his saliva glands into a mountain stream at snow-melt.

He sawed off a small piece with his incisors and just let it sit at the back of his mouth, feeling it slowly soften. He sucked on it and reveled in the taste of the tart pepper and the brothy spit-juice that formed on his tongue. He started chewing slowly, savoring the texture, taste, and after-taste.

"Thank you kindly," was all he said.

The Reb stood upright, stretched his back again, and Charles heard a faint *snickey-pop*. The soldier eased himself down next to Charles, sharing the same tree as a backrest.

For the longest time, neither said a word, the only sounds the bite-and-snap of bits of hard jerky torn from the mother slab, chewing, swallowing, all mixed with the returning night wood noises—a squirrel barking over territory or a would-be mate, the sighing of night birds, rustling leaves moved aside by an opossum or raccoon.

"I got a boy 'bout your age," the soldier said, weariness clinging to his voice like moss on a tree.

"He in the war?"

"Not hardly. I jined up so's he kin not be in this shootin' mess. He's watchin' his mama and three sisters, learnin' to be a man." He signed. "A man that's not about to get to fightin' in no war."

He made it to "fightin'" before he started crying. Not much sound. Just uncontrollable shaking and little gasps as he hauled in stuttering breaths.

Charles turned his head and listened to the fluttering of leaves stirred by the night breeze. He shut his eyes and conjured up images of the leaves during daylight hours.

Such pretty leaves, all the same, pretty near.

His head, cocked to pick up the sounds better, followed a critter...
Fox? Raccoon?
that was working its way down the hill.

Charles chanced a look at the soldier. He was still. Asleep. His chest rose and fell in regular fashion. Charles eyed the rifle leaning unattended against the tree beside him.

Without a word, Charles quietly lay down beside him, placing his head near the tree truck and ever so gently, reached out with two fingers and gently touched the Reb's coat sleeve.

Sleep overtook him like a dropped anvil.

It was well past midnight, closer to dawn—the full harvest moon was halfway across the horizon—when Charles opened his eyes. A sound—the crinkling of leaves and a huffing noise—pulled him from a dream about sitting down to Christmas dinner with a family he didn't know. He thought that odd as he checked on the Confederate soldier, who was sleeping soundly, little noises coming from his lips with each exhale—*flubbbbbmmmm.*

Charles sat up, rubbed his eyes and ruffled his hair frantically. He knew this would get the lice jumping, but, heckfire, some of them might just jump off. He sensed, rather than saw, a fog layer hovering several feet off the ground.

How does it do that, hover like that, like a ghost?

He looked around him; the night was ink, with white scratchings where the moonlight slid through the tree canopy. He heard the huffing noise again, and another noise: Heavy footsteps on leaves.

He wanted to get up and run, but he couldn't tell exactly from which direction the noise was coming.

Right, definitely the right. Maybe just a bit behind, too.

Then he heard the voices, filtering through the wispy fog.

"Can't see nothin'. What we doin' stompin' around? It's darker than inside a black cat's ass."

"We got to get back to the unit. We need to find the boys."

Peter! That's Peter Falen's voice, the boy who just joined up back in the spring.

Charles eased up off the ground and crawfished sideways until he was ten feet away from the sleeping Reb. He slipped toward the voices, staying low, sliding one foot forward at ground level, pushing leaves and sticks gently to the side to diminish the chance of noise.

Peter and his companion were chattering away like magpies in the dark and Charles knew there was little chance they would hear his approach.

When he was close enough to thump Milton on his ear, he whispered: "Peter, it's me, Charles."

One of the men let out a yip of surprise; Charles repeated the message.

Death could not be any quieter.

"Charles? That you?"

"Shhhhhh. It's me, yes. And I'm not dead. Let's get outta here."

"That's what we was tryin' to do," the other soldier said, "when you scared us almost to the grave."

"This is Ben," Falen said. "He's separated from his outfit too. He's a private with the Massachusetts—"

"Hush!" Charles said emphatically. "Be quiet. There's a Reb soldier asleep behind that tree." He threw his arm out in an "over-there" gesture toward the darkest part of the night.

Peter hummed softly and tightened his grip on his rifle. "A Reb soldier, you say. How you know that?"

"I was sleeping. He came up and kept me steady with his bayonet. Then he gave me food and water. Then we just laid down and went to sleep."

"A Reb did that?" Ben said. "Why? Wait! Don't make no difference. He's a Reb. I ain't never kilt me no Reb. None that I know 'bout, anyways."

"Not gonna kill you this one neither," Charles said, biting the words at the end so the two could hear he meant business. "That soldier is tired of war, and he's got a son about my age. He's not gonna hurt nobody tonight."

"What about tomorrow?" Ben said. "If we kill him tonight, he won't be trying to kill nobody tomorrow or the tomorrow after that."

Charles waited to snap. But he calmed quickly and held his tongue.

Tomorrow never comes, 'cause when it does, it's today.

He didn't want to think about tomorrow or the tomorrow after that. He just wanted to leave this place and the Reb alive in it.

After a few more words, calmer words, the three hit out through a small stand of hickory trees, feeling their way like blind men in a hedgerow maze.

As the sound of their footsteps receded, the Reb soldier relaxed, his finger sliding off the trigger of the old cap-and-ball rifle. He thought of his son, back home taking care of his wife and daughters. And of Charles thrashing away through the underbrush.

He smiled, filled his old field cap with leaves and grass, punched it into a ragged ball to make a tiny pillow. He lay down with his head on a mossy root and dropped over the edge into restful sleep.

CHAPTER 24

Recuperation and Reflection

Common sense is judgment without reflection, shared by an entire class, an entire nation, or the entire human race.
Giambattista Vico

Charles had been summoned to the command tent for an important chore: Fetch the officers a jug of liquor from the surgeon's tent. He ran to the tent, took one of three jugs hidden under the main operating table, wiped it off with a bloody towel and raced back the group of officers and non-commissioned officers with the prize in hand.

He wasn't formally dismissed so he stepped back in the shadows and listened to the officer-talk, which was pretty much like that of men around any campfire: Life, love, and the war. He listened to the fire crackling; it was a small fire with an abundance of shimmering red embers, more for staring into than for warmth. After taking a mighty pull off the jug and passing it along, Lieutenant Colonel Richard Fitz Gibbon said, "The Army of the Shenandoah owns the whole damn valley. Jubal Early, be damned! And may that old goat die a slow and painful death. May the rest of life be inflicted with ugly women and a blanket of pus-boils."

Laughter and more than a few shouts of "Here! Here!" followed the statement. Two battles. Two decisive victories. The stories reverberated around the campfire were the same Charles was hearing among the enlisted men. Officers or enlisted, the stories got better with every telling. Two weeks ago a sniper with the Second Brigade, Thirteenth Connecticut, had cut down two of Early's brigade commanders at Winchester, and a third at Fisher's Hill. Now was credited with seven officer kills, all center kill shots, two at an uphill angle at more than three hundred yards.

It was hard for Charles not to grin at the palatable exuberance of the officers and his comrades in the enlisted ranks. Victory was in the air and the men were celebrating, mentally and physically. Just last night Charles had heard the Army of Northern Virginia had 32,000 men in the valley; he wasn't for sure of that number but the tents and campfires stretched from here and gone.

Normally a placid soul with what he considered a calm head and heart, he found himself riding the inevitable emotional wave that naturally comes from men doing what has never been done.

Talk in the camp was limited to three subjects: Victory, the army's next move, and Gen. Sheridan. Charles liked to listen to the battle banter; he wasted little time in worrying about those things he could not control—troop movements or hypothetical battles. But he found himself buying into the building legend of the funny-looking, lop-headed little Union general who looked gawd-awful ill at ease on top of that giant horse with the funny name.

What's that horse's name? Oh, yeah. Rienzi.

The story was the horse was named from the town in Mississippi where the officers of the Second Michigan Calvary presented it to the diminutive general. Charles didn't much believe the story.

Who'd name a town in Mississippi, 'Rienzi?' Who'd name a town located anywhere that?

Charles eased back from the fire and leaned against a sagging sapling. He recalled seeing General Sheridan a half-dozen times in the last few weeks. But only once at eye level, off his horse and walking among his men.

The general was the strangest, tiniest little thing. Depending on which piece of Army paper you look at for me, I'm either five foot two inches to five foot seven inches. And I'm half-a-head taller than The Littlest General.

His mind wandered to earlier that day, when, en route to the surgeon's tent to deliver some dressing and powder, Charles stopped by a circle of men playing a rousing game of Pig's Knuckles. He listened to a rawboned New York guttersnipe go into his personal version of Charles's "single-handed attack" of the Rebel breastworks at Fisher's Hill.

"Data boy, data drummer from the Ninth, charged up that hill by his lonesome, chargin' the entire Johnny Reb army, screamin' like a rape-ed banshee. And, as God is my witness, them Rebs thought that crazy drummer boy was leading up Ol' Abe hisownself and enough soldiers to get shed of them pretty quick-like. They shat their pants and hightailed it down the 'tether side of the hill. Boy's gonna get the Confessional Medal of Honor, is what I heard the captain tell the chaplain."

A heavy-set man with a bushel-beard tongue-slapped him: "Now, that's a lie. You wouldn't know a chaplain if'n he came up and baptized you, much less get close enough to hear him tell a captain a damn thing!"

The soldier reddened. "Well, when it happens, 'member I told you as much!"

Shaking his head and trying to hide a smile, Charles ambled off toward the field hospital.

Can only imagine what Ian would do with that story.

And then he laughed out loud, before looking around quickly to see if anyone noticed.

Sah-so, old sot, ya gonna get the Cah-confessional Medal of Honor? That right? Tha-that'd be like putting a frock coat on a pah-pig!

CHAPTER 25

Some Deaths Just...Stand Out

Tears are sometimes an inappropriate response to death. When a life has been lived completely honestly, completely successfully, or just completely, the correct response to death's perfect punctuation mark is a smile.
Julie Burchill

Charles was attending to business at the latrine, having set up on the south end of the pit; the early evening southern breeze carried the nose-hair-curling smell in the opposite direction.
Small victories make for happy soldiers.
He smiled at the thought.
A noise from the tree line behind him—a small, muffled thump, followed by a miniscule squeak—caused him to look in that direction. Cupping his left ear, he waited for a repeat. Other than the nattering of a couple of squirrels and lonely bleat of a magpie, the forest was quiet.
Something, it assuredly was. But what?
He finished up with a handful of fallen leaves, still pliable enough to use without falling to pieces, when he heard the same, high-pitched squeak.
What is that?
Buttoning his pants and arm-wrestling his galouses into place, he walked to the edge of the tree line, stopped, listened.

There! To the left!

Three steps later, Charles stopped. Listened. Three more steps. He repeated that procedure four times before his eyes followed his ears to the ground beside a fat-trunked, silver-leafed maple. He saw a brief movement and watched as a leaf seemed to skitter slowly, unaided by wind, toward him.

A little early for snakes to be out, but you never know.

Using a nearby dead limb as a poke rod, he cautiously pushed the leaf aside. Under it was a tiny, gray thing, long-limbed and lean, powering through the ground cover.

A baby squirrel! It's a baby squirrel! Probably fell out of the tree. Or pushed out by its mama or bigger brothers.

Charles bent over and looked the squirrel over carefully.

Its eyes aren't even open. Its abandoned. Poor little thing.

He carefully picked it up, and brought it up to eye level. The squirrel squirmed out of his loose grip, digging into Charles' fingers with its tiny claws and levering itself onto the back of his hand.

It was an overcast early spring morning; a chill, held close to the ground by a low cloud cover, settled into the valley. Without conscious thought, Charles plucked the squirrel off his hand and stuck it inside his coat, between the wool outer garment and his longhandles. Without hesitation, the tiny critter crawled up Charles' chest, finally settling just under his left shoulder, where he seemed to be either very comfortable or just petered out due to the effort.

Feeling the bump to make sure the squirrel was secure, Charles started walking back to camp. His mind ran amok with endless questions?

Where's his mama?
How'd he survive the fall?
How can I keep him alive?
Where can I get squirrel's milk?

Back in camp, he went straight to the surgeon's tent, where he found Surgeon Avery asleep on a frayed cot. "Mister, er, Doctor Avery," Charles said, gently shaking his shoulder. Charles was greeted with heavy-lidded eyes.

In a matter of seconds, Charles had the bad news: Wild animals don't do well in captivity. A squirrel needs squirrel milk, although the doctor had heard of squirrels surviving on cat's or goat's milk. There are no cats in the regiment, and no goats. The squirrel is going to die.

Dejected, Charles walked back toward his tent, cuddling the still squirrel inside his rough wool coat.

A thought hit him as he walked along the creek bank near the command tent.

I've got to get some milk.

There was none to be had in camp; the last milk he had seen was from a cow confiscated by a Massachusetts company on a foraging trip several weeks ago. A half-bucket of milk was drawn before the cow was slaughtered and divided up among the regiments bivouacking in the valley.

Then he remembered something: Several days ago, he had gone exploring, back up the Valley Turnpike. Just walking, looking. At a ramshackled house right on the road there had been a yard cat, huddled in a box on a porch. He distinctly remember the sounds of mewling kittens and wondered what it would be like to have a real pet, something he could take care of, something that would love him...unconditionally.

He hollered at Sergeant Burke as he started jogging up the road, "Be back in a bit, just going for a look-see!"

The house was further than he had remembered and it took more than half-an-hour to get there; it was as he remembered, perched right in the bend of the road. He hello-ed the house from the road, not wanting to enter the property, especially when asking a favor was in the offing. The front door opened, and a young woman stepped from the dark into the porch's shadow. She was plain in appearance, and a baby, girl maybe, clung to her neck like a small, hairless monkey. Dressed in a patterned shift of indeterminate age, the woman automatically touched her bun, checking for stray hairs, before shielding her eyes from the outside brightness. She stood stock still, staring at Charles.

"Excuse me, ma'm, but I am in dire need of some milk."

Taking a step backward, the woman pulled the baby closer and put her free arm across her chest.

Embarrassed by his abrupt introduction, Charles stammered: "What-what I mah-mean, ma'm, is that I need some milk from that mama cat yonder. Or a cow, if you got one." He reached into his tunic and pulled out the tiny squirrel. "For my squirrel. Elseways, he's gonna die."

"Don't have no cow. You Yanks done took her. Bull and baby, too. The squirrel, where'd you git him?" the woman asked in a voice just barely louder than the sound of a bare foot scuffing across a hardwood floor. Not the sound of emphatic statement, more of an after-thought.

"Sorry about your loss, ma'm. I truly am. The squirrel, I found it in the woods back at camp. Reckon he fell out of a tree. I would've put him back, but the tree was kinda lean at the top, and I heard wild mama won't take back babies that's done been touched by a man."

"So, what do you plan on doin', milk the cat?"

Charles hadn't thought through that part. His anguish was apparently obvious.

"Bring him up on the porch. What's yore name, boy?"

"Charles Andre, ma'm. What shall I call you?"

"Mrs. Lancaster will do. This is Honor," she said, nodding at the baby.

Without another word, she took the squirrel in her free hand, simultaneously handing Honor to Charles. Without a word, the woman bent to the cat-filled box, pulled the five sleeping kittens away from the mama cat and put them on the porch, replacing them with the squirrel. Calming the cat with one hand— "Easy, Sadie, it's all right."—she thrust the squirrel toward a middle nipple. Charles watched as the squirrel simply sat there, obviously sniffing, but taking no action.

Mrs. Lancaster grabbed one of Sadie's nipples and gently massaged it; a single bubble of milk appeared, which she gathered on her fingertip and massaged it gently but forcefully on the front of the squirrel's mouth. A heartbeat later, the squirrel sucked in and the milk mustache disappeared. Retracing previous movements, the woman eased the squirrel's mouth onto a teat, and this time the squirrel latched it, holding its base with tiny, skeletal hands, and started sucking.

Charles almost cried out in joy and he watched the squirrel...
My squirrel!
drinking his fill.

The woman looked at him with a puzzled look. "You gonna rub all Honor's hair off, iffen you don't stop rubbin' her so hard." Without even realizing it, Charles had been rubbing the baby's head, his ministrations increasing with his excitement.

In less than a minute, the squirrel rapid sucking motion had stopped; its claws relaxed, body went limp as it fell into a hard sleep.

The woman lifted it gently from the box, stopping to let Sadie smell the squirrel. The cat didn't seem to care one way or the other about the visitor.

Exchanging Honor for the squirrel, Charles started thanking the woman profusely. She held up a hand, stopping him in mid-sentence: "Whatcha gonna do with it's time to feed it again?"

What am I gonna do?

Charles placed the squirrel inside his coat and it nestled once again just beneath his left shoulder. He sat down heavily on the porch and just stared at the woods beyond the road.

"How far is your camp? Is it the one past the brook?"

"Yes, Ma'm, Mrs. Lancaster. I'm with the Ninth Connecticut. A fine bunch of boys, they be."

"Can you leave camp and bring the squirrel here three or four times a day to let it feed? Sadie apparently don't mind the squirrel nursing. Two kittens died and there seems to be plenty of milk."

Camp life was regular for regular soldiers, as well as for the drummers—drilling still going on, chores to be done for the quartermaster and surgeons, errands to be run for the officers.

But...maybe.

"Let me go back to camp and check with my sergeant, ma'm. Is it okay if I come back this afternoon?"

Mrs. Lancaster stopped bouncing the baby and cast a glance in Charles' direction. "You better. Or the squirrel won't make it till dark."

She turned to go in the house, but Charles stopped her by blurting out: "Mrs. Lancaster. Your man? Is he in the war?"

She didn't turn around. Her head dropped by degrees until her chin was almost on her chest. "He was. Not any more. He's up on the hill now, under that lone tree. At least that's where I put my memories of him." With heavy steps, she entered the house and gently closed the door.

Charles turned to go, but a slight door squeak caused him to turn back. The woman, still clutching the baby, was standing in the doorway.

"The squirrel? It got a name?"

"Not yet," Charles answered. "I thought I'd think on it on the way back to camp."

"Squirrel needs a name. A name makes things more permanent, somehow." Neither of them moved during a long pause. "My husband's name was Edward. Edward Eugene Lancaster." Without seeming to move, she closed the door.

The entire way back to camp, Charles rolled a litany of what he considered proper squirrel names around in his head. By the time he reached camp, he had the perfect name picked out.

Less than a half-mile from camp Charles met Private Joseph Dronant, a Texan who had signed on with the Ninth in New Orleans about six months before Charles.

The young soldier had just emerged from a stand of trees at the side of the road. The two had had several conversations about life in New Orleans over the past year or more so Charles was not surprised when Dronant said, "Andre! Where you been? We all thought you had runned off to join Jubel Early and his boys?"

Charles joshed back: "Been feeling a little squirrely at that, Nawlins Joe." Without another word, he hauled the squirrel out and put it on display in the palm of his hand.

Charles recounted the tale of finding the squirrel, of getting its meal from a cat named Sadie and the sad-faced woman who was so accommodating.

"Ya named it yet?"

"Yep. Eugene."

"Eugene? What kinda name is that for a critter?"

"It's just a name, is all. But I'm gonna call him Johnny Reb."

"Why, Andre, that's just plain queer. Why Johnny Reb?"

Holding the squirrel up to eye level, Charles smiled and said: "Why, it's a plain as the nose on your face, Joe. He's kinda skinny and helpless, like them Rebs we been pushin' all over these mountains. But mostly it's because he's got a little gray coat. Get it? Gray coat? Johnny Reb?"

Put back inside Charles' coat, the squirrel went back to sleep immediately. And the two soldiers walked side by side into camp, laughing at the tiny irony.

Two hours later, after getting permission from Sergeant Johnson to visit the Lancaster household—"But no more than once a day. Is that understood?"— Charles approached the farmhouse. The woman was sitting on an old, flat-bottomed chair, holding a sleeping Honor in her lap.

"Back so soon?"

Charles stopped at the porch's edge.

"Named the squirrel."

"Really? That fast? Well, boys are always making decisions fast. That's why they get in so much trouble."

She looked at Charles and cocked her head. "Well, you gonna tell me the name or not?"

"Eugene."

The woman's eyes widened. She mouthed, "Eugene?"

Charles nodded.

She cleared her throat, startling Honor. "Funny name for a squirrel, don't you think?"

"I thought it was a fine name. Thought about naming him 'Edward,' but Edward seemed like a funny name for a squirrel. So it naturally fell to 'Eugene.'"

There was a short, quiet pause, then Mrs. Lancaster started laughing. Waiting a heartbeat to see if it the laughter was real or forced, Charles quickly joined in. The belly-shaking laughter of her mother woke up Honor, who did a happy wiggle dance as the peals of laughter washed over the front yard.

It was Mrs. Lancaster who came up with a workable plan for keeping the squirrel alive. ("Feeding it once a day just won't do.") Charles agreed to leave Eugene (*Johnny Reb*) full time at the Lancaster farm to let it nurse with the five kittens. Mrs. Lancaster made it clear Charles could visit whenever he could and stay as long as he liked.

Upon returning to camp, Sergeant Johnson seemed a bit disappointed that Charles didn't have the squirrel, but clapped him on the back: "That was a mighty grownup decision you made, Andre. Mighty grownup."

Over the next three days—two of which were overcast, chilly and rainy—Charles made the two-mile trip to the Lancaster farm six times (Sergeant Johnson eager to approve the squirrel-visit requests), reveling in the thought of playing with Johnny Reb and visiting Mrs. Lancaster and Honor.

The fourth day was bright and sunny and it was dew early—the morning dew still covered the fields—when Charles approached the Lancaster place. He was surprised to see Mrs. Lancaster out on the porch.

"Mornin', Mrs. Lancaster. How's Honor?"

"She's fine. She got up early, but is sleepin' again. The squirrel had a bad night. It's real poorly."

Just like that. No preamble. No warning. No "Eugene." Just "squirrel."

"What's the matter with Johnny Reb? Where is he?"

Her eyes widened at the "Johnny Reb" reference, but she let it pass. "He's havin' trouble gettin' air. He's not eatin' right. His stomach is all pooched out. It's what wild animals do sometimes. They get sick and die for no good reason. Like some people."

Charles bent over the cat box, and picked up the tiny squirrel. It was mostly limp and mostly cold. "Oh, Sweet Mary, he's really sick." Without a word, Mrs. Lancaster went into the house, but didn't close the door despite the chill north breeze slipping over the mountains and down the valley.

She watched through the cracked door as Charles cupped the squirrel tightly to his chest, rubbing it gently on his stiff wool coat. She heard his plaintive whispers as Charles bent his head and breathed words into the lank fur: "You're going to be okay...you're going to make it...you're a fighter. *Please.* Come on!"

He held the squirrel up chin high and rubbed its legs, brought him back down and cradled him, rubbing his chest, trying to warm him. Charles extended his arms, raising the baby squirrel up, offering him the lank sun's warmth.

And, just for a moment, Mrs. Lancaster saw Charles look directly at the early morning sun, seeming to try and mentally gather its power for a miracle.

Charles' thoughts tumbled around like a piece of driftwood in a swollen creek:

Don't want much. Just a bit of good luck. Never asked for much. Now I'm asking. Come on, Johnny Reb!

He gathered a large breath and blew into the squirrel's face and rubbed its chest frantically. The squirrel's legs straightened. It took a breath, and went completely limp.

Charles said nothing more. His mind went blank; his eyes filled with tears that he refused to let fall. He looked at the tiny squirrel stretched out in an unnatural position in the palm of his hand. It did not move. Its black eyes, open and unfocused, stared blankly, seeing nothing.

Since he had joined the army, Charles had lived near death daily. Men died for vile diseases, of consumption, in camp accidents, and in the rigors and throes of battles. He had watched gut-shot men curl up and die, and had seen animals killed and butchered—large and small, domestic and wild—and he had never blinked an eye.

But today was different; there was no reason for Johnny Reb to die—there was no hunger, no way of life to fight for, no belief to defend. There was no blood; there was no reason.

It's just a dumb ole' squirrel.
And...he's gone.

Mrs. Lancaster watched as Charles placed the squirrel on the edge of the porch and walked away, his eyes facing down to the ground and away from the sunshine. He walked to the edge of the road, stopping to kick a rock into the field across the road, like that was his mission all along.

Neither said a word for what seemed like a long time. Finally, Mrs. Lancaster said, "I am going to put Eugene in an old sock. There's a hoe around back if'n you want to bury him."

"It don't make no difference. It's just a squirrel."

"Don't you talk that way!" she said, stomping her foot forcefully on the porch. "Don't you dare talk that way atall! He was yourn and he had a name. Now, go git that hoe and git it quick-like."

There was no argument left in Charles. He turned to the house and fetched the hoe. He picked up the sad sock, cradled it in his left arm and turned toward the hill.

"Hold on a minute. Let me get Honor and I'll go with you."

Charles waited until she returned with the fussy child, who obviously would have preferred to sleep rather than go on a grave-digging jaunt.

As they walked around to the back of the small house, Mrs. Lancaster said, "Got any special place you want to bury the squirrel?"

"Haven't given it much thought."

She stopped abruptly at the corner of the house and leaned her head on the bare boards. Reflected sunlight off the parched field caused her to close her eyes.

She looks tired, tired as I feel.

Her voice was soft and thready: "I think a good place might be under that oak on the hill yonder."

Charles had seen the spot before, but now looked at it with a discerning eye. It was a small knoll, capped by a majestic, spreading oak tree and a single, simple, wooden cross.

"I can't think of a better place in this whole valley, Mrs. Lancaster."

It was three days before Charles could work enough energy and want-to to walk back to the Lancaster farm. Even from a distance, he knew no one was home. More of a feeling than a fact. When he got closer he saw the porch chair and the basket of hanging flowers were gone; there was a vacancy on the north side of the barn, where the wagon had always been.

As a matter of courtesy, he announced his presence. When there was no answer, as expected, he walked up on the porch and peered through the single-paned window. Empty. He walked through the skinny front yard, rounded the corner of the house and started up the hill for the tree.

Stray thoughts skipped around inside his head like a flat stone slung on a calm pond.

Feeling this way about a squirrel is just dumb.
Wonder where they went?
Didn't have it long enough to become attached.
Wished I could have said goodbye.
It was just a dumb squirrel. Why'd it have to up and die?

He was topping the rise when he looked up and saw that the flimsy cross on Mr. Lancaster's grave had been replaced with a round-topped slab of barn board. The hand-painted letters were in a bold, clean hand:

Edward
Eugene
Lancaster
b. June 3, 1841
d. July 10, 1864
Good man, husband, father

Blinking back the tears, Charles turned his attention to the smaller, wooden grave marker with small, pinched writing next to it.

Eugene
One of God's fine squrels
In his short life,
he was loved

There was a tobacco tin between the two crosses. "Chas" was printed on it with what looked like (and felt like) a mixture of honeycomb and boot black. It was closed tight, and it took some working with a small stick to pry off the lid. The note was short:

Dear Chas:
Me and Honor gon back to MaryLand to live with my Foks. No thing left for us Here. Sorry I didn't get to say Goodby. One of the soljers told me about you calling Eugene Johnnie Reb. Those are too Fine names to my way of Thinking. Don't be too Sad! Eugene had Food and Warmth and a Place in the Light for the best part of his Life. Unlike too many of us, he didn't Worry bout a World thout him, but wuz jest fine being a Squrel and content to be. As long as that was the thing to do.
Mrs. Edward Eugene (Hope) Lancaster

Charles had never felt as alone in his whole life as he did at that moment. He sat down between the two little wooden tombstones—one small, one smaller—and didn't get up until the sun had set over Manussetten Mountain.

CHAPTER 26

Early Wants "His" Valley Back

> *Nothing is too high for the daring of mortals:*
> *we storm heaven itself in our folly.*
> Quintus Horatius Flaccus

October 14, 1864.
Four companies of Ninth regulars were on what the soldiers called a "minor march." Just marching from one point to another with no purpose other than to keep them sharp and in shape. Charles and his new drummer-mate, James McGuire, were lucky; stuck at the front of a new, reconfigured C Company next to the flag bearers, they were in mostly clear air. The gap in the ranks from company to company gave the dust just enough time to settle or be blown to the slight ditches that bordered each side of the Centerville Road.

Charles still did not know what to make of the mix-and-match of the four new companies—A, B, C and D. He didn't understand soldiers leaving in the middle of a campaign, even though he was told a lot of enlistments were up. He didn't know why the structure of the companies were all botched up, men transferred from here to over there for no apparent reason other than match up company numbers. He didn't ask why and he wasn't told.

Charles made a point of not keeping track of the comings or goings of men and material; he had no thought of how such movements might affect him on a personal level. He did his job, and tried to do exactly what he was told while ignoring the constant mini-conflicts and controversies swirling around the regiment. He was an observer of life, for the most part; extra-curricular personal investments in why people did what they did was not his way.

Two days ago, Wednesday, October 12, 1864, the entire regiment was abuzz with talk of Special Order No, 59. Signed by Brevet Major-General Emory Upton, the order put Charles and almost a hundred others from various companies (D, E, F, G and H) into C Company with Captain William A. Lee as commander. Now, the entire Ninth, the newly re-organized Irish Regiment, was part of the king-hill Union Army that had driven the Rebels back south, out of the Shenandoah Valley, away from the Potomac, away from Washington. The Confederates had *owned* the valley for three years; Captain Lee told his men they should be proud for taking it back. Now, he said, "we get to keep it. For good. And forever."

The Union's XIX Corps, Brigadier General William H. Emory, commanding, had set up an extensive bivouac centered on short bluffs overlooking Cedar Creek. The Ninth was set up toward the right flank; Charles and McGuire put their tent within hollering distance of the command tent, which was just slightly to the southwest on a downhill slope to allow for quick drainage.

As a defensive warfare rest stop, the camp position was not a bad one. The corps line extended from Valley Pike Bridge up and over the hills and on to Meadow Brook. The Army of the Shenandoah was spread all over the upper valley, with good flank protection from cavalry patrols, and from natural barriers, like the North Fork of the Shenandoah River and the rough-and-tumble landscape of Massanutten Mountain and the nice-to-look-at-but-hard-to-get-up-and-down Hupp's Hill.

What the soldiers didn't know, and what the Union commanders could not fathom, was that the Union's two down-and-dirty victories within the last month had not only set the Rebs back more than a step, but the rollicking, hard-fought, but one-sided victories embarrassed Ole Jube Early in the eyes of the one person every manjack in the Confederate Army wanted to please—Robert E. Lee.

Outmanned, outgunned, and on the run with a disheartened half-army of tired, hungry, bedraggled, and depressed fighters, Early had not a single thought about withdrawal to safer climes. As a strong, proud leader, Early didn't think about revenge in the most elemental sense. He was operating under the most simple of emotions: He wanted his pride back. He wanted *his* valley back. Lee had given the Shenandoah to him to defend, and he was dead set on regaining the ground entrusted to him.

October 17, 1864.

Just after dawn, two men, Major General John Gordon, regarded by both sides in the conflict as one of the most stable of all Southern officers, and Captain Jedediah Hotchkiss stood behind cover on Signal Knob. Their vantage point was perfect for looking down on the Union line. Neither man could understand why a picket line had not been set up on the mountaintop, but were glad for the shortsightedness of Union commanders. It was, in this war that demanded righteous intelligence in all planning, the perfect place to watch the enemy up close.

Hotchkiss was often called a mapmaker. He was that; he was also much, much more. A New Yorker who had taught school in the Shenandoah prior to the war, he was a gifted cartographer who knew this country well. As the former personal topographer of General Stonewall Jackson, his reputation for accurate maps needed no embellishments. It was Jackson, who, two years earlier, had routed what seemed like the entire Union army and drove them out ass-over-teakettle out of the valley. The Union Army had arrived twice before with the heralding of one-nation angels; both times they had retreated a demoralized army that had been lopsidedly out-generaled and solidly whipped. Humiliated, even.

It was through the eyes of this master mapmaker, local resident, and terrain specialist that Gordon was able to see possibilities of outmaneuvering the Union Army. The pair quickly devised a plan to retake the valley.

The entire plan centered on a local landmark: Fisher's Hill.

The next day, just after dark, three divisions of the Confederate Second Corps, Army of Northern Virginia, forded the North Fork River several miles upstream of Fisher's Hill. Following Hotchkiss' maps with precision, six thousand men followed a ledge-path on the face of Massanutten Mountain—often in single file—then turned down the Manassas Gap railroad track back to the North Fork of the Shenandoah River. Since there was no thought, no hint of any Rebel activity in the area (after all, the Rebs were beaten and hiding off somewhere to the south and east licking their sizeable wounds) stealthy Reb point soldiers captured the string of Federal pickets along the river without raising any alarm.

Early risers on the Union's left flank were greeted with a cat fur-thick wet fog. Men asleep, wrapped tight in wool blankets, or just barely awake, or on sleepy guard duty, or doing early breakfast time chores, were surprised with a musket volley crashing out of the fog bank. It was quickly followed by second wall of minie balls. Gritty-eyed soldiers, some fully dressed for warmth, others in home-spun or sutler-bought longjohns, popped from thousands of tents up and down the line. Within seconds, a Reb division swept through camp, shooting, bayoneting, and clubbing Union soldiers, some of whom were scrambling to retrieve weapons. The majority of soldiers, outmaneuvered, outmatched, and overrun, settled for any avenue of escape.

Within minutes of the first volley, survival instinct won out over bravado. The Union retreat was pell-mell, with the only consensus being the direction in which to run: Away from rifle fire and attacking Rebs, into the cloaking, life-saving fog.

Some Union soldiers, urged on by screeching, sword-waving junior officers, tried to make a stand; a second unit stood fast in another section. Officers not already out of play due to being swallowed up by the fog and not being able to communicate with their men, pleaded for the men to "hold the line." A secondary charge by another Reb division in a pincer movement threw what was remaining of two Union divisions into an uncontrolled panic and retreat, with many of the fleeing soldiers taking nothing with them but whatever they were wearing. It seemed to be a consensus that lives were more valuable than clothes, provisions...or weapons.

Elsewhere along the Union line, Confederate artillery, perched on the heights above Cedar Creek, opened fire, directly into the dense fog. Soldiers trying to set up a defensive front were shredded.

"How can they see in this fog?" one officer screeched to another.

A sergeant, checking a dropped rifle to make sure it was loaded, screamed over the cannonade, "They musta lined us up before the fog settled, aimin' in by the campfires."

The Union had its own artillery at another high point overlooking the creek. Those guns were barely unlimbered when a third Confederate division barreled up that slope; more than fifty men and seven guns were captured within minutes. The guns and captured power and shot were put to immediate use against Union troops.

REVEILLE

The men of the Ninth Connecticut awoke to the first volley. Charles had been hovering toward awake, thinking, dreaming, wondering about Ian and Sister Bloody, sweet Sarie Beth, New Orleans, the Connecticut furlough, and Lucy, the pretty girl in the tintype. The first crack of direct gunfire into the Ninth's ranks came from the right of camp. The volley of minie balls cut through the fog like a scythe. Charles heard the sound of close-up cannon fire, then felt the percussion slam into his sternum.

Lots of guns. Somebody's doing some powerful shooting.

"Andre! McGuire! Drummers! Get 'im up and in formation. Now!" The strong voice of Major Frederick Frye pounded the drummers' ears.

Since both boys slept in their clothes to hold the autumn night chill that invaded camp at bay, in less than fifteen seconds they were standing in front of the command tent, pounding out the long roll in synchronized rhythm. McGuire, who was mustered in last winter, followed Charles' lead, mindful of seniority in the musician ranks.

The first sounds of fighting roused many of the brigade's soldiers. The continuing cracking of rifle fire, plus the long roll, had the soldiers moving at a fast clip.

"To the breastworks!" Colonel Cahill screamed, his order echoed from major to lieutenant to sergeant, from sergeant to corporal, from soldier to soldier. Keeping a steady beat, the two drummers of the Ninth, echoed by the drummers of other units, followed the men toward the defensive line, unconsciously keeping in step with the bouncing sticks.

In less than two minutes, the Ninth was ensconced behind their breastworks barrier, which just yesterday seemed formidable, but now, with Rebel soldiers swarming in their direction, seemed like a barrier composed of mere splinters.

Officers, some with pistols and a few dandies with drawn swords, were screaming orders, some comprehensible, some well-seasoned babble. As protocol dictated, McGuire had gone down the line, while Charles stayed put, closer to the high-ranking officers. In case orders had to be relayed by the drummers, a fair amount of space between the two would guarantee as many soldiers as possible would hear the call.

Charles cracked an ear listening for a change in his fellow drummer's cadence, but heard nothing but the thumping of the long roll and its echo off the hill's crest.

The crackle of rifle fire continued unabated to the south, and was soon joined by the sound of more gunfire, this time to the southwest. The sounds from the newest battle was muted by the series of pimple hills that swung in a lazy line to the rear.

The attack was a complete surprise. The previous night, reconnaissance teams had reported that there was no sign of the enemy within miles of the main camp. That report—"erroneous as all git-out," General Merritt would proclaim loudly days later—set the stage for a retaking of the valley by Early's forces.
"Sleep well, boys," Captain William Lee said as he made his late night rounds. "The Rebs have left our beautiful valley and all's right with the world." The soldiers—junior officers and enlisted men alike—took him at his word.

It's not that there were no warning signs that the Rebs were still in the vicinity. For one, no less military geniuses than Lee and Early had emphatically stated the Shenandoah would never be left in Union control. For another, Early's history as a commander should have pointed to the certainty of a surprise attack. And, finally, at least one officer of the day reported hearing noises that brought up images of troop movement. The officer went to investigate the muffled noises...and did not return; it was later learned he had been captured by Rebel cavalry. The disappearance of such an important cog in the military machine should have raised pointed questions, and set internal alarms a-ringing in the minds of the North's seasoned officers.
The XIX Corps' bivouac—which included the Ninth Connecticut—was west of the north branch of the Shenandoah River, within a mile of Middletown; the tents of the Eighth Corps was just off its left flank, south about five hundred yards. The Ninth's tent city faced Cedar Creek, whose banks at this point were overgrown by hearty hardwoods. As bivouac areas go, this section of the valley did not provide any semblance of ideal cover, being fairly open to the front and rear. Stretching along the valley for almost a mile, the XIX Corps' left flank extended past the Valley Turnpike, its right just short of Belle's Grove. Company C anchored the left flank, its men in shouting distance of men of the Eighth Corps.
Preceded by a cavalry charge which drove Union pickets streaming toward the rear, eleven Confederate divisions smashed into the Eighth Corps, sending the entire contingent of men racing pell-mell north up the Valley Turnpike.

Within minutes of the initial attack, several Rebel divisions made a successful end run around the Eighth Corps' left flank, which was non-existence since soldiers were "rapidly advancing to the rear," as one Southern officer put it.

What seemed like the entire Johnny Reb army went barreling straight down toward the Ninth Regiment. The regiment was driven from the breastworks in quick order, but at the urging of Colonel Healy, regrouped at the bottom of the hill. Urged on by the drummers' riffs, the Ninth counterattacked in an attempt to retake the hill. Pushed back by blistering fire from two Confederate regiments, and within a cat's breath of time, Colonel Healy's command, along with every other division of the Nineteenth Corps was in full-flight retreat. Many of the frightened soldiers, believing the entire Confederate Army was pounding down the valley bent on total destruction, simply quit the battle, running for their lives. In their headlong dash to escape the attackers, they left virtually all camp gear behind—tents, food, knapsacks containing personal items, pots, pans…and weapons

Leaving their camp intact and retreating quickly not only saved lives for the moment, it inadvertently created a perplexing dilemma in the minds of the attacking soldiers. Continue the attack? Or stop and plunder? To the minds of the war-numbed, hungry, and poorly outfitted Rebels, the choice was a simple one. The retreating army's camp leavings stopped more than half of the attacking Rebs in their tracks. Wholesale ransacking of the abandoned camps of both corps began and the vast majority of men from the Nineteenth and Eighth Corps escaped unscathed.

Charles and McGuire, through training, instinct, or blind dedication to duty (in future years, they would question the reasoning themselves) ran along with the rest of their retreating comrades, drums slung to the rear, banging against their backsides.

Due to the wrap-around attack of the Rebs, the men of the Nineteenth funneled out of the fire zone to the southwest through closed-in, hilly stands of hardwoods, and burned-over patchwork quilt patterns of pasture or farmland. Hundreds of dazed men of the Nineteenth and the Eighth Corps fled without even picking up their arms; almost twenty heavy guns were captured before they could be fired.

After running for more than a mile, Charles, surrounded by hundreds of his comrades, hit the banks of the slow-running Middle Marsh Brook, and plunged across it without breaking stride. Many of the men—those with guns and leather pouches of ammunition—stopped on the northwest side of the creek, took up positions behind trees...and waited. Charles slid down behind a deadfall...and waited. Captain Lee, a Bridgeport man who had moved over to C Company from H Company with Charles and others just a few days previously, hollered: "You with rifles, take up defensive positions along the creek. Those of you without rifles but with powder and ball, pass them to those with rifles. Get ready for a charge, but don't fire at jest anythin'. We're all by our lonesome with no supplies comin' any time soon that we know of. And we may have more of ourn comin' in behind us."

As if on cue, the forest became alive with other soldiers, fleeing the battleground. In spite of the forest gloom, the defenders breathed again when they identified the soldiers as Union from the color of their uniforms.

"Hold your fire!" Lee screamed, and then repeated his orders—loudly and profanity-filled—to the newcomers about setting up a defensive line. Defensive line? It was more of a fantasy than a reality. Many of the men had no weapons, and those that had only enough powder and ball to fire a few shots. As more and more men from various units of the Nineteenth Corps crossed the creek, officers—Colonels Cahill, Lieutenant David Warner of C Company, Captains Lee, John G. Healy, and Garry Scott, Sergeant Major John Bolger, and G Company's Captain William Wright, among others—worked to put the Ninth Regiment into the proper fighting units. It was a textbook example of controlled chaos.

Expecting an attack from either the east or south, the Nineteenth Corps staggered into approximate regiment fashion—company by company when individually assigned soldiers could find their units, picking out a good defensive position when they couldn't—under the relentless brow-beating of his subordinates by Major General Wright. The general had no sure way of knowing what was taking place to the south and east of the defensive position taken up by the Nineteenth. He could hear spatters of rifle fire, the *whoooof-pah* of large cannon fire at various distances from his position, but the sound swirled around the valley, bouncing off stone cliffs and wooded highlands, making it appear they were surrounded.

The heads of the officers and soldiers were set on a communal swivel, each man constantly searching in every direction for any movement that wasn't natural to the terrain.

Wright's immediate thoughts were for the safety of the men hunkered down in the woods around him; stray thoughts were reserved to think about—and silently pray for—the fate of the Sixth and Eighth Corps. In regard to the Sixth, his prayers were most appropriate, because those men were facing sure defeat, if not outright annihilation.

The men of the Sixth were in dire straits—those that did not flee quickly and earnestly earlier—hung up in a defensive battle around the Valley Turnpike. All the Confederates had to do was coordinate cavalry and ground units…and roll right over that isolated segment of the beaten army. But the Sixth was fighting tough, and had repulsed several frontal assaults without giving up much ground.

Despite the stringent recommendations by several Confederate field commanders to "Fight on!" (including the always-intense General John B. Gordon, who spoke his mind in every situation from parlor to battlefield), the Confederate attack was stopped in its tracks. When faced with the decision to attack the splintered, but still-fighting Sixth (down to but one division, two cavalry units and two artillery batteries) or declare the action to this point as a victory, Early elected to effectively stomp on any plans for a coordinated, full-out attack.

With Gordon hammering on his commander for a combined assault, Early replied: "This is glory enough for one day. This is the nineteenth (of October). Precisely one month ago today we were going in the opposite direction."

To the Rebel firebrands, especially since the outnumbered army had been whipped solid twice in the past month, this type of passive thinking was, at best, dull-headed, at worse, military blasphemy. It would prove to be a decision every commander and solider on the field that day under the Stars and Bars would dearly regret at the end of this day and many days to follow.

Fighting raged for miles up and down the valley in isolated pockets, near the rivers and creeks and turnpikes, and in the hills. It was cavalry pitted against cavalry, cavalry against artillery, Rebel units driving straight down the throats of Union soldiers fighting more of sheer desperation than for a hope of winning…anything, ground, skirmish, or battle.

For the Union forces, at mid-day, those that were still fighting, the only battle they fought, mentally and physically, was to simply stay alive. For those who had left the field, the primary objective was exactly the same thing.

CHAPTER 27

Grasping at Straws

> *The human animal dances wildest*
> *at the edge of the grave.*
> Rita Mae Brown

While the Rebel Army was sneaking around in the dark to get into position to attack his army, General Sheridan was sleeping on a down-filled mattress at a private home in Winchester, twelve miles to the north. He was en route to joining his troops after being summoned to Washington for a look-in-the-eye assessment of the Shenandoah campaign. Sheridan had opted to stop to sleep on a real mattress indoors rather than spend another hour in the saddle and try to sleep on a camp cot.

As the Confederate attack began and his troops were being scattered across the Shenandoah hills, Sheridan was awakened by a duty officer who reported hearing artillery firing in the vicinity of Cedar Creek. There was no worry in Sheridan; he knew that General Wright has scheduled a full-bodied reconnaissance mission that morning and surmised he had jacked up a Rebel battery or two.

Shortly thereafter, something caused his battle instincts to kick in; he roused himself, dressing hurriedly, and ordered a speedy breakfast and saddled horses.

Not an hour later, to the discordant tune of the distance sound of cannon,

Sheridan and his officers hit the Valley Turnpike and hooked up with the 117th Pennsylvania Volunteer Cavalry, his official escort unit, at Mill Creek.

Hearing the sound of battle increase from sporadic hiccups to a steady rumble, Sheridan became increasingly more agitated as the riders headed south at a steady gait. Hitting a rise above Mill Creek, Sheridan and the officers came upon a sight no commander ever wants to witness: Hundreds of wounded men, alongside perfectly fit soldiers in various stages of undress (few, it was evident, with weapons) and supply and field wagons and caissons, rushing out of the valley.

An army on the run, shaken, shattered, demoralized.

It was more than an organized retreat from a superior opposing force; it was full-fledged soldier-flight. Sheridan's first order was to halt the retreat by throwing a cordon of troops bivouacked in Winchester across the road and fields approaching the city. That duty was left to one of his accompanying colonels as Sheridan and a contingent of a dozen officers and soldiers started the long ride to the battle. "Stop them and turn them around," Sheridan shouted at Colonel J.W. Forsyth, his chief of staff. "This day isn't done. Not yet and not in this fashion."

The small group of mounted men, all bunched up in a trotting wad, started south along the road. Sheridan stood in his stirrups, waved his tiny, round hat and shouted to the retreating soldiers: "You're goin' the wrong way, boys! We're goin' the right way. Follow us! We'll be all snug in our old camp by nightfall!"

Some soldiers did turn around as if on a greased shaft and started walking back toward the distant rumble of cannons and small arms fire. Some had their rifles. Some who were empty handed followed the general's plea based on drummed-into-them military discipline, instinct, and faith. For as long as possible, the mounted officers stuck to the road or to the side of it, extolling the retreating army to turn around and "make an accountin' of yourselves!" But the going was too slow due to the backlog of wagons and masses of men still heading away from the battlefield. Without a sign or order, Sheridan spurred Rienzi off to the west, heading straight for the covering forest; his men followed at a gallop, thinking he knew where he was going. Sheridan, they knew, in all things military never questioned his instincts. They knew, too, he had been proven right more times than wrong.

Laying out the ground around the Cedar Creek bivouac areas in his head,

Sheridan knew that Early's troops must have approached his army from the least likely route—around the base of Massanutten Mountain.

Impossible, he thought. *Probable,* he re-thought. *That's the only way the Rebs could have made a surprise attack. That, or some officer or officers were dead in the brain.*

Assuming—*knowing*—the point of the initial attack, Sheridan also knew—*assumed*—the main force of Union soldiers would have been driven to the east and north. By cutting across country just south of Kernstown, a tiny hamlet whose main business district was comprised of a blacksmith shop and a general store, he would save time getting to the battlefield. Sheridan was also hopeful by taking that route he could avoid a full contingent of the enemy, and, hopefully, intersect chunks of his retreating army.

Sheridan thought kindly of Kernstown as they passed through the town. It was the site of one of the few Union victories in the Shenandoah, and one of the few times General Stonewall Jackson and his southern boys had ever been defeated. Colonel Nathan Kimball had met Jackson's forces head-on and sent them running east in a mighty hurry.

Helped that Jackson had faulty information on our strength. Helped that Kimball had more than eight thousand men instead of the three thousand number Jackson thought was right that had him attacking in high spirits.

Might be a good sign if we met Early today on this lucky stretch of ground.

The thoughts did not stick around long. Sheridan knew the battle was still miles to the south and west and the likelihood of retracing his steps to this community was not logical reckoning.

After traveling several miles in a more or less perpendicular route to the Turnpike, the image of the hundreds, thousands of soldiers streaming toward Winchester haunted the commander, and, without warning, without explanation, he turned back toward the road. As expected, it was packed with soldiers, but this mass of blue coats was different from those just outside Winchester; these men had been corralled and mentally hog-tied by berating officers. They had regrouped in loose fighting units by company and regiment and seemed to be leisurely awaiting further instructions.

One of Sheridan's officers commented on the "strangeness of the scene before us." Sheridan was quiet. The scene was, indeed, not what Sheridan or a single one of the men accompanying him thought they'd see on this ride. A strange, tentless camp had been set up along the roadside, a few campfires were blazing, coffee pots set blackening at their edges. Some of the men were "apparently tuckered out from all that retreatin'," one of the accompanying officers stated rather loudly. Sheridan silenced him with a stern look. "Now's not the time for recriminations. Now's the time for healin'." A poignant pause—long, drawn out—followed. "Now's the time for believin'. Then comes the time for fightin'."

He stood up in his stirrups, yeehawed to the troops, and started forward. And he looked over his shoulder at his support guard, smiled and said, "And, by God, WINNIN'!"

More than a few of those officers and soldiers accompanying thought he had gone daft. They knew Sheridan was good. But nobody was that good. Not here. Not now. Not in this situation. And, certainly, not with an entire army of broken and disheartened men.

CHAPTER 28

Time to Retreat in Another Direction

> *Yield and you need not break,*
> *Bent, you can straighten,*
> *Emptied, you can hold,*
> *Torn, you can mend...*
> *Disappointed, you can be fulfilled.*
> *Defeated, you can be victorious.*
> Passages, the Tao

The men of the Ninth, after their counterattack had been repulsed and they were pushed further away from familiar ground (and not knowing the fate of other regiments, with little or no communications between brigades), found themselves bunched up. They milled about in a stand of hardwoods, waiting for orders, some words of inspiration, a direction in which to turn.

Colonel Cahill opted to order his men to double-time back to the north, around Hupp's Hill, which housed Rebel artillery. As luck would have it, the southern gunners were preoccupied, being more interested in the peppering the scattering soldiers of the Eighth and Sixth Corps.

Once around the mountain, the regiment, gathering up fast-running comrades along the way like iron filings lining up on a magnet (along with strays from the other corps) turned due east toward the Valley Turnpike. Cahill surmised the Confederate forces were concentrating on ground west of

Middletown and up the Cedar Creek hollows and ravines. Heading away from those particular places, at least for now, seemed the logical thing to do.

Spying the Turnpike a half mile away, clogged with retreating comrades, Cahill ordered the Ninth to form up in companies in an open field; he could find no personal comfort in joining hundreds of defeated men rushing to God-knows-where.

Cahill instructed his officers and non-commissioned officers to make "sure your boys rest, 'cause I suspect we'll be headin' back. If not this day, then the one that follows."

Charles was dog-tired, and was comforted by the thought of resting a bit. His knapsack had an adequate supply of jerky and hardtack, and his canteen was full. Informal orphanage survival lessons are hard to forget. Other soldiers, who ran from their camp with nothing but whatever clothes they were wearing at the time, made their hunger known. Some with food, shared (including Charles); others, thinking about the immediate, and assuredly uncertain, future, deferred by ignoring the not-so-subtle signs from their fellow soldiers. A couple of supply wagons, trying to work their way down the road, caught the eye of the Ninth men. A large handful of soldiers ordered themselves to go to the road and get all the supplies they could carry from the wagons' storage areas.

It was an action readily accomplished despite the admonitions, screams, and curses of the drivers. Coffee pots, big tins of coffee and small tins of sugar, and sacks of hardtack were pulled off the wagons and carried to the waiting troops. Fires were quickly struck, and canteen water and coffee grounds started boiling.

It was Lieutenant Colonel Fitz Gibbons who first spied a small knot of Union officers coming toward them from north end of the road.

"It's Sheridan!" he cried loudly. "Li'l Phil is here, boys. Everthin' will be put right. It's General Sheridan."

The horsemen stopped briefly and talked to Sixth Corps leaders. After a few minutes, salutes were exchanged, and the horsemen headed toward the Nineteenth at a temperate speed.

The Ninth soldiers rose up as one and their collective yells could be heard up and down the valley.

Sheridan pulled up tight to Fitz Gibbon, who saluted smartly. After formally returning it and surveying the gathering men, Sheridan said, "I got something to say to your boys, Colonel, if that's all right with you."

Fitz Gibbon smiled, turned toward Charles, who hovered close-by, awaiting orders, as always. He nodded and Charles thumped out a raucous "assembly" call. The troops rushed forward quickly. Before he was ordered to do so, Charles stopped the roll, quieting the reverberations of his drum with his fingertips.

Sheridan took the time to eye the gathering, moving his head left to right over the several hundred gathered close in.

"Are we done yet, boys?" he said, in a voice barely above a whisper.

The men leaned in.

Sheridan fairly hollered: "Are we done yet, boys?"

The group, mostly Ninth men but a few from Ohio and Massachusetts companies who were separated from their units, raised up a resounding, emphatic "NO!"

"Is this the best we can do?"

"NO!"

Sheridan paused and then shouted so he could be heard at the furthest edge of the crowd: "If it's all the same to you, I'd like to spend the night where you boys spent last night. How's that sound?"

The answer was emphatic and positive.

"Well, then, let's get to it. How about you join me and we retreat in the other damn direction!"

It almost makes me want to drop my drum and take up a rifle. Almost.

Less than a mile away, more than six thousand Confederate soldiers, resting before a push to mop up scattered pockets of Union resistance, paused as the cheers drowned out even the heavy *poo-chu* of small-bore artillery firing from Hupp's Hill. They didn't wonder about the sound; they knew what it was and didn't have much use for it.

As Sheridan made ready to turn his horse toward the sounds of battle, Fitz Gibbons stepped forward. "Care for a cup of coffee before we go back where we belong, General?"

Sheridan put his right hand on his hip and gave a short bark-laugh. "Well, Colonel, I think a cup of coffee would go pretty good right now." He admired the calmness in the man and said as much.

A cup with a double-wire handle was quickly brought to him. As if by magic, other cups appeared and were dispersed to his men.

"To your health, gentlemen," the general said, raising the tin coffee mug high. "And to the bad health of any Reb soldier that gets in our way this day!"

CHAPTER 29

Turning Losing into Winning

> *The battle is won by the player who sees the furthest, the one...who can see through his opponent's move, can guess his plan and counter it, and who, when attacking, anticipates all the defensive moves of his opponent.*
> Game of Wei-Chi

News flew up and down the line about Sheridan's arrival and the stories were again miles ahead of the truth.

"He rode hard all the way from Winchester, changing horses three times 'cause he wore 'em out."

"I heard he got wind of the Reb plans yestiddy and rode all night from Washington, changing horses three times!"

"He's going to lead us back to Middletown and we're gonna push them Rebs all the way into next week."

Sheridan sent out riders to gather up officers for a general war council, which was held in a field to the side of the Valley Pike. His orders, after giving instructions for division and regiment locations for the upcoming battle, were simple and explicit: "Get your men ordered up and get them pointed in the right direction. We are going to recover our camp, every damn inch, and in doing so, by God, Jube Early will regret this day the rest of his life."

After asking for and getting the nods of agreement from all officers, Sheridan sent an orderly for his horse, climbed aboard and spun him around in a circle for effect and galloped back toward the nearest group of soldiers. "Come on back, boys. Follow my lead. We will give 'em hell, that I promise you. Gawd damn 'em. Gawd damn 'em all. We'll make coffee out of Cedar Creek tonight!"

Sheridan started down the side of the road at a regular trot, his contingent of officers and soldiers hurrying to catch up. Officers dispersed to their own units, and elicited cheers from their men as they hear a recounting of Sheridan's promise to retake the ground lost earlier.

Within the next hour, time allotted to him by the reluctance of the Rebels to put up any meaningful pursuit and attack, Sheridan met with all available commanders—Major General Albert Torbert, Custer (who, the men later would learn around campfires gave Sheridan a big bear hug), Captain DuPont (with two ready-for-battle batteries), General Emory, Cahill, and Fitz Gibbons, and a handful of junior officers.

His plan to retake the lost ground was a strategy steeped in military history: Counterattack on several fronts, regain ground lost earlier in the day when the opportunities to do so arise, move forward but never backward, and if attacked, bend but don't break...and immediately counterattack.

An hour after the general staff meeting, assigned units were in the proper position, more or less, for a coordinated counterattack. Always careful, even when making hasty decisions, Sheridan ordered Merritt's cavalry to capture some prisoners. In short order, Merritt returned with three captives, part of an informal Rebel picket line set up as an early warning system. Sheridan interrogated the men personally. His main concern—that the divisions of General James Longstreet was part of the attacking force—was put to rest quickly. Longstreet's main fighting force was nowhere in the area. It was time to counter-attack in full force.

The plan Sheridan devised was not a new and exotic military maneuver, just one the Confederates weren't expecting. The entire Union line, three miles long now and ever-extending as new companies rejoined the fray, was set to advance in a swinging line, pivoting on the Sixth Corps, which would advance slowly toward the Rebel lines. The Nineteenth was the movement's scythe. The Sixth was ordered to push the Rebs off the wooded hillocks that dotted the northern section of the valley. When the Nineteenth became fully engaged all along its line, the Sixth Corps, using several cavalry brigades as battering rams, would redouble its efforts and launch a straight-ahead attack into the heart of the Rebel forces.

Despite the morning's misadventure and despite the humiliation of being driven from their beds by the surprise attack of Early's men, the enthusiasm of the men of the Ninth Connecticut was running high. Sergeant Reilly screamed at his charges more than once to make sure they got the message: "We get it done today or by gawd, we'll be back here in the morning to do it all over again! With Sheridan leading us, it's victory, boys, nothin' but bloody victory!"

The attack did not go smoothly. Artillery shells from several hilltops rained down on the Ninth Regiment. The crack of muskets from both sides was deafening; smoke roiled across the valley like wind-whipped fog, slicing visibility to within mere yards.

Beating out the regular marching beat at the outside of the long line of men, Charles was knocked down twice by exploding canister shells. Both times he lay there for a time, doing a personal inventory check for injury. Finding none each time, except for severe ringing in both ears, he climbed unsteadily to his feet and pushed on, drum sticks pounding.

Out of the corner of his eye, he saw men fall, a couple from what was assuredly canister. Off to his right, he saw three Ohioans go down at once, as if slapped by a giant, invisible hand.

Grapeshot?

He saw Sergeant Reilly stumble and fall, then regain his feet and push on, a bit unsteady, but still leading his men.

'Course he got up. It's Reilly.

The first hard push by men of the Nineteenth ended up by coming eye-to-eye with Confederates holed up behind a wall near an apple orchard. All along the front the charge gained momentum, as a few Confederate soldiers, then a handful, a company, and finally, an entire Confederate regiment took flight.

It was the intent of the Union charge to "domino" the length of Early's line, to knock it down, soldier by soldier, company by company, regiment by regiment. Their intent was not a surprise: Signals from members of Early's flag company on Three Top Mountain had relayed the Union position and probable intent by noon. Gun batteries were moved hither and yon and were fully expected to be able to stop the expected onslaught. What was not taken into consideration was the whipped-into-a-battle-frenzy condition of the Union soldiers, and the long line of attack.

In short order unit after unit of Confederates were rolled up and scattered like wheat chaff in a high wind. Uncertainty and fear struck every Rebel unit like a raging infection. Strong units faltered; weaker units left the battlefield, some without firing a shot. As word spread about the orchestrated, controlled, full-force Union attack, Confederate units up and down the valley took flight.

James Caffrey, a corporal and a new transfer into C Company, grabbed Charles and, above the screaming of the shells, banging rifle fire and screaming soldiers, said something... Charles couldn't hear. He shrugged and pointed at his ears. Caffrey pointed to the rear, propped his gun against his left leg and made a carrying motion with both hands.

Stretchers! Go get stretchers!

Charles back-slung his drum and plunged through the pockmarked field, stepping over abandoned knapsacks and a few dropped rifles. He mentally noted the location of wounded men. He was almost in clear ground when he noticed one man down—Sergeant Reilly. The sergeant was on his back, eyes closed, right leg bent at an unnatural angle, blood seeping into the grassy field.

Dropping to both knees, Charles grabbed the sergeant by both shoulders and shook him frantically. Reilly's eyelids fluttered, then opened, his eyes unfocused. Blinking with the rhythm of the wings of small bird in flight, Reilly widened his eyes in an attempt to focus. Finally, Charles was certain, Reilly recognized him. A slight smile, followed by an eye-clinching grimace, slid across his face.

His mouth moved but no sound reached Charles' ears. He yelled, "Can't hear. Ringing in my ears." Placing a hand on Reilly's chest, Charles said loudly, "I'll be back. Don't you worry, I'll be right back."

The sergeant nodded slowly. His tired eyes closed.

Ten minutes later, Charles and John Rohr, a soldier from New Orleans who had a minor scalp wound recently tended to by a surgeon, double-timed back up the hill, found Reilly, and carried him to the surgeon's tent for treatment.

The leg's bad, that's for sure. Then, what wound isn't?

Back on the battlefield, there was a precipitous shift in momentum. Anticipating that Sheridan's plans would succeed by watching his leader and knowing his ability to accomplish difficult tasks through sheer will, as well as feeling the excitement of the troops, Captain DuPont, chief of artillery, followed his intuition and training. Without direct orders, he quickly moved nine big guns—an assortment of rifled and twelve-pounders—to a hill overlooking Cedar Creek. From that vantage point, he could clearly see, six hundred yards away, that the retreating Confederate Army was jammed up on the Turnpike.

DuPont smiled and ordered. "Fire at will. Take 'em out, men! It's a gawd damn turkey shoot!"

Initial fire was so fast and so accurate that the retreat became a flight for survival. Soldiers left artillery, caissons, supply wagons, ambulances, enough rifles to outfit several companies, and more than a hundred horses in the road as they took off in every direction to escape the cannonade.

After three rounds of fire, DuPont's battery came under fire from a Confederate battery on a neighboring hillock less than a mile away, causing DuPont to redirect two of his cannons in a long-range cannon duel.

Just as DuPont launched his cannonade, the Ninth was storming up the hill toward intricate breastworks that had been overrun by the Rebels eight hours previously. Withering rifle fire poured down at the advancing men, but many of the bullets were high as shooting downhill was a tricky business. The first attack was repulsed. The regiment quickly regrouped. The second charge was without hesitation as the Ninth swarmed up the hill.

The terrain C Company was slotted into was fairly free of big boulders and other natural obstructions. The advance went quickly and returning fire from the breastworks, while heavy early on in the assault, diminished rapidly as Confederate soldiers left cover to find escape routes to the south.

First to reach the breastworks was Private John T. Morrow, a fairly new recruit from Waterford, a transfer from F Company just six days previously. He captured the Confederate unit and battle flag, and waved it frantically from the topside of a fallen tree.

Darkness settled over the valley as men of the Ninth sank to the ground inside the protective wall they had built…and from which they were evicted that same morning.

It had been a day of scalding defeat…and glorious victory, as well as professional and personal vindication.

The South's four-year reign as master of the Shenandoah was over. Forever. While neither side yet knew it, the three battles for ownership of the Shenandoah Valley in the last month spelled the true beginning of the end of what the Union called the Southern Rebellion.

After a fitful night's sleep filled with nightmares about canister and grapeshot, and piles of arms and legs outside a surgeon's tent, Charles and McGuire carefully loaded a wounded man on a flatcar. The soldier, unconscious from the pain (or the opium-water slipped him by the surgeon), was eased up onto the second from the end of a thirteen-car train on the Manassas Gap Railroad line.

They carefully moved him toward the middle of the car and stacked heavy, rectangular supply crates around him to minimize movement. Sergeant Reilly didn't move. In fact, he hadn't moved since they carried him from camp, not even when loaded on an ambulance and bounced over more than two miles of ditchy road to the railroad crossing.

A soldier from the Twenty-third Massachusetts, missing his left arm at the elbow, assured them he would watch over their comrade, make sure he got water, and was handled proper when the train got into Washington. The soldier's eyes burned with fever. Despite the relatively coolness of the day, riverlets of sweat coursed down his stubbled cheeks.

"Thank you," Charles said, and meant it, wondering if the soldier would remember the promise when it was time to keep it.

Quitting the flatcar, they watched the engineer board the train by grasping the two metal rods attached to the engine and dragging his bulbous body into the dark, hot interior. Without fanfare, without any human noise at all—just a mechanical groan—the train started moving. It moved slowly at first, then faster, as fire pushed steam onto pistons, which spun the wheels on the slick tracks in a search for friction.

Charles and McGuire stood there, silent, until the last car disappeared from view, each man lost in individual and collective thoughts.

"He won't make five miles 'fore he's gone," McGuire said. He looked at the ground, holding his gaze on a burrowing doodlebug between his scuffed boots. "At least, we won't have to watch him die."

Closing his eyes to the awful truth, Charles fingered Sister Bloody's rosary, sewn into the deep crease of his pants pocket. He stared at the emptiness of the tracks, and thought about his life in general and the wounded man on the disappearing flatcar in particular. He thought about what his drummer-mate had just said.

Wrong. So, so wrong. We've already watched him die.

Jesus God! When will this war ever end?

CHAPTER 30

News. Glorious News.

> *News of battle! News of battle!*
> *Hark. 'Tis ringing down the street*
> *And the archways and the pavement*
> *Bear the clang of hurrying feet.*
> *News of battle. Who has brought it?*
> William Edmonstoune Aytoun

Early November, 1864

Charles had been waiting on the peddler for two days. The old man with the youngish wife who always sat beside him on the high-seated wagon usually showed up on Tuesdays or Wednesdays. Here it was Thursday and there was no sign of him.

"Wonder where he be?" Brean said, passing by Charles en route to fetch the company's rations from the cook tent.

"I don't know. I hope he comes today."

Stopping, Brean put a hand on Charles' shoulder. "You sure like to read, don'cha? Have you read every single *Harper's Weekly* that's been published since you joined up?"

"I missed some, but I sure do like to read *Harper's*. Those pictures are somethin'. I bet they have somethin' on Cedar Creek this time."

"Well," Brean said, "if they do, you'll have to read it to me and the boys."

After getting some water and a Quaker shingle to gnaw on, Charles went back to the Mooresfield Road. There! In the distance, coming over the slight rise, was the peddler's wagon.

Within minutes, the peddler, a bear of a man with a chest-length gray beard, hard, black eyes, and a guttural way of spitting out words, pulled up in front of the boys.

"Jah, it's da boy again, Mootilda. Betcha I know vhy he vaits for oos? He lacks to read da pahper, jah?"

Charles started to nod but caught himself when he noticed the peddler's wife smiling at him.

The peddler drew himself up as tall as possible. "So, Union soljer boy, cat's gut yore tong. Or, mavee, somting else, jah? Lack my Mootilda?" His voice contained a smile; his face was a thunderhead.

"Oh, er-oh, no, sir. I was just thinking about what I needed from you this week."

"Andre, right? I betcha I know vhat you vant, right Mootilda? You vant hod candies and da new newspobber, jah? Gots just vun Harber's left." He reached in a big box behind the spring seat and drew out a wadded up twelve-page paper and handed it to Charles. *Harper's,* November fifth, 1864.

"Dat's tah-vinty cents, Andre. I been savin' dat pobber for you for fit-ty mills."

"Twenty cents? But *Harper's* has always been ten before?" Charles quickly glanced at the top of the front page. "It says right here, ten cents."

"I know. I know. But it's tah-venty cents if you vant it. But you read it and keep it nice und clean und I buy it back next veek for five."

A line of men had formed behind Charles and the volume of grumbling started to rise. Two minutes later, with six sucking candies in his pocket—two mushies like the saltwater taffy he had longed for in New Orleans and three spongy, licorice rocks—and the *Harper's* folded under his arm (and indecent thoughts of "Mootilda" swimming in his head*)*—he marched back to camp. He was twenty-three cents poorer and not a bit happy about it.

Matilda. What's she want an old thievin' coot like him for, anyway?

The campfire nearest his tent was crowded with about a dozen soldiers hovering close to the fire to ward off as much of the late afternoon chill as possible. But they made room for Charles when they saw he had a *Harper's* or as one soldier called it, "The picture paper."

The questions came fast.

"What's the news?"

"Anythin' in there 'bout us?"

"Did they ever say anythin' about Fisher's Hill or Cedar Creek?"

As he was waiting for his candies, Charles had glanced over the small headlines and had already picked out a couple of articles to read to the men. Normally, a quiet, shy boy, Charles enjoyed sharing his reading ability with his comrades, and even took pride in his growing confidence to speak in front of his peers.

He stepped to the middle of the circle, near the blazing fire and held the paper in front of him. "There's a story in here about a dust-up out in San Francisco—that's in California—about some men tore down a statue of Buddha for some reason or another."

"Buddha. What's Buddha?" a voice called out.

"Has somethin' to do with religion. The picture shows a little fat China statue-guy sittin' and smilin'."

"We don't want to hear about no Buddha," a man sang out.

"Read about us whippin' the slobberjaws out of Early and runnin' him out of the valley!"

A mighty cheer went up, but ceased when Charles held up the front page of the *Harper's*, turning it in a circle for all to see.

An etching of General Sheridan, alone on a galloping horse on the Winchester Road dominated the page. The hazy background showed two ghost-like gun-bearing figures waving him on. Charles read the short title: "Phil Sheridan riding to the front."

Loud talk fluttered up like heated air bubbles from a boiling stew.

"He did that at Cedar Creek, he sure did!"

"Rode right down here from Winchester and gathered us all up and we whupped the damn Rebs, we did!"

Charles held up a hand and shouted to calm the chatter, "Here's one short one everybody will like," he said. "It's from the 'Executive Mansion, Washington, October twenty-second, 1864.' It's addressed to Major General Sheridan. 'With great pleasure I tender to you and your brave army the thanks of the nation and my own personal admiration and gratitude for the month's operation in the Shenandoah Valley.'" He paused for effect as the men clapped and shouted. The shouts drew more men to the campfire.

Clearing his throat to shush the men, Charles read on: "It continues on: '...Shenandoah Valley, and especially for the splendid work of October nineteenth. Your obedient servant,' (long pause and a slight smile), Abraham Lincoln."

The shouts of the gathering echoed off the surrounding hills. There was much back-slapping and yelps of sheer pleasure.

Shouts of "Read some more!" pushed Charles into reading accounts of Fisher's Hill. "The Nineteenth Corps on the right, the Sixth in the center, and the recovered Eighth Corps on the left.... The rebel line was completely broken...all lost guns were recaptured.... More than thirty-five hundred prisoners were captured includin' three hundred officers."

As each number was tolled, the men cheered. But the biggest cheer of all blasted forth with a single line, which Charles delivered with a sense of unmistakable pride: "The entire rebel loss is estimated at about ten thousand."

The men clamored for more. "Cedar Creek. We want to hear about Cedar Creek!"

"Right here. It's right here," Charles said, pointing to an inside page.

For the next fifteen minutes more than a hundred soldiers sat enthralled as the slight drummer boy read the newspaper account of the battle of Cedar Creek. Even though they knew the start, middle, and ending of the battle, each man hung on every word.

"...Sheridan came on the field, ridin', says one of his staff, 'so that the devil himself could not have kept up.' A staff officer (Charles' aside: 'Who shall go unnamed,' was met with derisive hoots.) meeting him pronounced the situation of the army to be 'awful.'

"'Pshaw!' said Sheridan. 'It's nothin' of the sort. It's all right, or we'll by gawd fix it right!'"

Charles paused for an offered drink of water.

He read on and on, about how Sheridan was greeted with a kiss on the cheek by the ebullient George Custer when the diminutive general arrived on the battlefield, how he rode up and down the line to rally his troops, and personally took charge of the field of operations, ordering first a cavalry charge, then a full advance by all troops.

The men who had lived that day, lived through that battle, sat enthralled. Eyes glazed over as they stared into the fire, each man lost in his own thoughts about his contribution during the decisive battle.

Charles read on: "The roar of musketry now had a gleeful, dancin' sound. The guns fired shafted salutes of victory." The rural volunteers hooted at the glorified images; those with classic prose studies in their background nodded knowingly and in appreciation of the mishmash of forced verbiage.

Warming to the appreciative audience and without even realizing it, Charles raised the dramatic bar little by little, lowering his voice to almost a whisper to quiet the men, then raising it for maximum effect.

"Custer and Merritt, chargin' in on right and left, doubled up the flanks of the foe, takin' prisoners, slashin', killin', drivin' as they went. The march of the infantry was more majestic, and more terrible."

He ended the last six words in a loud voice, pounding each word with tongue haymakers. The shouting was at fever pitch when he held up his hand for quiet. All eyes were on him as he read on.

"Beyond Middleton, on the battle-field fought over in the mornin', their columns were completely overthrown and disorganized. They," he said with a overstated flair, "fled along the pike…(he paused) and over the hills like SHEEP!"

The resulting tumult spooked the caisson horses in a nearby make-shift corral.

There was more, lots more, but Charles knew enough to quit when he was ahead. As he was pushing his way through the crowd of men, a soldier from the Thirteenth Connecticut that he knew from working with him on surgeon tent duty, said, "I'd like to borrow your paper, if you don't mind. I can read some."

Charles told the man he still had a lot of reading to do himself, but had a second thought: "I'll rent it to you for five cents. It's a good deal. You get to read it for half price," he said, quickly pointing to the front page price. And what do you do with a paper you done read? Use it to start kindling, no?"

No hesitation: "For how long."

"Two hours."

Within the next two days, Charles "rented" the Harper's Weekly to six different soldiers.

Ten cents profit, seven, if you count the candy. Not bad. Wish I had thought of it sooner.

For almost two months, the Union army stayed put in the valley, in minicamps, scattered but close at hand in case the Rebel Army decided to take offense of the new neighbors and stir up new trouble. The comings and goings of army units had never made much sense to Charles and many of the other men. They followed orders, going in the direction they were told and stopping when ordered to do so.

But the movements of the Ninth from early December 1864 to January 1865 made less sense than usual.

Encamped along Cedar Creek more than a month, the unit was finally ordered ten miles northeast to Camp Russell. It was a depressing march. Mile after mile of burned-over cropland and pastures, blackened remains of barns, grain storage sheds, small grist mills, and more than a few houses reminded the soldiers they were part and parcel of the Union's "torched earth" policy. The intent of the distasteful practice was to deprive the Confederate Army of the agricultural bounty for which the valley was known. The end result accomplished that, without a doubt.

But the scenes the marching army saw that day did not sit easy on the collective mind's eye. It was a hard man indeed who, when first catching sight of the devastation, did not think of his own home and hearth.

How would I feel if this were done to my land, my home, my family?

There was an uncommon quiet to this army's movement; it was almost as if the soldiers were afraid to make any noise in fear of offending...

Who? What? These people know who burned them out. It's not like it's a secret.

In a distinct break from the norm, sad smiles briefly formed on many faces as the Blankenship farm came into view. Neighboring farms to the north, south, and west of the farm were blackened and bleak. The late fall lushness of the rolling pastureland and patch of sweet corn of the Blankenship farm was a rainbow of color.

When the cavalry had passed through, torching everything in its path, they had leap-frogged the Blankenship farm. As was promised.

Mrs. Blankenship apparently saw the soldiers out the window and came onto the porch. Just like when the men first saw her, she was carrying Sarah.

Some men helloed and waved. She may have nodded, but there was no outward display of appreciation for the conquering army leaving her place intact in the midst of so much wanton destruction.

It's good to see her place spared. But, why do I feel worser than ever.

January, 1864,
Three weeks later, just enough time to get settled and feel somewhat at "home," they marched through Camp Sheridan, Virginia, and bivouacked just up the road at Stevenson Depot.

Ten days passed before the battalion was loaded on the *General Sedgwick*. This time Fort Monroe in Hampton, Virginia was the destination. Upon arrival, the troops disembarked and made night camp nearby. During the night, rations for fifteen days was loaded on the transport and at seven o'clock the following morning, the soldiers were ordered to reboard the ship.

Rumors spread like wildfire as the battalion's destination was not immediately communicated from the commanders nor non-commissioned officers. Healy opened his sealed orders at sea and sent his officers around the ship to tell the men the destination was Savannah, Georgia. On the trip south, the men could easily see the results of other battles: Masts of the sunken Rebel blockading ships stuck out of the water off Charleston, South Carolina; the skeletal remains of burned seaside homes dotted the shoreline; a solitary Rebel flag, flapping gaily from the uppermost branches of a majestic oak, waved defiantly at passing ships.

Nearing the mouth of the Savannah River, the steamer dropped anchor off Tyree Island, home of a stunningly beautiful lighthouse. Several men, Charles included, sat on the foredeck well into the night. They watched the lighthouse and talked, much as they did around a campfire when in camp.

The next morning the large transport stopped at the river's mouth. Deterred from entering the river by a line of sunken vessels and felled trees left as a farewell present from the retreating southern army, they waited as armies do when plans devised far away go awry.

Arrangements were made to ferry the men to the town located several miles upriver. A flotilla of small craft—fishing boats, skiffs and bateaus—transferred the Ninth soldiers upriver. Once in the city, commanders separated the companies, then slid the units into groups of twos and threes to march to various bivouac locations throughout the town. Companies A, B, and C set up camp just a couple of blocks from the river, in a small wooded park in the center of town. Nearby buildings included a general mercantile store, laundry, livery stable, and hotel. A cemetery abutted their campground to the south; they faced their tents away from more than a hundred graves, new earth still evident.

The next few weeks were uneventful: Daily drills, including uniform inspections and drummed marches through the streets of the town, kept the men occupied for part of the day. Most of the men had regular chores, but afterwards it was a lazy existence. They cleaned up the campsite, played games, took walks around town, or went fishing in the river.

Charles worked hard to be of help to the surgeons and aides. Even when battle wounds were not the order of the day, soldiers were a sickly lot. Always focused on learning whatever he could about the dark mysteries of "healing," Charles was constantly tested by Surgeon McNeil or one of the long-term aides on his growing medicinal acumen.

When time allowed, Charles and Brean and other men tested their mettle by swimming across the Savannah River to one of two islands. Fig was a small island slightly downstream with only a few fishing families attached to it via boats tied to trees on the banks; Hutchinson was a larger island just across from the city center that was lush with well-appointed crops of corn, wheat, barley, and rice.

No 'torched earth' plan here. But this ain't the Shenandoah.

A new camp meant new information flowed in; a settled army was an army that could be found and long-held mail finally reached the Ninth. A new camp also meant new campfire tales. One of the soldiers who had a Georgia cousin fighting for the Confederacy named off some of the southern regiments fighting in the Shenandoah campaign. When he got to "First Louisiana Volunteers," Charles said, a bit too loud: "Where'd you hear that? Was that for certain?"

Before the man could answer, Charles stormed off toward a small creek, deep in thought.

First Louisiana. Ian's outfit. We was fightin' against Ian. I wish I could have seen him. But I'm glad I didn't. Not there.

A favorite story concerned a letter sent to President Lincoln from Major General William Tecumseh Sherman, who sent a telegraph on the previous Christmas Day that read:

His excellency
President Lincoln
I beg to present you as a Christmas gift the City of Savannah with 150 heavy guns and plenty of ammunition and also about 25,000 bales of cotton.

Victory in battle and stories about victories in camp can create a strange euphoria. The boys of the Ninth hoorahed about that story for a long spell.

Charles was doing chores around the command tent in early February when Colonel Healy was reading aloud a claim of a "Mrs. Delannoy" against the United States of America to a group of young officers. It was the lady's claim that Sherman's army, at the end of their Path of Destruction campaign across the heartland of the South, had confiscated the following items: "a horse, twelve hogs, 200 gallons of syrup, 250 bushels of corn, 100 bushels of peas, twenty-five bushels of rye, 300 bushels of sweet potatoes, a hundred poultry (chickens, ducks, and turkeys), grain, carpets and rail fencing carpenters tools."

Turning to a subordinate, Healy said, "See if you can find the carpenters' tools and carpet, among our ranks. If found, return them to the lady. No need to look for the food. If you found any of it, the lady probably wouldn't want it back in its new condition."

CHAPTER 31

Goin' Home...Wherever Home Is

*Home is a name, a word, it is a strong one;
stronger than magician ever spoke,
or spirit ever answered to....*
Charles Dickens

April 18, 1865.
The war was officially over with the surrender of Lee's army at Appomattox Courthouse in Virginia. It would be more than four days before the word reached the Ninth Connecticut; it would be almost four months before the regiment was cut loose from the District of Port Royal, S.C., Department of the South. The soldiers were going home.
Wherever home is.

Charles was already feeling lonely, even though the regiment had not even left yet. His chest felt constricted; there was a fluttering inside, the flailing dark wings of anxiety—or fear.
The men of the Ninth, more than three hundred strong, stood in slouchy formations, waited in scattered bunches for the order to board the ship. As excited and giddy as teenage girls at their first cotillion, they awaited the order to board the *J.R. Spaulding,* a hulking, low-waver of a ship bound for New York, then Hartford. Then home, wherever that might take the individual ex-soldiers.

Despite offers from several of his comrades—McGuire and Brean and James Grady of Norwich, plus other not-close friends but older soldiers concerned about the young man's future—Charles had decided to head home. His home. The only home he knew: New Orleans. In that decision he was not alone. More than twenty soldiers were going back to Louisiana, most having left at daybreak, walking east to the railway station. They planned to catch the first train west, if there was room. A couple of men—Peter Devlin and Benjamin Joram—were going to walk for a "spell," as Devlin said, "just to shake the army dust off my boots and the confounded orders out of my head. Then, I'll figure out what to do."

Charles didn't want to spend any of his money on train fare just yet. He had three hundred and eighty-six dollars and thirty-six cents—nineteen twenty dollar gold eagles, a five dollar gold piece and a dollar and thirty-six cents in pocket-rattling money—from saved pay, clothing allowance, and his sign-up bonus. He was free to do what he liked for the first time in almost… well, forever, it seemed, and especially the last two-plus years. He was determined to not make quick decisions.

His plan, bubbling around in his thoughts for more than a month, was to head out toward New Orleans at a leisurely pace, resting when he felt like it, working when he needed to, moving on when it suited him.

When he had told Brean of his plans, his friend said he was making a mistake. "Think about it, boy-o, afore you go walkin' yourself off back to Kingdom Cotton. After what General Butler did to the town, and what with the toll the war took on your city, after what we did in the Shenandoah and what Sherman did to Georgia, do you think they want an orphaned Union soldier showin' up on their doorstep? And what about gettin' home? In that uniform, carryin' that drum, do you think you will be greeted warmly by those that was made to suffered during the war?"

Charles took the questions as rhetorical, nodding pleasantly at the appropriate places, but without commenting.

Home may be something less than perfect. But it's still home.
Or at least it used to be.

He wondered what New Orleans was like now.

How much did St. Mary's suffer through the hard times that always accompany war? Was Sister Bloody still there… and still the prettiest and kindest and sweetest lady-saint-nun on the planet?

Did Ian make it through the war? And Sarie Beth...?
Sweet Lord. So many questions. So few answers.

Charles was jerked alert by a call to arms by the bugler from the Thirty-Fifth Massachusetts, on loan for the day. Eager to be on their way, the men started pushing and shoving toward the single-file gangplank from the dock to the break in the ship's railing. But Captain Lee barked an order: "Men of the Ninth. We came here as soldiers and we will go back to our wives and sweethearts—and we all hope they never meet—" The happy shouts of long-abused and tired men going home stopped his speech solid.

He raised his hands for quiet. "As I was a-saying, we came from the Great State of Connecticut, most of us anyway, this great bunch I'm proud to call the Irish Brigade, as soldiers. We rode out proud and, by gawd, we will return the same way. Quit fighting like school boys and get in your companies and prepare to board ship, starting with A Company."

With no more complaints and more than a modicum of testosterone-laced jocularity, the smiling men pushed and shoved their way through irregular man-clusters, jostling for prime boarding positions and joking with soldiers from their respective companies.

It was easy to see, on some level, that Charles wanted to join them. Brean gave it one last try, shouting, "Come on, Charles, join us. Bring that confounded tiny, snapping drum and beat us a tune so we can march up that board without falling in the damn ocean. And then you git yourself onboard so you can go back and keep your promise to Lucy!"

Charles nervously grinned to hide a creeping sadness. He straightened his back, shifted his drum from the sling he had rigged so it lay flat against his back, marched to the gangplank and starting beating out the tune to *Molly McCree*. Happy faces splashed down on him from the ranks and from the officers hanging on the ship's railing as first one, then two, then six drummer boys—McGuire, Brean, Edward Dillon, Thomas Cavanaugh, and Michael Otis marched up alongside Charles and quickly picked up the rhythm.

Charles noticed several of the drummers didn't move out of their clustered companies to join them.

Could be they just tired and want to go home. Or they just tired of drummin'.

Don't blame them. Much.

"Well, what'cha waitin' for?" a sergeant shouted. "An engraved invitation from the Duchess Her Own High Self from Savannah? On my order: Forward, march!"

Led by the flag bearer of A Company, and following close on the heels of its officers, the first group marched up the gangplank, followed by the remaining companies. It took almost an hour for the men to get on the ship via the narrow gangplank.

The drummers kept up a steady beat. As the last man marched past, Brean hollered across three drummers. "One more time, Andre. Come with us. You can stay with me and my family for a while. You know you'd love it there. In her last letter Lucy asked if you were comin' home with me!"

Keeping his eyes straight ahead and his shoulders straight, Charles said, "You didn't say nothin' afore about Lucy askin' about me. You're just makin' it up, s'all!"

Brean smiled large. "Well, maybe she didn't come right out and want to know if you were comin' home with me for a spell, but I knowed she wants you to."

Keeping a perfect beat, Charles winked and thanked him. "Go on, Mister Brean. March up that plank and beat that skin all the way up there. You're on your way home, friend! I've got to do what I've got to do. Tell Miss Lucy I may make it Connecticut some day, not to see your sorry hide, but to come courtin' her in a proper manner. But not this trip. I've got people I've got to see first."

Within minutes, the steamship's lines were untied and tossed aboard. Belching smoke like a ripe pipe, the ship started slowly moving toward the main channel. Charles stood there, watching friends and acquaintances, waspish campfire liars and nimble-fingered dicemen, surgeons and drummers…all heading home.

He didn't plan on watching the ship until it disappeared. But he did. And even after it disappeared around a left hook in the dredged channel, he stood there.

There goes a part of me. A life now past.

Turning to face the main road leading toward the bustling town center, he thought he had never seen a more lonely place.

What's down that road for me? What now? Qu'après? What next?

Two hours later, Charles walked out of the Sturgess Emporium on River

Street a new man. At least he thought so. Besides, that's what Emmerett Sturgess, the proprietor, had told him as he was sizing him up in his new clothes. Spending twenty-eight dollars was a hard decision, especially on store-bought clothes and traveling gear.

But he was proud of his purchases and thought he had done well in his first major retail transaction. His lot was a hefty bundle: Two pairs of linsey-woolsey pants; a pair of two-button, pullover shirts, one off-white, one dark blue; a pair of Amsterdam longjohns; two new pairs of carded cotton socks; a pair of high-topped brogans with extra-thick soles; and a creamy nightshirt with a nice feel to it. Presented with the total bill, Charles nodded, then went to the other side of the store and turned his back to store clerk. He withdrew an old, worn-out sock, which had more hand-darned stitches than thread count, and carefully unrolled it. Palming two twenty dollar gold pieces, he rolled the remaining hard money back into a tight sock ball and replaced it in his knapsack. He silently cursed himself for not getting the money out before entering the store.

He had already calculated that one set of new clothes, plus his uniform and shoes, would not fit in his knapsack. The well-worn, dirt-and-sweat decorated bag was already busting at the seams from trail memories, as he referred to the booty. In addition to holding his one extra shirt and pair of holey socks, Surgeon Rollin had given him a sheathed surgeon's knife as a keepsake. He also had a fistful of minie balls he had plucked from the bloody ground around the surgeon's operating table.

Some things you want to forget, but shouldn't.

He also had his prized tintype of Lucy, whom his friends kiddingly called his "New Haven darlin'." He had shown it sparingly, not liking gummy fingerprints on the faded image. The stiff, wool blanket was rolled up tight around a short rope, and cinched at both ends with twine so it would lie on his back to cushion his drum.

After studying on it a spell, he plopped down seventy-five cents for a like-new Confederate knapsack to sling alongside his own and ninety-five cents for a hat with a tiny curled brim and a rounded crown.

Not as good as the Messkin gigolo, but it'll have to do.

Turning his attention to what he would need over the next several days, Charles picked out a smallish, shiny tin pot, a slightly larger skillet, a folding fork-and-knife contraption, a pound of dried beans, half pound of coffee, two handfuls of sugar (dumped in a tightly woven sack), one of salt in a tobacco pouch, a pound of salted beef rib meat, and a small sack of flour.

He added a sweet potato, two apples and a small tin of sweet crackers to his booty, paying out an additional eighteen cents.

That'll get me through several days and let's see how far I can get down the road.

Two knapsacks filled with necessities and assorted treasures, a bedroll, and a drum.

It's not a tidy kit and caboodle, but it'll get the job done.

It was getting late. Facing the pinkish glow in the western sky, Charles figured he had walked close to thirteen miles since leaving Savannah. It was not a typical march, more like a leisurely stroll. A real long, leisurely stroll down a narrow, rutted road. At first, traffic heading into town had been steady. But the further he walked, the number of buggies, horsemen, and wagons dwindled from a steady stream to a trickle.

Charles inhaled a headful of air.

River-scrubbed laundry.

The air was uncluttered by the nose-hair wrinkling smells of thousands of unwashed soldiers. It was clean and clear. Charles took it as a good sign.

He eyed an approaching stand of trees—mainly oak and hickory—as a potential campsite. A lonely, sad-looking farmhouse, drooping from age and possibly concussion blasts from artillery bursts that had split the nearby ground, sat about ten big steps from the road's edge. A shadowy figure was leaning against one of the four tree poles holding up the porch roof. Charles flopped a casual wave and nod; if there was any response, he didn't catch it. Walking just a few steps, he thought that the woods probably belonged to the family at the house, so he retraced his steps. The leaning figure had not moved.

"Excuse me, sir," Charles said. "I was wonderin' if you mind if I camped in those woods up yonder. I'd be real careful and not leave nothin' but my footprints when I leave in the mornin'."

A blast of silence was followed by: "I mind."

"Excuse me?"

"Are you deef? I said, 'I mind.' I mind because I figure you don't want to drown. If you want to stay there and get wet, go right ahead 'cause it's gonna come a frog-strangler tonight, that's for sure."

Charles looked at the woods, which were disappearing in the spreading gloom. "Well, thank you, anyway. I'll find another place to stay."

The figure cleared his throat. "You can stay on the porch if you want. The rain is comin' from the backside of the house, so the porch should be dry. I'd invite you to stay in the cabin but I have two young daughters and it's a small place so it wouldn't be seemly, you understand."

"Yessir, I surely do. That's right kind of you. And I thank you for your hospitality."

The tall man struck a store match to light his pipe. In the flickering flame, Charles saw a gaunt face with a frightful headful of hair and a flowing beard that dropped almost to his waist.

Charles stayed where he was, awaiting further invitation.

"You a Yankee." A statement, not a question.

"Ninth Connecticut. Drummer. Originally from New Orleans. Heading home."

The obvious question emerged from the swirl of pipe smoke. "You got a name?"

"Charles Andre. Father and mother were French. 'Fore the war I lived in New Orleans."

"General Butler ran that place, didn't he?"

"Yessir, he did. 'Beast' they call him down on Canal Street. He didn't have no friends give him a send-off party when he left and that's a fact."

"Name's Henry Matthew Gilroy. Come on up on the porch, Mister Andre. Got anythin' to eat?"

"Oh, yessir. I bought some things in town, a potato and crackers and such."

He drew on the long-stem pipe clinched in his teeth. A mountain of smoke billowed from the topside of the beard. "We're having stew. Marcy made some fresh bread. We have milk and well water. Save your potato and crackers." With that, he quit the porch, leaving Charles standing at the edge of the lane. After fighting on several fronts of self-doubt, Charles opened the plain wood latch-gate and hesitantly made his way to the porch. He sat down to the right side of the short steps, careful not to walk on the bedraggled daisies and cornflowers lining the porch. He noticed the steps and the porch were in need of repair.

Forearms on thighs, in the failing light he watched a meandering earthworm skirt scruffs of grass, looking for... *what, exactly?* The worm's movements mesmerized Charles—starting, stopping, bending its body in acute, curved angles, searching, always in motion, searching.

Not unlike an army regiment on the hunt looking for a scrape. Or a place to hide out.

The opening of the front door caused him to jump. Two quick giggles. His head swiveled toward the noise. He couldn't see her features, but he instinctively knew she was pretty. Maybe it was the way the backlight from array of candles on the mantle glowing through the half-open door halo-ed her hair. Or the way she was standing, the toes of her simple shoes together, hands clasped in front of her, head cocked to the left ever so slightly. Maybe it was just because she was a budding female and he was about to turn eighteen.

"I didn't think a soldier would scare so easy." The voice was lyrical and breathless and full of promise.

"Well, I'm not a soldier, just a drummer. And I was studyin' somethin' on the ground. When I get to studyin', I sometimes block out things."

"Just a drummer? But didn't you wear a uniform and everythin'? What were you studyin'?"

Charles hesitated before answering. "I had a uniform but I call them that fights 'soldiers'. Me, I'm just...was just...a skin-beater. That's what real soldiers call us what drum in the army. As far as studyin', nothin' much. Just a tirin' day, that's all."

That's just what I need! To tell this girl I was watching an earthworm trying to find...something!

The girl hadn't moved from the spot just outside the door. "I normally don't talk to young men without proper introduction." It was an invitation, pure and simple.

Grabbing his new hat off his head with his left hand, he stood quickly. "Charles Andre, formerly with the Ninth Connecticut, C Company, at your service, ma'm." He gave a short bow from the waist, never taking his eyes off the intriguing half-shadow.

"Martha Lou Gilroy, but everybody calls me Marcy, and pleased to meet you, Charles Andre. My sister's Matilda, but she goes by Maddie. Do you have a middle name or will just plain Charles have to do?"

Confusion slapped him back, triggering a coughing fit. "Sah-sorry," he stammered, trying to catch his breath.

Middle name. Why don't I have a middle name?

She wants a middle name!

The fight by the river floated into his thoughts. "I'm Charles Montgomery Andre. So very pleased to meet you, Miss Marcy Lynn Gilroy."

"Lou?"

"Who? What?"

"Lou, my middle name's Lou. You said 'Lynn.'"

Charles' eyes lit up. "There's nothing worse than calling some pretty girl by the wrong name. I need a knife. Do you have to have a fairly sharp one in the house, if it's not too much trouble?"

The girl looked at him strangely, her brow knitted until her eyebrows almost touched. "Knife? Why would you be needing a knife?"

"Why, to cut out my tongue, of course. My tongue offended you and I shall cut it out and feed it to the crows."

Marcy Gilroy dissolved in laughter and Charles joined in, self-conscious as always but happy at making his new acquaintance laugh.

A shadow blocked out the candlelight. "Marcy, you and the young man come on in to supper. Matilda has the table set, something you should have been helping with." The tone was stern, but carried with it an undertow of caring.

"Sorry, Paw," the lithe girl said, darting between him and the door jam.

"Come on in, Mister Andre. And welcome."

Simple as the dinner was—meatless stew, skillet-seared potato and onion hash, bread with fresh-churned butter, sweet milk, and hot, dark, syrupy coffee—to Charles it was a feast.

Not one Quaker shingle in sight. Now, that's a fine meal indeed!

In strong, direct candlelight, Marcy was a stunning girl: Hair the color of damp straw, light blue eyes with what looked like golden flecks enhanced by the light from the bobbing candle flames, and a blanket of freckles across a slightly upturned nose. Her sister was...different. Maddie had darker, straight hair that ended well below her waist; she had doll's eyes—dark, shiny buttons. A tall girl (several inches taller than Charles), she moved more like a man than a woman, taking big steps and clomping with each one. When Charles entered the room, Maddie smiled and nodded in his direction. It was, he decided, a fake smile, one that darkened her entire face.

Unhappy. And rather pleased to be able to hold onto the feeling.

Marcy Lou asked Charles question after question. Maddie Elizabeth seemed to brighten at his answers and finally joined in:

"What was it like growing up in New Orleans?"
"How did you come to fight for the North?"
"What was it like being in battle?"
"Do you have a girl back in New Orleans?"
"Where are you headed now?"

Between bites, Charles answered all of the questions, most honestly, and some filled with information intended to paint images. He answered all in a way he hoped would ingratiate himself to the three Gilroys. He knew he was the night's entertainment and wanted to uphold his end of the bargain. As was his social style and bend, he chose his words carefully, saying little to impart sympathy or disgust in his benefactors.

He didn't mention St. Mary's, just noted that (without giving a year) his father, mother and older brothers died during a regular New Orleans "plague" along with hundreds of other folks.

He joined the Ninth Connecticut because one of his friends was from up that way and he just needed to get out of the city.

"But why didn't you join the Confederacy, bein' from the South and all," Marcy asked.

"He probably had his reasons, child," Henry Gilroy said, gently chiding his younger daughter in a measured tone.

Charles explained that New Orleans was a worldly city, with as many or more free negroes as there were slaves. He parroted the words of Sister Bloody, saying, "I was brought up to believe this was one nation and I didn't think it could survive as two. Too many takers in this world, especially the English and the French. Divide it up and somebody is gonna try and take part of it or all of it. That seems to be the way of the men."

Silence slid across the room, which seemed to get darker. Charles felt the air close in tight.

"Thoughtful answer," Henry nodded. "Not one I particularly agree with in this case, but it was...thoughtful."

Clearing his throat, Henry abruptly stood up, with all three teenagers following his lead. "I better get Young Andre situated 'fore the rain hits."

Biding goodnight to the Gilroy girls, both of whom flapped eyelids in a nervous way, Charles stepped back on the porch and started to unfold his blanket. Horizontal lightning split the sky. He couldn't see it directly, coming as the storm was from the back of the house; the front yard, road, and the woods to the other side of the rail fence lit up from Nature's fireworks. Charles walked to the edge of the porch and looked back to the south. Booming thunder—which sounded nothing like cannon fire—beat a fluttering rhythm against his chest.

The old man came to the door and handed him a fat quilt in the Drunkard's Path pattern. Charles mentioned the pattern to Henry, who nodded and said, "Josephine made it years ago. She died last spring." Charles didn't ask, figuring the man would elaborate if he were so inclined. He wasn't. The quilt was twice as big as his bedroll. "Here, take this for a ground cover. Some damp will edge up through the porch, and that's a fact. And, I'll put your drum in the house so's it don't get wet."

Without another word, he picked up the little, cloth-covered package, turned and went into the house. Charles threw a "thank you" in his direction but the door was already closed. He thought he heard a soft thud as the drum was placed on the floor just inside the door.

I hope I didn't offend him. He has been awfully generous and kind, inviting me into his home and all.

Folding the blanket over twice, Charles carefully placed it up against the cabin wall, beneath the single window. Using the knapsack that held his clothes for a pillow, he snuggled in. He let out a single, long sigh that coincided with the first sound of fat, dipper-sized splashy raindrops on the porch roof. Within a few seconds, the rain, aided by a straight, strong southern wind, slapped against the back of the house. The driving rain sounded like flapping sheets in a cyclone. While the edges of the porch got damp, the old man had been right: Charles' sleeping place was dry as a dusty road.

Without realizing it, he dozed off and awakened to the cool crispness associated with a recent rain, and the occasional drip from water puddling on the porch roof before running off. Mutterings from inside the house edged him closer to full-awake. He looked up at the window and could see what he took to be the shadows from a single candle slip along the glazed glass.

At first he couldn't make out what was being said, although he knew without knowing it that it was the old man talking to one of daughters.

Bits and pieces filtered through the cracks in the cabin wall; snippets of conversation flowed under the warped window and over the mismatched sill.

"But, Poppa," he heard *Marcy? Maddie?* say, "he seems…nice boy."

"…he is," the old man said in chopped phrases, "…he's got something inside I don't understand. His...are, well, away somewhere. He has a hard time looking...the eye. That's never...sign. War does strange things...man. He's young and seen way...of what's not right about the world. Besides, he has a different look that's hard to place. He looks like he don't...anywhere. No...arcy

Marcy!

it's best that when the...best be on his way."

Charles clutched the blanket close to his chin. His heartbeat rippled like a bird trapped in a cage in a roomful of cats. He didn't know why. A shroud of sadness fell over him; his chin fell, eyes closed slowly, face relaxed...and silent tears of the lonely ran down his cheeks.

Two hours before dawn, before the false dawn even, Charles eased open the cabin door. He felt to the right of the door and immediately touched his drum. With it and everything else in place, he headed west. Something in him wanted to talk to Mister Gilroy and his daughters and try and explain who he was and what he was looking for. But sharing feelings was not his way, never had been. Too much hurt, too much rejection. Too much chance of more hurt, more rejection.

As he scuffled down the heavily rutted road, staying to the slight crown between muddy ruts and water-filled ditch, he thought about the note scratched with a pencil nub he had left for the Gilroys on the porch, held down by a small rock. He went over the words in his mind.

> *Gillroy Fambly:*
> *Thank you for your Hospitalty. The Dinner last night was Good and as close to having a Family gathering as I had in my Life. You will be in my Thoths. I am gone Home to New Orleans. Wish me Luck. I wish you the Same.*
> *Chas. Andre*

Several weeks later Charles was still heading west, getting closer to Macon, Georgia, and getting concerned about the route he was taking. His going had been slow. Virtually every large plantation house, every spacious farm, had been burned over as part of Sherman's "scorched earth" march less than a year ago. Looking like lost souls searching for Purgatory, rail-thin former

Rebel soldiers, wearing tattered bits of gray uniforms, eyed Charles with suspicion, with more than a few challenging him in a menacing manner.

"Where you from, boy? Where you headed?"

"Dressed good 'nuff, you is. I need some money to eat. Give it here."

"Say, what'cha got wrapped up in that bedroll? Let's have a look-see!"

He had taken to walking off the road, near the edge of woods when cover was provided, or well off the road to avoid direction confrontation. When approaching a homestead or upon seeing or hearing an approaching horse, wagon or buggy, Charles made every effort to pass it unseen. He went around six small towns and took to keeping odd change (adding up to just a tad more than two dollars) in his pants pocket in case someone he didn't care to fight or couldn't run from demanded money. He wanted no truck with those seeking revenge for deeds done. His singular goal was to pass unnoticed by local residents, regardless of feelings, regardless of wartime loyalties—evident or hidden.

He replenished his rations—two pickled eggs, pound of salted beef, two potatoes, two apples, coffee, a handful of sugar and one of salt—from a peddler he spied from his hidey-hole in a viney thicket just off the road near Griswoldville. He hello-ed the peddler from the woods, and in so doing scared the elderly traveling merchant in the process. But Charles was quickly able to assure him his intentions were to buy provisions, not steal them.

"Where you headed?" the peddler queried. After hearing "New Orleans," he offered: "Best keep headin' north a bit. There's been some trouble with Yankees travelin' south over the past several weeks. At least, that's the road word."

How did he know I fought for the North?

"You did fight for the North, right? I can usually tell. You still got a little sand in your craw yet and don't looked whipped like the Johnny Rebs around these parts. You don't look mad 'nuff to spit neither. That's another sign the losing side gives out."

Sand in my craw? What's a 'craw,' anyway?

Charles chose his foodstuffs from baskets and wooden boxes in the covered wagon and dug out a silver dollar from inside his small cooking pot, one of seven hiding places for his hoard of money. The peddler took the dollar and after studying it front and back, he popped it in his left vest pocket and counted out twenty cents in change from a small, tightly stitched cotton bag hanging from his belt. Charles carefully counted the coins: three copper nickels, a three-center, and two bronze pennies.

"Thank you, kindly," he said, touching his hand to his hat brim. He stepped back from the wagon.

"I'm heading up the road about four miles, then cutting back to the main road toward Atlanta. You're welcome to ride if you want to?"

Charles eyed the peddler and his mind put the simple offer through a mental colander. "I bet Atlanta is worse off than these parts. That's where Sherman did the most damage, true?"

The peddler shook his head to get rid of a sad expression that had grown on his face, out of place, like a flower growing out of a split rock.

"True enough. Not much left up that way. But it's still good business for a businessman like myself, and if you were to ride along with me, and help out when I need it and put your knapsacks in the back so people don't question that drum-shaped parcel, then it might be a better route for you, don't you know."

Usually Charles studied a spell or two on such proposals but in two heartbeats, he was up on the spring seat and his gear was tucked in a front corner in the covered wagon bed.

In the first mile, Charles knew the peddler's story. Ramer Pious Watkins was a born-agin peddler. His grandfather and father had been peddlers, and he had been on the road with his own rig at fifteen. One night, bored of his own company, he attended a stump revival north of Cahaba, Alabama. The traveling Bible-thumper had touched some deep-down chord and in an eye-blink Watkins had been "washed in the spirit" and swore he heard the Lord commanding him to be a traveling preacher. Selling all his merchandise and outfitting his wagon with a big, folding tent, twenty or so chairs and a small, twelve-by-twelve, pop-up stage he built himself, he went on a self-ordained circuit. He went by the name of Brother Pious and "was doing quite dandily, at least in the spiritual way," as he put it, "when the Lord quit talking to me when I quit talking for him and started talking for myself."

He enjoyed being on stage, talking to people, to have them respond in a positive manner. But, "Dammit to hell, I damn near starved."

The aftermath of war—"This'un anyway."—and getting folks to spend money to get a dose of religion when food is hard to come by at any price "don't work together. I tried every trick in the book, but didn't do no good."

So, Watkins told Charles, "I rededicated my life…to being the best damn peddler there is. And, I like to think I stuck with my calling a bit, carrying several real good Bibles for sale. And I just charge what I paid, not a penny more. That's my tithe, if'n you know what I mean?"

As Watkins talked, Charles learned more and more about the man, who, at one point, confessed to be a sutler for a Confederate division during the early stages of the war. As he did with most things in life, he studied Watkins intensely. The older man looked to be about forty, maybe could have been a bit younger, with dark, wiry muttonchops and shaggy hair. A small, thin-lipped mouth stood atop a straight, strong chin; alert, dark brown cow-eyes sat close together astraddle a long, thin nose. It was hard not to notice and focus on his ears; they were largish, with the top of the left one dew-lapped at the top and standing at a ninety-degree from his head.

A closed buggy with both doors open.

The questions he did ask Charles were answered, straightforward for the most part.

After a couple of hours of talking and listening, mainly listening, and three stops for residents who seemed mildly interested in the wagon's contents…and the chance of possible credit…Charles fell asleep to the rhythm of the jostling wagon.

A particularly rough jostle of the rig passing over a bad rut jerked Charles awake.

"Glad to see you're still alive," Watkins said. "You musta been one tired pup."

Charles didn't take kindly to being called names, any names, but, as always, he let it pass.

Over the next several days, the peddler drove along the busy dirt road, stopping at every house and the occasional miniature tent city. Confederate soldiers who returned home to find their homes and crops burned, livestock gone and families scattered from here to yonder, seemed to congregate in selected open spaces in mutual misery. They lived off the land for the most part, some trying to grow fall crops—late cabbage, stunted and apt to stay that way, a few stalks of puny corn poking up, hidden potatoes in high grass (identified only by flat green tops) they knew wouldn't make it but were planted in a flash of hopeful futility.

Watkins knew they didn't have folding or rattling money, but he stopped just the same—to barter if they had something for exchange, to sympathize if they didn't. Charles began to admire the man; he was a honest businessman who gave nothing for free and didn't seem to give preferential treatment to one customer over another. His demeanor, however, seemed right-on in his expression of grief for the losses of the people he met. White and colored alike.

It was not just the white populous that was hurting. Some former slaves, not knowing what to do or where to run to, had simply stayed put. It was hard for Charles to imagine being a slave, much less staying where you were one when you do longer had to be or were forced to be.

But some, many, did just that.

The devil you know vs...

Without it ever being discussed, Charles started helping Watkins at every stop: Listening to the conversation, fetching items of interest without being told, carefully packing up after some small transaction was completed. He listened to the patterned dickering, learning the nuances of conversations of the deal, saw how the peddler seemed to reach out and find an immediate connection with everyone he met. He complimented one man on his "fine beard. You keep it in shape, that's easy for even a stranger to see." Words directed to women always centered on the "fine young'un" hanging on their apron, or "such a pretty dress. Surely, it's store-bought," when it obviously wasn't.

Charles listened and learned the patter of the businessman who fought the road wars.

"I'm in need of a new skillet. Whatcha got in the wagon?"

"I have the finest skillets in the South (or the Confederacy, never the "United States"—not yet, not for years to come)," Watkins would say. "They are also mighty cheap this week. You got hard money or want to barter."

"Barter. I got some fine skins—deer and beaver and coon, mostly, and two red fox."

"Not much call for skins where I go. But, let's have a look."

Looking. Jawing. Sharing a tobacco plug. Chewing. Spitting. Dickering. More dickering. Until...

"Deal and done."

After one such bartering marathon in which Watkins exchanged a pound of coffee, small sack of sugar, ten double handfuls of flour, and a tin of hair pomade for four supple deer skins, three beaver pelts, and a tanned cow hide with an unusual pattern, Charles asked, "Was that a good deal what you made back there?"

Watkins slid back in the wagon seat and gave him a sideways glance. "You don't stay in business if you don't make good deals. You don't have to steal somebody blind doin' it, but you got to make a profit."

He paused to spit a globule of tobacco juice at a droning wasp. He missed. But not by much.

"The coffee, sugar, flour, cloth and pomade is worth about, oh, say, a dollar and two bits, maybe as much as two dollars at a town store. That's with a little profit for me built in. Now, I can sell the deer hides by their lonesome for up to a dollar each if I get someone who really needs a well-tanned deer hide. The beavers and coons will go for two bits each, and the cow hide I can sell to a furniture maker down in Atlanta for seventy-five cents, or thereabouts. The foxes will go for four bits each."

He paused to spit once again; the juice that ran down the left side of his chin was ignored.

"So, Young Charles, what would that come to, eh?"

Having been doing the sums in his head, Charles re-checked his mental math and said, "Six dollars and six bits." He added, "Or thereabouts," to be on the safe side.

The peddler laughed. "Right you are, Charles. Now, does getting more'n six dollars for less than two dollars worth of goods seem like a good deal to you? Uummmm?"

Choosing his words carefully, Charles said, "It would if I was the one who ended up with the skins. If I was the other fellow, I might think I got took."

"That's one way to look at it," Ramer said. "But here's another. We have to assume that feller didn't have no use for them hides or he wouldn't be gettin' rid o' them. And we have to also assume that he didn't have no other prospects for sellin' at a higher price or he wouldda done just that. And we have to also assume he needed them dry goods and was just as set on makin' a barter as I was."

Another pause. Another stream of tobacco juice.

"And, then you ought to allow me to figure in my time and storage expenses in settin' the price. How much do you think the work I do is worth per day, Charles? I mean, if you owned this wagon and all these goods and I worked for you, how much is my labor worth to you?"

More figuring on Charles' part. "Thirty, maybe forty cents a day. Maybe more if we was up North."

"Well, we ain't up North, so let's stick with the South wages. And let's take the lowball number. Thirty cents a day. Well, I picked up those goods 'bout five weeks ago and as you know I sell six days a week, and only on Sunday afternoon if people want something, got money, and I happen to be around.

"So let's take the five and multicate it by six—not takin' into 'count sellin' sometimes on Sunday after noon—and that comes to, what...five times six?...Thirty. Now, thirty days multicated by thirty cents a day is...what?"

Charles traced out the times problem on the wagon seat between them. "Ninety cents. No, nine dollars. I forgot the extra naught."

"Nine dollars for my labor. Now, how much for storage? If you leave somethin' somewhere that's protected, you got to pay for storage. How about ten cents a day. Can we use that? It's easier to figure anyway."

"Ten cents is okay," Charles said. "That's another three dollars."

Ramer scrunched up his face. "Nine dollars and three dollars is...ten, eleven, twelve dollars."

"So, I made almost, what was it? Almost seven dollars on the barter? And my costs so far in the dry goods is twelve dollars. Good Lord, Young Charles! I'm losing money! I gots to find me 'nuther line of work!"

Watkins started laughing. In less than three beats of a bee's-wing, Charles joined in. The pair filled the late afternoon with guffaws and chuckles for more than a quarter mile.

Without talking it over with Watkins, without any conscious decision-making thought at all, a month, then two, then six, passed with Charles easily settling into the routine of assistant peddler. They traveled the main turnpikes of Georgia, Mississippi, and Tennessee, once straying into eastern Arkansas from Memphis. For the most part, routes were retraced and major stops became monthly routines.

Wherever they stopped Watkins latched onto the men folk; Charles settled into conversing with the women and children, giving them a running inventory of what was on the wagon and showing wares when asked.

It was Charles who started the practice of selling some items—tinned foodstuffs, dry goods, tools—and throwing in a piece of candy to the family's children. At first Watkins frowned on Charles' apparent generosity at giving away his merchandise.

"Tell you what, ma'm, you buy the pot and the bolt of cloth and I'll throw in some hard candy for the children. One each. How many you got there? Six? And two are in the fields? Eight, it is then."

But Watkins watched and marveled at how many times Charles was able to get the wives to pester their husbands to buy some needed kitchen implement or material or household whatnot just to make sure their children got a treat.

Over a cozy campfire, with the two men sitting back, lazing, drinking coffee so hot they had to blow it so they could sip and swallow quickly, the peddler said, "I wouldn't never of thought about giving something for nothing in order to sell more. I still get a tad squinchy when I see you giving away candy. But giving away four-for-a-penny candy to sell a forty-cent pot sure seems to up the number of sales."

Charles tried not to overtly show the pride he felt in the words.

January, 1867.

A teeth-jarring north wind whipped straight down the road into the men's faces. Pulling a wool rag tight across this face, over the clomp-clomp of the horse he called "Horse," Watkins, who got in talkative moods several times a day, said, "Charles, you have a gentleness about you that womenfolk seem to relate to. You'd make a good peddler, you know? I been thinkin' 'bout expandin' my route, buyin' 'nother wagon, takin' on a full-time hand. Or partner. You ever think about goin' into business."

Charles was quiet. After all these months, Watkins knew to let him sit. He'd talk in his own good time.

"That's prob'ly the nicest thing anyone ever said to me, Mister Ramer. To be honest, I don't know what I want to do. I don't mind the peddlin' at all, travelin', seein' new places, meetin' new people. Talkin' to folks is somethin' I have to work at. I don't warm up to people quick enough, maybe, to do this type work."

Watkins clucked at Horse and pulled him back from the rightside ditch. "Dang it, Horse. Stay awake. One of us has to.

"I think you may be too hard on yourself, Charles. Like I said, you got somethin' that folks seem to cotton to. Well, as you can see from my peddlin' spiel, I ain't pushy. Sleep on it and we'll talk later."

The subject did not come up for the next three days. The pair, having come up from the south, pitched camp in a small thicket in southeast Mississippi just off the lee side of a crossroads. Charles knew the road well, having traveled it twice previously. Watkins was going to head north toward a small community called Slick Lake; the west road headed northwest into Arkansas, where it turned into a major East-West turnpike called, simply, Camden Road.

That night, over a campfire supper of side meat, beans and water cornbread with a little lard, Charles started talking and he said more in the next hour than he had in all the time he had been with the peddler.

He talked about growing up in New Orleans, Ian, Sarie Beth, Sister Bloody, trying to join up with the Rebs, life on the march, and the Shenandoah campaign. He even told the story of Eugene the squirrel, Sergeant Reilly, furloughing in New Haven and meeting Lucy Brean, mustering out, and life on the road before hooking up with the born-again peddler.

"I know I need to start thinkin' about what I'm goin' to be doin' down the road," he said, in an almost whisper. "But I have too many things runnin' through my head, too many things I think I need to be doin'. I need to find out about Ian. I need to go to New Orleans and see if Sarie Beth is still there. She'd be sixteen now. I bet she'd like to see me, with both of us all growed up. I need to go see Sister Bloody to let her know I made it through the war and see if I can help out in some way and to let her know she did a good job raisin' me.

"Leastways, I think she did and I hope she would agree."

Watkins scratched his chest through his heavy coat and spat. "She did, Charles. Or, well, somebody did."

Charles took a sip of coffee and cleared his throat for about the hundredth time. "About your offer to work with you. Let me think on it a day or two more, if that's okay?"

"Whatever suits you, suits me."

In Watkins's business, reading people fast was the first priority of success. He already knew what Charles' answer would be.

Two days later, the peddler woke up, stretched, unwrapped from his blanket and two quilts, and climbed over the back gate of the wagon. He found Charles sitting by the stoked fire. The morning coffee was on the edge of boiling and smelling smart. He couldn't help but notice Charles' kit and caboodle sitting near the front wagon wheel.

"Up early, Charles."

"Yessir. Got up early. Got my thinkin' done. I'll be leavin' today, Mister Ramer. Not that I don't 'preciate the offer, 'cause I do. It was mighty nice and more than generous. But there's some places I need to go and people I need to see. Wouldn't feel right inside till I get those things out of the way. I hope you understand."

Watkins took his time answering. He grabbed a tin cup from the customer stores, wiped it out with two fingers and filled it to sipping height from the bubbling pot. It was so hot that blowing on it didn't seem to matter.

Deciding to let the coffee cool for a spell, he sat it on a rock pulled up last night for just such an occurrence. "I been studyin' on what to tell you, Charles, what I can say to change your mind. Came up with just south of nothin'. You are a man what follows his own mind, and heart, too, if my readin' on you's right. I got a feelin' 'bout you and it's all good."

"Thank you kindly for the words. They are warmer to me than a buffalo robe. Haven't ever had one, you understand, a buffalo robe, that is, but I seen two and do they ever look warm."

"Buffalo robes? Now wonder why I never thought of carryin' them in my stores?"

They both laughed at the image of a wagon piled high with buffalo robe coats. Covered up by hides of deer, beaver, coon, fox, and cow.

Charles helped pack the wagon up tight before saying his goodbyes.

"Sure you don't want to ride a day or two more," Watkins said, climbing on the wagon seat.

"Nosir, thank you just the same. I'm headin' back down south, then east up the Camden Road. Heard a feller a few days back say there's some nice people on that road. I haven't fully made up my mind yet 'xactly how I'm getting' to New Orleans. May go to Texas and then head south. I've got a hankerin' to see Texas. I heared it's big."

"I heared it was bigger'n that," Ramer said, waking Horse by popping the reins. "Take care, Charles. The best the world has to offer to you and the rest to myself."

The wagon moved only a few yards, before the peddler showered down on the reins. "Charles, come up here. I forgot somethin' I wanted to tell you."

When Charles was abreast of the wagon seat, Watkins said, "What I'm 'bout to tell you is none of my business. But I been thinkin' on it a spell and I want you to think about it. You got a fine name, but, to be blunt, it's a foreign name. Andre. It sets you off different right from the start. Sometimes it helps to start off new, to be on even footin' with people. Before you head back down south, and surely before you head to Texas, you might think of a new name. A new name for a new future, a new direction in your life."

"A new name?"

"Andrews, or something like that. Some people don't cotton—makes no difference whether it's right or wrong—to people bein' different. It might help smooth that road you're goin' to be walkin'. Take care now, Charles. My hopes and prayers go with you."

Charles watched the peddler's wagon move slowly up the north road. Throwing his knapsacks and bedroll on his shoulders, and propping his wrapped drum in the pitch-cover blanket on top of them, he steadied his load before cutting left and headed west.

Charles Montgomery Andrews. Charles Montgomery Anders.

The sun was trying to burn its way through the heavy, chilled air, but Charles didn't notice. He set his eyes on the southern horizon and started down a new life-path in fine fiddle shape.

Sometimes not knowin' what's goin' to happen is better than knowin'. Leastways, by not knowin' there's no way to be disappointed.

Charles Montgomery. Charles Montgomery Anderson. Charles Montgomery Andres.

CHAPTER 32

Fate...or Blind Luck?

*Fate will bring together those a thousand miles apart;
without fate, they will miss each other
though they come face to face.*
Chinese proverb

Early March, 1867.
It was a lion day: Rain puddled around peeking jonquils, a bone-chilling wind hacked through the forests surrounding Washington, Arkansas. It took Charles more than a month to get to this bustling town from Camden, down in the south central part of the state. He often worked a day or two for room and meals, saving money, meeting new people.

He had a plan but important parts of it kept changing. He was going to Texas, but which way? Straight south through Shreve's Port? Or southwest into Texas and then head due south, coming up toward New Orleans from the west. He truly wanted to see Texas. But he kept feeling the pull of New Orleans and things and people familiar.

Being a major east-west commerce connection, the Camden Road was heavily traveled, but just a year and some after the war, friendliness had not again taken up residence in many of those who had lost loved ones, property, or land due to the war. The current to-the-grafters-go-the-spoils political climate set well only with them that had the economic and political upper-hand.

That sentiment was true for most of the people Charles encountered.

After a not-pleasant meeting with three former members of the Twenty-second Arkansas Volunteers on a lonely section of the Camden Road just south of a small community called Kale, Charles opted to change direction. The three loud-mouthed ruffians wanted to know what he had wrapped in a shelter-half he had purchased along the way and he was not obliged to tell them it was Union drum.

Cutting into the woods just down the road from the encounter, he half-expected to hear the men in pursuit. If the men did stalk his trail, the woods absorbed the noise.

After going some distance weaving in and out of stands of pine, sufficed with strangler vines and poison oak, he headed northwest along isolated wagon trails. In two days of easy walking, he hit the Southwest Road, the acknowledged proper entrance to Texas.

Texas. Charles had heard it was an open land with open people. To a tired and lonely traveler who had fought in a war, rambled around for more than a year searching for...something so elusive he didn't know what it was exactly...Texas sounded like the Promised Land. Was its hazy promise a myth, or fact? Charles had a hankering to find out.

I can always go back to New Orleans on down the road. Don't have to go there right yet.

An icy scythe of wind whipped through the isolated community as Charles sat at a small table in a grouping of small tables on the south porch of the Tavern Inn. Tucked down into his heavy coat, he was plotting his leaving. He had spent the last two weeks in Washington, working for food and a place to sleep—sharing a horse stall with a pregnant filly—for the local blacksmith. The smithy, James Black, claimed he had built a special knife for Jim Bowie, the frontiersman who fought the Mexicans and died at the Alamo about thirty-odd years earlier. The burly smithy seemed quite pleased about the fact. Charles didn't much believe him. He thought Black a braggart and Charles didn't cotton much to braggarts.

Except Ian. Ian bragged, but he was funny doin' it.

Black was an old man, almost seventy, but still powerfully strong in his right arm—his hammer hand. Shaking hands with him was like being caught in a calloused vice.

He looked at Black in a new light after he heard other folks pointing the old man out on the street, repeating the story about Bowie killing more than twenty Mexicans at the Alamo with a design of Black's called the "Arkansas Toothpick."

Charles was, as always, a hard worker, but keeping the forge white hot was not his idea of a long-term commitment. Baking on one side of his body with ice forming on the other was not to his liking. He had his fill of that particular feeling in two winter army camps. He didn't mind being hot or being cold; being both at the same time was more than slightly uncomfortable and more than slightly mentally confusing.

His thoughts wandered back to the previous night. He was sitting in a quiet corner in the tavern, drinking a warm sarsaparilla. A banjo player started plunking in the drop-thumb style a quirky, toe-tapping tune that was unfamiliar. The duded-up dandy...

By jingo! He was wearing spats!

kept the banjo humming to the tune of "Bonaparte's Retreat," but it was the words that caught Charles' immediate attention, being it was a familiar subject.

Met the girl I love in a town way down in Dixie
Neath the stars above she was the sweetest girl I ever did see
So, I took her in my arms and told her of her many charms
I kissed her while the fiddles played the Ol' Jub Early's Retreat

All the world was bright as I held her on that night
and I heard her say, "Please don't ever go away."
So, I held her in my arms and told her of her many charms
I kissed her while the fiddles played the Ol' Jube Early's Retreat.

It was the end of the second verse when a few men, apparently Reb veterans, began hooting and hollering. Not in a good way, at all. The banjo picker was saucily moving into the next verse when a half-filled shot of whiskey hit the wall near his head, followed by a few more glasses and a spittoon. As Charles hit the door, he looked back in time to see two men grab the musician and heard "tar and feathers" and "rail" before he struck the porch.

The wind licked underneath his coat collar and refocused his attention. Looking south across Washington, Charles was amazed at the number of beautiful homes and substantial commercial buildings speckled across the rolling hills. Families with the names of Trimble, Monroe, Royston, May, and Couch had constructed magnificent homes in flower-strewn open fields; the county courthouse (which the tavern-keeper had told him served as the Confederate Capitol of Arkansas until Union soldiers captured it in 1863) stood at the center of town. It was surrounded by offices housing doctors, lawyers, and land brokers.

Charles thought the town was a bit smallish and tawdry, but there was a rumor a railroad was coming soon and land speculation was a booming business.

There are probably some opportunities here. Surely are. But, ahhhh, Texas!

As he was considering his options, a man walked over and sat down at the next table. Charles felt the man's eyes look him over before he said, "Where you headed, boy?"

Charles looked at the man cautiously. "I may stay around here, may head south, or I may go to Texas."

"Why Texas?"

"Why not?"

The man studied Charles and Charles studied him back. "You don't have to get uppity," the man growled through a full, bushy, black beard. "I was just makin' conversation, 'sall."

Charles did what he did best and said nothing.

"I was just wonderin' if you were interested in work? A friend of mine has a goin' enterprise down the road apiece and he's looking for spring and summer help. Thought you might be interested."

The silence lay between the men like a hog in a public bathtub—totally out of place and totally unacceptable.

The man levered himself up and started for the porch steps. Charles said, "Mister! I'm sorry for my bad manners. I didn't mean nothin'. I just like to think things through before I talk. It's just somethin' I do."

The man turned and threw Charles a half-smile. "That may be a good thing. I wouldn't know. Ain't never found a word that I didn't like and believe it needed to be spoke."

He came over, stuck out his hand: "Charles Winnock Ridlings. And you are…?

"Charles Montgomery…Andres. Now, about this job…?"

Two hours later, Charles was sitting tall on the spring seat of a fashionable buggy. Without any questions, Ridlings had motioned Charles to the left side of the conveyance. Under the watchful eye of his new acquaintance he held the reins loose in his hands like Brother Pious had instructed the one and only time Charles had been allowed to rein a horse-drawn wagon.

It was a quiet ride for the first hour; both men seemed content to let the horse (a sparkling piebald gelding with the unlikely name of Julius Caesar) pick a path on the skid-smooth roadbed.

Heading out the south road as they did, the slide top on the buggy protected the men from a bracing north wind. After an easy hour and a restless half-hour, conversation started to flow like a new roof leak during a monsoon…slowly but promising to pick up speed and volume quickly.

By the time they reached Hope, a village with buildings smashed together on each side of the Cairo and Fulton Railroad tracks, their recent personal histories were laid out. Ridlings had served in the Twentieth Arkansas Regiment, been captured when Vicksburg fell, was pardoned within two days, and came home "as quick as can be, done with fightin'." When Charles said "Ninth Connecticut, drummer," the older man looked at him but didn't comment. Ridlings came from a big family that stretched clear back to Georgia; Charles declared he was an orphan and joined the Union because other options were cut off.

In the four or so hours it took to get from Washington to Hope, an easy bond between the two developed. As the train depot came into sight down the wide lane that passed for Hope's main street, Ridlings said, "Wish I could ask you to come on down to Ozan and work with me. But we've got a small place. The Waddles own a lot of farmland and even have a goin' sawmill and flourmill. Both horse-drawn, but good just the same. Their place is about the center of commerce in that part of Hempstead County."

As it was getting late, the two pulled up at the Hempstead Inn, a boarding house near the tracks. Usually full of comers and goers who worked for or used the Cairo and Fulton Railroad for a living, Ridlings was surprised the boarding house was almost empty.

"Slow week," the owner said, after Ridlings commented on the vacancies.

"Railway bridge over the Ouachita flooded out several days back. It'll be a couple of weeks or so before the regular runs start up again. I hear they're pullin' double crews, pushin' them hard to get done. Can't be too soon for me."

Ridlings started to sign in and Charles pulled on his shirtsleeve. "I really don't have the money for a room stay, even at two bits for the night. I can sleep in the buggy and keep watch on the goods if you don't mind." He hated to say it since it wasn't the whole truth (he still had more than two hundred dollars plus some hidden among his belongings).

"Have you ever cleaned a hog?" Ridlings asked.

"No, sir. But I seen it done. Two old boys back in the Shenandoah caught a pig one night—they called it an 'enemy pig'—and I watched what they did. I'm a quick learner."

Ridlings' beard hid his smile, partially. "Well, tomorrow I'm stopping on the way to the Waddles place to get a pig off'n a man what owes me some money. Help me clean it and I'll stake you to a room. And," he said with emphasize, "I'll throw in a bath ("Just a nickel more," the boarding house owner said.) "not because I'm generous, but because you need it."

At another time, with another companion, Charles would have been embarrassed. Ridlings' easy nature made that feeling impossible to grab, much less to hold onto.

A couple of hours later, after being settled in a corner room with two sets of windows overlooking the main street, and a bath in water that had been used only a couple of times that day, Charles was in good shape and in a better mood. Hair slicked back the best he could without pomade, and in clean clothes for the first time in more than two weeks, and getting ready to sleep in a real bed for a change…he felt better than middling.

I need to take a bath more often. Easy to forget how good you feel when you're clean.

He and Ridlings walked down from the second floor room to the big dining room. Since they were the first to arrive for the evening meal, they stood at the sideboard, Ridlings drinking coffee, Charles sweet milk. They talked about tomorrow's weather, the hog killing, what the future would hold for the South. Charles offered few opinions, just flat statements. He was content to listen to his companion make observations about anything and everything.

After a dinner of chicken and dumplings, beans, boiled okra, and an odd black bread, the two men walked around the small town for a spell before ending up back at the boarding house. It was a quiet night, so they sat on the porch in rocking chairs.

"In this part of the country, we're not as hard hit by the northern carpetbaggers as they are back in Georgia, Alabama, and Louisiana. I hear tell Georgia has a nigra governor and almost all the legislature is colored. New Orleans used to be an open city with friendly people. Now's I hear it's a dumping ground for degenerates—nigra, Mexican, Cuban, and white. You said that's where you're heading, well, I'd think that move over more than a spell, if'n it was me."

Charles asked about "carpetbaggers," a term he had heard but did not totally understand. "Them's men who paid somebody high-up in the Union gummit for a gummit job—federal land commish, martial law examiner or whatever they call it, or commish of commish something or other. It's a mess. They come down South and act like God Almighty, giving orders, making up laws, working with the nigras against any white man. They take land, homes and what valuables are left. Whatever they want to do, they do.

"The law don't stop them 'cause they are the law; they make the laws and enforce them, too. There's lots of resentment over the war—on both sides, I reckon—but the South, despite us out-generaling the Yankees at every turn till the last—just ran out of men and shot to win the war."

Ridlings paused and cast an eye on Charles. "Nothing personal, you understand."

"None taken. The war was hard on both sides, but the South got the brunt of it for sure."

His host paused and let out a mournful sigh. "We're gonna pay for what one carpetbagger called our 'aggressive sins' for a long time, I can tell you that."

Charles hesitated. "You sound like you had some first-hand truck with the carpetbaggers."

"Did, once. Sure as I'm sittin' here. A man showed up at my farm one day in a big buggy with brass fittin's. Had three men a-horseback with him. Told me he was the district governor, appointed by Andrew Jackson hissownself. He had a piece of paper that he said gave him the right to cut out two cows and a horse from any farm that had more than five head each. I had ten cows, so he took two. Don't know what happened to those cows and don't want to know."

Later, in the room, Charles obligingly said he would sleep on the floor, but

Ridlings told him he'd "do no such thing. I like the right side. And, I'd appreciate it if you'd keep on at least some clothes."

Charles was used to sleeping fully clothed, but stripped down to his longhandles. Because of the newness of the relationship with the older man, he didn't expect to sleep much. He was wrong. He awoke the next morning to Ridlings standing in the corner, using the thunder mug. Keeping his eyes averted until his host had finished, Charles splashed water on his face, got dressed, and went outside to the privy, a nice-sized three-hole affair.

Breakfast was homemade biscuits, slab ham, pepper gravy, hot coffee, and sweet milk. Charles ate his fill and even slathered some peach jam on a biscuit and stuck it in his pocket for later.

Two hours later, Ridlings' buggy quit the Camden Road, turned back south for a mile or two, then turned back east at the first trail. The buggy bounced down a slim lane lined with pines leading to a house at the edge of a clearing. He hello-ed the house and a bedraggled man followed by an extra-lean hound with extra-full jowls came around from the back of the house.

"Hello, Jacob. Came to get that hog you got for me," Ridlings said. The man didn't acknowledge the greeting. He looked at the ground and turned and went toward the back of the house.

Ridlings tied the horse's rein to a lead frog weight that was under the spring seat and dropped it to the ground. He motioned Charles to follow him. When they rounded the side of the house, the man, tall and spare as a winter sycamore, was standing near a wooden pen where three hogs rooted around in the dirt.

"Take yore choice," the man said in a whiskey voice.

"Which one of the females is the youngest?" Ridlings asked.

The man called Jacob cast him a suspicious look. "The one with the upright ears. Why?"

"Want to leave you the best breeding pair, now don't I?"

Jacob's eyes softened. "Obliged."

Three hours later, the fire-building, killing, scalding, scraping, and slaughtering was done. Salted from a bag Ridlings had in the buggy, the meat lay in double tow sacks in a neat line near the scalding pot.

Charles had done whatever he was told to do, and his instincts and memory helped him anticipate some requests and wants. Heavy packing gauze was used to wrap up the meat, and that, plus the salting, would keep the meat "fine and dandy until I get it home in the smokehouse," Ridlings said.

There were twelve packages of meat and Ridlings took the last two, a forequarter and ham, and gave them to their host. Jacob shook his head but after Ridlings talked to him quietly, the man nodded, took the two meat parcels and went into the house.

Nothing was said for the first mile or so. Finally, Ridlings offered: "Whenever you bargain with a man, keep the bargain. That means both ends. But, if you got the upper hand, try and temper the bargain with generosity. It won't hurt you much atall, and it always helps the other person. It eases you in his mind."

Words worth remembering, that's for sure.

"There she be," Ridlings said a couple of hours later, jolting Charles out of nice daydream about Sarie and Ian and how one day they'd all be together.

The Waddle place was certainly not your run-of-the-road South Arkansas farmhouse. It was a freshly painted, rambling, white dogtrot with several outbuildings and a cotton gin off to the southwest. A good-sized open building with a short, peaked roof and open sides to the west of the main house protected the flour grinder. An A-topped shed out a piece toward the back of the clearing Charles took to be the cotton gin. A largish, two-story bareboard barn stood like a sentinel, flanked by two of the largest horse apple trees Charles had ever seen.

With his eyes bouncing like a fishing cork over a bed of minnows, Charles finally focused on the main house, which was situated just a few yards off the single dirt lane.

"Why's the house so close to the road?" Charles asked.

"That's a question you'll have to ask Mr. Arch. But I reckon he didn't want to mess up his planned fields by having a road and a house sitting at the backside of his property."

There was a healthy pause. "But like I said, you'll have to ask him.

CHAPTER 33

The "Feeling" of Family

> *Family—the sense of belonging, of being part of something important and long-lasting—means everything. Until you don't have it. Then it means more than that.*
> Author
> During research for *Reveille*

    Charles focused his attention more keenly on the Waddle house. It was a healthy house, a wide dog-trot affair with what looked like shotgun add-ons to the back, two probably, maybe three. The house was accented by an expansive, straight-across porch with an abundance of chairs—four-legged, straight-backs and rockers—lining the front wall. A gaggle of kids, a couple colored, more white, ricocheted around the front yard, playing tag or "It" as Charles knew the game. More children were up in a huge oak, set just outside the right front corner of the porch.
    There could a hundred more up there. Hard to tell.
    As was the custom, Ridlings hailed the house. Having taken care of the societal niceties, he got down and looped a single rein through the lead frog weight and dropped it at Julius Caesar's feet.
    A door banged open. Charles' head jerked toward the direction of the sound from where he had been studying the tree-climbers. The doorway to the

Waddle house was filled with the outline of a huge man. "That's Mister Archibald, right there," Ridlings said.

"Charles Ridlings," the tall, broad-shouldered man on the porch, hollered. "Welcome and come up on to the porch. Who's that you got with you? That one your sister's boys?"

"No, Arch, this here is another Charles, Charles Andres, in fact and in person." Charles doffed his hat and nodded agreeably. "I came across him up to Washington and he was deciding whether to head south or into Texas. He mentioned he was lookin' for work and knowin' you said last week you might be needin' help, I decided to give him a lift over just in case."

"Let's sit a spell and talk then," Waddle said, eying Charles like a hawk checking out a scurrying field mouse. When they were seated—Waddle, in a extra-large slatted rocker, Ridlings on a hung swing, and Charles in a smaller chair he had seen here and abouts and knew to be called an "Adirondack,"—the big man said, "Where you from, boy?"

"Born and raised up in New Orleans, Mister Waddle. Till I was about sixteen. For the past two years and then some I served as a drummer boy until the end. Then I spent a year on the road, working and walking, trying to get back home."

He inwardly winced as the omission of having served in the Union Army. He flicked a look at Ridlings, who was busy studying the fingernails of his large, heavily veined, left hand.

"Your folks in New Orleans? Family?"

"Nosir. All died before the war in the plague. I guess I am headin' back to New Orleans 'cause it's all I know."

Waddle seemed to study on that for a spell, then yelled, "Martha. We got two for company. Some water would be good. Do either of you want coffee? No? Just water, Mother."

Ridlings and Waddle talked about corn prices that could be expected with the fall harvest and about a hundred-acre plat Waddle was thinking of buying with mill money.

A scuffling noise from inside the house caught Charles' attention. The front door was opened and two girls bounced through. Taking the lead was a girl of about ten and the second Charles took to be about his age.

"Ah, here's the water," Waddle said, taking two glasses from the younger girl and handing them to the visitors before taking the proffered glass from the older girl.

"Charles W., you remember Lizzie, I'm sure," he said, and the younger girl curtsied, "and Nancy Ann. Lizzie, Nancy, you both know Mister Charles Ridlings from over to Ozan. This young'un is Charles Andres from New Orleans. He's just passing through. Gentlemen, two of my daughters."

Both men were on their feet, hats in their hands.

"Of course, I know both girls and all your children, Archibald. And, how are you girls this fine day?"

Lizzie tee-hee-ed, hiding her mouth with a tiny, cupped hand. Nancy Ann threw a thin-lipped smile in the direction of the two visitors: "We're fine, Mister Ridlings." She fixed her gaze on Charles, looking him up and down.

Like a horse at auction.

Charles met her eyes, tried to hold his gaze steady, but quickly looked away. Nancy Ann was about an inch taller than he, and had the same stern look as her father. She did not have the easy carriage of many of the women Charles had seen. She was a bit thick through the shoulders, with the outline of meaty arms under the wool dress and shawl pulled tight across her bosom. Her dark eyes fairly crackled, but Charles could not tell whether her personal examination of him was from crass amusement or exasperation.

She took a step toward Charles and held out her hand.

She wants to shake my hand. What kind of woman is this?

Not knowing what to do, Charles looked to Ridlings, then Waddle, for help. Ridlings had curled his lips inward to hide the beginnings of smile; Waddle sat stone-still, a rural Buddha in a rocker.

Certain he was violating a social code of some sort or, maybe, several social codes, he took Nancy's hand and lightly grasped it. She gave a curt nod, a quick up-and-down with her hand, dropped his hand, and quickly went back in the house.

Waddle and Ridling looked at the puzzled expression on Charles' face and both men started laughing. Lizzie, who had plopped herself on the arm of her father's rocker, joined in.

"If you stick around a spell, Charles, you'll find most all my children are independent and none worse at it than Nancy Ann."

Stick around a spell? Does that mean I've got the job. Whatever it is?

After Lizzie was shooed back in the house, but before the three men had finished their glasses of water, Waddle had offered Charles "work at forty cents a day, room and found" and Charles had accepted, agreeing to stay on at least through the fall harvest.

The next hour was spent with Waddle in pontification mode, telling Charles and Ridlings the family history—descended from Scottish kings, English princes, and earls—ending when the Waddle clan had moved to South Arkansas just seven years ago "and doin' pretty good, if I do say so myself."

There were ten children in the Waddle household, four boys and six girls, with Mary Jane being the oldest (twenty-three) and Henrietta being the baby (six). Charles didn't ask, but Waddle mentioned where the children were born, including Nancy Ann, who was born in Tennessee. She was a year old when the family settled in Arkansas.

Before he could stop himself, Charles heard himself ask, "How old is Miss Nancy?"

Waddle squenched up his forehead and cast a pair of snake eyes in his direction. "She's my third oldest. She's eighteen. Why do you want to know?"

Charles' brain scrambled for a suitable answer. "I had just met her and was just curious, that's all. My 'pologies if askin' was out of line, Mister Waddle."

"So, I guess if you asked how old she was 'cause you just met her, then you'll want to be knowin' how old Lizzie is, since you just met her." The following pause seemed to last a year. "She's ten."

"Uh, thank you. I was just gettin' ready to ask about Lizzie. Yes, I was."

Without acknowledging the statement, Waddle went into a litany about chores around the sizeable farm: Tending to livestock (cows, horses, pigs, chickens, plus several goats—"Henrietta is partial to goat's milk."—tilling, planting (corn, cotton, maize, potatoes, plus a large family garden); tending to young apple, pear and peach trees; helping at the mill and gin when needed; doing odd chores as they came up.

As his new employer ticked off the chores, Charles nodded both understanding and acceptance. Ridlings sat quietly, studying the pair between sips of water.

"We're a church-goin' family and we expect our hands to be the same. That a problem?" Waddle said.

"Nosir. It's surely not. During the war, we only had chaplains and church services were catch-as-catch-can affairs under trees, in the hospital tent when we could, or in old barns. I like to learn and I seemed to have learned a lot of new things listening to preachers and such."

Quiet descended on the porch, each man lost in his own thoughts.

Waddle broke the silence with a loud clearing of his throat. "Joseph! Joseph! Martha, where's Joseph?"

A voice from inside the house: "He took the wagon to the Bynam's to pick up those laying hens. You told him to go. Don't you remember?"

"Course, I remember. I also told him to be back by three. And, by my reckonin', he's late!"

A plain woman in a plain dress came to the door, and said, "Not much, he's not. You never give the children enough time to finish chores. You judge them by what you can do, not what they can do."

Waddle stood up and stretched, "I was going to get Joseph to get young Charles situated down at the potato shed since he's going to work for us. I was going to talk some more with Charles W. here for a spell. Charles, this is Mrs. Waddle."

Already on his feet, Charles nodded politely. "Pleased to meet you, Mrs. Waddle. I surely am."

The older woman, hair pulled back in a strict bun, bright eyes hooded under bushy eyebrows, hands wrapped in a printed apron, nodded.

A voice from inside the house said, "I'll show him, Papa." Nancy Ann edged pass her mother and came up directly to Charles, who took a step backward, coming dangerously close to the edge of the porch.

"You'll do no such thing, Nancy Ann," Waddle said. "It's not seemly."

The young girl swung her head around toward her father. "Not seemly? Not seemly to walk from my house to the potato shed and show a new hand where he's going to stay? Papa, that's just silly."

She pointed past the barn to a small, solid shed by the nearby stand of pines. "The shed is right over there. You can watch us the whole way if you want. Come on, Mister Andres. I'll show you."

Charles was in a panic, looking in turn at Anne as she stepped off the porch, then stopped and looked back at him over her shoulder, then at Waddle, whose face was a thunderhead, to Mrs. Waddle, who looked…amused, to Ridlings, who was no help at all.

Looking hard at his daughter, Waddle seemed to inhale an extraordinary amount of air and then expel it in one long *whoooosh.*

"Do what you want to do, Nancy Ann. You're going to do it anyway. Charles, I expect you to be the perfect gentleman at all times around my family. Do you understand me?"

Mrs. Waddle quietly went back in the house. Ridlings went back to studying his fingernails. Charles tried to think himself small…then smaller still.

"Poppa!" Nancy Ann's cry escaped in a cracked voice. "Come on, Mister Andres." She stomped off and disappeared around the edge of the house.

Charles' panicked eyes searched for an answer to the dilemma.

"Go, boy. She'll show you where you will stay. Make her hurry back now, you hear?"

Charles nodded and took off at a scared trot after Nancy Ann, who was almost halfway to the shed. She didn't turn around when he caught up to her; he opted to trail in the wake of her billowing crinolines.

She stopped at the shed door, turned and said, "It's not much, but it's solid. Mantooth is…was…the best. Mantooth was our nigra carpenter. He died a year or so back. He was the best carpenter anywhere around. Daddy hired him out to other folks for making desks, cabinets, dining tables, and such. He built this shed for storing potatoes, apples, pears, and onions."

She swung the door open and stepped aside, allowing Charles to look past her to the dark cabin's interior. Nervously, he glanced back at the house and noticed the two men were standing at the edge of the porch, staring in the shed's direction.

Not stepping inside, but looking the interior over carefully, he noticed that it was a up-and-down structure, lower front room with a scrapped dirt floor and a built-up back room. Except for a small, foot-wide trail from the door to the back room, the entire floor of the thirty-foot-wide cabin was covered with potatoes, onions, and a few apples and pears bearing dark spots.

"The back room has a bed built against the north wall, a small two-pot stove, and a built-in stand for a pitcher, towel, and such. We've had others stay here and, while it's a bit sparse, nobody much complained."

Thinking about sleeping outside in hardwood thickets, in two-man dog tents, and under a peddler's wagon over the past three years, the shed looked "much more than tolerable," he said.

"Good, then let's go back to the house and get you some bedding." Without another word, she turned and started walking back to the house.

Not walking, really. More like stepping over a low rail fence. Seems she's mad all the time. Wonder what about?

While Nancy Ann was getting two half-sheets, two heavy quilts with random patchwork patterns made from what looked like old shirts and pants, and a horsehair pillow and pillow glove, Charles gathered up his two knapsacks, drum, and canteen and deposited them on the ground just off the porch.

He thanked Mister Waddle for the job and, without being asked said the shed was "just fine." He thanked Ridlings for the ride and opportunity and told him "I'll be thankin' you for a long time and I hope to see you again soon."

Nancy Ann came out of the house bearing the bedclothes. She was about to bypass her father without a word, but he reached out and stopped her, took the bundles from her arms and said, "I'll take him back. We got some talkin' to do."

It was obvious to the three men that she didn't like it, but she bit back any words she was thinking about saying and went back in the house. She did not close the door gently.

Ridlings took his leave and after goodbyes and promises to "come visit" Charles followed Waddle toward the shed.

Reaching the door to the shed, Waddle stopped. "Is it all right if I go on in?"

Confused once again, Charles blinked rapidly several times before stuttering, "Ah-excuse mah-me?"

"This is your house now, boy. You don't enter a man's house without permission. Mine. Or yours. It's a good rule to remember. Can I go in?"

"Sha-surely. Please. Go in anytime you want."

The big man shook his head. "No, that's not the way it works. I don't enter your house without your say-so, and you give me the same courtesy. Is that clear?"

The method to Waddle's seemingly madness came into sharp focus. "Oh! Yessir. It's clear. It's real clear."

The big man walked a tight line to the back room. "You can fix it up any way you like, only when you leave, everything goes back the way it is now. We leave it spare on purpose, so every hand that stays here can make it his own. Is that clear?"

"Yessir."

"Good. We start to work early. And you being in the army, I know you are used to that. One of us will hit a wagon wheel rim hung near the back of the house three times and three times only. That's the only warning you'll get for meals."

He stopped and looked around the small room.

"I'll have one of the boys fetch you a lantern. I forget we took it up when Jeb Hoskins—the last man who was here. Stayed more than two years. Then left. Anyway, we take just enough time to eat and then get to work. We got a big place, big anyways for around here, and lots to do.

"I'll have you work with Tote—he's our colored hired hand—for a couple of days while we see what all you can do. We work six days, and try to take off a bit early on Saturday. That's payday. After work, just come by the house and collect your pay."

Charles had already figured his first week's pay in his head.

It's Tuesday, so I start to work on Wednesday. Four days work this first week would be...a dollar and sixty cents.

It'll add up over time.

"Sundays, as I said, we go to church. We take a wagon but most of the young'uns like to walk. It's only a couple of miles by the road, shorter through the short field and woods at the front of the house."

He walked over the room's only window and looked out. Without turning around, he said: "Charles, you seem like a nice young man. I wouldn't have hired you on if I didn't think that. And I'd be a fool if I didn't see that Nancy Ann has taken a likin' to you."

Charles started sputtering but was cut short by a look from Waddle.

"You didn't do nothin', nothin' atall. She's about your age and has a mind of her own. She says things she shouldn't. All the time, in fact. She thinks she's as good as a man at just about anything, and that includes me. She's got a lot to learn."

Waddle blew out a huge sigh, which wallowed around the room. "What I'm tryin' to say is this: You are here to work, not to diddle. You are here to make me think you are worth keepin' on every week, not someone who is interested in bein' here for a better reason, a higher callin', if you will, just because I happen to have a daughter of age.

"Charles, I have high hopes for all my children, and that includes Nancy Ann. I don't mean nothing personal, son, but we don't know one single thing about you other than what you told us today. That don't make you a liar but what I heard don't come across as the whole truth."

Charles felt light-headed. He wanted to sit down but opted to just lean as casually as possible against the door jam.

"I'm telling you straight, boy. I don't know you and you don't know us. But I want more for my children, for Nancy Ann, than for her to marry somebody just passin' through. She's better than that and I just want you to know my feelin's straight up."

Waddle headed to the door. Charles quickly stepped aside.

The big man stopped inside the outside door, turned and said, "If you're here in the mornin', we get to work. If you're not, and I have a feelin' you won't be, then there's no hard feelin's."

Charles' first night in his new "home" was a sleepless one. Too much to consider. Too many new experiences, emotions, opportunities, problems. Too many perceptions, sensory and mental. Visual and mental overload.

He thought of the meeting with the Waddles' eldest son, Joseph, when he brought a lantern, a small tin of kerosene, and some stick matches. He, too, asked permission before entering the vegetable and fruit shed.

Lessons of the father...

The two young men talked a while, Joseph asking questions about New Orleans, the war, and Charles asking questions about everything on the farm except Nancy Ann.

In the dark, with the call of a lone poorwill william filtering through the cabin chinks, he revisited his first supper at his new home. Mrs. Waddle—not Nancy Ann nor Lizzie nor the other girls (Elizabeth, Emma, Mary Jane, Henrietta) had brought two plates to the back porch at suppertime. She handed Charles and Tote the plates and then returned quickly with two splatterware cups of scalding black coffee.

"When you get done, Charles, just put the dishes on the porch next to the door. Tote knows what to do."

Tote nodded and motioned Charles toward the barn, where they sat on nail barrels and talked while eating field peas, fried hominy grits, two slabs of pork side meat, and a huge buttermilk biscuit slathered with wild strawberry jam.

Tote didn't ask many questions, and none of a personal nature. But Charles answered the obvious ones—New Orleans, drummer in the war, heading back home, needed to work for a while to build up a little purse.

Before the war, Tote owned up to being a slave on a Mississippi plantation. His master had been "nice to a fault" to his chattel before the war. But the fighting and looting and burning had changed the old man, made him bitter.

Almost overnight, for some reason or another, he seemed to enjoy taking his frustrations out on his field hands and house slaves.

"He beat me some, Mister Ransom did. The last time he beat me, I got up off'n the dirt, looked him in da eye, and just walked 'way. Never said a word. And he neva raised a hand to stop me. I guess we both feared what would happen if'n he did."

Tote said he walked north until he ran into a Union brigade from Ohio. "I worked with the quartermaster and cooked, cut wood, whatever they wanted done just to get by. When the war ended, I been headed to Mississip, when I happened along the road yonder. Mr. Waddle hello-ed me and asked if I wanted to work.

"I swear I never had anyone ever ast me if I wanted to work. He pays a fair wage—twenty cents a day—and Mrs. Waddle feeds good. I got no complaints."

For now, Charles didn't either.

The next morning Charles was up and dressed before the ringing of the breakfast bell. He met Tote halfway to the house and they greeted each other with a nod.

Mister Waddle was waiting on the porch with a single plate and cup of coffee. He handed it to Tote and told Charles, "I'll fetch your breakfast," and went back into the house. Tote smiled openly, sat down and started eating. Mister Waddle brought out another plate and cup and handed them to Charles without a word. He turned to go back into the house, but stopped at the door, turned, and said, "When you two are done, we'll get to work."

Charles quickly fell into a comfortable routine at the Waddle farm. There was always something to do and when there wasn't, Mister Waddle found something that needed doing. There was little time for anything else but work and working "can-to-cain't" was not a lot different than being in the army. It was something Charles was used to and accepted with a natural enthusiasm and energy that belied his quiet demeanor and small stature.

He prided himself on his ability to mimic almost any action. Once an instruction was given or action was observed, he would not only mimic it with startlingly similar results, but his mind was constantly looking for ways to improve upon it.

That trait did not go unnoticed by Tote or Waddle.

After showing Charles how to rasp a horse's hoof—one front hoof—and then watching Charles finish off the other three (with just a stumble on trying to figure out the proper way to raise a back hoof as compared to a front one), Tote said, "Law's sake. You could be what Mister Waddle calls a ferrier."

Charles didn't know what a ferrier was, but, based on the pride in Tote's voice, he took it as a compliment.

Tote was not one to keep good news to himself. Later that same day Waddle looked up Charles, who was checking fence on the west side of the farm. He was using smooth wire and sections of green saplings chopped with a machete to tighten barbed strands affixed to wobbly posts loosened by recent rains.

Waddle rode up on his piebald gelding, Tom. "How's it goin'?"

"Fine, Mister Waddle. Fine. That rain really loosened a lot of posts. I used a little wire to tie some of them off to trees so they'll be straight when the ground hardens. When it dries out, I'll come back and fetch the extra wire."

Waddle thought about what Charles had said, finally nodding. "Makes sense. Don't forget to come back and get the wire though. We're not growing no wire this year and it costs too much money to have it just laying around."

"No problem, sir. I'll take care of it."

Waddle said, "What I came down here to do is tell you that Tote is mighty impressed with your work. He said you could be a ferrier. You ever done work with horses before."

"Nosir, never did. I watched some fellas in the cavalry workin' on their horses, but they were mighty particular about their mounts. Wouldn't let nobody touch 'em."

"Well," Waddle said, wheeling Tom back toward the house, "keep at it. You're doin' fine work."

Well, if that don't beat all. A good word from Mister Waddle. Gotta remember this day for sure.

Due to the proximity of certain chores and the main house, and the regular comings and goings of family members, Charles was constantly running into Nancy Ann and her sisters and brothers. All the Waddles had chores, except Henrietta, and often it took Tote and Charles and a handful of Waddles to complete certain heavy-lifting chores.

Henrietta had taken a particular liking to Charles, who thought Nancy Ann was using her baby sister as an excuse to visit every so often. Or, at least he hoped so.

Henrietta called him "Chash" and laughed when he blew his lips at her. Every time.

Charles was particularly polite to Nancy Ann, and purposefully standoffish. He answered her questions perfunctorily, making eye contact only when he thought it proper.

I like my work and need the money.

Headstrong was not a common word used to describe women of the time, but Charles thought of Sarie Beth and Lucy and Mrs. Blankenship.

Seems I attract headstrong women.

And Nancy Ann fit the mold perfectly. If she was in a mood to talk, she wouldn't allow him to ignore her. Knowing her father like she did, and assuredly knowing his mandate to Charles, she took no offense at his reluctance at meaningful conversation, but also wouldn't allow the behavior of either man to dictate her actions.

"What do you want to be doing five years from now, Charles?"

A typical fly-away question from Nancy Ann. Straight. True. Unexpected actions and words. Complex.

Charles was chopping firewood—"Makin' little sticks out of big 'uns," as Tote called it—when she asked the question. It unnerved him so that he missed the small log's center with the axe, causing the piece of wood to jump sideways, barking his shin.

"Oh, Mary, Mother of Jesus!" he cried, grabbing his shin in both hands and sitting down on a big piece of oak trunk. He frantically tried to rub the pain away.

"Ohhhhhh, are you okay?" Nancy Ann gushed, rushing to his side and grabbing his right arm with both hands, squeezing gently.

"No, ma'm, I'm not okay. Oh, my, that really smarts. Can't believe I missed the durn log."

Nancy Ann's hands tightened perceptively on his upper arm. "You were doing so well, too. You have the smoothest axe stroke, Charles. You really do."

Aware of her words, her caring demeanor, and her hands on his arm, Charles scurried to his feet and picked up the axe.

"Better get back to work. No time to take a break." He began rhythmic pounding the big pieces of wood into leaner chunks.

Nancy Ann watched him split four or five pieces, then turned and started walking purposefully toward the house. But not before Charles heard her say: "Boys! They are all just plain dumb. All of them. No exceptions."

She may have a point. More than likely, a good one.

Having being raised as a "forced" Catholic, Charles was not looking forward to attending church with the Waddle clan. Organized religion, at least that he had experienced, had too many painful memories. When it came to religion in general, he was unsure about his feelings, about what he wanted, or needed, from "church." These thoughts had jelled while in the army. Field church services were unstructured affairs that didn't suit his internal need for organization and common sense. Faith was fine, he thought, in its place. But growing up where he did, and striving to survive as he did from an early age, he had always opted to think about what Sister Bloody to him and Ian one time: A bird in the hand is worth two in the bush. Be satisfied with what you have because what you don't have may never come to you.

Charles was a bird-in-the-hand man; promised rewards meant little. What you have is what you have. What you might get might not be there when you expect it to be. Personal gratification and individual fulfillment based on one's own merits…now, that he could understand and appreciate.

But, he was pleasantly surprised when, after the first Sunday church service attended with the family, he found himself not put off, but happy at being included in the gathering. He especially liked the pre-church social activities (walking to the church with most of the Waddle children and meeting other young people who joined the group en route). He got to listen to Nancy Ann talk along the way. And he got to show off occasionally with his knowledge of medicinal plants growing wild in the countryside.

For the most part, the Bible teaching classes and the sermon by a circuit-riding preacher were entertaining, if not necessarily enlightening. A rousing sermon about Samson and Delilah he-ing and she-ing was unsettling, especially the part about fornicating, which the preacher seemed to dearly embrace since he spent so much time on that particular part of the story.

Free-will Baptists did a lot of amen-ing, a new experience for Charles. They even had a special corner for it. Waddle and ten to twelve other men sat in three pews and amen-ed to beat the band for the hour and a half that preacher was going on about the sin of fornication.

Charles, sitting between Henrietta and a large woman who squeaked when she breathed, made a point of not looking at Nancy Ann. And he could feel her not looking at him.

I don't know about anybody else, but I couldn't stand to hear this sermon more than once a year.

On the way back home, Charles had a belated thought.
Tote! What does he do on Sundays?
He thought badly of himself for not thinking to ask.

After church, he went to barn and hello-ed the loft for Tote, but there was no answer. An hour later, after changing from his church clothes, he heard the dinner clanging and joined up with Tote on the walk to the back of the house.

"Whatcha do this morning, Tote?"

"There's a church for colored folks about a mile or so south of the Harmony Church in the woods. I go's over there just about every Sunday. It's a lively place and people bask in God's spirit more'n a little. Makes me feel good the rest of the day, that's for sure."

I'm glad he has somewheres to go. I'm glad I have somewheres to go, too.

Over time Charles started feeling more comfortable around the family. They were accepting of him as a non-central part of their lives, but a part of it just the same. The Waddles began recognizing certain givens about Charles. For one, he was a studious sort, reading anything and everything he could get his hands on. The Waddles started saving newspapers, including *Harper's Weekly* for him. Even catalogs were handed down to him.

He was a hard worker. Regardless of the cold of dreary Januarys or the suffocating humid heat of Augusts, he never shirked any duty handed to him or any chore he saw needed doing.

After several incidents involving Charles whipping up home remedies foreign to the Waddle clan, the family started looking to him as a healer, of sorts, a holistic practitioner who seemed never at a lost for a cure for a common ailment. Concocting up cure-alls from local plants or roots was not an unusual trait. Every family had its own remedies mixed up from wild herbs and roots and such. Some worked all the time; some worked some of the time; many didn't seem to help at all, anytime, or on anybody.

Charles' talent as a healer came into the light one hot summer's night when he heard a commotion at the house and went to investigate.

Standing on the porch, he could hear the family lamenting the fact that Henrietta was sick, mighty sick. The child was coughing, and between coughing spasms, she had trouble catching her breath. She had been given two big doses of sugar, sulphur, and molasses, but seemed to be getting worse.

"Anything I can do?" Charles hollered from the porch. Nancy Ann came to the door in a neck to ankle nightgown, which she tried to cover up with her mother's shawl. "Henrietta is sick. Choked up. Mama's doctoring her. It don't seem to be helping."

"Tell Mister Waddle I'm going to go round up some herbs and will be back directly."

Before Nancy Ann could reply, Charles was running to the barn.

Within minutes he had roused Tote and they picked up two hatcheted pine knot limbs piled with pitch. The makeshift torches lit up the path toward the property's southernmost pond.

"What we lookin' for, Mister Charles?"

"I need to make a cough elixir. I've got a little bit of hyssop in my haversack. It don't grow around here. But I need aniseed. It don't grow around here either, but I saw some wild fennel down near the pond and it's close enough I reckon to maybe help Miss Henrietta."

In a short time, Charles found the billowy green tops of wild fennel plant, and he and Tote dug out three bulbs with a sharp stick, then headed back to the shed. Reaching the shed, Charles dug around in his haversack until he found several cloth sacks. "One of these has some hyssop, I think."

He found the right dried plant flowers and headed back to the main house.

"Thanks, Tote," Charles said in the retreating darkness.

"Don't thank me," Tote said, just steps behind Charles. "I'm comin' wid you."

Charles knocked politely on the front door, which was quickly opened by Nancy Ann.

"I think I can help," Charles said, nodding at Tote, "me and Tote, that is. May we come in?"

Nancy Ann pulled the shawl tighter around her and opened the door. The

Waddle clan was gathered around the purple velvet settee where a red-faced Henrietta was lying down. Her body was constantly wracked by one coughing fit after another. Her face was red and splotchy.

The family looked up and saw Charles and Tote. The displeasure was evident on Waddle's face.

"Please forgive this intrusion. But I have some medicine that I think will help Henrietta, if I may."

"Medicine?" Waddle bawled. "What are you now, Charles Andres, a doctor? And you, Tote? Are you a doctor, too."

Tote turned to leave and Charles caught his arm. "Mister Waddle, I know you're upset and I don't blame you. But I learned some things in the Army that just might help Henrietta. Tote here helped me get the plant I needed and can help me mix it up."

"What do you need, Charles?" Mrs. Waddle's voice was eerily calm.

"Not much. Boiling water and honey and something to cut up and crush some plants with. That's all."

"Mary Jane. Nancy Ann. See to your sister. Charles, Tote, follow me."

Tote stoked the wood stove, and moved a cool kettle to the front stove lid. Mrs. Waddle gave Charles a bowl and a honey pot. He took out the dried hyssop and, using a spoon, crushed the flowers into tiny bits. He diced the fennel into the smallest possible pieces, crushed them with a spoon, and mixed it with the hyssop. He alternatively mixed a couple of spoonfuls of honey and hot water until the mixture was the consistency of cream. Taking a pie tin, he gave the medicine to Tote to put on the stove and let it come to a boil.

After it boiled for several minutes, Charles poured the dreary-looking mess into a dainty china cup with a handle too small to put a finger through, and handed it to Mrs. Waddle. He stuck the tip of his index finger in to test the temperature, then licked his finger.

"Let it cool down some, and give it to Henrietta, all of it. Despite the sugar, she won't like it."

Mrs. Waddle looked at him with pleading eyes.

"I truly think it will help, Mrs. Waddle. I saw men in the army with consumption so bad they were coughing up blood. After takin' several batches of this they were runnin' around trying to catch cows to ride. That's the honest truth."

While Mrs. Waddle was giving Henrietta the cough syrup, Charles and Tote started making up two more batches. Nancy Ann wandered in.

"Is she going to be all right?"

"Nobody can answer that, Miss Nancy Ann. But, I can say I've seen that medicine do wonders. I can tell you that as God's truth, and with men lots worse off that she is. Me and Tote're making up a couple of batches for later tonight if she doesn't improve and one for in the morning. Is there something we can put it in, something that can be corked up tight?"

Without a word, she left the kitchen and returned in a few minutes with an empty bottle with a wire-and-glass stopper contraption. "Mama said you could use this."

The next morning, Charles was with Tote at the barn, mucking out stalls and doing general chores when Waddle appeared at the double doors.

"Charles, Henrietta is much better this mornin'. Thank you for what you did. You too, Tote. Whatever that was you fixed up seemed to have helped. I'm much obliged."

"It was our pleasure, Mister Waddle, surely. Wouldn't do to have Henrietta sick. She's my helper around the place, you know?"

Waddle shook his head and gave a pleasant, grunting laugh as he turned and headed back to the main house.

Tote leaned his pitchfork up against the stall door and came over to stand by Charles.

"If that don't beat all. I've been working here five summers now and I've never seen Mister Waddle laugh."

Sometimes the fear of losin' somethin' that means a lot will do that to a man.

CHAPTER 34

Time to Change

Maturity involves being honest and true to oneself, making decisions based on a conscious internal process, assuming responsibility for one's decisions, having healthy relationships with others and developing one's own true gifts. It involves thinking about one's environment and deciding what one will and won't accept.
Mary Pipher

Late February, 1870.
It was going on three years as a hired hand when Charles realized he needed to make a move in his life. He aimed to take charge of it and forego riding the comfortable current. Since arriving at the Waddle farm one month shy of three years ago, he had worked alongside Tote, learned new skills, and performed every task assigned to the best of his ability. Without even realizing it, he had become attached to the Waddle family.

Mister Waddle was stern, but, for the most part, fair, especially if you worked hard and followed orders to the letter, which was never a problem for Charles. Mrs. Waddle was aloof most times as might be expected of women in general, but she never was condescending or mean-spirited. The Waddle boys treated him well, not as a brother, but not exactly as a hired hand either. Henrietta became Charles' constant companion whenever her parents allowed. She and Charles shared a commonality of spirit—quiet, introspective, thoughtful. They could spend hours together with few words passing between them: The grown, quiet man...the small, quiet girl.

And then there was Nancy Ann.

When Charles came to the Waddle farm in early 1867, he expected to fulfill his obligation to work till late fall. But eight months had turned into a month more, then another month. And twenty more after that.

The reason was Nancy Ann.

She was no longer a round-faced, headstrong, obstinate girl. She was a headstrong woman, not pretty in the traditional sense, but more than pleasant to look at...coming or going.

She liked him, he knew this instinctively and by her less-than-subtle on-again, off-again flirtations. But, she was now twenty-two and more than a few local hairlegs had "come a-calling," as she told him more than once.

"John Westmore came a-calling Sunday afternoon. I surmise you saw his buggy at the house."

And, "Benjamin Craner is a good man. His poppa is a banker in Hope, don't you know. A little birdie told me he's going to come callin' Sunday next."

Charles knew the drill. He was expected to show anger, to give a visible whit about what Benjamin or John or a chorus of other callers would or would not do. He had figured out Nancy Ann wanted him to do something that was not his nature—display emotion.

It just was not his way. He just sniffed at the baited conversation, and refused to bite.

Nancy Ann did not consider herself a patient person; no one who knew her did. But there was something about Charles that intrigued her, made her think about what could be, what might be.

And, what *would be* if she had her way. Charles smiled. Most times, she had her way.

It was a blustery March day and Charles was taking a wagon of grain to the east pasture for the cattle. He was climbing aboard the wagon when Nancy Ann hailed him from the house.

"Wait! Wait up." He held tight reins on Buck and Doe, the matched dray horses Waddle had picked up the previous fall at an auction down at Summerhill.

Without another word, Nancy Ann climbed up on the wagon via the front wheel spokes. Charles held out a hand but she bounced up unassisted and settled into the spring seat next to him. He just sat there, staring at her, waiting for an explanation.

"I'm bored. I'm going to help you feed."

He just sat there, his hands limp on the reins.

Nancy Ann turned to him, pulled her shawl up tight around her face and held it firmly at her throat. "Charles, I'm in the buggy, and I'm going with you to feed Papa's cows."

He just sat there, mesmerized. Nervously, he glanced back toward the house.

"Now."

He looked at her, then cast a second hasty look at the house. Mrs. Waddle's face, an older version of her daughter's, was framed in one of the kitchen windowpanes. He couldn't tell if she was happy, sad, or concerned.

It was a short trip to the pasture, less than ten minutes. But in that time, Nancy Ann told him four things, which she precisely ticked off on her fingers.

First, he was a good man. She could feel it. And Henrietta liked him and that was a good sign. He was a hard-worker, no shirker, and could do almost anything that needed to be done. What he didn't know how to do, he not only learned it, but mastered it.

She told him without an ounce in pride in her voice that she was a good woman, deserving of a good, hard-working man.

And, she was emphatic that he was a fool. Her exact words were "a danged fool" for taking too much time to make important decisions.

Charles listened to her verbal laundry list and said nothing.

He shoveled the feed into the short-sided, wooden feed barrels. Nancy Ann talked. He listened, and didn't say a word.

However, he did, start plotting his next move.

That same night, dressed in his Sunday-go-to-meeting clothes he walked what seemed like a death-march to the Waddle house. He had earlier confided his plan to Tote, who wished him well. "It's been nice knowin' you, Mister Charles. I'm bettin' you'll be out of her by mornin'."

Charles stood by the front door of the Waddle house longer than he realized. He finally boldened up and knocked firmly three times.

Henrietta opened the door. "Chash! Mama, it's Chash! And he's all dressed up like on Sunday."

Charles blew his lips at her and she laughed.

The shape of Mister Waddle filled the door, blocking out most of the light coming from the inside.

"Charles?"

"Mister Waddle. Nice evening."

"I guess. What can I do for you, Charles?"

"If you don't mind, sir, I'd like to talk to you, man to man."

"Man to man?"

"Mah-man to man."

Waddle's face darkened and he looked back inside the house. "Just a minute," was all he said before he closed the door with force.

Charles didn't know what to do: Stand there. Sit. Run away. He opted to just stand, hands clasped in front, eyes on the door, ears on alert.

He could hear voices, but not words. He imagined the absolutely worst possible scenario into the unintelligible conversation inside the house.

Without warning, the door swung open and Waddle burst through it, dragging on a long, brown, canvas duster as he swept by Charles. He stopped at the edge of the porch, his back to Charles.

"What do you want, Charles? Spit it out."

Charles had a dry tongue and itchy heart, but nonetheless took a tentative step forward to close the distance. He saw Waddle's back tense.

"Mister Waddle, I've been working for you for almost three years. Three years, next month, in fact. And, every day, I've tried to do right by you and your family. I hope I've been a good hand to you."

Silence greeted one of the longest sentences he had ever spoken to Waddle since he first set foot on the place.

"I have come here, in the most respectful way I know, to ask your permission to come callin' on Miss Nancy Ann."

"And if'n I say no…?"

"What?"

"What are you goin' to do if I say 'No, Mister Charles Andres, you may not call on my daughter, Nancy Ann?' What would you do then?" He swung around to stare into Charles shadowed face. He grabbed him by the arm and swung him forcefully in front of the window, in which filtered lamplight trickled onto the dark porch.

"What would you do then, Mister Andres?"

Charles firmed his back. "Mister Waddle, I respect you as much as any man I ever met. If you told me I could not come callin' on Nancy Ann, then I would go pack my things and leave here tonight. I respect you way too much to go against your wishes."

"You just sayin' that?"

"Nosir. You been fair to me. More than fair. You set the rules early on and I abided by them without any reservations and knowin' what was expected of me. I have done nothin' to make you regret hirin' me on in early sixty-seven and I never would."

Waddle stood there, a giant, tired oak. He moved slowly to his favorite rocker and motioned Charles to a chair beside him.

"I told you way back that I wanted the best for my kids and I didn't want Nancy Ann to become attached to someone just passin' through. That still holds true. But you, Charles, are a sticker. I'll give you that."

There was a long pause. It seemed like Waddle was thinking, choosing words carefully.

"You got anything else to say to me?"

Charles drew himself up as tall as he was able. "Mister Waddle, I just want you to know that I was a Union soldier during the war, drummer actually. I tried to join the Confederate Army in New Orleans and that's the honest truth. They thought I was too young. I either had to go back to the orphanage or just leave. To go someplace else. I served in the Ninth Connecticut Regiment for more than two years."

He took a deep breath. "I did the best I could and was the best drummer I knew how to be."

Waddle got up quickly, pulled his duster tight across his broad chest and said, "You didn't have to tell me that, Charles. But I'm glad you did. You have my permission to come callin' on Nancy Ann Sunday next."

Mr. Waddle. I do have a question, if you please?"

"Spit it out."

"Why did you choose to build your house so close to the road, when all the other houses are way off the road."

"A fair question deserves a fair answer. But, first, why do you think it was built right on the road?"

"To let folks know this place was the Waddles's and that they had to go through you if they was goin' to take anything."

Waddle's mouth angled up at one corner. He turned and went into the house without another word.

Now, what have I gone and done?

It was two months more—two months of Charles "callin'" on Nancy Ann Sunday afternoon, which was nothing more than sitting on the porch with the entire family—before Charles and Nancy Ann were allowed to sit on the porch on a Saturday night without being chaperoned.

As Nancy Ann walked out on the porch, wearing a new, pink dress with little embroidered blue birds on the bodice, her father handed Charles a sturdy piece of an oak limb and his personal pocketknife.

"Here," Waddle said, thrusting the wood and knife into Charles' hand. "Since you aren't planning on doin' much except exchange pleasantries, you'll have no problem carvin' Mrs. Waddle a good, sturdy spoon."

"A spoon?" Charles asked, while Nancy Ann giggled into a gloved hand.

"A spoon. A good stirrin' spoon. Carve it. Finish it tonight."

Two hours later, Waddle came to the door and told Nancy Ann it was time to come in. He eyed the pile of shavings on the porch as Charles handed him his handiwork, which was examined closely.

"Not bad. Mrs. Waddle always has a need for good spoons," was all that was said.

The next Saturday night, the ritual was repeated and, for the second week in a row, Waddle complimented Charles on his carving ability.

The next day, as dusk was hard at work settling over the west piney woods, Charles was down at the pond, line-fishing for bream. Waddle rode up on Tom and said, "We got to have a talk, Charles," he said. He made no move to get down from the horse.

He held up his off hand. In it was the spoon Charles had given him the night before.

"Nice spoon. But the wood I gave you was hickory. The spoon you gave me was carved out of oak."

Charles almost died on the spot.

"Charles, what you did was wrong. It was, I hate to admit, also clever and inventive. You'll go far if you keep usin' your head like that. Just don't use it with me like that ever again. And, never with a man to get close to his daughter. Is that clear?"

"Yessir. Very clear. And I am sorry and I promise to carve you or Mrs. Waddle as many spoons as you want out of whatever wood you want whenever you want them."

Two nights later, after all the candles and lanterns in the main house were out, Charles left the shed and walked due south for a hundred yards to the edge of a stand of short-leaf pines. There, under the defused light provided by a half-moon, Charles used a short-handled spade to dig a foot-deep hole. In it he placed a small cracker tin holding a tintype wrapped in an old sock, the rosary and the cross, and a piece of paper with three names written on it: Sarie Jane. Ian. Sister Mary of the Five Wounds.

He covered the tin carefully with the dirt and patted it down firm. He stood alone in the moonlight. Tears of sadness mixed with tears of expectant joy.

That October, in the front yard of the Waddle farm, Charles Montgomery Andres married Nancy Ann Hines Waddle. There were more than a hundred friends and neighbors in attendance, including every single member of Charles' new family. Charles said his section of the wedding vows in a loud, assertive voice, and smiled openly, winked and blew his lips at Henrietta when she handed him the ring.

During the entire service, Charles held tightly to Nancy Ann's hand. And she held his just as tightly. Because they both could think of no other place they would rather be.

Family.
I'm home.

EPILOGUE

Charles Montgomery Andres and Nancy Ann Hines Waddle were married for more than fifty years. The sturdy, stoic, and hard-working couple had seven children—six sons and a daughter.

All of the children took after the Waddle side of the family: All the boys, when grown, were more than six feet tall; the single daughter was not dainty, standing about five-foot-eight.

The youngest child, George Logan Andres, was, like his father, a special man. He married Mattie Bright Hamilton, who "lived down the road a piece." The "odd couple"—as a young man George stood slightly taller than six-foot-two, and, with heels, Mattie was an inch over five-feet-tall—had nine children, all exceptional and loving in their own way.

One of those, the third-oldest daughter, was Mildred Brownie Andres, who married a handsome soldier named Edward Dale Smith during World War II. Brownie was certain about most things and outspoken in all things, like her grandmother; the man she chose as her life's companion was accommodating in most things, like her grandfather. They had two children—Andrea Dale and her older brother, who gleefully continues to torment her to this day.

It makes no difference to any of the later Andres generations what name Grandpa Andres was born with, what forces—internal or external—caused him to change it, or what mistakes (if there were any of consequence) he made in his life.

When he died in 1929, Charles Montgomery Andres was buried under a name that was not the one given to him at birth. But it was a name of which he was proud, one he had grown into, one he had earned through trials of war and life.

What matters to his family is that he lived a meaningful life and loved those around him with an abiding, albeit quiet, passion.

What matters to them most is that he lived his life to his expectations and abilities, and that he discovered and fiercely held onto what he truly sought his whole life—family.

THE GLORIOUS NINTH

By George S. Smith and Dr. C. Jason Smith, great-grandson and great-great-grandson respectively, of Charles Montgomery Andres, aka Charles Andre, musician, Ninth Connecticut Regiment, 1863-1865.

Today we call them heroes,
that band of men and boys.
They gave up lives they knew
for a war they did not yet know.

The men of the Ninth Connecticut:
adventurers, bounty-men,
husbands, brothers, and sons:
Some were running away,
some were running to believe,
some just went to see.
They are all patriots in the end,
marching to different drumbeats
of their impetuous, broken nation,
two sides, out of step,
out of spite, out of pride.

The Irish Regiment, they were,
although by that name others were known.

But here redheaded boys rubbed shoulders,
shared tents and pots and pans and spoons with
tow-headed boys and dusky, harder men
whose fathers bore the yoke,
with men raised on sowbelly and grits
who scanned enemy lines for cousins
uncles, and brothers.
They were all searching for justice,
perhaps, or simply looking for a home.
All sought a reason
for the unreasonable times.
Together, they cleaned guns, boiled beans,
peeled wild onions, broke hardtack,
built campfires, and fought like banshees
when called upon to do so.
Believers and not.
This gathering of brothers,
working, living, fighting, dying
beside one another
at a time when Truth
had to wait for History.

These ancestors made room
for us to be proud.
They fought at Vicksburg, Baton Rouge,
Winchester, Fisher's Hill, Cedar Creek,
and other battles of man.
They fought for freedom
because freedom sometimes means
you have to give it up.
You will find their mark still
on places high and low,
In history, on paper,
in remembrance, and in rumor.
Their bones fertilize our very ground.

REVEILLE

*They left their youth, their farms,
their loves and dreams...and blood
on hundreds of hills and fields
from the swamps of Louisiana,
to a big ditch at Vicksburg,
to the rolling hills of the Shenandoah,
building a legacy forged from
faith, determination, necessity,
inner strength, courage,
and, finally, brotherhood.*

*We honor them now
just as they honored themselves
with difficult, faithful service
those long years ago,
when this nation was still enduring
the horrible pains of growing.*

*These heroes didn't think
of themselves as heroes.
Heroes never do.
Just soldiers
doing what they came to do.*

They did it well.

ACKNOWLEDGMENTS

A quest begins with a single step. The journey to ferret out additional information about a distant relative began with the study of a single photograph of Charles Montgomery Andres. For some unexplained reason, the old photograph spoke loudly to my natural curiosity about closeted mysteries. In studying the photograph, there was no hint of the expedition that lay ahead.

On the almost three-year journey to uncover what official information about this solemn-faced man, literary works were read, academic and governmental websites were visited time and again, and correspondence with wonderfully giving people interested in the past became part of the routine to ferret out every tidbit possible about the Ninth Connecticut and the men who were a part of it.

It's impossible to thank them all, but some stood above the rest in helping smooth out the curves encountered in the research for this book. This is a paltry attempt to thank them.

To Betty Ann Andres White, Jack Wayne Andres, and Wanda Ruth Andres Collins, the grandchildren of Charles and Nancy Andres. Though exploration of the life of "Grandpa Andres" uncovered deviations of beloved family stories, they were supportive in the tale finally told.

To Thomas Hamilton Murray, whose 1908 book, "The Ninth Connecticut—The Irish Brigade," is the beginning and end if one wants to learn about the heroic exploits, missteps, foibles, and heroism of a special band of men that came together at a defining moment in the nation's history and made themselves proud. I can not adequately express the feeling that came over me when the name "Charles Andre, musician" was first seen in the book. It was the first step to unraveling a part of the mystery.

To Jack Belsom with the New Orleans Archdiocesan Archives and the redoubtable Dorenda Dupont, for searching for, and finding, baptismal records and other information for the central figure of *Reveille*.

To Joel Craig, editor of The Bivouac Banner (www.bivouacbooks.com), who published draft chapters from novel (under the working title *The Long Road*). Seeing the work in print created a need to improve each ensuing installment, and make the ones Craig published online better.

To Robert O. Larkin, whose comments, gentle critique, and encouragement during the writing process added much clarity to the final product. His dedication to the mission of erecting a monument to the Ninth Connecticut at Vicksburg is a shining example of goal setting, determination, and execution. Larkin is an expert on the Ninth Connecticut; one of his ancestors died during the Civil War as a soldier in that esteemed regiment.

To Chase Perryman, whose illustrations, cover art, and jacket design added a professional feel to this work and helped bring "Reveille" to life.

To Mattie Smith Cummins, Ron Andres, and Deanna DuVall, who took time out of their busy lives to read "Reveille" and offer insightful, gently worded critiques. This work is better because of their efforts.

To Gayle, who has encouraged me to write and never wavers in her support of my efforts. A reluctant critic in all things, she nonetheless is a driving force in my continuing efforts to write something that will please her.

To my children—Jason, Mattie, Brandie, and Cameron. Without even knowing it, they have all inspired me to work hard to be a better writer—and a better person—than I could ever hope to be on my own.

BIBLIOGRAPHY

Thomas Hamilton Murray, *History of the Ninth Regiment, Connecticut Volunteer Infantry, "The Irish Regiment," in the War of the Rebellion, 1861-1865, The Record of a gallant command on the march, in battle and in bivouac,* The Price, Lee and Atkins Co, 1903. Reprinted by Higginson Book Company, Salem, Massachusetts, 1998

Edward J. Stackpole, *Sheridan in the Shenandoah,* The Stackpole Company, Harrisburg, Pennsylvania

Richard O'Shea and David Greenspan, *Battle Maps of the Civil War,* Smithmark Publishers, New York, New York

General John B. Gordon, *Reminiscences of the Civil War.* Charles Scribner's Sons. 1903

Jeffry D. Wert, *From Winchester to Cedar Creek,* Stackpole Books

Jim Larkin, *www.jimlarkin.com/9thRegiment/History.htm*

Bell Irvin Wiley, *The Life of Billy Yank, The common soldier of the Union,* Louisiana State University Press

Louis-Philippe-Albert d'Orléans, *History of the Civil War in America,* Paris, 1876

E.B. Long with Barbara Long, *The Civil War Day by Day: An Almanac.*

Stormy Stuler, Seventh Michigan Volunetter Infantry, *Civil War Medicine at Home*, Great Lakes Military and Civilian Civil Water Conference

Readers Digest, *Magic and Medicine of Plants,* 1986

U.S. Census Bureau, Archives, 1850-1860 Census.

U.S. Military Archives, Civil War, Union Army, Ninth Connecticut Regiment.